The Plantation House

Parallel Lives, Secrets Revealed
The Story of Adria and Elizabeth

Sherry Erickson

Printed in the United States of America
Published in Hellertown, PA
Cover design by Anna Magruder
Library of Congress Control Number 202 492 5987
ISBN 979-8-89420-036-1
For more information or to place bulk orders, contact the author or the publisher at Jennifer@BrightCommunications.net.

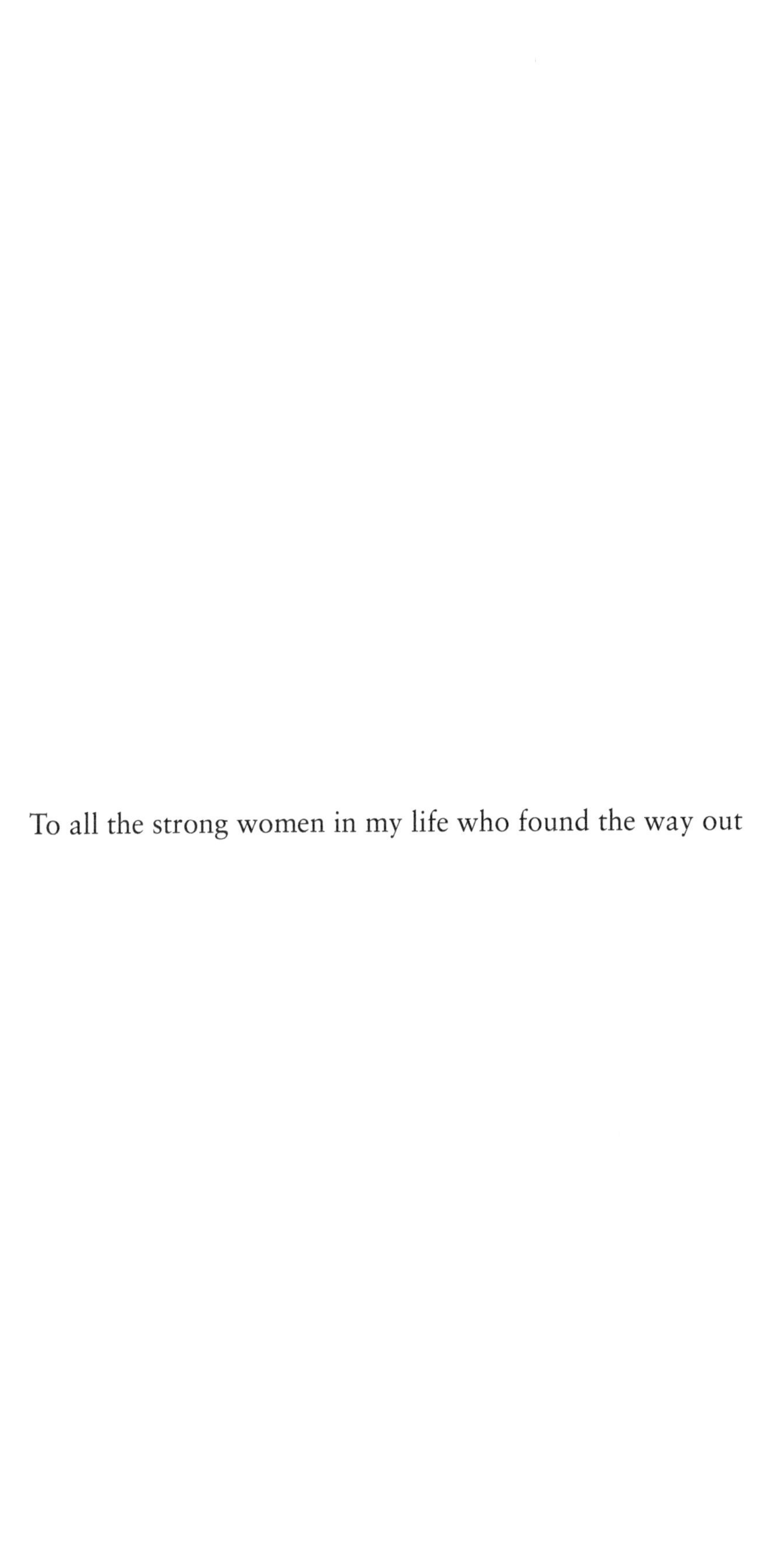

To all the strong women in my life who found the way out

Chapter One: The Wedding

Elizabeth stood facing the man she hoped would be her husband for the rest of her life. She didn't know him, really, and as she stood in the shade studying her future husband, images of the past few months flashed before her eyes—their first meeting, then the courtship that led up to what she now acknowledged had been a hasty proposal.

Her friends had cautioned her, but she'd been smitten and their warnings fell on deaf ears. For one brief moment, she had the urge to run. She took a deep breath and then her first step as the wedding march began, the live band cloistered beneath a pergola, shielded from the glaring summer sun.

She held a lavish bouquet of white lilies wrapped with a lavender ribbon. The dress that had taken months to complete was covered with thousands of tiny pearls. Her hair was swept up in a lavish, coiffed swirl, beset with strands of the same small pearls. Swans swayed in the adjacent lake as if to the music, with two in the front leading their graceful dance across the water. Two young girls with white ribbons in their braided hair held the edges of Elizabeth's bridal train, keeping step with her as she walked slowly toward her destiny.

Charles stood stone-faced at the altar, a look of admiration in his eyes; however, any semblance of love was difficult to discern. His chiseled, high cheekbones and prominent jaw line emphasized his tan face, as did the white collar that protruded from an immaculate tuxedo. Elizabeth felt as though she were floating. Charles's steely stare drew her forward step by step but she didn't let her eyes meet his until she stepped in front of him. She didn't remember saying the words that would haunt her just days into their marriage.

Once the bouquet was caught by one of Elizabeth's bridesmaids, the festivities began on the veranda. The parties were seated at tables according to either their status in town or the amount of money that flowed from their companies through Charles's bank account on any given day. As the heir to the firm, bestowed by his father upon his death just three years prior, it was his responsibility to make sure the 1980s and beyond were as successful as the past thirty years had been. The music continued as waiters circled the tables with silver carts, offering champagne, wine, and fine Tennessee whiskey.

The clinking of a spoon on glass indicated that it was time for a toast. Charles's brother stood at a microphone in front of the band, looking out across the crowd as they grew quiet. Finally, the patio settled, and his brother, Bryce, cleared his throat. His mother, Dehlia, gave him a slow nod, so he began.

"Well, it is no secret that there has been pressure to produce an heir to the Freeman family fortune," he began, eliciting murmurs from every table and laughter from some. "But seriously, Charles has chosen well."

Bryce continued, "Elizabeth, it is my honor to welcome you to the family. How you will put up with my brother we can only imagine, but you have my undying respect from this day forward." He turned to Charles, locking eyes with his older brother. "Charles, I have two things to say." Then after a long pause, "One, take care of her, dammit, and two, it's about time! Dad would be proud."

Dehlia Freeman sat at a table adjacent to the bride and groom, dabbing at a tear that formed in one eye. She turned and smiled at Charles, then gave Elizabeth a nod. She lifted her glass of champagne, and the room erupted in a unanimous, "Cheers!"

Dehlia—Mrs. Charles Freeman the third—sipped her champagne, watching as Charles and Elizabeth touched glasses then raised them to each other and then the crowd before taking a small sip and returning them to the table. Dehlia had spared no expense in dressing for the occasion; her lavish hat adorned with the same but smaller lilies as were in Elizabeth's bouquet, a tight strand of pearls that had been passed down from her grandmother, and her shirt showing gold threads running through the fabric that no one doubted were the real thing. A thick mink stole sat draped around her shoulders, defying the Georgia heat while watching the proceedings with vacant, beady eyes. Dehlia decided then that if Elizabeth produced an heir on the first try, the pearls would be passed to her. Otherwise, they would go to Aimee.

Charles turned to Elizabeth and took her hand, bringing her to her feet and leading her to the dance floor that had taken all week to construct, made of smoothly sanded red oak planks. With one hand on her waist and the other holding hers high, outstretched, he led her around and around to the music, locking eyes with her in an apparent gesture of the connection she'd been searching for. But when she mouthed the words "I love you," he simply smiled.

When the song was over, Bryce—who had been waiting at the edge of their table—led her back out onto the floor, standing in for the father-daughter dance because Elizabeth's father had also passed away three years prior. Her mother had died when Elizabeth was young, and she wished for them both right now, desperately. They danced to a song, one that her father never would have chosen, Elizabeth noted. that Dehlia had selected. Dehlia sat watching, letting her tears flow freely now. When the song was over, she excused herself and walked across the lawn to the rear entrance of the mansion, ignoring the extraordinary dinner that was now being served. She motioned to one of the servants to bring her food to her room.

Small talk and chatter consumed the rest of the evening, some dancing to the slower songs. Elizabeth wistfully thought of the few weddings she'd attended, noting the absence of upbeat dance tunes, laughter, and the air of celebration. Friends and colleagues of Charles and Bryce stopped to extend well-wishes on the way back to their tables, congratulating Charles while barely acknowledging Elizabeth—and without the exuberance one would expect from well-wishers sincerely joined together to honor the commencement of a lifelong union. As dusk fell, the vast expanse of the old plantation twinkled out into the distance, revealing soft lights that had been placed in ancient oak trees. The swans rested at the edge of the great pond, and the band switched to melancholy background music, befitting of the great Southern ball that it almost was. Elizabeth had the fleeting thought that it sounded like a funeral march she'd once heard in New Orleans.

When Charles noticed Elizabeth's eyes grow heavy, he stood, announcing to the guests that he was taking leave to walk his new bride through the home that he'd purchased just before their wedding. She hadn't seen all the rooms yet, and just that day workers moved her from her modest apartment on the outskirts of Atlanta, although she would find out later that most of her things found their new home in an outbuilding on the back of the property.

Elizabeth rose, and Charles took her hand firmly. Some who watched the couple as they approached the mansion's great doors wondered—how long would this last? They knew how arrogant and cruel Charles Freeman was known to be, how his narcissistic behavior had alienated most of his former friends, and mosed that although many were present, it was likely for appearances only.

The doors were opened by two attendants and closed behind them.

Chapter Two: The Plantation House

Elizabeth wandered the halls of the mansion alone the next morning, taking in all that had transpired the previous day during the carefully planned wedding, down to the details of who could and would not sit at the same tables due to politics or previous business disputes. The fact that no children were allowed meant her nieces and nephew had not been invited.

Her sister and brother-in-law came, but they only stayed through the first dance, then took their leave. Elizabeth knew they had a nanny at their hotel and had promised not to stay late. At least that was their excuse. Truthfully Elizabeth's sister, Penny, despised Charles, and her husband made reference to him as *that man* in private conversation and wouldn't say his name. They wanted to be happy for Elizabeth but knew that the arrangement was anything but normal. Elizabeth was going to be living miles from the center of town, miles from her former friends, was not going to be given a car nor allowed to drive—although she would, of course, have a driver—effectively cutting her off from the outside world for anything but that which Charles approved, they suspected.

Elizabeth stopped by an overly large painting of a man and woman in the dress of the past century. He stood tall with his arm on the back of the chair where his wife was seated, both looking at the artist but neither smiling. The metal strip at the bottom of the painting identified the couple in calligraphy as *Sir John and Lady Clayton, Noble Oak Plantation, 1850.* Elizabeth noted his coat, tails, and tophat as being of that era. Dark, unsmiling eyes peered out from beneath the brim of the hat, while his jaw was sharp and set at an angle mimicking that of his high cheekbones. The woman's name was not mentioned. Elizabeth peered more closely at the woman's face, noting the sharp features and harsh determination in her eyes. Her dress flattered her curves, a corset pushed her breasts up high, while the folds beneath the waistband exploded into a waterfall of finely patterned expensive fabric.

Continuing past the great dining room, Elizabeth noted the overly long dining table meant to seat at least twenty. A large fireplace at the head of the table would hold a crackling fire filled with hard wood in the coming winter months. She shook off the chill that ran down her spine, although the temperature by mid-morning was already nearing 90 degrees outside. There were currently only two chairs at the table, one at each end facing each other, seemingly miles apart. Her breakfast setting was still waiting for her arrival. Charles had taken his and left for the city hours earlier.

Elizabeth wasn't hungry and had no desire to dine alone in this vast, empty room. She would ask the housekeeper—what was her name—Gwendolyn? Yes, that was it, and she was not allowed to call her Gwen. She would ask Gwendolyn to bring breakfast to her room.

The most she'd seen of the place had been after their wedding the previous day when Charles had taken her arm as they strolled from room to room, citing the history as a plantation house. He seemed to know quite a lot about the family who had built the plantation, some he already knew and some he learned from the real estate agent who had managed to milk an immensely large sum of money from him for the place, citing the history as the reason for the over-inflated price. Charles went on and on about John Clayton, that he had been a slave owner who wielded a great deal of power in the day, and that the county they currently resided in was named after his father.

Right up your alley, Elizabeth recalled thinking to herself as they'd stopped briefly at the painting. But she turned and smiled at Charles as he stared up in admiration at the slave trader. When she asked Charles what Sir John's wife's name had been, he turned to her with a slight sneer and said, "Hmmm, there is no mention of her, nowhere that we know of, although I'm sure we could find out. I guess she wasn't that important." As much as Charles purported to know about the estate and history, Elizabeth highly doubted that he didn't have that information.

Charles then steered her away from the painting past the formal dining room and parlor and down a dimly lit corridor where tall, gilded double doors opened into the master bedroom. A large chandelier hung in the center of the room, casting light in every direction, accompanied by large torch-like wall sconces that had been electrified at some point in the past century.

There Charles let go of Elizabeth's arm and watched while she walked through the room, peering outside to the southern lawn where the last of the guests had been lingering, noting who stayed to overconsume the whiskey, those who had drivers to take them home, and those who were likely conducting business in their absence. She walked up to the enormous four-poster bed, admiring the fine coverlet and heavily beaded pillows.

The bathroom was almost as big as Elizabeth's previous apartment. An ancient, wrought-iron bathtub had been refinished and sat in a corner with adjacent windows that peered out across the garden. Sheer curtains lined the windows to give one the privacy of a bath even at night but allowing for a view that was priceless during the day. The tiled floors were still perfect after more than 100 years. Elizabeth imagined feeling her bare feet slide across the cool tiles as she walked to her bath. She turned to see Charles in the doorway.

"Ready?" he smiled. "Let's continue. I'll show you to *your* room."

Elizabeth startled, a shiver running up her spine, which erupted in a surge at the base of her skull. What was he proposing? That they would not share a bed? Not even a room? The dread that she recalled feeling earlier was now returning. Her sister had voiced her concerns, as had her brother-in-law, months and again just weeks earlier, as they tried to convince her that it wasn't too late to back out. Penny suggested that their parents would have been horrified had either of them been alive. Yet Charles had done an excellent job of calming Elizabeth's fears, convincing her that he did indeed love her and that she would be happy with him. She would now have the family that she'd all but lost when her father died in a fatal crash years earlier and after her sister's husband had been relocated to the northeast. He would give her a fine home and children, and she would want for nothing. *Except a husband?* she now wondered.

"But I thought…" she started.

"Come, darling," Charles said, taking her elbow and leading her down the corridor, around the corner, and up a flight of stairs.

The corner suite was lovely. Although it was not nearly as large and lavish as the master, it was ornately adorned with another, smaller four-poster bed with a lace canopy, a beaded, lace coverlet, and gilded French armoires and dresser sets. The floral rugs that covered the floor were extravagant, and she wondered briefly what part of the world they'd come from.

A sitting area off one end opened onto a small patio, the doors standing open to reveal the view that took in the lake. Moonlight bounced off the backs of the swans, now sleeping with their heads tucked under one wing.

The double doors that led to the bathroom were smaller, as was the room itself. The bathtub was set up on a raised platform to allow one the ability to wash the hair of the bather should she choose, while hardly bending over. Although the bathroom had a view of the grounds as did the master bath, the windows were tall and narrow and did not afford the luxury of peering out while bathing. The room was on a higher floor, so no one on the grounds could see in, no matter the lighting nor the time of day.

Elizabeth turned to face her husband. "It's lovely," she said, unable to muster a smile.

"Elizabeth, please let's go sit down," he said, gesturing to the patio. Once there, he pulled out a cigar, seating himself on the opposite end of the patio so that the smoke would not waft through the open doors. He lit the cigar as she seated herself, stiffly, watching him and waiting for what was to come. It surely wasn't going to be a romantic, wedding-night roll under the comforter of either of the giant beds—that she understood immediately. He took a pull off the cigar, exhaled over the railing, and turned back to face her.

"My darling," he started out, accentuating his Southern drawl. "I do hope you will find the plantation to your liking and that you will make it your home. I've assigned several people to you who will be in your employ. You will meet them all in the morning. Most important will be Faye. Her family worked for my father, so she can be trusted. She will be a great help to you and will get you settled in the morning. You can give her daily tasks from shopping for your favorite foods to bringing fresh flowers back from the market, daily if you wish."

He took another puff, this time letting the smoke out slowly. Elizabeth studied him with dreaded anticipation as the cigar smoke swirled around, nearly obscuring his face. Without so much as a faint breeze, the smoke lingered, creating the illusion of two lone eyes shining from a wispy, dark veil. Elizabeth shuddered while Charles continued.

"I do want to let you know that while we will have separate rooms, we will still sleep together from time to time. At my age, I'd rather not toss and turn with someone else in the bed, lest neither of us be able to sleep. And my days, as you know, start early. Living out here means I will start earlier to beat the traffic into the city. I will also likely work late and will have business meetings and such, but I'll always call to let someone know when you can expect me."

He continued, "While you will have a driver, Branson, at your beck and call, his instructions are to call me for approval as to your wishes for outings, to see if they are necessary or if someone else can take care of your needs."

Elizabeth sat stone-faced, unable to comprehend all that she was hearing and trying to understand the gravity of the situation in which she'd just placed herself by marrying this man. This was not how it was supposed to be. Although he had said that she would not need a car and that a driver would be provided, she thought that it would be *she* who would do the shopping, *she* who would go to town for flowers, not that she would need approval to leave the property. Elizabeth had to breathe deeply to calm the panic that was stirring inside of her. She sat quietly, waiting for him to finish.

"Gwendolyn—you may not call her Gwen, she detests the shortening of her true name—is the house manager. She will address you in the evening and every morning. You may let her know the night before what your wishes will be for breakfast, and she will instruct Nettie—I've hired her to be our cook—of your daily meal plan. There are chickens out on the far edge of the property by the stables, so fresh eggs will be brought up each morning. You may select from a variety of menus that Nettie is proficient in making for our nightly meal, and I will take it with you when I can.

Barely taking a breath, Charles continued, "Gwendolyn will tell Faye what to bring you back from the markets and will have flowers changed daily in locations throughout the house, wherever you desire. Faye will also bring you the morning papers, and you may request any other reading materials from town or the library. She will also tend to your laundry and instruct the maids as to the care of your suite. She will draw your bath for you, and should you desire, she will wash your hair for you, as has been customary for the women of this house the past 100 years, longer actually."

Elizabeth blurted out suddenly, "Yes but they had slaves, didn't they," immediately wishing she'd not said what she did. Elizabeth then thought of his last name, Freeman, and how ironic it was that his family for generations had been slave-traders, yet the name *Free-man* seemed to be the antithesis of a family that kept people in a way that was anything but free.

Charles looked as if she'd slapped him, and his face flushed. He grew angry and was trying to figure out how not to get into a row with his new wife on their wedding night. His own family had been slave owners, yes, and although he didn't boast of it—it was no longer politically correct to discuss in most circles—he was proud of his family's heritage and how they had immigrated from Great Britain then built the family dynasty from scratch. They made their money first by tobacco farming, acquiring slaves as needed, then watched their wealth grow as his great-grandfather dug deep into his pockets to acquire more slaves than almost anyone in the adjacent counties, except the Claytons of course; they'd been rivals at the time. And now here he sat in their house, feeling smug about his purchase and the acquisition of a new wife who would give him an heir to all of this.

Charles took another moment to collect himself, then smiled insincerely at Elizabeth, giving her a loving look that took a great deal of effort to conjure up.

"Yes, darling, they had slaves. We have servants. Some of them are black, not all. But we employ them; they are not slaves. They will go home each night to their families and return in the morning. We will treat them properly, and they will take good care of us." He stood and calmly stubbed out his cigar on the railing, leaving it for whomever it would be that would come remove it in the morning.

"Now while I know that it is typical to consummate a marriage by jumping into bed, we are going to wait. I hope that doesn't offend you. We will reserve our lovemaking for the times when we feel an heir could be imminent, and Faye will advise me of when that might be. I promise that you will not be disappointed." He smiled, crossed the patio, kissed her lightly on the lips, and squeezed her hand.

"Your boxes have been unpacked, and Faye has put things in dressers and where you might find them easily. If you wish, she will move them around to your liking in the morning. Rest well, Mrs. Freeman. I will see you tomorrow. Would you like me to have Gwendolyn send up a glass of champagne?"

Elizabeth sat staring out at the pond, watching as the moonlight caught ripples of water being blown about by a wind that came up ominously from nowhere, offering dazzling patterns that she could not fully appreciate in the moment. She felt a tear sliding down her cheek and turned her head away.

"No, thank you," she said in a small voice.

Chapter Three: The Staff

Elizabeth passed the doors of the master suite that now stood closed and walked up the stairs to her room. The light that streamed in through the immensely tall windows should have brought her joy, but in the moment, she felt almost nothing at all—except for the knot at the bottom of her throat that wasn't there the day before. She stood looking out at the lake when she heard a knock at the door. She jumped.

Gwendolyn stood in the open doorway. Faye peered out from behind her. Gwendolyn was tall and thin and wore her hair back in a tight bun. She wore a stylish pantsuit and dress shoes. She looked at Elizabeth over the top of horn-rimmed glasses. Faye styled her dark, curly hair back in a version of Gwendolyn's bun, wisps of loose hair framing her face. Faye had olive-colored skin, an extremely round face, a turned-up nose, and olive-colored eyes flecked with gold that darted back and forth between Elizabeth and Gwendolyn, waiting for direction. She had on a plain black shift that had white sleeves and a lacy white collar, with a black apron tied around her waist.

"May we come in, Mrs. Freeman?" Gwendolyn asked.

"Yes, of course," answered Elizabeth.

Gwendolyn entered, followed by Faye, who looked at Elizabeth in a way that she found disconcerting. She watched while Faye pulled a small notebook and pen from the pocket of her apron, then handed it to Gwendolyn.

"Please, sit down," Elizabeth said, gesturing to a set of chairs clustered around a tea table.

Gwendolyn and Faye each took a seat on one side of the table, and Elizabeth sat on the other. Gwendolyn started, "We've not met yet, as Mr. Freeman asked us to introduce ourselves when you came down for breakfast. I am Gwendolyn and the house manager. Faye here will help me with household tasks and will attend to your needs…primarily of course."

Elizabeth looked at each of them, noting that neither of them smiled, and that although Faye had the look of a deer in the headlights, she felt it to be feigned. She was, after all, the one whom Charles had tasked with deciding when they would sleep together. She couldn't be that innocent.

Gwendolyn continued, "As you did not take your meal downstairs, we thought we should come up and see if there is anything we can get started for you, then we can make a plan to help you get settled in your room. Can we bring some breakfast up for you?"

Elizabeth looked from one to the other. "Yes, Gwendolyn, that would be nice, thank you. A soft-boiled egg, toast, some grits, and a fruit plate. And some tea would be nice. Earl Grey if we have any."

"Let me step into the hall and call down to Nettie," Gwendolyn said, rising from her chair while pulling out a small walkie-talkie from her jacket pocket. "Faye can go down and fetch it for you when Nettie has it ready. She's looking forward to meeting you, but she doesn't really leave the kitchen. We'll go down and see her after you've had your breakfast."

Gwendolyn walked into the hall. Faye sat looking at Elizabeth, the weird smile back on her lips—almost like she was stifling a laugh, like maybe she knew something that Elizabeth did not. They could hear Nettie's voice on the other end of the walkie, saying "uh-huh, uh-huh" after every item she wrote down on her chalkboard in the kitchen.

"It's nice to meet you, Faye," Elizabeth said. "How do you spell your name?"

"With an 'e' on the end. F.A.Y.E." Faye looked over at Gwendolyn, who was coming back through the door.

"That's nice," said Elizabeth. "Pleased to make your acquaintance. Seems as though we will be spending a good deal of time together. Charles told me that there is a history between your two families; let's talk about that someday." She took note of Faye's mixed skin color, suggesting that their families were perhaps more intertwined than what could be called a work relationship over the decades. Faye noticed the scrutiny, wiggled in her chair, and looked over at Gwendolyn, who had taken her seat once again.

"The two families go back almost 100 years," said Gwendolyn. "Faye's mother worked with Ms. Dehlia, and Faye's grandmother with Dehlia's father, and so on, all the back to the war. The slavery war." She looked over somewhat sternly at Faye, indicating that she should wipe that silly smile off her face. Faye caught the look, and her smile turned to a thin line—not a smile but not a frown.

"I call it the slavery war instead of the civil war because really, we all know that was exactly the purpose of all those poor souls being killed…for nothing really, and it was anything but civil," Gwendolyn said sadly while slowly shaking her head. "Could have just left us Southerners alone with our cotton and tobacco and made themselves a different country if they didn't agree." She knew she wasn't supposed to talk about such things, and she caught herself short of continuing, changing the subject.

"Faye, why don't you run down and get Mrs. Freeman's breakfast. It should be about ready. You'll need to make two trips anyway. You can bring her tea first." Gwendolyn nodded toward the door, dismissing her. Faye jumped up and walked out the door and toward the stairway, without looking back.

"That girl is a keeper," Gwendolyn said. "She needs some training, but she's a keeper. I've run quite a few households, and I can tell. She'll learn. She will do you right. You just let her know what you need, and if she don't hop to it, you let me know, and I'll set her straight real quick."

Elizabeth's eyes grew wide. "I'll try not to be too hard on her. I mean: I don't need a lot. I'm just trying to wrap my head around the fact that everyone is going to be doing everything for me that I'm used to doing for myself."

"You'll get used to it. People with money like the Freemans, they're used to it. They'll expect you to get used to it too and to start telling us what to do pretty quick now, so you need to plan to take control, or at least act like you're doing so." Gwendolyn sat with her pad and pen now poised to take notes. "You are the lady of the house now, like the lady in the picture downstairs. Now she sure 'nuff took control of things back then!"

"The lady in the painting? Downstairs in the hall? Sitting next to Sir John Clayton?" Elizabeth asked. "What was her name?"

"Her name was Helen Clayton. She died a hundred years ago, after Sir John built this house using his slaves. They say he was awful mean—to her, to everybody. She had four children, then died with the fifth. The baby didn't make it either. By then their first son, also named John, was old enough to marry, so his daddy put him up to marrying his sweetheart. Her name was Adria. They were young, but his daddy, Sir John, helped out. Together they ran this place for a long time. The son was nicer than his daddy, so they say, but still mean. Then the North and South started fightin' over the idea of having slaves, turned this place upside down. Adria had to run things when John went off to fight since Sir John was too old and frail by then."

"John got hurt real bad in the war and had to come home. Adria had one more baby girl just when he got home. I guess he put the seed in there when he came home for Christmas, and she was born right after he got back. After that, he got meaner, then he died. Adria ran this place on her own until her boy turned eighteen and could officially be the man of the house." Gwendolyn was proud that she knew enough to catch Elizabeth up on some of the details. She leaned in closer and lowered her voice. "Rumors were that she poisoned him."

Elizabeth sat up, her first thought being Charles's words about Sir John's wife, Helen, *not that important.* Not so true, she guessed now, as being the lady of the house, running the largest slave plantation in the area, she surely had immense responsibilities, the least of which likely being the parties she would have been expected to organize. She didn't know anyone else in the county, and she wasn't sure how she could get more detail on the Claytons—except perhaps at the local library. Elizabeth was dying to know how Sir John got the title of *Sir*, but was ready to release Gwendolyn to her duties of the day, and she wanted to have her breakfast and go down to meet Nettie.

"Gwen—Gwendolyn, if you would, please find a book for me from the library on the history of this place. And of the Clayton family. And if there are any on the Freeman family, and both of their families' businesses, I'd love to get more of the details. There must certainly be something in the local history section."

Gwendolyn jotted down a few notes as Faye walked through the door with a tray. She set the tray in front of Elizabeth. There was a China teacup on a floral saucer and a silver pitcher with hot water, a smaller pitcher of milk, a silver bowl that held a meager bit of sugar, and another saucer with two wedges of lemon in the center. A silver spoon sat beside the saucer.

"I forgot to ask how you take your tea, so I brought it all. Next time, I'll bring just what you need," Faye said. "Your breakfast is almost ready, so I'll be back real quick with the rest." She walked back out the door, looking over her shoulder at Elizabeth, watching as she poured milk into her cup, leaving the lemon and sugar.

"Gwendolyn," Elizabeth began. "After I have my breakfast, I would like you to take me on another tour of the house and then the property. I would like you to tell me everything you know about this place and anything you've heard—whether you know it to be true or not."

She took a sip of her tea after blowing across the top, in a gesture to cool it although it wasn't as hot as she preferred. "Then I would like you to introduce me to Nettie, and then to Branson." Gwendolyn was nodding. "After that, we'll sit in the kitchen and make a list of what we'll need from town so that we have dinners ready for Mr. Freeman every night whether he makes it home or not. How does that sound?" She was trying to slide into her new role, although she knew she would find it uncomfortable for a while.

"Sure nuff, Mrs. Freeman. Yes, we can do that," Gwendolyn replied.

At that moment, Faye entered with another tray, and Gwendolyn rose. "I'll leave you to your breakfast and let Miss Nettie know that we'll be coming down shortly. She'll want to make sure the kitchen is in perfect order."

Gwendolyn gestured to Faye with a nod, who turned and followed her out the door.

"Oh, please, wait," Elizabeth continued. "When we go to town for supplies, on second thought, I'd like to find a bookstore and browse a bit while you two are shopping for groceries."

Gwendolyn stiffened. "I'll run that by Mr. Freeman," she replied.

"Now why in the world would we have to ask his permission to go to town?" Elizabeth asked tersely.

"Those are the rules, ma'am. Mr. Freeman gave us all a set of rules."

"That will be all for now, Gwendolyn," Elizabeth replied. The two women walked out her bedroom door.

Elizabeth took the silver covers off the plates on the tray and inspected the array of food in front of her. She wasn't really hungry now, but she wanted to see how things were prepared and how it was presented. She dunked a piece of toast into her tea, taking a bite and shoving back the tray.

What in the hell have I gotten myself into? she thought as she leaned back with her teacup in both hands.

Chapter Four: Dehlia, Nettie, and Married Life

In downtown Atlanta, Charles Freeman sat at his large, shiny walnut desk with a green felt desk pad in the center, where his calendar sat open to his appointments for the day. The large expanse of glass behind him revealed the Atlanta skyline and beyond—even some of the hills leading toward his home in the country. His phone buzzed, and his secretary's voice came over the intercom.

"Your mother is here," she said.

"Send her in," Charles replied, closing his book and running his hands through his hair.

His secretary held the door open to let Dehlia pass, closing it quietly behind her. Dehlia stood for a moment clutching her handbag, one hand rising to smooth her silver hair back under her hat. She dressed as many women did who lived through the fifties and sixties in the South. She still wore a dress and hat when she ventured outside her house, no matter where she was going. Her stern hazel eyes took in the room. She looked out at the skyline and back at Charles who remained seated, recalling when her husband occupied that chair. Dehlia walked to the couch on the other side of his office and sat, motioning to the chair across so as to say she expected Charles to sit right there. It wasn't an option. She wasn't going to sit on the other side of his desk like one of his clients.

Charles rose, walked around his desk to where his mother sat, leaned to kiss her on the cheek, then took a seat.

"Would you like a bourbon?" he asked.

"Why not," she replied. "It's after noon." She glanced at her watch. "Twelve fifteen to be exact."

Charles rose again, walked to the liquor cart, and retrieved two glasses. He poured two measures and sat one glass in front of her on the coffee table. He went back to the chair and sat with his glass in both hands, exhaling deeply. He knew why she was there.

"Have you told her yet?" his mother asked.

"No, Mother, we just got married yesterday. I thought perhaps it would be appropriate to give her a few days to settle in before letting her know that my mother is coming to live with us."

"Well Aimee has an offer on the house in Peachtree Hills. I'm going to take it. How long do you think it will take to remodel the quarters?" Aimee was Bryce's wife, now a real estate agent and her daughter in-law, so of course she got the listing. Dehlia took a stiff gulp of the bourbon, wrinkling her nose as she swallowed, although it was the smoothest available.

She was referring to the old slave quarters that sat out away from the main plantation house. It had once housed up to four families of slaves, although it only had three small bedrooms. Charles promised her when he bought the plantation that he would completely gut the building and have it remodeled as a cottage for her. He wanted her close, and before she got any older, he wanted her to be in a place that had no stairs.

He intended to tear out the wall between two of the bedrooms to give her a decent-sized master bedroom. The third bedroom would be her study. He would have to start from scratch on the kitchen because the slaves had mainly cooked outside. There had never been any indoor plumbing nor appliances, which meant electrical would have to be upgraded, and plumbing would have to be added.

"You're going to have to give me some time," Charles said. "I have the crew starting on my master bedroom next week, and it will take them a few days to replace the carpet and reinstall the old baseboards." He took a sip of his bourbon. "After that, two months on your cottage. Best I can do."

Dehlia rolled her eyes and leaned her head back. She sighed, emptied her glass, and set it down with a thud.

"Another?"

"No, my driver is waiting," she said. "I'm going to lunch with Bryce and Aimee. Please tell her soon, okay? Let her get used to the idea. She's surely not going to like it much." Dehlia put her purse over her arm, and Charles opened the door for her, nodding at his secretary, who then buzzed her driver to let him know she was on the way down.

~~*~~

Elizabeth finished her breakfast, as much as she could manage, and then wasn't sure what to do with the trays. Should she carry them to the kitchen? Was that Faye's job? The maid, who she'd not yet met, apparently was not to be allowed in her suite without Faye present to supervise. It wasn't a security measure per se, but to make sure that everything was done to Elizabeth's liking, once Faye knew what that was exactly.

Elizabeth had never lived this lifestyle, and it was only by accident that she was even sitting in this very room. She had run into Charles just a year prior—at one of his summer parties—where she had been her friend Beth's plus-one. Charles had been taken by her immediately, partially because she was pretty, and after he spoke to her for a few minutes, he saw that she was also well-composed and very smart. He had been hosting regular parties with the hope of meeting more available women, disguising them as work events, office parties, or client-appreciation functions at high-end rooftop restaurants, one of which being where they met. Charles had rented the entire rooftop, hired a band, and had an open bar for a July fourth party. From there, they could see fireworks all around town, at the baseball stadium, and out into the suburbs.

Charles had been bent on finding any excuse to throw a bash because the pressure had been mounting to find a mate. His little brother was married, and Aimee was expecting a baby boy. If he didn't get it together, and Bryce bore the only male, Charles would lose his place to pass the baton to his son as the controller of the family fortune. It terrified him. He would not have admitted that he was desperate, but indeed he was.

Elizabeth was shocked when the day after the party she received a call from Beth, who was shrieking. Once Elizabeth was able to calm her, she realized the reason for the call was that Charles had contacted Beth to ask for Elizabeth's contact information.

"Do you even know who he is? Really?" Beth nearly shouted into the phone. Elizabeth only knew that he had money, that he'd hosted the party, and that he'd been really nice to her when they shared a glass of red wine while leaning against the rooftop railing and talking about Atlanta's different skyscrapers. It had been small talk. She never got the impression that he was actually interested in her.

After giving Beth permission to send Charles her last name and number, she immediately got a call from someone at Charles's office inviting her to lunch the following day with

Mr. Freeman at a restaurant near her office. It was kind of him to consider her work location and schedule, yet she wondered how he knew where she worked exactly, as he only had her name and number.

The lunch went nearly two hours, after which she begged out, saying that she although she'd had an amazing time, she couldn't lose her job over an extended lunch. He called for a car to whisk her the three blocks back to her office. It was only later that Elizabeth learned of his massive connections in the downtown district and that it had taken him merely minutes to figure out who she was and where she worked, and in that same amount of time he had been able to call in a favor and have a quick background check performed before noon. Charles had also placed a call to the head of the advertising agency where she worked to let him know about their "casual" lunch date and that she would be late in returning. People wanted to stay on Charles Freeman's good side, so of course, this was no problem at all.

Their second date was at the country club, and on the third he kissed her but not on the lips. After dinner back on the same rooftop where they met, Charles had his driver take them to her apartment building where he jumped out, opened her door for her, then walked her to the entrance. He took Elizabeth's face in his hands and leaned down, kissing her eyebrows, one at a time. After the eyebrow kisses, he bowed slightly, taking her hand and bringing it to his lips, kissing it while looking into her eyes, then wishing her a good night and to sleep well.

That was it, but it was enough to find her floating through the office the next day, unaware of the murmurs as she passed her colleagues. Word traveled fast that she was dating perhaps the most eligible bachelor in all of Georgia.

Elizabeth sat wondering what to do with the trays, deciding in the moment to leave them and figure it out later. She found her way to the kitchen. It hadn't been hard, as the smells emanating from Nettie's oven had permeated every nook and cranny of the house. She was baking some kind of bread—nothing that Elizabeth had asked for yet, but it would be on the menu for that evening's dinner, without a doubt.

When Elizabeth entered the swinging door of the kitchen, she saw the back of an enormous black woman with a large headscarf wrapped up high with a white bow on the top. She was singing as she stirred a pot of some kind of stock, perhaps chicken, Elizabeth thought by the smell, although with the blend of garlic, onions, and herbs, it was slightly difficult to discern. Elizabeth cleared her throat to announce her presence, and Nettie jumped and screamed at the same time, dropping the spoon on the floor.

"I am so sorry!" Elizabeth said loudly, running to retrieve the spoon where it landed, at the same time as Nettie bent down to do the same. Their heads nearly collided in the process, and they both came up laughing. Nettie's laugh was deep and boisterous.

"Child, you scared the daylights out of me!" Nettie exclaimed, still laughing.

"Oh my God, you must be Nettie," Elizabeth clamored to find words while Nettie washed the large spoon.

"Well, honey, you are correct about that, and I know who you are, so let's talk about food!" Nettie stuck the freshly washed spoon back in the simmering pot and turned to face Elizabeth. She opened her arms, inviting a hug. Elizabeth melted into her large embrace, feeling as though she'd encountered the arms of a mother she'd never known.

"How was your breakfast? Can I get you anything more?" Nettie stood still holding both of Elizabeth's arms, with Elizabeth in a bit of a shock over the encounter but still feeling the warmth.

"Maybe some tea?" Elizabeth replied weakly.

"Here, sit down right here, and I'll make that happen," Nettie said as she led Elizabeth to a large wooden chopping block that had been cleaned and freshly oiled that morning. She moved over a stool and directed Elizabeth to sit while she pulled out a cup and saucer and set it in front of her.

"Earl Grey again?" Nettie asked.

"Yes, please, and just milk, thank you." Elizabeth sat down and watched Nettie as she moved about the kitchen. She *owned* that room. It was obvious that she could move around and even cook in the dark in that kitchen if she had to; it was that familiar to her. Elizabeth wondered how that could be the case since they'd all presumably moved in just days earlier.

Within seconds, Nettie had a teabag in her cup and near-boiling water filling it to the brim. A small silver pitcher appeared, and before Elizabeth realized what had happened, her tea was ready.

Nettie pulled another stool over to the chopping block and placed her enormous bulk upon the seat, causing Elizabeth to peek down slightly to see how in the world she managed to do so without spilling off onto one side or the other. Nettie folded her hands on the chopping board and looked at Elizabeth.

"Welcome to Noble Oak Plantation, daughter. You gon' be happy here if I have anything to do 'bout it."

Just then, the kitchen doors swung open, and Gwendolyn walked through, startled to see Nettie and Elizabeth sitting casually together in the kitchen.

"What in the…" she began.

"You just relax, Miss Gwendolyn. Everythin' fine here," Nettie said back.

"But we're supposed to have the meeting together to discuss the weekly dinner plan," replied Gwendolyn, flushed and worried.

"Yes, dear, that is your job, to keep track of everything, and my only job is to cook and keep people fed and happy. Miss Elizabeth here wandered in, scared the daylights outta me, and now we're havin' a little moment if that's okay wit you."

Nettie smiled while she said it, but the authority in the words was clear. This was her domain, and Gwendolyn was merely a visitor.

Gwendolyn stuttered, "Of course, of course, no problem at all. Do you want me to come back?" She looked at Elizabeth for guidance.

"Yes, I think that would be a good idea," said Elizabeth. "We need to finish this conversation. Can we start the meeting in fifteen minutes?"

Gwendolyn looked from Nettie to Elizabeth and back to Nettie, suddenly concerned that her position as house manager may have shifted a notch. Nettie was supposed to answer to her, not to Elizabeth, not to anyone else. But she knew better than to rock the boat this early in the game. This was not her first time in this position, and she knew that things needed to settle in before she could establish hierarchy. She nodded, turned, and walked back out the double doors that were still swinging slightly from her entrance.

Elizabeth turned to Nettie. "I'm new at all this, okay?" she started, then continued. "I'll get the hang of it. I just need to know the rules. Like for instance, me bursting into the kitchen this way unannounced. Is that allowed?"

Nettie let out another belly laugh. "Child, Mr. Freeman, he set out the rules when we all hired, but you in charge now, okay? You can change the rules anytime you want. You the first lady of this house since Miss Edna died in 1929. There have been other families that have come and gone since the crash, but none what was from the South."

"Now Lady Adria, she was the first woman to take over a plantation in these parts, but she died back in 1884. She ran this place for years after her husband died from injuries he got in the war." She didn't mention the rumored poisoning.

The name *Adria* sent a slight shock through Elizabeth's body. There it was again, another name that everyone seemed to know except her husband, who claimed to have very little history on the place, but only when it came to naming the women.

"What do you know about her?" she asked.

"Well, Lady Adria and John Clayton were the second family to live in this house after his daddy died and left the place to him. My great-great-grannie sat right here where we sittin' at one point when she was little, servin' up grits for Lady Adria's little ones. My mama worked for one family that owned this place for a while in the forties, and I sat right where you sittin' and helped her knead bread nearly every day. And here I am again! We all family 'round here, like twisted branches on a big ole tree. We all growed together at one time, then apart, and here we are together again. Little Miss Faye, her family one of them branches. You be the newest little sprout." She smiled and gazed into Elizabeth's eyes, conveying a look that warmed Elizabeth to her core.

"But one thing fo sho, and that is when you walk through those doors," she gestured to the swinging kitchen doors, "You the boss o dis house. And one mo thing," Nettie wrapped her big hand around Elizabeth's on the table. "In here, in my kitchen, there are no rules where you concerned."

Elizabeth smiled and nodded; the weight of Nettie's hand on hers was comforting. She had so much to learn, so much to figure out, and she knew in that moment there was so much her husband wasn't telling her.

~~*~~

Elizabeth was in her room with the windows open wide, enjoying the breeze wafting off the lake. The curtains billowed, and frogs were rejoicing, welcoming the moon as it rose over the lake to illuminate their nightly chorus. The swans were once again heading to the reeds to take themselves off water and sleep for the night.

Charles hadn't called as promised and had not shown up for dinner. Their settings still sat at the table, and Elizabeth decided that rather than wait she would skip dinner and go to her room to read. She'd found the library on a walk with Gwendolyn through the mansion as she'd requested and had pulled out a few books that she might be inclined to read at some point. She found it curious that in Charles's extensive library there were no books on the history of the county nor of the Claytons and their building of the plantation house where she now lived. She made a mental note to ask him about that later, when she heard tires on the gravel outside.

Elizabeth went to the bathroom where she could get a partial view of the entry if she craned her neck. The driver was holding the door open as if at attention. Charles stepped out with his briefcase and umbrella. He took an umbrella everywhere he went in Atlanta because no matter what weather was predicted, there was always, always a chance of rain. She saw him walk from the car and shortly heard voices downstairs in the foyer. She elected to stay put and wait for him to come to her room.

Elizabeth sat down out on the patio, in the same chair where just the night before—her wedding night—she'd been delivered the unexpected news that she was quite literally a prisoner here, having been *installed* apparently for no reason other than to provide an heir for her husband's fortune. Although he'd been generous in the prenuptial agreement, she would want for nothing should they divorce or in the event of his untimely death, by no means would she come close to touching the family's wealth. That was made perfectly clear, and it came with a timeline: nothing if they divorced within the first year, ten percent of her separation alimony if within two, and so on. She would have to remain in the marriage ten years minimum to receive the full amount.

It was clever of him, really, but then again, he *was* quite clever. He made sure that if all else failed, they would have enough time to start over if their first child was a girl, and their second as well. In the event of a divorce, the children would stay with him. In the event of his death, they would go to her, but with stipulations regarding where they would live and what schools they would attend. In that case, she would have access to a larger sum of money for their care, but when they each turned eighteen, that sum would be turned over to them, and their inheritance would then be managed by his firm and family. Once the youngest was an adult, Elizabeth would be put out of the plantation house, and it would be sold. His mother—if she were still alive—would of course be taken care of but would have to leave the plantation. Charles did not want the children to bear the responsibility for the upkeep of such an estate, and furthermore he did not want to chance them fighting over the place. He'd thought of every detail with regards to the children. Her needs were secondary, but alas, what had been written in the agreement for her was more than she would make in ten lifetimes if even a pittance to the family, so she'd agreed to all and signed willingly.

At the time, Elizabeth had thought that they were in love—a strange, distant love, but love nonetheless. She chalked it up to his being older and involved in such serious financial and business dealings that he had little time and energy left to devote to his personal life. She had not been anxious to marry, nor had she given it any thought when they first met.

Before meeting Charles, Elizabeth had but one serious relationship in college with a handsome, intelligent boy from a good family that ended when he went away to study for his post-doctoral degree in environmental studies. He had a year-long adventure planned that would start in the Amazon rainforest and end in Antarctica. It was not a journey that she wanted to embark upon with him, nor had she been invited, so they decided to go their separate ways.

Following that, she had experiential relationships with a couple of men, both of whom she met through colleagues, and each she viewed as a potential life partner, but neither relationship had progressed to the level where she felt she would be safe and stable—nothing like when she met Charles. Stability was a given, without a doubt, and she thought the safe aspect was part of the deal, but now she was forced to redefine *safe*.

Looking back on the past year, she followed the trail of crumbs that Charles had left. From the first kisses on the eyebrows to the fancy dinners, including charitable events that led her now to own a trove of gowns, to the moment he proposed, it seemed now that every step had been perfectly calculated to lure her to this place, to this moment, to this balcony.

The purchase of the plantation had begun days after she agreed to marry him. It took months to close the deal, then weeks more to clean, remodel somewhat, and furnish. Simultaneously, the planning of the wedding took up a good deal of her time. Such a whirlwind of events that led her to find herself the night after vowing to love until they parted in death in a marriage that had not yet been consummated—they'd both agreed to wait to have sex until they were married—alone on a balcony in a fairytale setting, without her husband. He'd even designed the suite to suit her tastes, not his, down to the lace, the wallpaper, and the carpets, knowing that this would be where she would spend most of her time. His master suite was much more masculine, heavy, and dark. It all made perfect sense now.

Elizabeth gazed out at the moon as it once again rose to illuminate the pond, knowing that she would spend countless nights sitting right there in that spot, alone. She felt as though she'd taken her first deep breath in a year but still found herself swallowing hard, fighting that lump in her throat again. She had stability, but was she safe? Or was it that she was simply imprisoned and not even as a concubine but as *breed stock*. The words rolled around her brain, rattling her. There was a knock at the door. She jumped.

Although Elizabeth had left the door open, he'd knocked.

Charles stood just inside the threshold, as if he needed permission to enter. He'd changed from his work clothes into something more comfortable and was holding a bottle of champagne in a bucket of ice and two glasses.

"May I?" he asked for permission to step farther into her domain.

"Of course," she called from the patio.

"I came to see how your day unfolded and if everything is to your liking," he said as he set a glass in front of her and filled it, not asking her if she wanted to drink. It was a Southern thing, or a Freeman thing, the drinking—day in, day out, and any time of day.

"It was nice, thank you," she said as he poured his own glass and set the bottle back into the bucket.

"Cheers, here's to us," he said, smiling.

Elizabeth raised her glass in his direction but did not swallow the sip she pretended to take. "How was your day? Did you have dinner?" She was of course referring to the fact that she had not.

"I had a last-minute client call to let me know he was in town. We met at the club briefly and had a bite there. What did you have planned that I missed?"

"Nettie made some bread." She paused. "You said you would call if you weren't going to make it home." She was smiling tersely and clearly agitated.

"Oh yes, Elizabeth, dear—I'm so sorry. As I said, it was unexpected, and I do apologize. Next time, I will make sure that my secretary gives you a ring." The comment was well-intentioned but hit her like a stone.

"Really? You'll have your secretary give me a call so as not to leave me sitting at that god-damned table all alone, or better yet, not eating at all, like tonight, because you have forgotten your home phone number or because, clearly, you just didn't give it a thought." She paused. "Charles, I am your wife now. And I expect to be treated with decency and respect, above all else, even if you don't want to come to bed with me."

Charles flinched. He clearly had a lot to learn about this marriage thing, even if he didn't plan to have sex with her until she was fertile. He had his mistress in the highlands, Annabelle, with whom he'd had a sexual relationship for almost ten years now. She wanted nothing from him, enjoyed his company, but liked her lifestyle. He made sure she was comfortable and received regular reports from her doctor regarding her birth control—part of their arrangement—so that there would not be any mishaps, and he could ring her up anytime he so desired and that was that.

"I'm going to go downstairs and see if Nettie can warm up whatever it was that you two had ready for me. I'm still a little hungry. Can I interest you?" He was trying.

"I'll pass. And anyway, she's gone home. I'm going to go to bed early and read. Goodnight, Charles." And like that, she dismissed him.

He turned; leaving the bottle, the bucket, and the still-full glasses on the table; and walked out the door of her bedroom. She picked up her glass and nearly drained it with one long swallow, resisting the urge to pitch the glass over the edge onto the patio below.

Chapter Five: Holden

Elizabeth awoke to banging that was coming from downstairs somewhere. She rolled over and looked at the time. Seven o'clock? Who could be making that much noise at this hour? She rose and put on a robe and slippers, walking out the door of her bedroom toward the sound. The door to Charles's bedroom was open, and she could see workers with toolbelts and hammers tearing away at the baseboards, pulling them off the walls and piling them into the center of the room. The ornamental carpets had been rolled and stacked in the hallway outside the bedroom door.

She continued through the foyer and past the dining room, to the double doors leading to the kitchen. She smelled coffee, and she thought perhaps cinnamon rolls. She pushed through the doors to see Charles standing at the butcher block with a cup of coffee in one hand and a cinnamon roll in the other. He looked up, startled. Nettie came around the corner from the giant walk-in refrigerator and saw her standing there.

"Oh, child, did those men wake you with all that noise?" Nettie came toward her, pulling a stool over to the counter next to Charles. "Sit down here, honey. I'll make you some tea."

Elizabeth took a seat, looking up at Charles.

"I'm so sorry, Elizabeth. I had no idea they were going to arrive so early. I would have warned you." Charles looked at her, sitting in the kitchen in her robe, her long hair mussed up and flowing every which way. She looked beautiful. He wondered in that moment if he could ever love her like she needed to be loved.

"What in the world are they doing?" she asked.

"I'm having the carpets replaced in the master. In order to do so, they must remove all of the baseboards, after which they'll rip out all of the old carpet and replace it with a new style that I've selected. Then they'll put the baseboards back in. The entire process should take only two or three days." He took a sip of his coffee and then took a bite of his roll.

"I've got a meeting that I need to run off to. I'll be home for dinner," he continued, then glanced at Nettie, who was giving him a look that said he'd better, unlike the night before when she'd cooked and had everything ready, and he never showed nor called. He looked over again at Elizabeth.

"I promise." He set his cup on the counter, wiped his hands on a napkin, turned, and kissed Elizabeth on the top of her head. "I'll see you at six." And with that, he was gone.

Nettie brought Elizabeth a teacup filled with hot water and a teabag, a warm cinnamon roll, a fork rolled in a napkin, and a pitcher of milk. "Lord know that man need to find balance in his life, o the good Lord gon' take him early," she said. "He work too hard."

Elizabeth poured milk into her teacup and stirred. "Yes, he does. But it doesn't appear that he is going to make any changes in his life anytime soon, so I guess it's just you and me here, Nettie." She took a bite of the roll, and warmth flooded through her. It reminded her of her childhood when her mother used to bake. The memory brought tears to her eyes, and she reached for the napkin.

Nettie came around the table and put an arm around Elizabeth's shoulder, the weight of which was surprisingly light.

"Now don' you go cryin' over that man. You gon be fine wit all this," said Nettie softly.

Elizabeth wanted to say it wasn't about Charles. It was that she missed her mama, she missed both her parents, and that the cinnamon roll triggered her tears. But deep down, she knew that she was indeed crying about her husband, her new life, and the despair that she felt so deeply.

Just then Gwendolyn and Faye came through the double doors. They'd arrived for their daily shift and were surprised at the scene: Elizabeth in tears and Nettie consoling her.

"Is everything alright?" Gwendolyn started.

"Yes, yes, everythin' jus fine," Nettie answered. "Miss Elizabeth here got woken up by those construction workers who came a way too early if you ask me. And I was just givin' her some tea and a roll to calm her nerves."

Elizabeth looked at the two of them and smiled. "Well now that I'm up and have had my breakfast, when you are ready, we'll talk about a plan for the day." Her weak attempt at trying to regain control of herself and the household did not go unnoticed as they noted her hair, her robe, and her tear-streaked face.

"Mrs. Freeman, if you would like me to run a hot bath for you, we can have our meeting a little later," Faye offered. "We need some time to get organized anyway, and if that would make you feel better, I'm happy to run up there right now and get it started."

"That would be lovely, Faye. I would like that," Elizabeth replied. She turned to Gwendolyn. "What do you think? We meet back here in an hour?"

Gwendolyn nodded. Faye turned and left the kitchen, and Nettie brought hot water to refill Elizabeth's teacup. Gwendolyn stood, unsure whether or not to pour herself coffee in front of Elizabeth to take to her small office off the kitchen. She'd never had a lady of the house sit in the kitchen taking tea and coffee with the cook nor anyone else for that matter.

"Gwendolyn," said Elizabeth. "Would you like some coffee? The cinnamon rolls are amazing. Please have one. I'll go up and take my bath and see you back down here." With that, she picked up her teacup, then turned to smile at Nettie. "Thank you. Those were the best cinnamon rolls I've had since I was a little girl." She turned and left the kitchen.

Once the doors stopped swinging and they were sure that Elizabeth was out of earshot, Gwendolyn relaxed and sat down on a stool. Nettie brought her a cup of coffee, sugar, and cream and set in in front of her.

"That girl has her work cut out for her, no doubt 'bout that," Gwendolyn said to Nettie as she set a roll in front of her.

Gwendolyn would choose her words carefully, as she knew that Nettie's family went back several generations with the families in the county, and no matter the race, politics of a household were protected. She, on the other hand, was only the second generation in her family to run a household for a rich family and was still learning the ropes, much less the politics.

Although Gwendolyn was thought to be white, a little-known fact about her family was that they descended from sharecroppers. Over the generations, they'd had so many children sired by white landowners that the light skin had become predominant, and she was often addressed as a white woman. Nettie knew this, but she would never bring it up. They were both employed by the same man and were both there to make sure the household ran smoothly and that Charles Freeman remained a happy man, if in fact they could. He was known for having his moments of anger, and both wondered if Elizabeth had seen any of that yet. Nettie saw a glimpse of the tenseness between them that very morning but would keep it to herself.

"She gon be fine, Miss Gwendolyn. She jus not used to all this bein' the lady of the house and all dat." She poured herself a cup of coffee and sat next to Gwendolyn, again managing to arrange her weight atop a stool meant for someone half her size.

"I just hope we can keep her happy enough to stay," said Gwendolyn. "I mean, we are all aware that Mr. Freeman is in desperate need of an heir. And we are here to make sure that all of this goes smoothly and that Mrs. Freeman stays happy enough to make that happen." She took a bite of her roll, rolling her eyes with pleasure and nodding her head. "These are the best, Nettie. Thank you!"

Nettie leaned in toward Gwendolyn and lowered her voice. "Listen up. She will be happier if we are honest with her, we treat her like a lady, and we teach her what she needs to do to run the house. She don know nothing 'bout this, but she wants to learn. Let's help her and not worry about Mr. Freeman. He got only one thin' to do to make it happen, and we both know what that is." She smiled, and Gwendolyn laughed.

~~*~~

Elizabeth dropped her robe on the bathroom floor, kicked off her slippers, and let her nightgown fall on top of the robe. The steam rose from the bathtub, and the scent of lavender wafted in the air. She noted the foam bubbles floating on top of the water as she stepped into the warmth. The temperature was perfect—hot but not too hot. She sank down in the water, allowing herself to appreciate for just one moment that there was someone right now who was paid to do just this kind of thing—to draw a bath for her, remove her clothes from the floor after she was finished, and to take those and her wet towel to be laundered and returned dry and folded before midday. And all she had to do was—*what exactly?*—she thought, *other than give this man children.*

She had always wanted children. She'd wondered many times if it would ever happen, as the years flew by and relationships did not develop to that stage. And now here she was, a kept woman but not a free woman. She stifled a giggle. She married a *Freeman* but she was not a *Freewoman*. It wasn't actually funny. It was sad, and it was scary. And it was made quite clear to her that she was to produce a child, but not for her, or for him, but for the family.

Elizabeth sunk down into the water, closing her eyes and going deeply enough to submerge her entire head. She could still hear the pounding downstairs, even under the water. Knowing that this was going to be anything but a relaxing bath, she elected to bathe quickly. After pulling the plug and draining the water, she turned on the shower that hung from a post at the head of the bath to rinse off before stepping out of the tub. Water went everywhere on the tile floor, but the drain in the center of the tiled floor was an indication that this was exactly how it was designed and so she wouldn't worry. She pulled a towel off the rack next to the tub and laid it on the floor so that she wouldn't slip, then grabbed a second for her body and a third for her hair. Why not?! She wasn't the one who had to do the laundry. She suddenly had the thought that she could probably get used to this.

Elizabeth toweled off and walked naked into her room, surprised that while she was bathing, Faye had set a variety of clothing options upon her bed—which she noted was now freshly made—but who was nowhere in sight. At least not that she knew of, causing her to wonder if Faye might be lurking somewhere watching her naked body as she walked around her room. She looked around, then decided that actually she really didn't care. Faye was in charge of her, more or less, and she was going to have to get used to it.

The thing that concerned her most was that it was going to be Faye who would report to Charles as to when she may be fertile, which meant she would be counting the days from the beginning of her period, then Faye would direct Charles to visit her room. That part was creepy, so creepy that she couldn't wrap her head around it. She wondered what part Gwendolyn played in all of this other than being the house manager, as she'd stated. Elizabeth knew in her heart that Nettie was at this point likely her only true ally.

Knowing the three of them were likely waiting for her in the kitchen, Elizabeth dressed quickly and slipped on some flat shoes, which had also been placed at the foot of her bed, and went out into the hallway and down the stairs. The workers had taken off for lunch, as they'd started so early—*too early,* she thought—and so it would be quiet in the house until they returned.

When Elizabeth walked into the kitchen, she saw Gwendolyn seated where she'd been sitting earlier, with a pad and pen on the butcher block counter. Faye sat beside her, and Nettie was chopping something over in the corner of the kitchen. Gwendolyn stood when Elizabeth entered.

"Sit down, please," said Elizabeth. "I'll sit over here." She took another stool and sat across the counter from her and Faye. "Alright, let's get started. Do you have any questions for me?" she asked, directing the question mainly to Gwendolyn.

"Yes, ma'am. I actually have a list." Her questions included everything from what she should put on the grocery list— although she and Nettie had not yet discussed even a single menu—to what kind of flowers she would like to see in the vases that were placed around the house as Charles had alluded. She also had questions about miscellaneous personal items that Elizabeth might need, including those for her monthly, what type of soaps she preferred, and if she wanted her laundry detergent to be scented or without fragrance.

Elizabeth answered every question quickly and without too much thought because she truly wasn't as high maintenance as most of the people Gwendolyn must have been used to dealing with. Then she turned to Faye. "And how will you be spending your days, when not attending to my needs, if I'm not in fact needy?"

Faye blushed. "I don't know, ma'am—I mean, Mrs. Freeman. I was hired to do whatever it is you need me to do."

Elizabeth thought about that for a moment. "Do you know how to knit?"

"Yes, Mrs. Freeman. I do. My grannie taught me."

"Alright then, Faye. I would like you to tell Gwendolyn what type of yarn we need and what needles I should start with, and I would like you to teach me how to knit."

Faye raised her eyebrows in surprise. "Um, okay, yes. I can do that." Then she turned to Gwendolyn with a look of surprise.

"It's okay, Faye. You can give me the list later," Gwendolyn said, then adding, "Maybe you should come to town with me since I don't know anything about knitting supplies. How about we go in about two hours?"

Elizabeth turned to Nettie. "Nettie, before they leave, can you and I spend a few minutes discussing what we might want to make for meals for the next few days, and I'll add those ingredients to their shopping list?"

Nettie turned from her chopping and smiled. "Yes, ma'am. Dats a great idea. Why don' you let me finish up here, and we can do dat. I jus need about fifteen minutes."

Elizabeth was pleased with herself. She'd managed to get through the first of her meetings with the household staff, give them the orders for the day with regard to shopping, *and* have a bath, and it was only noon.

"If you'll excuse me, I'm going to go to my room for a bit," Elizabeth said, then she turned back to Nettie. "I'll see you back here. How about thirty minutes?"

"Sure 'nuff, Miss Elizabeth," Nettie said, smiling.

Elizabeth sat in her room on a chaise lounge that had been placed in a corner. She dragged it over by the window next to the patio doors where the light came in the strongest. She picked up one of the books that she'd retrieved from the library, then settled in to rest.

To rest? Although it was just a few hours ago that she'd been awakened by the sound of hammers, it still seemed weird that here she was, wanting to lie down, and it was just after noon. She had worked her entire life up to this time. Weeks before the wedding, Charles insisted that she quit her job. He paid the last two month's rent on her apartment and told her that he wanted her not to worry about working to cover bills when there was so much to prepare for and a wedding to plan.

The office had thrown a going-away party for her at a local downtown pub. Charles begged off, citing a last-minute client who had flown in, but in reality, he had no desire to spend time with the likes of her colleagues. He'd known her friend Beth, the one who brought her to his party where they'd met. She'd only been on the invite list to broaden the types of women that he might meet and felt that she was too simple for Elizabeth, surprised that they were friends outside of work. He'd secretly requested also that she not be invited to the wedding, citing to Elizabeth some cap on the number of guests due to the space that they'd already allowed for.

She'd not seen Beth since that party, and she knew Beth was hurt. Now that the wedding was over and things had calmed down, she thought she might reach out to her, invite her to the plantation house for a weekend. They could watch movies and paint their toenails. But somewhere deep down, she knew that it would never happen.

Downstairs, the hammering resumed. The noise of the demolition was too much to take, and Elizabeth could never read with all that going on. She decided instead to take a quick walk. She laid down the book, changed her shoes into a pair that were a bit sturdier, and walked down the back staircase that led to the south patio. Once outside, she headed straight for the pond. It was more of a lake, she guessed. She didn't really know how big a body of water had to be to graduate between the terms.

The swans were floating in the middle, all together as they usually were, but barely moving. She thought they might have been napping, which she might be doing if it weren't for those workers downstairs. She stood on the water's edge for a moment, tempted to pick up a rock and skip it across the water as she had as a child, then changed her mind. She turned to survey the great home, taking in the ornate detail that adorned the facades over each door and window, and that ran the length of the building just below the roof. "The stories that could be told if these walls could talk," she thought. Her gaze shifted to the many buildings that sat near and farther away from the main house. One in particular caught her attention. It was a modest cottage, set a short walk from the entrance to the estate but over a slight hill so that from the first floor one might not really notice that it was out there. She headed in that direction along a lightly wooded path.

Elizabeth walked onto the modest front porch, noticing that the door was open just slightly, so she pushed gently, feeling it give way with a creak. She stepped just over the threshold and stopped. The inside was dusty, and there were outlines on the floor where furniture that had been recently removed left shapes of dust, showing the location where each piece had been. Cobwebs hung in the corners of the great room from exposed rafters. The doors to what looked like three bedrooms sat open, and each also appeared to be empty. Elizabeth looked around, noting that there was no kitchen nor any smaller room that would have been a bathroom. She turned to leave and came face-to-face with a man she'd never seen before. She let out a short scream.

"Mrs. Freeman, I'm so sorry to have scared you. I saw the door to the quarters open and came down to shut it. I didn't realize you were here," the man said, tipping the fingers of one hand to his beret and sticking out the other. "I'm Holden, Holden Grady Harding, ma'am. I'm your groundskeeper. I can also fix anything that's broken."

Elizabeth straightened, regaining her composure, and took his hand, noting his piercing blue eyes, deeply set dimples, and brown curls that peeked from underneath his hat, those in front tinged reddish-blond. He had a firm grip. Holden held her gaze and her hand for just a moment too long, long enough for her to feel the strength of his character through his penetrating eyes and in his hands, the strength of a working man. He was wearing a long-sleeved, tightly woven shirt that revealed the ripple of every muscle in his arms and shoulders. She caught herself allowing her eyes to linger on the buttons at the top and the slight amount of chest hair that protruded, then pulled her hand away.

"Very nice to meet you, Holden. Please call me Elizabeth. Everyone around here is so formal; it's driving me mad."

"In the company of others, ma'am, I'll need to call you Mrs. Freeman, but since it is just the two of us, I'll call you Elizabeth, not a problem." He grinned, revealing perfectly spaced, white teeth. "Nice to meet you, Elizabeth. How did you find yourself down here? Can I help you in any way?"

Elizabeth flushed. "I saw the building from the lake and was curious," she said. "What is this building, or what *was* it?"

"It was an old slaves' quarters, used to house I imagine at least three families who would have lived here together, worked the plantation. Hasn't been anyone living here probably since the end of the war, and no one ever fixed it up." They were now standing on the porch.

"Where did they cook? And use the bathroom?" Elizabeth asked.

"Well, back then the slaves all cooked outside. There's a brick fireplace and oven around back. The outhouse was torn down when Mr. Freeman bought this place. I supervised that. They filled in the hole for sanitary reasons." He looked over at Elizabeth. "Want me to show you some of the other buildings?"

He turned to walk away, Elizabeth noting the muscles in his back showing prominently as they had in the front. "Come this way," he said when she didn't answer.

He led Elizabeth around the side of the quarters where she could see the crumbled fireplace and the small oven that was built into the back side, where she imagined slaves cooking and baking their own bread. But year round? It got cold in Georgia. She remembered the exposed rafters inside and that there had been no insulation.

"I imagine they had a hard life," Elizabeth said.

"Yeah, I imagine life was hard for most slaves, but I've heard that Miss Adria was kinder than most, especially after her husband passed. One of them ended up living here. He was a son that the master—her husband John—sired, who came back around after the war, once he was a free man, and the family let him live out on the property until he died."

Elizabeth looked over at Holden, surprised. *How in the world did the gardener seem to know more than her husband?* She suspected now that Charles knew everything about the family, and that there was a reason he didn't want to share anything about Adria or the Claytons with her at this time.

Elizabeth looked back at the quarters as they walked together down the path she had taken to get there. "It must have been a nicer house at one time," she said. "Seems to be in an awful state of disrepair."

"Not for long," said Holden. "Mr. Freeman has plans for the crew to move out here after they finish his room. He has a lot to do on the place before his mother moves in this summer."

Elizabeth stopped on the path, unable to believe what she'd just heard. Holden stopped and turned to look at her. "What? You didn't know?" he questioned, thinking he had revealed something that he shouldn't have, something that might get him in a lot of trouble.

Elizabeth stiffened and shifting her gaze from the path below up to Holden's face, where she caught the level of concern.

"Of course, I'm aware," she said, smiling. "It will be good that she'll be out here with us," she lied. Inside though, her anger grew sharply. She started walking. "Show me more," she said.

Holden walked her down the path, past the lake to the other side of the main house, where a small cottage sat in the woods, completely out of sight of the main house.

"This one here is where the half-brother to Master Quinn lived when he returned a freed slave. His name was Henry."

"Master Quinn?" Elizabeth asked. "Henry?"

"Quinn was Lady Adria's oldest son, whose real name was John Clayton the third. He took over a few years after his father died. He was named after his father, yet he chose to be called Quinn, his middle name. Perhaps because he recalled his father's ire and anger and didn't want to take his name. I hear tell Quinn was much kinder than his father—so much that when the slaves here were freed after the war, a few begged to stay on. Of course, it was not like they had anyplace to go; most of them were born here and had never lived anywhere else."

Elizabeth was taken by Holden's knowledge of the history of the plantation. "Where did you learn all of this?" she asked.

"There's an old plantation next door that is a museum now. From the roof of the house here, you can sometimes see tour buses in the parking lot. People come down from Atlanta to tour the plantation and learn all about the history of the area. All of this is written in documents that you can read for yourself on the tour. It talks about the history of all the great plantations of the area, including Mr. Freeman's great-great-grandfather's estate, which was on the other side of the county." Holden was happy that Elizabeth was curious and delighted that he could fill her in on so much of the history.

"If you'd like to take a tour and if I can get Mr. Freeman's permission, I could probably have Branson drive us over there someday."

Elizabeth shuddered. There it was again, another of the employees—*servants*, Charles had called them—referring to the need to get her husband's permission before taking her off the property. "Thank you, Holden. Now if you don't mind, I'll find my way back to the house. I have a meeting with Gwendolyn to prepare for shopping in town. *If we can get my husband's permission*, I'll join them," she said, haughtily.

The tone of the comment did not go unnoticed. Holden tipped his hand to his beret again, smiling broadly.

"Have a good day, *Elizabeth*." The way he drew out her name, the way it rolled off his tongue so slowly, stirred something in her. She liked it.

Elizabeth turned and walked to the main house, entering through a back door once reserved for slaves who worked in the kitchen. Nettie, Gwendolyn, and Faye were seated again at the butcher block counter. They appeared surprised to see Elizabeth use the rear entrance.

"Hey, sorry I'm late!" she said. She was flushed and smiling, a look that none of them had seen yet on her.

"We were a bit worried about you, Mrs. Freeman, when we couldn't find you in your room. You said we'd meet back here and then you didn't show up." Gwendolyn took the lead in admonishing Elizabeth for her tardiness. It didn't faze her.

"Well, when I didn't get a tour of the grounds, I decided to take myself on a little stroll. I couldn't read due to the noise in the master bedroom, so I went out. I ran into Holden, who gave me a short walking tour and shared a little more history of the place with me." Elizabeth grinned at Gwendolyn to let her know that she wasn't calling her out in a negative way, but she did in fact ask for a tour of the grounds that never materialized.

The three servants sat somewhat stone-faced, unable to comprehend the fact that the lady of the house just went on a walk alone with the groundsman. Mr. Freeman would be appalled if he found out, but none of them sought to mention to her that things like this were simply not allowed. Gwendolyn patted the stool beside her.

"Come, sit down. Let's plan the meals and shopping for the week." She gave Nettie and Faye a look that told them to let it go this time.

~~*~~

After a grueling hour and a half session in the kitchen, Elizabeth found herself back in her room. Not only did she wish she were not in charge of meal planning, but she couldn't care less if the flowers were changed daily—or weekly for that matter—and she was sizzling over their insistence that she stay home, at least for this shopping trip, and let Mr. Freeman warm up to the idea of her going to town with them. She still hadn't met

Branson, who was the one charged with driving them—and her eventually—if ever her husband decided he would let her out of the house.

She was extremely happy to have met Holden, though, and in the manner that she had, although his revelation that Charles planned to move in his mother *before the end of summer*, and that he was keeping it from her, was infuriating.

Elizabeth had taken care to pretend that she was already aware of the plan to move the aging mother onto the grounds, but she was shocked that Charles had not told her so himself. What other surprises were in store for her? She shuddered to think.

The image came back to her of Holden tipping his hand to his beret. His tan skin and dimpled cheeks—and his rippled torso—completed a picture that was hard to shake. And then there was the way he said her name. It gave her chills as she sat down on the chaise lounge, again thinking she would read.

Charles hardly ever said her name any longer, although he had when he was courting her. He would now say "dear" if he was feeling she needed to hear it, but he never called her by her name. Elizabeth opened the book to the first page for the second time, then again closed it shut. She just wasn't in the mood to read, or relax, or for anything at that moment. She got up and went to the hallway, listening for sounds in the house.

It appeared that the workers had gone home for the day. There were no sounds coming from the kitchen although from the smells, she knew that Nettie was cooking up her version of the chicken potpie they'd discussed. The crust would be homemade and would overflow the individual serving dishes, and it would not go into the oven until they received a call from Charles telling them he was truly on his way home. Gwendolyn and Faye were still out on their shopping trip, so Elizabeth decided to wander the house alone once again.

She walked down the main stairway that led to the great hall where she saw what were surely Persian rugs still rolled up outside the master suite. The doors had been left wide open, and as she approached, she saw a huge pile of base in the middle of the room, which had been removed earlier in the day. She looked around, then entered the room, something she would not dare to do if anyone but Nettie was in the house.

Nettie never left the kitchen, she imagined, and she knew that she came and left via the rear entrance as the slaves once had.

Elizabeth had not been in the master bedroom since Charles had given her the tour, showing her the room that would not be hers to enjoy. The room had been emptied of the furniture, a feat in itself, and she wondered where it had all been taken and where her husband was sleeping. Far be it for him to suggest sleeping with his wife for a night or two until the construction was completed might be an option. These new circumstances were already wearing on her, and it had only been two full days since the wedding.

Elizabeth noted the places where the baseboard had been pulled away from the walls, leaving gaping holes where the plaster had come off in the process. Some of the boards had been left in a pile; others were still sitting up against the wall that they'd been pried away from, waiting to be replaced the next day. She was walking through the room toward the bathroom when something caught her eye. Sticking out from behind one of the loosened boards was what looked like a ribbon. She bent over and could see that the ribbon disappeared behind the loose board. She tugged on it, but it held firm to something in the wall. She took hold of the board and pulled on it—it came away easily—and then saw that the ribbon was attached to a book. She pulled the board back completely, then loosened the book from its place nestled in a carved-out space in the plaster.

The book was leather-bound, its bookmark ribbon was faded, and on the cover was a picture of the plantation house— her house! It had been etched, or burned into the leather, and the inscription below read "Noble Oak Plantation, 1857." Elizabeth was ecstatic. She tucked the book under her arm and left the room, heading quickly back up the stairs. Once inside her room, she shut the door and turned the lock. She wasn't really sure why she'd done that other than not wanting to take a chance that someone might walk in on her and catch her with the book in her hands.

She went to her chaise lounge for the third time that day and laid down, this time covering herself with a shawl and settling in to read.

Chapter Six: Adria

On the first page of the book, in a flowing cursive were the words:

Private Writings of Lady Adria Clayton
    September 15, 1857

Elizabeth turned the page, where the cursive continued, apparently in Adria's hand.

As I begin this first entry, I must announce that I am with child. My marriage to John Clayton and the nights following have immediately produced what will be our first offspring, the first of many I suppose. A surprise, really, that this is coming so soon, motherhood that is, but it was to be expected by all. John is so excited! I had hoped to have time to settle in to the routine of running the household without also planning for the design of the nursery so soon, but I am happy and content to have this take my mind off of the daily chore of keeping such a grand home and the daily management of the servants and slaves.

I'm thankful for the attention of Rae and of her mother, Hattie, both who will be in my company for the birth. Hattie will take care of the daily needs of the child and will most certainly be able to find someone to provide the milk when I am called back to the duties of the household. Rae already tends to my every need. She is a dear child and is learning fast as not all slaves are want to do.

John and I were married in a small private ceremony—he requested that we have the ceremony here on the large stretch of grass out by the lake. It was May 16, my mother's birthday, and we were blessed with a perfect spring day. We thought it would be a beautiful gift for my mother—to marry on her birthday, and she so agreed.

John's father built the house where I sit now by the window and write. The Noble Oak Plantation. What a beautiful name he chose, as beautiful as the oak forest that surrounds the property and as protective as the large oak that stands alone in front of the house, a perfect place for a home and to raise a family. His father carefully gave thought to the views when he constructed the house, so that as I write, I am able to watch the swans on the lake and feel the peace of their presence.

Elizabeth put the book down. She could not fathom what she was reading. It was unbelievable what she had just found: a history book, really, one that belonged to Adria's descendants and to the house—and someday in a museum. But she decided in the moment that she would keep it a secret. She no longer needed a trip to the library in town, that was for sure! She curled up on the chaise lounge and continued to read.

John's father has moved on to purchase another plantation when Sir John's wife, Helen, died in childbirth, deeding this property to my husband in order that he raise a family here. His siblings were not happy about this, apparently, but John being the eldest and named John II gives him heir's rights, I imagine. They moved on to the new plantation and although they were in attendance at our wedding, did not speak to me.

I think a lot about being the lady of a household at such a young age. But with John's guidance, I'm able to learn about things like how to make sure the head housekeeper, Opal, who is a slave, does a good job so that she's not subject to a beating.

I don't like the idea of beating people. It doesn't seem like the Christian way to do things. From what I've heard, people here did not always have slaves, but John's father made his fortune trading them. I'm not sure what that means, really, but something about buying and selling black people. It gives me the chills. John has just started working in his father's business. They farm tobacco mainly, but this slave trading is going to be his main source of family wealth from what he says. The business made enough money to build this house, and from what people say, we are rich. I don't really know how to tell because we don't live much different than the people around us. The only difference is that we have more slaves, so I guess that makes us rich. John wants to have a party soon, before it shows that we have a child on the way. It might be our last chance for a while, he says, and we need to socialize I guess so that people know how rich we are. I've been to some fancy parties but haven't ever had to plan for one. I guess now I will have that opportunity.

John is a good husband, but he sometimes gets very angry. The servants seem to tiptoe around him, I've noticed. The slaves tiptoe around him too, but they tiptoe around everyone. They get very nervous sometimes, and sometimes so do I. He's never hit me, but he does turn red and clench his fists when he's angry. Now that I am carrying his child—his little seed—I'm hoping that he will be nicer to me. The baby will be born in the spring. Hattie thinks sometime in March.

Elizabeth closed the journal and laid back on the chaise lounge. She shut her eyes, imagining Adria and that she might have at one time been in the very same room, lying on a couch or chaise similar to what Elizabeth was lying on now. She imagined Adria holding her belly, not yet swollen but knowing the *little seed*, as she called it, was growing inside—as she would hopefully experience, she supposed, sometime soon. But first, that would require having sex.

She looked at the time. She was getting hungry and knew that Charles would be home for dinner soon. After last night's no-show, he didn't dare give a repeat performance. Even Nettie was upset with him. She had gone home by the time he finally arrived, but Elizabeth knew that she resented having cooked all that food for nothing. When Nettie finally realized that he wasn't going to make it, she'd put it all away in the refrigerator and had to make plans for using the leftovers for something creative the next day. She would always be able to concoct something for the staff for lunch, but the disrespect irritated her.

Elizabeth rose, placing the book underneath a velvet pillow that rested on the chaise. She would need to find a better hiding place for it. She could not risk Faye finding it and turning it in to Gwendolyn or worse, to Charles. She tossed her shawl over the pillow and went downstairs to see what the state of dinner was looking like. When she passed the formal dining room, she noticed fresh flowers in the center of the table and candlesticks holding candles waiting for a match. Two places were set, one at each end. The distance between her plate and Charles's spoke volumes about their relationship. She wondered who was doing all this. It wasn't Nettie; she was busy cooking. Gwendolyn and Faye had both gone home. Was there another servant who she'd not yet met?

Nettie was humming an old gospel tune when Elizabeth came through the doors. She cleared her throat, not wanting to startle her. Nettie turned around.

"I heard you come in, child. Come sit yourself down here. I won tell you somethin'." She patted the stool. Elizabeth sat, waiting for what it was that Nettie needed to discuss. She could smell the chicken potpie in the oven, which meant Charles must have called to say he was on his way.

"About our little meetin' earlier today and the reason you was late." Nettie turned to open the second oven door, nodding approval that the chocolate cake was almost done. She quickly shut the door and turned off the heat, turning back to Elizabeth. "My grannie used to make dis same chocolate cake in dis very kitchen."

"How lovely. I can't wait!" Elizabeth replied.

"This boy Holden." Nettie said, changing the subject.

Elizabeth's faced turned bright red. *What about him?* she thought.

"It din' escape none of us when you come in this afternoon after takin' your little walk round that you was downright flushed in the face, an if I din' know better, I'd say you were a little taken wit him."

Elizabeth tried to keep a stoic face, letting Nettie continue.

"Now I know it's none my business, but I need to tell you now that Faye said somethin'. You know how I said Mr. Freeman done gave us all rules when he hired us. One of his rules fo Faye was to keep a good eye on you, and that's what she gon' do. I told her she better not say nothin' to Mr. Freeman, that it was just a walk, but child, watch yoself. She's his eyes and ears."

Just then, the front door opened, and they could hear footsteps in the foyer that then disappeared down the hallway. Charles had come through the door and gone straight to his bedroom suite to check the progress.

"Thank you, Nettie, for your concern. But a walk was all it was. Trust me. If I appeared flushed, it was because I haven't hardly been outside since the wedding, much less for a hike around the property, and it was hot being midday and all." Elizabeth smiled warmly, appreciating the fact that Nettie was looking out for her and apparently willing to do what she needed to in order to keep her out of trouble. She took Nettie's big hand in hers and squeezed it, then stood. "I think I'll go try to find my husband." She turned toward the door, then stopped. "Nettie," she started.

"Yes, ma'am," Nettie replied.

"Who sets the table and clears the dishes away? I know Gwendolyn arranged the flowers because she told me she was going to do so, but the rest?"

Nettie responded with a smile, looking down slightly. "That's my daughter, Miss Elizabeth. Her name is Twyla. She comes in and helps once an' a while. I'm tryin' to train her so that she can have a job like Miss Gwendolyn someday. She's not officially staff, and I don' know if Mr. Freeman would approve. When he's around, Faye helps out."

"Secrets are safe with me," Elizabeth said, smiling, then walked out the door in search of Charles. She found him standing in the middle of his room, turning in circles, looking at the mess. He was seething.

"Everything okay, darling?" She felt it weird to call him darling all of a sudden.

"Pigs," he said. His jaw was clenched, and he was visibly angry. "I gave them explicit instructions to clean up after the end of each day, stack things neatly, vacuum. This place is a disaster."

Elizabeth didn't know what to say. But the thought occurred that if they'd done too much cleaning after themselves, they might have found the diary that was safely stashed in her room right now, full of information that she had no intention of sharing with anyone, especially not her husband, not at this time. "Dinner is almost ready," she said, calmly.

"I'll be down in a minute," he said tersely. "I'll go change and be right down. Please tell Nettie I need fifteen minutes," he said, dismissing her with his words.

Elizabeth turned back toward the kitchen, feeling a little angry herself. A little bit of "Hello, dear. How was your day, my new bride?" would have made her feel more like a wife and less like one of the servants. She walked back through the kitchen doors and delivered the message to Nettie, visibly shaken.

"Is he havin' one of his moments?" Nettie asked.

"Oh, so you know something I don't?" asked Elizabeth.

"Word is he's prone to have fits once in a while, but I ain' never seen one," replied Nettie. "Come here, Miss Elizabeth. I have somethin' special that might make you feel better." Nettie walked to a locked cabinet, pulled out a key hanging from a chain underneath her blouse, and opened the cabinet. There sat a decanted bottle of wine with a crystal stopper. She pulled the bottle out and set it on the table in front of Elizabeth with a small crystal glass.

"I just pour'd this an hour ago but lock'd it back up because those be my instructions about the alcohol. This wine comes from another plantation not too far from here, from grapes that are hundreds o years old. Mr. Freeman say dis bottle here go for more than a hundred dollars, but once it's open if you all don' drink it, I have to use it fo a gravy or somethin', so here, have a taste." She poured wine into the glass, which Elizabeth took and raised to her mouth.

"No rules," she said, smiling.

"You have fifteen minutes to finish that," said Nettie with a grin.

~~*~~

Elizabeth took her seat at the dining room table. Charles walked in a minute later and took his. It was the first time they'd been seated together at the table since moving into the house, since the wedding. Her first thought was to wonder whether or not to raise her voice to speak to him—if she spoke in a normal voice, would he hear? He seemed so far away. He answered the question by greeting her, now calmer than she left him in his room.

"Good evening, darling," he started in what seemed to be a normal tone.

"Good evening, Charles." She didn't know what more to say, although a number of things came to mind. *How was your day? Why were you so angry? Are you going to ask me what I did today?* But she said nothing. She waited for him to continue.

Faye had set a fine spread in front of Charles and was waiting for him to give her the nod so that she could pour the wine. He looked up at her and gave her a half-smile, which must have been the signal. She stepped forward, poured a taste of the wine into his glass and waited while he sipped, swirled, swallowed, and nodded. She finished pouring his glass then walked to the other end of the table and poured a glass for Elizabeth—her second, but the way Charles went about making a show of tasting, he obviously hadn't noticed any missing from the bottle. As Charles dished a helping of each side next to his potted chicken pie, Faye would take the bowl and bring it to Elizabeth to do the same, which continued until each of them had a plate ready, at which time Faye disappeared into the kitchen. *Always serving him first*, Elizabeth noted.

"Listen, Elizabeth, I'm sorry that I got angry about the workers; it was certainly uncalled for. It's just that I gave them specific instructions, and they left the place a wreck."

Elizabeth nodded as she took a bite of the potpie. It was amazing, and the crust was blue-ribbon worthy. She didn't have a response. She was thinking about Adria, that Adria had likely sat at this very table, maybe exactly where she was sitting now. She'd learned that this table was one of the pieces of furniture that had been sold with the house when the Clayton family left after the turn of the century. It was impractical for any house that wasn't immense, and the style wasn't suited for a modern house, that was for sure, so she understood why it was still here.

"Elizabeth?" Charles said, his voice slightly raised—not because of the expanse between them but because he was irritated that she seemed to be daydreaming.

"Our first night dining together as husband and wife, how delightful!" Elizabeth quickly recovered and feigned joy in the fact that she was alone with her husband for the first time since the patio discussion. "It's alright. I understand."

He continued, "It's just that, well, this master bedroom was a test run for them. I have more projects that I'd like to do around here, and I want to know that I can count on them."

"Such as?" she asked, wondering if he would come clean about the servant quarters.

"Oh, I have a list of things, here and there." He did not intend to tell her about his mother, apparently, not just yet.

Elizabeth wondered how long he was going to keep that a secret. "Are you going to be interested in dessert?" she asked. "Nettie made a beautiful chocolate cake from a recipe she said has been in her family for decades."

"I would say no, but in that case, yes. I'll have a small slice. I don't want to insult her."

Charles smiled at Elizabeth from the other end of the table. She recalled the nights when he was courting her, and they would have romantic candlelit dinners where he would hold her hand across the table. *Certainly nothing like that could happen now,* she thought.

After dinner and cake and a very small glass of cognac, Elizabeth grew sleepy. She excused herself from the table, walked to Charles to take his hand, and looked down at him while noting the balding spot on the top of his head. Yes, he was older, and yes, he needed an heir, but why in the world would he not consider getting in a little practice? It baffled her that after four days of marriage, they'd still not had sex.

"I'm going to my room to read," she said. "If you find yourself in need of a little nightcap or just want a snuggle, my door is always open."

With that, she kissed his balding spot to let him know she'd noticed, turned, and walked down the hall, leaving him to wonder how much longer he could keep the secret about his mother's impending arrival and how Elizabeth would take it—likely not too well, he guessed. He recalled the way his mother treated her at the wedding—like another guest or even a servant he'd thought then, after catching the way she barely acknowledged Elizabeth's presence. It had been painful to all who had noticed.

Charles also knew deep down that he was betraying Elizabeth by keeping a mistress in town, which of course was the reason he did not need to visit her room. And he wouldn't, except when he knew she was fertile; he was counting on Faye to advise him of her monthly and to help him calculate when that might be.

~~*~~

Elizabeth walked into her room and after changing into her nightclothes, went straight to the chaise and pulled the book out from under the pillow. She pulled a floor lamp over to the head of the chaise, switched it on, then laid down, covering up with a light blanket that had been folded at the foot. She settled in and opened the diary.

September 17, 1857

I asked John if he could have Atticus ask Liam to hitch a wagon so that Rae and I could go to town.

If I'm going to start growing, I'm not going to fit into any of my clothes soon and will need to buy fabric to make new dresses that I can wear until the baby comes. John got angry and told me to send Rae. He said there was no reason I needed to be running around town in my condition. But heavens, no one would have to know. There is not so much as a bump where the little one is growing. I only know that the child is there because I've missed two of my monthlies, my bosom aches, and I feel sick in the morning. Also, Hattie says she can tell.

We fought about it, and I won. I told him under no circumstances was I going to let a slave pick out fabric for my dresses and for the baby's nursery. We will need to start making quilts soon, and I told him I was not going to use scraps of old fabric the way Hattie did. I said I also needed to buy soft fabric for baby blankets and the baby will need dresses as well. All babies, even boys are dressed in frocks until the boy starts to wear britches, and truthfully I've never understood why boys wear dresses although it is easier to change their soiled cloths. Finally, John gave in and said I could go and that he would instruct Liam to go slow over the bumps.

Liam is our liveryman. He takes care of the horses and tack and welds the iron on the buggy wheels when they break. His family came to America all the way from Ireland about a hundred years ago when they had a thing called a potato famine. I don't know what that means except that famine means people were starving, so I guess that is why they came over on the boat. He said it took them months to get here. I can't imagine being on the sea for that long. And imagine doing this while pregnant! I've never been on a boat except on the lake and when the wind comes up, it's hard to get your footing and you rock back and forth. It would make me very sick, so no boats for me right now.

I watch Liam drive the horses into town. He has a very strong back, and his hair is curly. It has just a little red in it, from his grandparents, he says. Most of his family back in Ireland had red hair, he told me, but they lost it here when they married into families with darker hair.

The trip to town took an hour, and Liam was careful not to hit the bumps as John told him. He turned around every once in a while, to ask me if I was doing okay, and when he did, he smiled, and I could see little dimples on his cheeks and the most beautiful blue eyes. For a moment, he reminded me of a little boy, but he's a man. He's real handsome, but of course I can't tell anyone that I think that. I can write it here, though!

My husband, John, is handsome, but in a different way. He's tall and has a mustache, which tickles when he kisses me, which is not very often. When he puts on a top hat, he seems even taller, although I know it is an illusion. But where Liam is nice, John is mean. He never smiles. He used to be nice, but I guess with all he has to do to keep this place running and with his business farming and trading slaves, he has too much on his mind these days. I don't hold it against him, but I wish he could give me the attention he used to before we were married. Those days were fun. This spring before we were married, we once took a buggy to the countryside with a basket of fresh bread, cheese, and apples. He knows a lot of places where there is shade beside creeks and lakes and where we were able to have a picnic and lie on a blanket watching clouds go by, blowing dandelions to watch the seeds fly in the wind.

Well, I must change into my nightdress now and get ready for bed. Rae will be in soon to brush my hair, and I need to put this book away someplace safe, especially now that I am already writing secrets. I will never get to go to town again if John finds out that I think Liam is handsome. Men can be so jealous.

Elizabeth yawned and stretched, feeling it was time for bed and knowing that she too needed to find a place to hide the diary from prying eyes. She thought of her safe. She'd asked Charles for a safe where she could store her pearls and other jewelry, some that he'd given her to wear to the lavish events so as to appear befitting to a man of his social stature, so he'd had one installed in her closet, showing her how he'd had it bolted to the floor behind where her dresses hung. It had a combination lock, so that she didn't have to worry about losing a key. She'd programmed it, using a combination of the dates of her birth month, day, and year but not in order.

She went to the closet and opened the safe. She turned the book over in her hands, examining the smooth leather and the stains that marked both the front and back. It definitely felt like something that was a hundred years old, she thought as she placed the book inside the safe and shut the door, spinning the lock.

Chapter Seven: Taking the Reins

Elizabeth woke early the next morning, hoping to catch Charles at breakfast to discuss a few things that were on her mind—like her going into town without his permission, which she found ludicrous. When she approached the dining room, she noted that there was no breakfast setting for either of them. She wandered straight to the kitchen. Neither Gwendolyn nor Faye had arrived, so it would be just her and Nettie.

She pushed through the doors and found the kitchen quiet, almost dark. Elizabeth turned the fire on under the tea kettle and pulled out a cup, saucer, and teabag. She wasn't really hungry but thought she might rummage around for a day-old cinnamon roll. As she opened the pantry door, the whistle went off on the kettle, and she turned to find Charles standing in the doorway of the kitchen. She startled.

"Charles, what?" she began, moving to turn the fire off under the kettle.

"There's been an accident," he said. "Nettie's daughter was on her way to town when her car was hit. Everyone is okay, but Nettie had to tend to her, so she'll be late."

Elizabeth took the kettle and poured water into her cup, adding the teabag. She found the rolls and brought them out, setting them on the counter. She took the plastic wrap off the tray, then found two plates, setting them down and retrieving another cup and saucer.

"Will you have tea or coffee before you head out?" she asked. She turned to find the milk pitcher in the refrigerator, placing it on the counter, then finding a stool to sit down. She poured milk into her cup with the hot water and tea bag and took a roll off the tray and placed it onto her plate.

Charles took in this sight, wondering what she would do if he said yes. Would she jump up and make him tea or coffee or was she simply asking for the sake of curiosity. Instead of waiting to find out, he decided to help himself. The water was still hot on the stove, so he took down a teacup and saucer and dropped in a teabag, pouring water over the bag. At that point, since the rolls were already on the counter, he decided to join Elizabeth and sat down with a small plate to dish himself up a roll.

Elizabeth found the sight rather curious. She'd never seen him wait on himself, nor help himself to anything for that matter. As long as she'd known him, there had always been someone around to wait on him. But here they were, their first breakfast together as husband and wife, and it was a makeshift breakfast in their kitchen in the dark on a butcher block countertop.

The thought prompted a giggle, then she stopped abruptly, realizing the inappropriateness of such an action but finding hilarity in the moment as she watched her husband trying to navigate the large pitcher of milk from the refrigerator, being careful not to spill.

"Is there anything I can do? For Nettie?" she asked.

"The family is all there, and her daughter was never admitted to the hospital, only checked at the scene for minor scrapes. Nettie will be here shortly and will bring her daughter with her so that she can keep an eye on her."

"Oh, great then," said Elizabeth. Then switching topics, "Will the workers be finished in your room today? And if so, then what?"

Charles shifted uncomfortably. "Yes, they should be finished by the end of the day," was all he would offer. He was not ready to tell her that they would be moving their tools and focusing their efforts on demolition in the former slave quarters. Not yet.

"Charles, I would like to go to town today," Elizabeth said, blowing steam across the top of her teacup.

He looked up sharply at her, furrowing his eyebrows. "And what do you need there that Faye cannot add to her list?"

"I want to go with her. I would like to find a nice gourmet store where I can find a few things, like imported brie cheese and dried black olives. And some smoked salmon. Faye looks at me blankly when I mention things like this; she has no idea how to shop for anything but staples." Elizabeth set her cup on the saucer, somewhat forcefully.

Charles had a feeling that this was not negotiable. He opened his mouth, then closed it again. After putting the last bite of cinnamon roll in his mouth, he picked up his cup and saucer and placed them next to the sink.

"I'll call Branson from the office," he said as he walked out of the kitchen.

Elizabeth sat staring at the double doors, still swinging. Her face was hot. Was that a *yes* or a *no*? She wasn't quite sure. She decided to wait for Gwendolyn to arrive, when she would press the issue. Gwendolyn would be in within the hour, so Elizabeth decided to go up to her room and wait there.

September 20, 1857

John let me know this morning that it is time to throw a party. Before I start showing and while I can still fit into my best gown, he wants to have the governor and his wife out for dinner. He says due to our status in the county, the governor will accept his invitation, and so then will anyone else he chooses to invite.

He said that in no uncertain terms I will be in charge of everything, from creating the invitations to planning the menu and the music. He will handle the guest list and told me to expect up to fifty people! He said he would tell Liam to come inform me as to how to instruct the guests regarding their carriages and that this should be part of the invitation and that we should tell them that he will have extra hands present to care for their horses during the event so they don't have to bring their help unless they want to. I had to hide a little blush when he mentioned Liam's name.

I think John has his sights set on being governor one day. He hasn't said so; it is just a feeling I have. I wonder what it would be like to be the first lady. I imagine it would be fun, but it would also carry a great deal of responsibility.

I used the party as an excuse to insist on another trip to town. Some things I can have Rae pick up when she is there, but I told John I absolutely must shop for others myself, and some things will have to be ordered well in advance for such an event, so time is of the essence. He agreed, and so this afternoon Liam pulled the buggy around, and Rae and I got into the back as usual.

Once we were halfway to town, I tapped Liam on the shoulder and told him I wanted to drive. I've known how to drive a buggy since I was a little girl. My daddy would have me drive to town when my mama was heavy with child. We didn't have any slaves, and we only had one man that helped us around our property, but we couldn't spare him for a whole day to go to town and back and trust him to get the shopping done. That was up to me when I got a little older. I would bring my little brother, and although he was a pest, he was also helpful. I would pay, and he would carry things to the wagon. He would also tie up the horses and watch them while I shopped.

At first, Liam thought I was kidding, but I tapped him again and told him that I insisted. He stopped the buggy and took my hand and helped me climb over the buckboard into the front. I have to admit, sitting so close to him made me feel warm all over, and when I looked back at Rae, the face she made was one of amazement. Her eyes were so big! And I don't know if it was because I was driving or that I was sitting close to another man, so close that our legs were touching! I don't think she approved, and also I doubt she'd ever seen a woman drive a buggy. The best part was when Liam gave me the reins, his hand lingered over mine, and he turned to look at me. I will dream about those blue eyes of his tonight.

When Rae was braiding my hair tonight for bed, I told her that if she mentioned one word of me driving or sitting up front with Liam, I would make sure she got a beating. Of course, I would never order such a thing to happen. I actually don't like the fact that we own other people, but I could never say that out loud to anyone. I feel bad when John gets angry and orders one of them to be beaten. Atticus is the one who has to do it, and I can't tell if he likes it or not, but it is part of his job.

I feel bad that I have such strong feelings for Liam, being a married woman and all, and with child. Things are about to change drastically for me and my role in

the household will never permit me to come any closer
to Liam, but I can dream.

Elizabeth heard pounding again coming from downstairs.
Then she heard voices in the foyer. She guessed that the
workers had resumed—thank God it was their last day in the
house—and Gwendolyn had arrived with Faye. Gwendolyn
often picked her up where the bus dropped her off so that she
didn't have to walk the last mile.

Elizabeth closed the diary and slid it back into the safe,
turning the dial just slightly to hide the last number of the code.
She changed quickly into clothes that would be suitable for a
trip to town and made her way down to find Gwendolyn giving
Faye instructions regarding the help she was going to need in
the kitchen since it didn't appear Nettie was going to make it
in at all. Elizabeth wondered how this would affect her trip to
town. She greeted the two of them as they headed toward the
kitchen together.

"Good morning, ladies. Have we heard anything from
Nettie?"

"Good morning, Mrs. Freeman," answered Gwendolyn
over her shoulder as they passed into the kitchen. "Nettie can't
make it in today. Her daughter is fine, just a little bruised, but
she needs to stay and care for her. She'll be in bright and early
tomorrow. Faye here is going to take over in the kitchen for the
day." Gwendolyn smiled at Elizabeth and gave a nod toward
Faye, who was already donning an apron and pulling food
out of the large refrigerator. Elizabeth was happy to hear that
Nettie's daughter, Twyla, was not hurt.

"Very well, then. I will be going to town today for supplies,"
Elizabeth announced.

Gwendolyn turned to her, surprised. "Is Mr. Freeman aware
of this?" she asked.

"Yes, Gwendolyn, he is. I told him this morning that there
are some things I need to pick up. He said he would call Branson
and advise him. I'll get the supplies we need if you give me the
list along with where you normally purchase things." Elizabeth
stood with her arms crossed, waiting while Gwendolyn pulled
out her notepad. She set it on the counter and began adding
some things to a list that had already been started.

"Don't forget to have her go by the butcher shop," Faye said to Gwendolyn. "Miss Nettie had me order some ribs cut just the way she likes. They should be ready." Faye then turned to Elizabeth. "Branson know where all of the stores are, Mrs. Freeman, and in what order we usually go so that the milk don't grow warm on the way home."

"Thank you, Faye," said Elizabeth as Gwendolyn handed her the list.

Charles had evidently given Branson the go-ahead because precisely at ten he pulled the long car in under the portico, came in, and took off his hat as he entered the front door, where he nodded to Gwendolyn then folded his very large frame into a petite bench in the foyer. He normally wore coveralls because he was usually working on cars or the tractor, but today since he was taking Elizabeth to town, he'd done his best to clean up. He'd worn his best pair of denim jeans and cowboy boots, along with a flannel shirt and leather vest, combed back his dark hair, and had donned a fedora, an odd combination but one he felt was befitting of driving the lady of the house into town.

Elizabeth was still in the kitchen watching Faye as she tried to figure out what Nettie had planned for the workers and staff for lunch when Gwendolyn entered to tell her Branson was waiting. Gwendolyn instructed Faye to start with lunch, then figure out the dinner menu once lunch had been served. Elizabeth and Nettie had written out the daily menus for the week, and supplies had been purchased, so her reason for going to town was truly self-serving. She needed to get out of there and take a ride. Shopping at a gourmet store had just been an excuse, but she could justify the trip now by picking up the ribs and getting fresh milk and eggs.

Grabbing her purse and the list inside, Elizabeth walked out the front door, stepped into the car while the door held open by Branson, and for the first time since before the wedding she was out of the house! Only a week had gone by, and she was already going stir-crazy.

The ride into town was much shorter than she remembered. She felt so isolated out at the plantation house that she imagined they were an hour or more from town. She then remembered that while the ride into town had taken Adria more than an hour, she had been in a buggy! The road wound through dense woods that every now and then would open up to reveal a mansion on a hilltop with a long, narrow driveway leading up from an overly large, closed gate.

Branson stopped at the gourmet store before making the usual rounds. Charles had evidently located the store on their route and called Branson with the address. Being that this was Elizabeth's excuse to go to town, she took her time while Branson waited outside, purchased more than she'd intended, and with Charles's American Express in hand, she cared not. If she were going to be a prisoner in her own home, she was going to eat well, and whether her husband joined her or not, she was going to start taking her dinner at the main table so as not to seem cavalier about the fact that Nettie spent long days in the kitchen, her sole mission being to cook for them nourishing, comforting, delicious food.

When Elizabeth left the store with two large bags filled to overflowing, Branson stepped forward to retrieve the bags and put them in the trunk. She stepped into the car, Branson coming quickly around to close it for her, and off they went. The butcher, the grocer, then a quick stop for something she presumed Charles had ordered—she didn't recognize the business and didn't pay attention to what was in the bag that Branson came out with—and quickly they were on their way back to the country.

Once the plantation house was in view, Elizabeth realized how much bigger it was than the newer mansions she'd seen on the way to town. She knew that the place was big, but coming up the long, narrow driveway, it suddenly came into focus as perhaps the largest she'd seen all day. She noticed the old slave quarters as they came near the house and saw Holden standing in the doorway. He tipped his hat as they passed. Her heart beat fast for just a moment, and she gave a smile and a brief wave, then looked up to see Branson watching her in the rearview mirror. Her smile faded, and she locked eyes with Branson.

"Thank you for driving today, Branson. I really appreciate it. We'll have to make it a weekly thing."

"Yes, Mrs. Freeman," he replied, knowing full well that Mr. Freeman would be the one to make that call.

Charles did not come home for dinner that evening, and once again, he did not bother to call. In fact, Elizabeth was fast asleep by the time he entered the foyer. With Nettie not there, she'd settled for a bowl of leftover soup that Faye had prepared for the staff earlier in the day. It wasn't as good as Nettie's cooking, but it wasn't bad.

Elizabeth dismissed Faye early and had Gwendolyn stay to discuss fabric for new curtains in the drawing room. By five o'clock, no one had heard from Charles, and Elizabeth wasn't going to have a repeat of the other night where Nettie cooked a fantastic meal and no one ate a bite of it, so she had Faye return everything to the refrigerator and told her to go on home. Nettie could cook it up the following day, and the ribs would have to keep another day.

After dinner, Elizabeth drew her own bath. She was half tempted to bring the diary to the tub and read until the water grew cold but thought better of it. One slip, and the diary would be ruined by the water. The paper was already fragile, and the ink would simply disappear if it got wet.

She slipped in under the bubbles, sinking to her neck in the deep tub. She recalled the day and how much fun a simple outing had become. It made her miss her friends and their happy hour gatherings after work—and her sister, whom she had not heard from since the wedding. Elizabeth imagined she could call her sister as well, but Penny was always so busy, with the kids and everything.

As I will likely be someday soon, she thought. She brought her hands to her breasts, imagining what they might be like full of milk, and what it would feel like to have a baby sucking on her nipples. Her breasts were tender, meaning her period would be coming in the next day or two. She was glad that she remembered to add tampons to the supply list on the way to town. She wondered where Charles might be at that very minute. She stepped out of the bath and toweled off, making a mental note to call her sister in the morning. She slid into bed nude, enjoying the crisp, cool sheets, and quickly fell to sleep.

Little did Elizabeth know Charles had been lying naked in the arms of Marigold, whom he loved perhaps more than his wife. She was stroking his hair, her milk-chocolate hands massaging his scalp, his head lying against her shoulder, exhausted after making mad passionate love to her. *But it wasn't making love in the sense that meant anything,* he would remind himself as he dressed, when he combed his hair and donned his jacket before he walked out the door.

It was just routine, he told himself as he drove home, a routine that had carried on for years, ten years to be exact. Their arrangement was that as long as she did not sleep with anyone else—only him and whenever the need arose—he would take care of her in every way. But if so much as a word came out about their affair, the support would stop, and her life would change forever. He went so far as to maintain contact with her doctor, to monitor her birth control and her regular checkups *down there*. It was another part of their agreement, and one that she didn't mind at all, as that was another bill paid.

The fact that she was of mixed race could be a problem for Charles down the road. He had aspirations of running for political office, which meant that if something like his affair with a woman descended from slaves on her father's side and an Irish Catholic mother whose family had been in the area for many generations came to light, he would be ruined before he had his first rally.

Charles cut his lights as he rounded the last corner of the drive, coasting up to the house by the light of the moon. He didn't want to chance his lights shining into Elizabeth's room and waking her. He dreaded what that conversation might be like and prayed she was fast asleep as he turned his key in the lock.

Holden sat on the porch of the barn, attached to a second garage that housed three of Charles's cars, which Branson was in charge of keeping in perfect condition, inside and out. Also inside the barn were two horses Charles kept in the event he ever might like to ride. Holden watched as Charles cut the lights on his vehicle. Holden turned his hand, cupping his cigarette so as not to take a chance of Charles seeing the glowing tip. He laughed when he saw Charles look toward the upstairs windows, creeping like a teenager who has been out too late, quietly and cautiously exaggerating every move. He wasn't fooling anyone but Elizabeth. Everyone knew about Charles's mistress except her. Holden stubbed out his cigarette on the railing and turned to walk inside.

Holden's apartment was also attached to the garage, around on the other side. It was very nice for a caretaker's quarters, small but with country-plantation charm. The wood floors were original and had been previously sanded and varnished by the same crew that just finished the master bedroom and had moved their tools that afternoon over to the quarters. They all still called the building "the quarters," but Charles had said that morning that before his mother moved in, they were going to rename the building the Cottage at Noble Oak Plantation. Holden was tasked with finding a sign maker in town to make a small wooden placard that would be mounted above the porch when the remodel was complete. Charles requested that they all start calling it the cottage, though, instead of the quarters because his mother was not keen on living in a building that had once been overcrowded with slaves and didn't need a reminder.

Holden recalled finding Elizabeth there at the open door the prior afternoon and remembered how taken he was by her plain but beautiful nature. She had a certain innocence about her, although he supposed she wasn't that young—likely they were the same age. He knew—everyone knew—that Charles had been forced to take a bride to provide the family with an heir and that his relationship with Elizabeth would likely be anything but love. Holden hoped for Elizabeth's sake that Charles could grow to love her because she was really quite remarkable and deserved to be adored.

Holden also knew—again everyone knew but Elizabeth— that Charles had laid out strict orders not to let her out of their sight. She wasn't allowed a car because that would mean too much freedom. Branson would be her driver so that he could be Charles's eyes and ears and watch her comings and goings. Elizabeth likely didn't know it yet, but she wasn't going to make any new friends, as friends outside of their elite social circle could be threatening to a family like the Freemans.

Oh yes, Holden knew a lot about the situation, as in the very first meeting with Charles, the rules had been clearly laid out, and they'd been told that the slightest infraction would result in immediate termination. Holden was paid very well, twice what the position normally paid, so the stakes were high. The apartment was an added benefit, as well as the fact that he had at least three cars to choose from anytime he decided to venture to town. But the irony of Elizabeth living in an old plantation house-turned-prison was not lost on him. And he had quickly become fond of the only prisoner.

Holden decided then and there that he would not only keep an eye on Elizabeth, but he would do everything he could to protect her—even if it meant losing his job.

Chapter Eight: Liam and Holden

September 30, 1857

I'm happy to report that preparations for the party are well underway. John insisted that we call it a ball instead of a party, so that guests would be inclined to dress in their finest. The musicians are known to be some of the most renowned in all the South. They have played for not only governors but for presidents!

I haven't had time to write in a while as my days have been consumed with getting out the invitations and menu planning. Since we will be serving alcohol (and hopefully lots of it!), it has become complicated. Alcohol can be very hard to get sometimes. John says something about supply and demand that I don't understand, but I guess if I did it would explain the current shortage. I've had to send out notices to local distilleries and winemakers that we're looking to make a bigger purchase, and I'm confident that they will answer since I dropped the governor's name. I hated to do it, but what could be worse than running out of booze when the governor is at your party? This is my first gala as lady of this plantation, and everything must be perfect. John is counting on me, I know, and I don't want to disappoint him.

My belly is just beginning to show, but the gown I'm going to wear is the one that I own that is the most forgiving. Rae has it hanging in the corner of my room, and I try it on every couple of days to make sure that it still fits. We have a plan to take out a tiny circle of fabric in the center and expand it if we have to, then we can cover it with lace and sequins or pearls and make it look intentional, as if the dress was originally designed that way. Rae is good at things like this, and I'm glad about that. I have enough to worry about right now.

Liam drove me to town yesterday, and it was just the two of us. Rae stayed behind because she was in the middle of a project with doing some deep cleaning, moving furniture, taking down drapes, and cleaning them then putting everything back up. It is a big project so I suggested that she stay behind and that I could handle the shopping on my own.

At first, John didn't like the idea of me traveling in the wagon all that way, and I finally heard from Hattie that he was concerned that the bumpy ride might be a danger to the baby. Just goes to show how little men know about how strong women's bodies are. Now he is fine with it, until it becomes obvious that I am pregnant. After that, I am expected to stay home and prepare the nursery, sew baby clothes, and in general just wait until the big day comes. I'm a little nervous to say the least, but women have been having babies for a very long time, and I'm young, so I'm going to trust that everything will be fine.

It is nice riding with Liam alone. When it is just the two of us, he lets me ride in front all the way to town. Sometimes he hands me the reins and watches me handle the horses. I know he is looking at my face although when I look over at him, he looks away. I'm so curious about him. I wonder why he isn't married and why he is content to live on the plantation and just work with the horses. He never goes out, at least that I know of, so he must be very lonely. The only other girls our age are slaves. You hear tell of white men bedding them, but I can't imagine that is something he would do.

Yesterday on the way back from town, Liam asked if I would mind if we took a little break at a place he knew of, a lake where the horses could rest in the shade. He said he doesn't get off the property much, and it would be a nice break for him. I told him I didn't care, but secretly I was a little nervous. If anyone saw us together and with me in the state I'm in, it would spell trouble if anything got back to John.

The place where Liam drove us was completely secluded. He pulled the horses up toward the lake and into the shade, where he hitched them to a tree. He pulled a blanket out of the back, and when he held out his hand to help me down, I lost my footing just for a moment, and he put both hands around my waist to steady me. Our faces almost touched as he helped me out of the buggy. It gave me chills, and I shivered a little even though it was hot out. He saw that and smiled.

He set out the blanket, plopped down, and gave it a pat, offering a spot next to him, and truthfully, I was ready to settle for a minute. It seems I've been going and going for days trying to organize this ball. Once I touched the ground, I wanted to lie down but resisted the temptation. He laid back and closed his eyes, chewing on a piece of grass. He didn't talk, and I didn't know what to say. We just sat there for a while, then I said maybe we should get back, and he agreed. He held his hand out to help me up, and before I could begin to get up, he leaned over and kissed me on the lips. Since I'll probably burn this book someday, I'll admit that I kissed him back, long and hard.

Although I'm John's wife, he isn't romantic with me like that, and I guess Liam found a weak spot in me. I needed to be kissed, and he could tell. Then he touched me. Not in a bad way, he just found my breast with his hand and then with his mouth, and I have to say I didn't want it to stop there. After a few minutes, though, we both realized that we would be missed if we didn't get back on the road. I sat up on the blanket, pulled my skirt down straight, and checked my hair to make sure nothing was out of place. Then Liam helped me up all the way this time, looking at me with those blue eyes. I smiled all the way home.

Elizabeth was lying in bed reading. She slipped the diary under her pillow before answering Faye's knock, getting up quickly to dress because she'd gone to bed naked. Faye set a tray on her table that held tea and milk, asking if she wanted to take breakfast in her room. Given that she was miffed about the fact that Charles did not come home the previous night—not that she was aware of anyway—she said she would.

After noting that Elizabeth was undeniably upset, likely due to Charles's disappearance, Faye said she would be back with breakfast and quickly left Elizabeth's bedroom. Elizabeth went to her table, taking a seat before pouring her tea. She was absolutely blown away by what she was reading in the journal and dismayed that she had absolutely no one—save her sister probably—that she could share the story with. Adria's tale was quickly becoming an obsession, and it was a thick book. She didn't know if she would possibly be able to keep it a secret until she was finished, but she knew she must. The details of Adria's life were beginning to feel all too familiar, and it made her uncomfortable, although she remained wildly intrigued.

Elizabeth rose from the table and went into the bathroom, suddenly feeling a trickle of what was surely her period beginning. She got out the box of tampons and set them on the bathroom counter next to the toilet. She showered off briefly then dressed again as Faye came through the door with her breakfast. Faye sat the tray down and picked up the teapot.

"I'll be right back with more hot water, Mrs. Freeman."

"Faye, honey," Elizabeth started. "Is it allowable to call me by my first name?"

"Yes, Mrs. Freeman, I suppose so," said Faye. "What is that?"

Elizabeth could hardly contain her surprise. "My name is Elizabeth. It used to be Elizabeth Anne Storey, and now it is Elizabeth Anne Freeman. And as long as we are together in private, I do wish you would call me Elizabeth."

"Yes, Miss Elizabeth, I can do that." Faye looked past her and noticed the box of tampons on the bathroom counter. "Can I get you anything else?"

"No, Faye, that will be all for now."

Faye turned to leave.

"Wait, Faye, one more thing. Is Mr. Freeman here? He wasn't when I went to bed last night." Elizabeth saw the look on Faye's face turn to one of concern. She wasn't supposed to talk about Mr. Freeman; that was one of the rules. "You are not to discuss my comings and goings with anyone," he'd told Faye, Gwendolyn, and Nettie when they were hired. Of course, they all knew that this meant not to talk to Elizabeth about whether or not he comes home or when, and what time he leaves in the morning. Faye didn't know what the big deal was about all that, after all they were a married couple and what each of them did should be none of her concern.

"I'm not sure, ma'am. His breakfast place setting is there waitin' for him; so is yours. But I'll go down and remove yours since you're having breakfast here. I will be downstairs when you are ready to talk about things. Gwendolyn said something about new curtains. If there is anything I can do to help, I'll be ready." With that, she smiled, turned, and left the room.

Elizabeth retrieved the diary from under her pillow and started reading from where she'd left off.

October 5, 1857

When Liam and I got home the other day with the supplies, he carried in the heavy woven bags and set everything in the entry, tipped his hat to me and backed out the door, closing it on his way out. Hattie gave him a sharp eye, noticing the way he looked at me. She went through the bags and pulled out things that needed kept cold. Our icebox is the best one John could find, good enough to keep food cold for days if we are careful. In this case, it means more ice and not opening it unless we have to. The help will start cooking later today, and they probably won't stop until people are walking in the door.

I was exhausted today and went straight to my room after talking to Hattie about the food one last time. We received back fifty-five responses from the invitations that I sent out, so Hattie has a lot of work to do! I finished showing the workers how to set up the tables and chairs around the grand dining hall. I had them move the long table outside in back and set up smaller tables, leaving the center open for dancing.

The musicians will sit just outside the patio doors, which we can leave open since the evening temperatures are lower now. Behind them, the guests will be able to see the lake and maybe the swans if the moon is out. Rae will bring her sister to help attend to the guests, taking their coats to the cloakroom when they arrive and showing the ladies to the powder room in the hall. I told them both to braid their hair with ribbons and make sure their uniforms are freshly washed and pressed.

I asked Rae to draw a bath for me. I wouldn't ask her for anything else as I know she had a rough day with the cleaning and all. I stood naked in front of the long looking glass that was propped against the wall. I turned sideways, where I could just barely see the little seed telling us he was coming. I say *he* because I hope it is a boy. I want girls too, of course, but having a boy is important as John is going to need help running this place, and the oldest boy will eventually take over this plantation when John is no longer able.

I guess I should have been honest with Liam and told him there's a baby coming. He probably would not have kissed me, though. John and I don't plan to tell anyone until after the ball. We don't need people looking at me like that, John told me. Truthfully, I think he wants to keep the focus on himself and the talk about business. Either way, if Liam tries anything like that the next time we are alone, I'll have to tell him.

Only two more days until the party. I'm nervous and excited. I tried the gown on today. Rae was able to pull the buttons together in the back, but it was hard. I'll only have to wear it for a few hours, then I can put it away for a long time.

Faye sat at the kitchen counter peeling potatoes, watching Nettie as she moved around the kitchen, first filling a large pot with water to boil, then pulling out a broiler pan for the ribs. Nettie was telling her what she was doing with each step and why, in case something like what just happened ever came about again, and Faye had to take over for her.

"How is your daughter?" Faye asked, noting the bowl was almost full of potatoes, certainly more than Mr. and Mrs. Freeman could eat at one meal but knowing better than to question.

"She's fine, thank you fo askin', child. She gon' be jus like new in a few days." Nettie took the bowl from Faye as she dropped in the last potato and after giving them a final rinse in the sink, dumped them into the now-boiling water. She pulled out the rack of ribs and set them on the broiler pan, then began brushing them with a barbeque sauce that she'd made earlier in the day.

"Miss Elizabeth asked me if her husband came home last night," Faye said, looking at Nettie, who gave her a disapproving stare.

"First of all, you do not call her by her first name in this house, and second, you better not have had an answer fo' her. You know the rules. What Mr. Freeman do is his business, not yours, not mine."

"And not his wife's," challenged Faye.

"Missy, you gon' work yoself up to get fired you keep that up," Nettie fired back. "That is correct: not even his wife's."

"His breakfast setting is still out there," Faye said, looking at the clock that read just before ten.

"Then go get it," Nettie said curtly.

"She's having her monthly," continued Faye. "I'm supposed to report to Mr. Freeman when this happens and when I think she'll come to be ready to make a baby. I always count the days from my first day so that I know when I could be in danger of this." She quickly added, "Should anything happen, you know."

"Then count the days and tell him what that day might be. Start a couple days early as sometimes that time comes faster. The sooner she is wit child, the sooner the pressure can be off all o us, and we can get this house ready for a little one! Now go get those breakfast dishes off the table." Nettie shooed Faye out of the kitchen with the towel that had been draped over her shoulder and went back to basting the ribs.

Elizabeth was standing in the great dining hall when Faye entered. She was looking around the room, imagining what it must have been like to have fifty-five guests in the room. The long table Adria referred to was the one that held the untouched breakfast setting. She envisioned the patio doors flung wide and a band sitting out there playing to the room. The lake shimmered in the distance, rays of sun hitting the rippling water blown by the breeze. The swans were nowhere in sight.

"Mrs. Freeman, you okay?" asked Faye, who'd been standing there watching her as she daydreamed.

Elizabeth started. "Yes Faye, yes. Why I was just looking out at the lake and wondering where the swans had gone."

"They go to the far side when it is sunny," responded Faye. "They swim under the shady side where the cypress trees overhang and take cover until the sun goes down a little."

Elizabeth wondered why she hadn't noticed this. Then she recalled that Adria also had swans, wondering if those on the lake now were descendants.

"We're having those ribs for supper," Faye said, changing the subject.

"Hopefully, my husband will come home to enjoy them," Elizabeth said without a smile. "I'm going for a walk, Faye. Please tell Gwendolyn to meet me back here in an hour, and we'll continue the conversation about the curtains. Maybe you and I can go into town tomorrow and get the fabric."

Faye liked the idea of that. She wanted to know more about things like this, about what it takes to run a big house. She removed the breakfast dishes and watched as Elizabeth walked out through the patio doors into the bright sunlight, wondering why she didn't wear a hat.

Elizabeth walked down to the lake, scanning for the swans. Just as Faye had said, they were nestled together under a cypress on the far edge. She continued around the lake on the path that led to the old slave quarters, where she heard banging and men's voices. She walked up onto the porch and noticed that the windows that had been there the other day had been replaced with brand new ones. They were white, the kind with divided panes, and they opened, unlike the ones they'd removed.

Elizabeth poked her head in the door. The voices were coming from the back room, when suddenly she heard what sounded like a chainsaw and a loud crash. Then laughter.

"Hello?" she shouted from the doorway.

A big surly man with an enormous beard came walking out of the back bedroom.

"Mrs. Freeman! What are you doing here? This is a construction zone and a dangerous place," he said, noting her trim figure and healthy breasts.

"Then perhaps you should be wearing a hardhat," she said with a grin. "I'm just checking out the progress."

"We're tearing out this wall to make one large bedroom out of two," he said. "Let us get the demolition done, then I'll have this place cleaned up, and you can come back for a tour when it is safer," he said, waving a hammer in the air behind him.

"Sounds like a plan," she said, backing away onto the porch. She turned and was suddenly face-to-face with Holden.

"Dangerous place, indeed," he said, almost laughing. "Let's get you a hardhat so that you can tour when they are ready."

"I was just out for a walk and…" she started.

"And you could not help but check out your mother-in-law's new quarters…or shall we call it the cottage, as instructed?" he said, amused. "It will shortly have a new sign above the door, inscribed with those words."

"What do you mean *as instructed*," she asked?

"Apparently the elder Mrs. Freeman had a real problem living in a space that once housed slaves," Holden mused. "But wouldn't you think that would include not only this plantation house but about every house in the South?"

He continued, "But she is the lady of the house—although she defers to you at this time—and only because you are destined to give her son an heir."

The comment stung, hard. Elizabeth gave Holden a scorching look. But she couldn't deny his words. Everything he said was true. She was housed here much like mating stock, and that she could not deny.

"And what if I don't deliver?" she asked, a quizzical expression on her face. "Do I stand a chance of being shunned, or even put out to pasture as might have happened a century ago?"

Holden looked around for anyone who may be able to hear this conversation.

"Perhaps, Mrs. Freeman," he started.

"If people do not start calling me by my name, *Elizabeth*, I think I may go stark raving mad," she said, then broke into laughter. "This is utterly ridiculous, and you and I both know it," she said. "But apparently, I signed up for this, and here I am." She paused. "Here *we* are."

Holden looked at her questioningly.

"Because you signed up for this as well, right? You are one of my keepers?" she asked.

"Let's take a walk," he replied, looking around again. There were no cameras on the property yet—although Charles had talked about installing them—so it was still safe to walk and talk, without the chance of being watched and scrutinized for any behavior that might be deemed out of the ordinary.

They took the path back toward the lake, but then Holden veered off to the left. Elizabeth followed, curious where this path led and happy to know more of the property's trails. They walked for some time, and a small cabin came into view in front of them. Holden stopped.

"Here we are," he said, pointing. "This one has been left as it was more than a hundred years ago."

Holden came around behind her and produced a key. Elizabeth stepped aside as he climbed the stairs to the porch and turned the key in the lock. The door swung open to reveal a landscape stopped in time. Elizabeth entered, taking in the small humble abode and imagining that she had certainly just walked in Adria's footsteps through this very door when she came here to meet her lover. For now, in the journal Adria and Liam were only sneaking kisses on their journeys to town. Elizabeth's heart beat with excitement at the thought, tempting her to skip ahead in Adria's writings. But she would not.

The wood stove held a kettle for boiling water. Pottery bowls sat on the small kitchen table as if waiting to be filled with freshly cooked beans or perhaps grits and cheese. Plates were stacked on shelves adjacent to the stove, and two chairs sat empty at the table, beckoning them to sit. A small bed sat in the corner, still made, the quilt ravished by mice throughout the years but nonetheless speaking of memories made.

Elizabeth walked around the room, taking in every detail, imagining Adria as she would have entered Liam's home and shared what he offered from the stove, then made love to him on this very bed. Adria hadn't revealed anything like that in her journal yet, but surely it was just a matter of time. Elizabeth was stunned, amazed, and taken by the entire scene.

"This is truly astonishing," she said.

"Yes, it is. I agree," said Holden. "Charles and I have spoken about what to do with this place, and we both agree that it should remain just as it is, a timeless window into this plantation's history. We call it the bunkhouse."

Elizabeth was relieved to hear that. The last thing that should happen here would be what was taking place over at the old slaves' quarters, a complete annihilation of what it once was. She turned to Holden.

"It will always be preserved just like this then? It should be," she said as she continued to walk through the room, touching the table, the kettle, the chairs.

"As the lady of the house, you can make sure that happens," he said, his hand intentionally brushing hers as it rested on the back of a chair. He continued, "The story is that this is where the liveryman lived, who was once the lover of Miss Adria, the lady of the house then, who took that man in secret when her husband left for the war—although rumors were that it had been happening long before he left."

Elizabeth paused, gazing over at the bed. *So I am right, I knew it!*

Holden went on, "Then John returned—severely injured but intact and apparently as angry as he ever was—and the entire household was in turmoil for some time upon his return. John apparently was never apprised of the affair, although he questioned why Liam was gone, and the couple tried to carry on upon his return and did so successfully, that is until Miss Adria had a daughter with red hair." Holden ran his hands through his own hair, nervously watching Elizabeth's every move, praying that no one walked in to see them in that moment.

Elizabeth turned to face Holden, the heat rising from her breast to her neck and up to her face, which now flushed.

They stood only a few feet apart, taking in the history of the place together, the transgressions that had happened there that had at times threatened the rule of the family plantation, and suddenly Elizabeth understood everything that Adria had once faced: her place in the family, the patriarchal rule of the times then that stood to this day, and the fact that she herself was now in a very similar situation.

"I will insist that this place remains exactly as it is now," she said, smiling. "I will make sure of that." She walked to the porch and stopped at the door, turning for one last look around the room.

"Come, let me show you my place. It looks a lot like this but much cleaner," Holden said, grinning broadly, showing her out and locking the door. They continued along the same path, turning left when it forked, leading away from the plantation house, which was just barely visible in the distance. Holden looked back nervously as he led her away from the bunkhouse.

First the stables came into view. Elizabeth was aware of them because she'd seen them from the main drive and had heard there were still horses inside although she'd never seen them. She might ask Holden to freshen her riding skills one day soon. She followed Holden around the stable doors to the side, where a porch roof sat over a small deck from where she could see the portico of the plantation house. An ancient but refurbished rocking chair sat beside the door, holding a quilt draped over the back. Holden swung open the door and stepped back to allow Elizabeth to enter.

"The man who ran this plantation when it was first built, named Atticus, lived here," Holden said.

Elizabeth was aware of Atticus, but only that he was in charge of beating the slaves, a painful reminder of the darker parts of the history of the South—and of her new home.

Holden stood watching Elizabeth take in the beauty and timelessness of his home. He had no idea to what extent she understood the significance of the moment. It was indeed very much like the bunkhouse, but it had running water, and she could see through an open door in the corner that a bathroom had been installed. And it looked lived-in, not so much a museum like the bunkhouse. She noted that Holden's neatly made bed against the window held another quilt, this one beautiful and well-preserved. A coffeepot sat on an electric burner, and a cup and spoon were in the sink. Elizabeth turned, standing only a few feet from Holden as he leaned in the doorway, watching her every move. She walked over to stand in front of him.

"Holden," she said. "Would you kiss me?"

Chapter Nine: Dehlia and the Ball

Dehlia arrived at two in the afternoon, knowing that Charles would still be at the office and well behind her. Her driver parked under the portico and held the door and her hand while she got out of the long, dark sedan. Her arrival caused quite a stir because no one was expecting her, so there was no afternoon tea nor hot biscuits ready. Nothing.

Gwendolyn ran to the kitchen to advise Nettie, then scrambled to greet Dehlia and welcome her into the house, not knowing if she would want tea nor what the purpose was for her visit exactly.

Dehlia's driver brought her bag to the foyer and dropped it there, waiting for further instruction. Faye ducked into the kitchen, not having any idea how to receive Mr. Freeman's mother unannounced. Elizabeth was nowhere to be found, so the entire household was in a quandary, not knowing what to do next.

Dehlia walked into the dining room, taking in the greatness, the long table, and the doors that sat open to the cool breeze coming in off the lake. Gwendolyn found her there, curtsied, then looked up and smiled.

"Mrs. Freeman, what a surprise and a pleasure!" she said somewhat inauthentically. As the house manager, she should have been more prepared and had a plan how to entertain and where to offer to put her. (For the night? She had come with an overnight bag, it seemed.) Gwendolyn was embarrassed that she had no earthly idea where Elizabeth was at that very moment.

"Thank you, Gwendolyn. I must admit I've arrived somewhat unexpectedly, and for that I apologize. I'd mentioned to Charles just days ago that I wanted to come and see the progress on the cottage, and he said that I should just come and have a look for myself sometime. So here I am!"

Gwendolyn first set Nettie about heating water and preparing a tray of cookies and was ready to host Mrs. Freeman until she figured out the purpose for the visit. Now she knew that Dehlia's goal was to inspect the construction, but she'd also brought an overnight bag, so what now? Gwendolyn so wished Mr. Freeman would come back quickly. She would call him as soon as tea was ready and Mrs. Freeman was settled in. She decided then to put her out on the veranda. Gwendolyn knew that if she needed to ready a guest room, she should be able to do that within a short time, but she had no idea if the elder Mrs. Freeman was here for the night or if she planned to stay for a week!

"Nettie will have tea ready within a few minutes," Gwendolyn said, still somewhat nervous.

"Where is Elizabeth?" Dehlia asked.

"She is either in her room resting or out taking a walk, given that it is a most pleasant afternoon. Let's make you comfortable on the patio, and I'll have Branson tend to your bag. Will you be spending the night?" Gwendolyn asked anxiously as she tried to think about which guest rooms were clean, which may be clean but perhaps slightly dusty, and which were off-limits due to impending remodeling needs.

Gwendolyn led Dehlia to the patio, arranging her in a comfortable lounge chair beside a table large enough to hold tea as well as an afternoon biscuit tray.

"I will go and request that Mrs. Freeman—Miss Elizabeth—join us promptly," Gwendolyn said once Dehlia was seated in a lounge chair.

Dehlia reclined, facing the pond and appeared to be enjoying watching the swans on the lake, answering Gwendolyn calmly. "Don't make a fuss, please. I'll rest here and take tea and cookies. When you find Elizabeth, please send her to me, and we'll take a walk down to the cottage." Dehlia was enjoying the view and looking forward to a time very soon when this would be *her* home and *her* view.

~~*~~

Holden stood face-to-face with Elizabeth, their hot breath exchanged freely and more rapidly as the kisses became more intense. Elizabeth's heart was pounding, and when Holden pulled her in tightly, she felt his stiff erection through his jeans, which he rubbed against her belly. Suddenly, she heard her name being called. She pulled back in a panic and stared wide-eyed at Holden.

"Shhh, don't worry, Elizabeth," Holden said, smoothing her hair. "I'll stay here. You walk back the way we came, through the trees until you get to the fork, then turn sharply left. That path will take you up to the kitchen door. I'll stay here. If anyone comes here looking for you, I'll say I thought I saw you out walking up that way."

Elizabeth looked into Holden's eyes, taking a deep breath and exhaling slowly. Then another. She leaned up and gave him one last kiss on the lips, and with that, she walked quickly out the door. As she moved along the path, she kept an eye on his porch and the stables, knowing that no one would have likely seen her leave, nor could they see her now in the dense woods. She emerged as Holden said, just steps from the back entrance to the kitchen, where she could see Nettie moving about.

"There you are, Mrs. Freeman," Nettie said excitedly as she came out the door. "We been lookin' all over fo you. Mr. Freeman's mother is on the patio. She don showed up without so much as a phone call, and she askin' fo you."

Elizabeth froze. She'd never spent as much as five minutes alone in the company of her mother-in-law, and she had the sense, correctly, that Dehlia didn't care much for her. She walked through the swinging doors, checking her hair in the hall mirror as she passed, and out to the patio. She could see Dehlia biting into a biscuit then nodding her head approvingly. Two teacups were set, but no tea had yet been poured. Elizabeth walked up to Dehlia.

"There you are!" Dehlia started, unsmiling.

"I was taking a walk," Elizabeth replied, forcing a smile. "When it is warm like this in the afternoon, I find the shadiest paths. It is pleasant and so much cooler in the forest."

"As long as it is safe," Dehlia replied, taking another bite of her biscuit. She pointed to the chair next to her, indicating that she wished Elizabeth to sit down.

"Of course it is," Elizabeth answered.

Faye came through the door onto the patio, holding a teapot of scalding water with a hot pad. Dehlia gave her a disapproving look. *Biscuits before tea is served. How uncouth.*

"Oh look, teatime!" Elizabeth smiled at Faye, who looked nervously from Elizabeth to Dehlia and back as she poured water into each waiting cup, covering the teabags with steaming water. Faye set the teapot on an adjacent table, then nodded to Elizabeth, who smiled and nodded slightly to indicate all was well.

Elizabeth dunked her teabag a few times, then added milk and reached for a biscuit. Dehlia left her tea sitting there, apparently disinterested—or simply trying to make a point about the order of service. Finally, Elizabeth decided to break the ice.

"Charles didn't mention that you were coming today. We would have had more prepared for you. Will you be spending the night? If so, I'll have Nettie add extra servings to the menu. I believe we are having ribs tonight. Nettie ordered a special prep from the butcher."

"I can't stand ribs," Dehlia said, looking out at the pond, unwillingly to meet Elizabeth's gaze. "Too messy."

"I will go see what else she has that she can make for you. I know the rib smoking is well underway." Elizabeth rose, intending to go speak with Nettie.

"Sit down, Elizabeth. I don't care. I'll have a peanut butter-and-jelly sandwich. I just don't like ribs. I came to see how the work on the cottage is progressing."

Elizabeth sat back down. A chill ran up her spine. She knew, of course, that her mother-in-law would soon be living on the plantation, but Charles wasn't the one who had told her. She'd have to feign surprise if Dehlia informed her of her plan to move in once the construction was complete and, of course, pretend to be happy about it, when nothing could be farther from the truth. It was perfectly clear that Dehlia didn't care for her. She was probably waiting for Elizabeth to have a son, and somewhere in her mind a plan was likely brewing to take the heir and push Elizabeth out of the picture. She likely had no idea that she and Charles had not yet consummated their marriage, and it had been two weeks.

Dehlia finished her biscuit, took the teabag out of her cup, tossed it on the saucer, then added a spoonful of sugar, stirred, and nearly drained the cup with one swallow.

"Let's go see how the work is coming along," she said, pointing a crooked finger toward the direction of the cottage.

Elizabeth could hear faint noises coming from that direction, so she was sure the workers were still there. She rose, straightening her hair again, aware of what she must have looked like when she came running into the kitchen. Surely, Nettie would begin to suspect something if she wasn't more careful. *Or she may already, who knows,* she thought.

Elizabeth waited for Dehlia to pull her body out of the lounge chair somewhat awkwardly and stand, turning toward the direction of the cottage. She walked slowly in that direction, and Elizabeth followed behind. Neither said a word on the path over to the building. They made their way up onto the porch—the door once again stood open—and Dehlia marched right on through into the front room.

"Who's in charge here?" she asked the first worker she saw.

"Um, that would be Tom," the man said. "He's in the back room, pulling up some flooring. It is dangerous in there. Can I go get him and have him come out to talk to you?" The man was clearly uncomfortable, and although he recognized Elizabeth, he had no idea who this old woman was who was acting like she owned the place.

"We'll go find him, thank you," she said, walking in the direction of the noise in back. Elizabeth smiled and rolled her eyes ever so slightly at the young man then followed behind Dehlia. When they arrived at the bedroom door, they found Tom bent over with a crowbar lodged under a piece of flooring. One of his legs had disappeared down into the crawlspace, and the other was resting on a floor joist. The muscles in his back were clearly tense as he pried on the wood. The piece of flooring he'd been working on suddenly gave way as they entered the room, surprising Tom and sending him reeling backward toward the two of them. Elizabeth jumped, but Dehlia stood perfectly still.

"You're not going to get hurt here on our job, are you?" Dehlia asked Tom, surprising him even more. He stood quickly, prying himself out of the hole, dropping the crowbar, and wiping his hands on his pants.

"Not at all, ma'am, not at all." He recognized Dehlia Freeman as Charles and Bryce's mother. He had known their father and had worked on the plantation house since the beginning, after Charles purchased the place and walked him through, showing him the full scope of work that would keep him and his crew busy for at least a year.

"Nice to see you again, ma'am," Tom said, extending his hand. "I'm Tom; we've met."

Dehlia smiled but noting his dirty hand, replied with disgust, "Show me around, Tom. I want to see the progress." She turned to walk out of the room and nearly bumped into Elizabeth, who quickly spun around and left the bedroom, heading back the way they'd come in.

Tom followed them and stopped when they stopped near the front door. "Well, here we are in the living room. The windows have been changed, otherwise it will pretty much stay the same. We'll be tearing out one wall and expanding to add a kitchen over there." He pointed toward the wall that faced the lake. "You'll have a view from the kitchen sink," he said, smiling.

"Yes, but I don't do dishes," Dehlia replied.

Tom awkwardly turned and walked back down the hall, expecting them to follow, which they did. At the first bedroom door, he paused and turned to Dehlia. "The wall between this room and the next bedroom will be torn out so as to expand and have one large bedroom. We will be adding a window here," he said. Then as he stood against one wall, he continued, "This window will have a bench seat, nice for reading, and will also look out onto the lake," he said, hoping to appease her.

"I don't read, either, but that is a nice touch," she said.

Elizabeth was beginning to grow angry at the way Dehlia was treating this nice foreman. As much as he tried, she shut him down, like she did everyone, Elizabeth presumed.

Tom paused briefly at the next door. "This is the second bedroom that will open to the first," he said as he continued to the back room where they found him originally. "I'm starting here in this room, which will be the study, as it needs the most work. The floorboards have had some damage—maybe a flood, maybe termites at one point. All the flooring needs to be pulled up and replaced."

"Where is the bathroom going to be?" Dehlia asked.

Tom turned and walked toward the living room again, pausing between the two bedrooms and pointing across the hall. "This wall will be torn out, and new construction will happen, taking the room out and away from the hallway here. Since there was never a bathroom, it has to be a whole new room, new plumbing, new everything. The kitchen is on the same side of the building, so the plumbing will serve both rooms."

Dehlia was satisfied, for the most part. "And are we still on schedule?" she asked.

"Yes, ma'am, still shooting for the first of October," he replied. "The leaves will be changing by then, and it should be beautiful."

"Very well, then," Dehlia said, turning to Elizabeth. "Come, let's go see what Nettie can dig up for me for supper." She then walked out the door, leaving Elizabeth and Tom standing in the living room.

Elizabeth turned to Tom with an apologetic look, and he waved her away. "Go on, then. She's your mother-in-law. She's the one you're going to have to make happy. Don't worry about me." He turned and walked back down the hall to resume his work, shaking his head, while Elizabeth chased after Dehlia, who was already halfway back to the house.

Elizabeth walked behind Dehlia silently all the way back to the patio, where the dishes had been whisked away, through the large doors—now closed—and through the great dining room to the kitchen where Dehlia pushed her way through, paying no mind to the fact that the swing of the doors would have caught Elizabeth squarely in the face had she not held up her hand to catch them. Elizabeth paused for a moment, taking a deep breath before entering the kitchen where Dehlia and Nettie were already in deep discussion with the refrigerator door wide open. They had apparently decided on something that would please Dehlia, so they shut the door and Dehlia turned to face Elizabeth.

"Nettie says Gwendolyn has my room ready, so I'm going to head upstairs and unpack," she said, walking past Elizabeth and out the doors once again, leaving Elizabeth standing there in shock.

When Dehlia was safely out of earshot, Elizabeth spoke. "What in the world?" she asked.

"Miss Elizabeth, we in fo' some trying times," said Nettie. "You probably mo' than anyone, since she needs somethin' from you, and lawdy if you don' deliver, she gon' go mad." Nettie stood still, wiping her hands on her apron and shaking her head.

"But...but she said she's moving in!" Elizabeth cried.

"I heard tell of somethin' like that, but rumors be rumors until you hear it from the source," Nettie said. "She tell you that today?"

"No, but she asked Tom, the construction foreman, to confirm the date when *her* place would be ready, and he said October." Elizabeth was nearly in tears. "How can this be happening? I didn't sign up for this!"

Elizabeth turned and nearly ran through the double doors, pushing so hard on them that they banged on the walls of the dining room, and went straight up to her room. She was devastated. Not only was she a prisoner in her own home, but now her mother-in-law, a self-serving hateful bitch, had just implied she would be moving in when the remodel on the old slaves' quarters was complete. The only saving grace at this point was Nettie. And Holden, of course. His kisses still burned on Elizabeth's lips.

Elizabeth went to the bathroom and drew a hot bath, deciding to skip dinner. Charles could dine with his mother, if he even came home. Surely, he would, especially once he found out that Dehlia was here.

The steam drifted above the tub of hot water. Elizabeth stood naked in front of the floor-length mirror, looking at her body and wondering what it might be like to stand in front of Holden naked—even more what it might be like to see *him* standing in front of *her* naked. My God, his body was so cut, so rippled; everything was tight. And the erection that he presented to her that afternoon told her that if it might happen someday, she would not be disappointed.

As a newly married woman who had not yet had sex with her husband, her desire for touch grew with each passing day— not to the point of desperation, but growing nonetheless, and she doubted her ability to resist Holden's advances if Charles continued to hold out. She was not a virgin, and Charles was quite aware of that. How weird would it be anyway in this day and age to marry a woman of thirty years who was a virgin? But to say that her sexual exploits were many would be an overstatement. Her college boyfriend—not her first lover— had been clumsy. He'd taken care of her needs but barely, and their sex was always somewhat awkward. Her next serious relationship before Charles had been with someone who was much more into himself and satisfying his own needs than worrying about a woman even when she lay moaning and unfulfilled.

She knew how to take care of herself in that way, but now she found herself in a situation. It was clear that her husband had married her for breeding stock, and now she was confronted by a man who was obviously willing to provide her with whatever she needed and perhaps more, in terms of sex. But the situation was untenable. If they went further, she could possibly lose her marriage, her household status, her home. It went without saying that if discovered, Holden would also lose his job, yet from his actions it seemed that he was not at all worried by that.

Elizabeth slipped into the steaming water, sinking down to her neck, and closed her eyes. She thought of her mother-in-law downstairs, trying to take control of the household, likely bossing Gwendolyn around and surely Faye as well, but she was unsure about Nettie. Nettie was not intimidated by the likes of Dehlia Freeman, and Elizabeth knew that she would do her best to stay on Dehlia's good side, while making it perfectly clear that she only answered to one person, and that was the current, younger Mrs. Freeman.

When the water cooled, Elizabeth elected to drain it and dry off rather than add more hot water and spend more time soaking. She wrapped one towel around her body and another around her hair and went to the chaise, pulling the diary from the bottom of a stack of books.

Elizabeth wanted to lose herself in Adria's world for a while. When she left off, Adria had just described a grand gala that she'd had to plan without any experience putting together such an event. From Adria's viewpoint, it seemed to have come off without a hitch. Elizabeth wondered if she would be so competent in a situation such as that. After all, she was also in a somewhat similar situation, being thrust into running a household, suddenly finding herself in charge of a completely unfamiliar world. She could get used to it, as long as she was able to retain control, as long as Dehlia Freeman didn't have plans to take her down. Oh, if she only knew.

October 7, 1857

The guests began arriving exactly on time, as the invitation was for five in the afternoon. We had set that time to allow everyone the opportunity to greet and mingle and then to settle into their assigned seats, giving the servants time to offer appetizers and alcohol (it arrived, all of it!) before the first course was served. Atticus made sure that Liam had extra help come in for the day, and every guest's buggy and horses were tended to carefully.

The music started as soon as the first guest arrived and gained in volume when the governor and his wife made their entrance, soon launching into a waltz. The governor and his wife were the first to take the dance floor after which many of the guests joined.

John came and took my hand, insisting that we dance while the governor danced. We had not often danced together before, but my attendance at the preparatory school paid off, as I must say in confidence, we were much more well-timed than any other couple on the dance floor. However, John slowed our pace so as not to show up the governor and his wife. Still, we circled the room I don't know how many times, and I was dizzy by the time John led me back to our table. I was not sure if the dizziness was due to the little one, who is taking much of my energy these days, or due to the excitement of hosting a ball with that many of Georgia's elite in attendance.

Hattie had done an amazing job of preparing the food, and the servants set out the portions, timed as I had requested in perfect order leading up to the main course—lamb with roasted potatoes and stewed greens.

I'd asked Hattie to make her special chocolate cake for dessert, a family recipe of hers that had been passed down from her mother. You can't go wrong with a good chocolate cake! In the end, everything was perfect—the company, the music, the food, and the conversation.

As I thought might happen, a lot of the discussion between the men was about politics, the slave trade, and tobacco and cotton farming. The women mostly wanted to talk about their charities and thankfully, not a lot of gossip. Gossip really bores me, as it always involves things that are none of my business, and I don't feel the need to listen, or especially to have an opinion in anyone else's business.

The night came to a brief pause with the governor and his wife leaving first as we thought might happen. They are busy and don't accept a lot of invitations, so as much as we were honored by their presence, we expected them to take an early leave. John and the governor shook hands, and the first lady kissed my cheek, looking down at my belly after she did—did she know? It was an exchange that we left between us and one that I will cherish.

The tension in the room eased a bit once they were gone, and both the men and the music became a little rowdier. I was tiring due to my condition, but I knew that I had to endure. The women suddenly became more boring, and I longed for my bed, but John begged for another dance once the whiskey took hold. I was obliged, as we knew we would have everyone watching. One turned into two, another waltz. Afterward, we were met with cheers and laughter, with some of the men slapping John on the back, congratulating him for having a spouse who could perform with so much enthusiasm. Little did they know, I couldn't wait for all of them to leave so that I could take my house back, get my dress off, go to bed, and think about nothing more than birthing my child within a few months.

Rae was exhausted as well once the time came to help me out of my gown. She had worked since the early hours of the day, and once I was free of my dress, I bid her return to her room and leave me to my private space.

As I lay now in my bed in my nightclothes, my thoughts turn not to the evening, the event, and my husband, who by choice will sleep in his own chambers and who is likely still downstairs drinking whiskey and making business deals, but to Liam. How I long to have someone who would wrap his arms around me while I drift off to sleep. And somewhat shamefully, I wish now that I might be lying next to Liam and not my husband. Thoughts of his muscular back and arms and my head lying on his chest will send me drifting off to sleep.

~~*~~

As Elizabeth was reading, Charles pulled into the driveway and parked, letting Branson take his vehicle to the garage. He walked through the front door with his briefcase and heard a familiar voice in the kitchen. This wasn't good. He overheard his mother discussing how those ribs should have been cooked with one who was expert at cooking ribs. He dropped his coat and briefcase on a chair and walked through the doors of the kitchen.

"Mother!" he said with a large, fake smile. He was disturbed that she'd arrived unannounced, having an idea as to why she'd come, which horrified him even more. He gathered Dehlia in a firm embrace, then pushed her back to hold her at arms' length.

"You look lovely, Dehlia. What brings you here this evening, when we were not expecting you?"

Nettie gave Charles a look congruent with his concern. Nettie knew that Elizabeth was not going to come down after her bath and lamented that her ribs were not going to be perfect, according to Dehlia, who had made it clear that she hated ribs, so why in God's name was she making a fuss about how they were prepared? Nettie was ready to toss in her apron and go home.

"Nettie, it smells amazing in here, and I've been looking forward to your ribs all day. Are they ready?" Charles was evidently trying to appease her.

Nettie had already pulled some homemade chicken noodle soup out for Dehlia that sat warming on the stove.

"Yes, Mr. Freeman, everything is ready. If you two would like to take a seat in the dining room, I'll have Faye bring the first course. Your supper will follow—your ribs and Mrs. Freeman's chicken noodle soup," she said attempting unsuccessfully to hide her disdain. "Miss Elizabeth is feeling a bit under the weather after a long walk today and is going to be skipping her dinner," Nettie lied, not having spoken with Elizabeth but knowing full well what was about to transpire.

"Very well, then, Nettie, thank you." Charles said then turned to his mother. "Dehlia, will you join me for a cocktail in the dining room, and we'll wait for dinner to be served?"

~~*~~

Elizabeth heard a light knock at her bedroom door. She stashed the diary back in the safe and answered the door, still wrapped in a towel. It was Faye, who looked frightened.

"Miss Dehlia, she's in the dining room with Mr. Freeman," Faye whispered. "And I don't know what I'm supposed to do. They are wondering if you're coming down to join them."

"Serve them dinner, then go home," Elizabeth replied. "You have my permission to do so. They're adults; they'll figure it out. Tell them I'm not feeling well, that I have a headache."

Faye gave a slight nod, looking at Elizabeth obviously naked underneath her towel with another holding her hair, and without a doubt not intending to leave her room. She turned and walked down the hall, glancing back slightly to watch as Elizabeth closed her bedroom door.

Elizabeth put on her nightgown and pulled the diary back out of the safe, reclining this time in her bed propped up with pillows, then covering herself with a light blanket.

October 11, 1857

It has been a few days since the ball, and I must admit it has taken me all these days to recover! It was delightful to host all of Atlanta's elite—some of Georgia's finest, including the governor—but it was so very tiring, the whole thing. And I can't stop thinking about the look the govenor's wife gave me when they left. How in the world did she know I'm with child when we have not yet announced it? Maybe once I have given birth, I will be able to tell with other women as well. We shall see.

I've not seen Liam for a few days. The cleaning up after the party and putting things back in order has taken as much time as setting it all up in the first place, so I haven't had time to spare to go to town with him.

And now the announcement party is next. I am looking forward to it but dreading it just the same. That party will be a small, informal gathering of family and close friends, which will be delightfully simple compared to all that went into the planning of the gala.

After John and I make our formal announcement about the coming birth of our child, I will be under tremendous pressure in so many ways—as I will be expected to prepare the nursery and go through lists of names—girl and boy. Please, God, let it be a boy. I can't imagine what the gossip will be if it is a girl and we have to start again right away to conceive an heir to the plantation.

I will be assigned a midwife, who will watch over every aspect of my daily life, from the food I eat to whether or not I am able to take walks around the lake. That will be dreadful in so many ways.

Also, after this announcement I know that my relationship with Liam will change. He will not want to put his hands on a woman who is with child—for a lot of reasons. If I am carrying the heir to the fortune of this family and he is caught causing a possible disturbance to all of that, his life would surely be in danger. I must make time to meet with him briefly before the announcement party to find myself in his embrace, to feel his kiss on my lips for possibly the very last time.

Elizabeth closed the diary, then her eyes. She was hungry but unwilling to risk sneaking into the kitchen or asking Faye to bring something to her room, lest she arouse the ire of her mother-in-law for not coming down for dinner.

She could just imagine her husband seated in his usual spot with his mother in her place at the other end of the very long table. They might be making small talk and exchanging pleasantries. Then, surely, Charles would come out and ask Dehlia why she'd come, hoping she would tell him the truth—the truth that he had not yet shared with Elizabeth directly although she'd heard it from not one but two other people now—that Dehlia had come to check on her future abode, to see the progress and secure her move-in date.

Charles must be writhing in his chair, Elizabeth thought, knowing that she was now aware of what he'd been unable to share with her so far. Why? Was it fear? If so, of what? It was not Elizabeth's place to tell Charles that his mother shouldn't join them on the plantation, that it might wreck a marriage that never was, really, and never would be. After all, it was his house—*their* house but never in a legal sense as Elizabeth was not on the deed—and so it was for him to decide. But she was still his wife, and deep down she hoped he felt terribly guilty in some way that he would never admit to her.

It was true that Charles had married Elizabeth for one reason only, and above all else he would stick to the commitment that he'd made to himself and to the family, forever. The Freeman legacy would continue in the name of Charles Freeman the fourth. It had to because the only other option was to disrupt the lineage of three generations and deliver the title of the foundation to that of his younger brother's eldest son, who was now six years old—and not named Charles!

Downstairs, Charles pushed his chair back from the table and rose, signaling to Faye that she could begin clearing the dishes. Dehlia picked up her glass of scotch and rose as well. The two stood looking at each other from a distance, silently.

Finally, Dehlia spoke. "Your father would be proud, Charles." And with that, she left the great hall and went up the stairs, past Elizabeth's door and around the corner into the room that Gwendolyn had prepared for her without saying goodnight.

Chapter Ten: Charles

Elizabeth woke to a light tapping on her door. She rolled toward the door with the diary still in her hand, realizing that she'd fallen asleep reading. She tucked the book under the pillow behind her and straightened her nightgown.

"Yes?" she asked softly.

"Elizabeth, it's me. I'd like to come in." It was Charles. This was not a request but a slightly veiled command. He'd noticed the light beneath her door and presumed she was awake.

"Come in, then," Elizabeth said, still half asleep.

Charles came through the door, noting the look of wonder on Elizabeth's face. She was propped up on two large pillows, and her hair was sprawled somewhat messily, a look that he rather adored. He walked to her bedside and sat down on the edge, taking her hand.

"I'm sorry," he began.

"For what?" she replied, although she imagined she knew full well the reason.

"For not telling you that my mother would join us someday here on the plantation," he said, looking her squarely in the eyes.

"Well, darling, it is your house and your decision. I just hope someday she comes to tolerate me and not look at me as though I'm a nuisance, although surely that is exactly what I am to her," she said, sharply. Her words stung Charles because they were so fitting, so true. He'd seen the look.

"She'll be out in the old slaves' quarters," he said, trying to soften the situation but to no avail. Elizabeth didn't pull her hand back although she wanted to.

"Like this evening? You mean to say she will be dining alone out there or will she be a nightly dinner guest?" Elizabeth meant to pry the truth out of Charles, but he couldn't answer. He knew that, of course, his mother would be present in their daily lives and that by October the elder Mrs. Freeman would be running the household.

Charles's answer was to lean over and kiss Elizabeth on the lips, shocking her somewhat. It was the first since at the altar. He kissed her again, and this time his hand went to her breast while his lips lingered. He expected to feel her rise under his touch, but she laid still, kissing him back but barely. He came farther onto the bed, prompting her to move away slightly, giving him space to lie down. He put his head on her pillow and laid staring into her eyes while his hand moved down and underneath her nightgown, where she opened her legs just enough to let him touch her. He said nothing while his fingers began caressing her, back and forth, up and down, finally entering her to check for her level of dampness.

He wanted to get this over with as quickly as possible. Faye had informed him of the dates of her last menstrual cycle and that she should be coming into her fertile time. He knew that he would have to visit her again this week, maybe even for the next two nights to make sure he captured the moment.

When Charles was sure she was sufficiently ready, he pulled his hand back and opened his shirt then swiftly unbuttoned his trousers and pulled his now-engorged penis out into the air, stroking it hard to make sure his entry was seamless. After pulling down his pants, he lifted her nightgown up around her neck then rolled over on top of her, the bare skin of their chests touching. He entered her quickly and pumped hard until he came in an explosive last push. She watched his face, his closed eyes not wishing to engage. Had Charles known that Elizabeth lay staring at the ceiling through the entire act of consummating their marriage thinking of Holden's much larger erection felt between them as they embraced earlier in the day, he wouldn't have cared.

After one last half-hearted kiss on the lips, he rolled over and sat up on the edge of the bed, pulled up his pants, and stood looking down at her while he buttoned his shirt.

"That was nice, thank you," he lied, a half-smile concealing his disgust. Disgust of what, exactly? That he was forced into a marriage he did not want? That she was strong headed and seemingly unappreciative of her current good fortune? Or that he couldn't accept her for the extraordinary woman who she was and embrace their marriage. He couldn't be sure. Elizabeth really was beautiful, and she was now his wife, so why couldn't he love her? He turned and walked out of her bedroom door, closing it quietly behind him.

Elizabeth got up and went to the bathroom, running water in the sink until it was hot then plunging a washcloth into the steaming water. She washed and washed until every drop of semen trickled out of her, then drained and filled the basin again with warm water. She took a fresh washcloth and washed her face and breasts—everywhere he'd touched her. She wanted his scent and touch completely washed away. She looked at herself in the mirror, hardly able to believe that her fairytale marriage to one of the wealthiest men in the city had taken such a dark turn. She'd been the talk of the office at one time, and her girlfriends eyed her with envy. If they only knew.

She brushed her hair and sprayed rose water on her face, in her hair, and on her breasts. She threw her now-soiled nightgown into the hamper and walked naked to her bedroom, finding another where Faye had folded them neatly in rows in her dresser drawer.

Faye, she said to herself, almost out loud. Faye had something to do with this. She'd asked too many questions around the time of Elizabeth's period, admitting then that her only form of birth control was counting the days and knowing when she might be fertile. She guessed that Faye had counted the days since her own cycle began and had likely informed Charles that she was within the window of fertility. Could that have been a part of Faye's job description when Charles hired her? Elizabeth wouldn't put it past him at this point. She would be very careful as to what she said to Faye going forward and what she allowed Faye to know in general.

Elizabeth pulled a fresh nightgown over her head, locked her bedroom door, and crawled into bed, feeling under the pillow where she'd stashed the diary and fishing it out. She plumped up the pillows and settled in to read a little more.

October 14, 1857

I met my midwife today. She's a nice lady, a little older than me, and she already has four children, so I guess she knows what she is doing. She's delivered quite a number of babies, I hear, and with good results, so I'm going to have to trust that John checked her out and that I am in good hands.

The midwife gave me a list of foods to start eating and things that I will need to stay away from. She wants me to increase my water intake, which is not a problem. In this heat, when even in the late fall it still feels like summer, I get so thirsty.

I sent out the invitations today for the announcement party, although the guests will think it is just a regular dinner party. We'll surprise them toward the end of the evening, I imagine. John will figure when the time is right and clink his knife on a wineglass and that will be my cue to come around to join him at the head of the table. And then he will make the announcement.

The party is in three days. I can use the excuse of another party to make a trip to town, and I'm still not showing enough to arouse any suspicion on Liam's part, and no one in town will notice since I'm just in for shopping. I'll make my rounds quickly so that I have more time with Liam. I'll ask him to take me to that nice grassy area by the lake where we went the other time. It is so private, and no one driving a buggy down the road would ever notice us parked back there in the shade. I do wish that we could just have a place to lie down together. I could not, would not consider letting him take me in a sexual way. With the baby being in there and all, it just wouldn't seem right. But I do long to know what it would feel like to lie with him, to feel his arms wrapped around me. I look ahead to after the baby is born when I have free time again, and I know that if I can, I will find a way to continue taking trips to town with him.

John is not a very warm person. When he beds me, it is all down to business. I guess it is just his nature. He's just never been a very romantic person, and he is never one to take his time with anything. He gets right to the point with everything. Even though I am with child, when he has a need and comes to me like he did tonight, I can't say no. It's not like it would harm the baby at this stage, and he knows it.

When John came to my room earlier tonight, I could tell he had been drinking. His nose was a little red and so were his eyes. And he didn't knock, which usually he would do. He saw me in my chair, sitting in front of the looking glass on my dresser brushing my hair, and he just crossed the room and ordered me to lie on the bed. I did as I was told, of course, not wanting him to have one of his spells if I should say I wasn't in the mood, which I was not.

John was hasty in the way he appeared to want to rub himself, even though he usually asks me to get him ready. Then he did something distasteful, I thought. He stood over me, parted my legs, and then spit into his hand, rubbing it on himself I guess so that if I wasn't ready, it wouldn't matter. Before I knew what was happening, he was already inside me and pumping away. It seemed like he was angry, and he was using me as a way to vent about whatever it was that he was mad about. It was over before I knew it, and he pulled up his trousers and left without saying a word.

I must admit I'm glad that soon it will be inappropriate for him to do such a thing, once the baby is growing in there, as it just seems it wouldn't be right. I'll have a break from that kind of behavior for a while, and I'm looking forward to it.

Elizabeth rolled over and turned off the lamp, again stashing the diary under the pillow next to her, not wanting to bother with the safe. She would hide the book in the morning.

The next morning, Elizabeth strolled down the hallway in her pajama bottoms and a T-shirt and slippers, headed toward the kitchen for some tea. Normally, Faye would have come up by now to offer, but Elizabeth had not seen nor heard from her, so she decided to get it herself.

When she rounded the corner toward the dining room, she heard Dehlia, loudly complaining about her eggs. Faye stood before her, and Elizabeth could hear her apologizing for something that she likely had nothing to do with.

"Yes, ma'am, sorry, ma'am. I'll let her know," she heard Faye say to Dehlia as she removed the plate then turned and headed back toward the kitchen.

By going through the foyer, Elizabeth could avoid the dining room and therefore her mother-in-law. She came quietly through the doors to the kitchen, presuming Dehlia would have no reason to intrude into Nettie's space after sending her a message via Faye, admonishing her about the difference between a soft and medium yolk on a sunny-side-up egg.

Nettie was visibly rattled, Faye sat at the counter biting her cuticles, and Gwendolyn stood looking out the kitchen window toward the lake, holding a steaming cup of tea. The normal morning stood in disarray.

"Good morning, ladies," Elizabeth said, taking great care to overemphasize the smile and connect with each of them warmly. She knew that the key to her survival at the plantation was to keep the staff on her side as much as possible, especially as the time grew near for Dehlia's permanent arrival.

Nettie mumbled something Elizabeth couldn't hear. Faye smiled then looked down at her hands, likely aware that Charles had paid her a visit, which Elizabeth hoped included a sense of betrayal. Gwendolyn turned and smiled sincerely, shaking her head.

"Not sure what we're going to do once that woman moves in permanently," Gwendolyn said, still shaking her head.

"Put a lock on the outside of the quarters' door," said Nettie before slapping a hand to her mouth. Such a comment could get her fired, although it would be Elizabeth who would have to make that call, and Elizabeth giggled instead. She came around the counter with open arms and brought Nettie into an embrace. She said nothing, just gave her a good squeeze, then held her at arms' length and gave a wink that only Nettie could see.

"Nettie, let's get Mrs. Freeman some tea," Gwendolyn said, nodding to Elizabeth. Now that there were two Mrs. Freemans in the house, they would have to find a way to differentiate.

"I tell you what," Elizabeth said. "When she is here," she said nodding her chin toward the doors that opened to the dining room, "you may call me Miss Elizabeth. I really don't mind. Just not in front of her. We'll keep it formal when she's around. Sound good?"

All three nodded, Nettie sporting a grin that revealed the wide gap between her two front teeth. "Yes, Miss Elizabeth, yes. Sounds like a plan." She set a teacup in front of Elizabeth that held a teabag steeping in scalding water. The milk was waiting on the counter.

Elizabeth dunked her teabag thoughtfully, recalling the visit from Charles last night and thinking about her mother-in-law sitting alone in the dining room waiting for her eggs—cooked properly this time—to arrive. She'd already finished off one piece of toast and held the other to eat with her eggs. Nettie set the plate in front of Faye to take out to Dehlia.

"I'll take it," Elizabeth said. She wanted to see the shock in Dehlia's eyes when she appeared in her pajames to serve her mother-in-law breakfast.

Nettie backed up and opened her mouth, thinking she should protest, then shut her mouth, turned back to the stove, and smiled, thinking, *This lady know exactly what she doin', and I's gon' leave it alone.*

Elizabeth came through the door with a plate of eggs and a fresh serving of hot grits beside them in one hand and her teacup in the other. Dehlia didn't look up when Elizabeth set the plate in front of her, but followed the hand up to the face, the hand that was not black like Nettie's—nor brown as Faye's skin was—and saw the face of her daughter-in-law. She startled.

"Wha...what is this?" she asked. "Why is it you serving me?"

"Because I was in the kitchen when they were ready and thought I would come out and say good morning," Elizabeth said with only a slight smile, on one hand trying to use it as a bonding moment, while on the other hand not caring one bit. She walked to the other end of the table and took the seat where Charles usually ate his meals. She wondered where Dehlia would sit when there were three of them dining together.

"Aren't you going to have breakfast?" Dehlia asked, awkwardly aware that Elizabeth had no food in front of her, struggling with picking up a fork and digging in while it was hot before the younger Mrs. Freeman had been served.

"Not just yet," Elizabeth answered. "I'll get dressed after I have my tea and return to have a little breakfast before I begin my day. Gwendolyn and I are planning to have a few things moved around and having some new curtains made. "Elizabeth said that to enhance the fact that she, sitting at the table half-dressed, still had some sway over what happened at the place, for some period of time anyway, over this prim and proper old lady who was quite apparently seething inside.

The very sight of Elizabeth sitting at the dining table looking the way she did set Dehlia on fire. But she managed to finish the eggs—not perfect but better this time—and the grits, then polished off her last piece of toast to which she'd added strawberry jam. Wordlessly, the two women sat in each other's presence, then Elizabeth decided enough was enough.

"How long will you be staying with us, *Mother*?" she drew out the word to convey the intended sarcasm.

Dehlia bristled. "I'll be returning home this afternoon."

Elizabeth stood, leaving her cup on the table. "Well, do let me know if there is anything more you need between now and then. I may see you back here in a few minutes, otherwise you know where to find me." She turned and walked toward the hall, a smug grin on her face.

Elizabeth: one. Dehlia: zero and gone.

Later that afternoon, back in her room after a brief nap, Elizabeth heard a car in the drive and peeked out just in time to see Dehlia being scooped into her car by Branson with her overnight bag on the seat beside her.

Good riddance, she thought. She'd had a productive day with Gwendolyn while the elder Mrs. Freeman stayed out of sight. They decided which furniture pieces should be moved in the formal living room, mainly to accommodate the light from the windows, an aspect that had apparently never been considered before. Large carpets would have to follow certain pieces to their new location, and now that the curtains covering overly large windows were going to be closed during the sunniest part of the day to protect the furniture from fading further, Elizabeth could see how hideous they were.

Elizabeth had asked Gwendolyn to arrange for fabric samples to be delivered the previous day, which had arrived already. They spent some time with each swatch, holding them up to couches and chairs and lying them on carpets to make sure that whatever they chose would tie in all the colors, finally settling on a moss green with a raised pattern but no other competing colors. While Elizabeth napped, workers had moved the furniture while Gwendolyn supervised, so Elizabeth was pleasantly surprised when after Dehlia's departure she entered the living room and found it completely changed.

"Do you like it?" Gwendolyn's voice came from somewhere in a far corner where she was replacing a vase that she'd moved to another room for safe keeping, not trusting the workers to take care of fragile items.

"It is lovely!" Elizabeth exclaimed. It was just as she pictured it might be, much cozier, with furniture groupings closer together to accommodate intimate conversation between guests. They would no longer have to shout across to each other to be heard. She smiled approvingly at Gwendolyn.

"Let's have a seat and test it out, why don't we?" Elizabeth took a seat on one of the couches, and Gwendolyn followed her, taking the adjacent chair. They were seated an appropriate distance apart, where even at a large gathering they would be able to hold a conversation at a reasonable level.

"So, how was it?" Elizabeth asked, looking somewhat excitedly at Gwendolyn. "Did Dehlia go mad watching the furniture being moved all over the place?" She had a grin on her face that Gwendolyn read perfectly.

Elizabeth did not actually realize that the reorganization would take place so quickly or she might not have chosen to rest in her room. Rather she would have enjoyed watching the action in the great room, and even more, she might have enjoyed watching Dehlia suffer while knowing that the management of the household was out of her control.

"She was…uncomfortable, let's say," Gwendolyn started. "She asked a few questions here and there as things were being moved into place, but the workers already had their orders from me, so they pretty much ignored her." Gwendolyn was calculated in her response, not wanting to gloat and understanding fully that someday she might have to answer to the witch. She would need to be careful to walk the thin line between the two Mrs. Freemans.

"Very good, then," Elizabeth replied. "It came together nicely, and quickly I might add. Thank you! Now we just have to get those curtains ordered."

"They have been ordered, Mrs. Freeman."

"Gwendolyn, please, call me by my name when it's just the two of us." Elizabeth smiled at her warmly and resisted the urge to reach out and take her hand. Gwendolyn was a servant and a professional, and a move such as that might cross a line that was so far invisible to her, but she had much to learn. She was happy with Gwendolyn's attentiveness to the situation, and the progress she'd made was phenomenal, given such a short period of time.

"Yes, Miss Elizabeth, as you wish," replied Gwendolyn.

Elizabeth rose and dismissed Gwendolyn with a nod and a smile, then headed to the kitchen where Nettie was busy stirring a huge pot with chicken quarters, dumplings, carrots, and the rest Elizabeth noted was hard to define.

"What's in the pot?" she asked Nettie. "Smells delicious!"

"Fixins' for mo chicken potpies," Nettie replied. "Everyone liked 'em last time so I figured I'd make 'em again."

"Anything wrapped in that crust of yours, savory or sweet, is what I want for dinner," Elizabeth replied. Nettie smiled and kept on stirring.

"Will someone let me know when—or if—my husband comes home? I'll take my supper in my room if he doesn't show." Then she added, "And if that is the case, please ask Faye to bring up a bottle of chilled white wine before dinner is served." With that, Elizabeth turned to leave through the swinging double doors.

"Yes, Miss Elizabeth," Nettie replied, amazed at how quickly she was learning to take control and let people know what she expected.

At seven o'clock, there was a tapping on Elizabeth's bedroom door. She went to answer and found Faye standing there with a bottle of white wine in an ice bucket and one wine glass on a tray.

"Thank you, Faye," Elizabeth said. "Please put it on the table. How long before you will bring my dinner up?" The wine and glass conveyed that either Charles had called to say he would be late, or he'd not called at all.

"Miss Nettie says when I get back to the kitchen, she'll have your dinner ready," Faye replied.

"Very well then, thank you. I'll see you in a few minutes." Elizabeth was fine taking dinner in her room once again. She was anxious to dive back into Adria's life and could do so in between bites of chicken potpie and sips of white wine. But first, she thought that she might like to call her sister, Penny. She'd only spoken to her once since the wedding, and since they'd left abruptly, Elizabeth never had the chance to show here around the plantation house. She would love to invite her for a weekend—a sister weekend—and decided that she should do so quickly before her dinner arrived.

Elizabeth didn't have a phone in her room, so she went to the library where she thought she'd seen one before. She took her glass of wine and wandered to the open doors, where there was a table, a comfortable chair in front of an enormous wall of books, and a telephone sitting in the middle of a desk.

Penny answered on the second ring. Hearing her voice almost brought Elizabeth to tears, and Penny as well, for different reasons. Elizabeth was still saddened by her sudden departure after the ceremony, and Penny was distraught with the suspicion that Elizabeth's marriage was in fact a sort of captivity. Neither of them knew where to begin.

"Penny, I miss you!" Elizabeth began. "Please come see me if you can."

"Elizabeth, we still talk about what a beautiful wedding it was. How is Charles?" It seemed Penny was deflecting.

"Can you come and visit me, please?" Elizabeth was trying not to beg but on the verge of doing so.

"What are you thinking, sister? You do have a birthday coming, but I imagine you would want to spend it with your husband." Penny was so bothered by her sister's situation. She was trying, but unsure as to how to proceed.

"Fine, after my birthday, but then you will come, yes?" Elizabeth was still trying to hide the desperation in her voice but somewhat unsuccessfully at this point.

Elizabeth sat back in the large chair, studying the glass of wine on the desk and looking past it to the wall of books, most of which would never be read. Was her sister going to be straight with her? Did she not actually want to come? Elizabeth knew how Penny felt about Charles and wondered if that would prevent her from showing up for her sister.

"Yes, honey, I'll make it happen," Penny said. "I'll look into dates that might work."

Outside the library door, Faye tiptoed away quietly. The next day, the library phone would be disconnected. One phone in the house was enough, and the library offered too much privacy.

~~*~~

Elizabeth hung up and returned to her room, where she poured herself another generous glass of wine and sat back on the chaise after retrieving the diary out of the safe.

Elizabeth had remembered to secure the diary there before going downstairs to meet with Gwendolyn earlier that afternoon. God forbid she should leave it somewhere, where Faye might find it and possibly confiscate it and take it to Charles. She really worried now about Faye, if she could be trusted at all, and what stipulations Charles had put on her employment. She wondered, but at the same time she was pretty sure where Faye held her allegiance.

Elizabeth opened the diary, knowing that within a few brief minutes she would be interrupted. She began reading, while sipping the wine perhaps too enthusiastically. She was without a doubt frustrated as to the unfolding of the past two days, the arrival of Charles's mother, and her seeming disapproval of almost everything and everyone she encountered. And to think her marriage was consumated with that witch just down the hall!

If, that is, one could consider the manner with which Charles planted his seed without any element of lovemaking, a consummation. He'd not even bothered to take off his clothes, after all, and had clearly not given a single thought to her level of enjoyment.

She was so curious about the parallels between her life and Adria's, and she wondered if it had always been so. Were all women, herself included, predestined to be dominated by powerful men—unless they chose to rise up and make spectacles of themselves? Were these women throughout history driven to be so weak, so servile throughout generations that they unwittingly indoctrinated their sisters, their children, and their daughters-in-law? Perhaps so, she imagined, still feeling Dehlia's eyes on her as she sat at the breakfast table "not properly dressed for breakfast" as she knew she had been judged.

Before Elizabeth could even start reading, there was a knock at her door. She went to the door, knowing that it would be Faye, who stood there as the door, opened holding a tray with a steaming potpie in a single serving dish on a plate. Instead of inviting her in, Elizabeth took the tray, thanked her, and bid her goodnight, closing the door and feeling a sense of control for perhaps the first time since she'd assumed the position as lady of the house.

Elizabeth set the plate on the table after taking a bite of the pie. She was starving but not hungry. She was craving more than food. For love most certainly. For touch most definitely. And for romance, without a doubt. Her desire to be caressed, to be held in a way that satisfied a primal need, not a desperate need but a need nonetheless, was paramount to her every waking moment these days. Her thoughts turned to Holden as she heard another knock at the door. *Faye certainly would not have been sent to retrieve my tray before I've had time to finish my pie*, she thought.

Elizabeth went to the door and opened it to find Charles standing there, an empty wine glass in his hand.

"Oh, my dear, have you come begging for a glass of wine?" Elizabeth asked with a giggle. She had finished one glass and was well into her second and was feeling a bit tipsy and empowered.

Charles remained aloof, the gesture and the implication that he might be begging certainly beneath him, yet still he walked to where the bottle sat on the table and held up his glass, which she filled.

"Let's do have a toast," he said.

Elizabeth's glass was still half full, and so she raised it in salute. "To Noble Oak Plantation," she started. "And to all the children and children's children who may come after. May we all rest here in eternal happiness." She had no idea what she meant by this; it was just the first thing that came to her mind.

Charles touched the edge of his glass to hers, taking a sip and eyeing the pie. She turned to sit back down on the chaise, setting down her glass and quickly covering the diary with another one of the books she had pulled from their library days before.

"Are you enjoying your room?" Charles asked as he took a seat in an adjacent chair.

"Do you mean do I enjoy taking my meals here, napping here, and sleeping in this very large bed all alone?" She caught his eyes and held them, refusing to have him deflect as he so often did.

He shifted uncomfortably in his chair. "Elizabeth, I know I work a lot—too much some say—but it is to provide for you, for us, to keep this place afloat."

"And to maintain your family's legacy, not mine," came her retort. "I will never be a part of this family. I'm a fixture—a concubine in many ways." She drained her wine, setting the glass back on the table with a little more force than she intended. Her giddiness had evaporated.

"Oh please, Elizabeth," Charles said, standing and walking to her chaise. He pulled her up with two hands and brought her to a standing position, then drew her in to his body, wrapping his arms around her. He began kissing her, first on the mouth then planting kisses on her neck while he walked her to her bed.

This time, he took more care as he removed first her shirt, exposing a lacy bra that Faye had found in town and tucked into her drawer. He continued to kiss her as she unbuttoned his shirt. He fumbled for the button on her slacks and laid her back on her bed as he did so, pulling them off to reveal the matching lace panties. He stood at the edge of the bed, smiling as he undressed completely while she watched. She pulled the covers back in anticipation, moving over on to the soft sheets as he crawled in beside her. He began kissing her breasts, then her belly, then pulled off both her bra and her panties as his tongue made the journey south, planting kisses along the way. She was truly aroused by the time his tongue found the sweet spot he was seeking. He lingered long enough there to nearly bring her to an orgasm before moving on top of her and entering her, this time more slowly and she thought more lovingly. Again though, his orgasm came quickly, but luckily this time she was able to join him—not with the enthusiasm she was capable of, but she did offer a couple of moans to appease him as she felt his hot sperm entering her body.

Charles lay beside her this time, allowing her head to rest of his chest for a few minutes, wondering what the window of fertility might be. He'd give it one more shot this month, then wait for Faye to tell him if her cycle began and that they'd need to try again. He gently pulled away from her, allowing her to move her head to her pillow, and got up to dress quickly again, leaving her to finish her bottle of wine alone.

Elizabeth once again went to the bathroom, this time not feverishly washing him away but still cleaning herself enough to put on a nightgown and return to the chaise to pick up where she'd left off in the diary. She'd opted not to take a full bath tonight but would take a quick shower before she went to bed.

October 15, 1857

Today John gave me permission to take one last outing to town. Liam hitched up the buggy, and I told Rae to stay home, that this trip would be quick and that she needed to help get the place ready for another party. Rae knew they did not need her help, and she watched while Liam took my hand and helped me into the back. I think she suspects something, but she also knows I am with child, so she assumed nothing would happen. But how wrong she was about that.

I shopped hurriedly for the few things on the list, all things that we would have for our party so that the trip appeared to be legitimate.

Once Liam and I were in the buggy headed home, I tapped him on the shoulder, asking him if we could take a rest in our same spot. He knew what "take a rest" meant and was happy to oblige. He pulled the horses into the shade and tied them then pulled a blanket from beneath the seat, which I supposed he'd put there for this very reason. He once again put his hands firmly on my waist to help me out of the buggy instead of simply extending a hand, and this time he surprised me by stopping before my feet touched the ground and planting a kiss on my lips. I was shocked and pleased and let out a little squeal of delight.

Liam spread out the blanket for us then helped me down to a sitting position. He sat down beside me and for a while he said nothing, just pulled up a long blade of grass and looked out across the lake, pointing out a blue heron that stood tall on a rock along the edge of the water.

When he turned to say something to me directly, our eyes met, and I couldn't stop staring at him. I am going to miss gazing into those clear blue eyes. I noticed a tiny scar above his eye and thought I'd ask him about that someday. Not today, though, today was just for drinking him in with my eyes. Finally, his hand came up and moved a strand of my hair back away from my face. As he did so, he leaned in and gave me one of the sweetest, longest kisses ever. Then he said, "We both know this is wrong, yet I cannot resist you, Adria." He kissed me again, and we laid back on the blanket.

We stayed there together like that for some time. He didn't try to find my breast with his hand; we just held each other. I could have stayed in that position for hours. I was sad knowing what he didn't know, that it would be the last time for a very long while, if ever again. We both worried that we would have no excuse for being late, not with the very few items that I had in my bags, and soon he rolled over on his side, stared at my face, and put his hand on my chin, drawing me toward him as he kissed me with what only could be described as a deep love. No one had ever kissed me like that, especially not my husband. Then Liam raised me up, folded the blanket, and helped me climb back into the buggy, in the backseat so that if we passed anyone on the road, there would be no gossip.

I know I was a little flushed in my cheeks when we got back to the plantation, and Rae noticed immediately, whispering something about it to me in the hall. I told her it was just from the ride and that I needed to go lie down for a bit. I don't think she believed me, but after my last warning, I knew she wouldn't say a thing to anyone. I watched out the upstairs window as Liam carried in my bags then drove the horses out to the stable. I could see him from there, disconnecting the buggy and putting the horses in the barn. He took such wonderful care of them, brushing each of them after removing the harness, bringing them buckets of water. He will make some woman very happy and no doubt be a great father someday.

The next morning, Elizabeth rose to the sound of Faye knocking. With Dehlia gone, the household had returned to normal. Faye stood with a tray that held her tea, a plate of cherry biscuits, and blueberry jam.

"Miss Nettie made these especially for all of us," Faye started. "She said she felt real bad about the way the old Mrs. Freeman treated everyone and wanted us to start our day with some sweetness." Faye gave her a broad smile, and Elizabeth opened the door wide so that she could pass.

"You can set the tray on the table, Faye, and thank you. I'll be down in a bit." Elizabeth watched Faye as she set the tray next to her stack of books.

"You sure like to read a lot, don't you, Miss Elizabeth… um I mean Mrs. Freeman." Faye had permission to call her by her name, but Elizabeth was sure she'd been rattled by Dehlia.

"Yes, I do, Faye. Do you read much?" asked Elizabeth as she poured hot water into her teacup.

"No, ma'am, I don't. I'm not a very good reader, didn't learn until late, and never went to school after the eighth grade."

That shocked Elizabeth somewhat, but then she understood more about why Faye was the way she was. Elizabeth knew how much Faye needed this job and that Faye was likely terrified of both Dehlia and Charles and would bend to their will over hers, above all. She also knew that she would work harder to keep many things from Faye because everything she said or did would travel directly back to Charles. That included when she had her menstrual cycle if possible.

The time spent with Charles the previous evening was sweeter than before, but she'd told him she felt like a concubine, and he'd not responded with anything that would change the way she thought. However, "concubine" wasn't exactly the right word. "Breed stock" was better, and maybe she'd use that the next time.

"Thank you, Faye," Elizabeth said, dismissing her. She wanted to take a walk after she had her breakfast and would think of a task to give Faye on her way out that would occupy her long enough that she might slip out without being noticed.

Faye gave Elizabeth a nod and lowered her eyes, sensing the growing distrust. She went out the bedroom door without a word, closing it softly.

Elizabeth was happy to hear that Faye wasn't a reader, but that did not give her enough reason to leave the diary out in the open. She quickly placed it in the safe and spun the dial.

Chapter Eleven: John's Cabin

Elizabeth finished her sweet rolls and tea, then she changed into long pants and a long-sleeved shirt to protect her skin from the sun. She donned a wide-brimmed hat, deciding that she was going to make today's walk a little longer, perhaps venture farther out into the woods than before. She found a fanny pack in the closet, and deciding it might come in handy, she strapped it around her waist. She stopped into the kitchen on her way out, taking a bottle of water from the refrigerator. Nettie was kneading bread on the countertop, humming as usual while she worked.

"Nettie, thank you for the sweet rolls; they were delicious!" Elizabeth said. "I wanted to let you know I'm going out for a walk. I didn't see Faye or Gwendolyn, but would you tell them when you see them so they don't worry? And would you please ask Faye to strip my bed and change my sheets? Oh, and please have her take my comforter out and hang it on the line. It could use a little freshening up."

"Will you be home for lunch?" Nettie asked with a grin, knowing that Elizabeth seldom ate lunch, that she mainly snacked and waited for dinner.

"Not likely, but don't worry about me. I won't get lost." Elizabeth tucked the water bottle into her fanny pack and headed out the back kitchen door. She walked in reverse down the path that led to the old bunkhouse where Holden had first kissed her. The padlock on the front told her that he was not there, so she kept walking. When she got to the water, she turned right instead of left, heading down a path that she thought might take her all the way around the lake. She could still see the plantation house in the distance as she moved along the water's edge. The sun was high in the sky, and it was hot. The hat offered some protection, and Elizabeth was happy that she'd thought of the long sleeves.

She came to a bench that someone had carved out of an old, downed tree. It was directly on the other side of the lake from the house, and from this angle she could clearly see the plantation house, the bunkhouse tucked in on one side, and the old slaves' quarters on the other. It would have been the perfect spot for someone to keep an eye on all of the comings and goings about the property, and Elizabeth did not doubt that was the reason for the bench. She took a seat, got out her bottle of water, and took a long drink. She heard rustling in the bushes and startled, turning to see Holden coming down the path.

"Sorry, I didn't mean to scare you," he said, smiling. "I saw you walk away from the bunkhouse and head toward this path; thought I'd join you."

Elizabeth looked up at Holden and felt the heat rise in her face.

"Do you mind if I sit down?" he asked, still smiling down at her.

"Oh, please," she said, embarrassed that he'd had to ask. She scooted over and patted the wood next to her. "I was just enjoying seeing the layout of the property," she said looking out again across the water, wondering if anyone curious enough could see the two of them sitting here together. "Can they see us down here?" she asked.

"Did you ever notice this bench out here before?" Holden asked her. He knew that the bench could not be seen even from the second floor because he'd looked for it from there. There were just enough trees on each side and more that hung over the top slightly, collectively disguising the bench and even now, the two of them. He'd been able to spot the bench once with binoculars, but never with the naked eye.

"Not without binoculars, which I doubt Charles issued to his staff. We know he wanted to keep an eye on you but doubtful he went that far." Elizabeth looked at Holden, who then reached over with his right hand and took her hand. With his other hand, he took her chin and brought it gently to his waiting lips. They kissed long and hard, and Elizabeth's heart raced. She wanted Holden more than she'd wanted anyone in a very long time. The fact that she'd finally had sex with Charles, and for the past two nights in a row, did not diminish the feeling but intensified it greatly.

"Elizabeth, I know why you are here. Everyone knows. You are simply to produce an heir, and then you will be cast aside. I will be waiting for you when that time comes."

Holden drew her in closer now, and she fought back tears. He was right. What did he mean by "everyone knows"?

"I should be going," Elizabeth said with a smile. "When I'm gone too long, they worry."

"Let them worry," Holden said, bringing her in again for another long kiss. "Okay, I understand. But would you let me show you something else you've not seen?"

"Of course, if it isn't too far out of the way," she replied, standing up.

He took her hand. "Come, this way."

They continued on the path in the direction she presumed circled the lake and would come out somewhere around the old slaves' quarters. Just before the quarters, the path forked off away from the water into the forest. He continued to hold her hand now, as the path widened and they could walk side by side. She was visibly nervous.

"Don't worry. I know where everyone on the property is at this very minute," he said, smiling. "Even that little troublemaker Faye."

Elizabeth stopped on the path. "What do you mean by that?" she asked.

"She was hired by Charles to keep tabs on you. She's not just your assistant; she's his little spy. You'd do well to ditch her at every possible turn." Holden raised his hands in the air, as if to wonder why she didn't also know this.

Elizabeth's suspicions were confirmed regarding what Holden had just said, her menstrual cycle, and how that coincided with the visits from Charles the past two nights. "I will do just that," Elizabeth replied. "Now what is it you want to show me?"

"Just around the corner, we're almost there," Holden responded.

Elizabeth walked silently beside him, her very being teeming with anger, outrage, suspicion, and pain. And she was considering Holden's remark, "I will be waiting for you when that time comes." Was he really expecting her to be booted out the front door as soon as she birthed a baby boy? The thought chilled her, but then she thought of Dehlia, and suddenly the prospect seemed very real.

The path curved sharply away from the plantation house again, and soon Holden stopped. In front of them was a very old, somewhat dilapidated house with a rickety front porch and windows streaked with tales of a time long ago, blackened from soot and stained with whitewash that had been splashed on the boards outside more than once. The door was attached, but Elizabeth could see that it was barely closed shut. Holden skipped up onto the porch, opened the door wide, and bowed, inviting her inside.

Once inside, Elizabeth was once again transported back into time. An old wrought-iron bed was made with a perfectly clean quilt draped across the top. A shiny tea kettle sat atop an old wood stove, and the kitchen cabinets held porcelain bowls, coffee mugs, old clay plates, and other pottery that had survived the war. An old kitchen table had a crude bench on either side, and the wood was polished and well cared for. A basin was set in the kitchen counter with a faucet of sorts, *but surely there is no running water out here*, Elizabeth thought as she wandered through the place.

"What is this place?" she asked.

Holden sat down in a rocking chair in the corner and rocked, smiling.

"This, my dear, is the secret place where John Clayton the second kept his lover. She was one of his slaves, and she bore him a child. No one knows of this cabin, not even your husband, I'm quite sure. I found it early on, shortly after I was hired to caretake the property, and I've been fixing it up. I come out here to escape, read, and be alone." He looked around, admiring the work he had put into fixing up the place. He intentionally left the outside looking somewhat abandoned to discourage the curious who might stumble upon it.

Elizabeth turned, leaning against the kitchen table. "A child?" The thought crossed her mind that either Adria didn't know or she'd not reached that point in the diary.

"Yes, a boy. He was hidden for some time, so the story goes. Slave owners sired children all the time back in those days, accidentally of course, and if they were sired by men of high status, they were typically whisked away to another state to be reared as a slave by another family. The mother and child were often separated, sometimes for life.

In this case, because John Clayton had deeper feelings for this woman, which was not acceptable at the time because she was a negro and a slave, he allowed the boy to be raised on a nearby plantation where mother and son could maintain contact, which they did until the war broke out. She died sometime in the middle of the war, never knowing her son as a free man."

Elizabeth was shaking her head, having a hard time understanding how in the world Holden could have all this knowledge, yet when she pressed her husband, he continued to offer nothing more.

"How in the world do you know all of this?" she asked.

"Again, the Stately Oaks Plantation next door," he said. "You should go sometime soon. You'll learn so much about your house and the family who built the place, you will be amazed."

Holden stood and walked to Elizabeth, who looked around, still taking in the beauty of the little cabin. She looked at him as he came close for another kiss.

"May I come out here sometime and read?" she asked. She came so close to admitting that she'd found Adria's diary, but she could not. It had to be a secret, hidden from absolutely everyone until she finished it, and then she would decide where it should go. She wanted so badly to tell Holden what *she* knew about the family, especially the second lady of the house, but she wouldn't, not yet. She wanted desperately to ask him if the slave's baby was born before or after Adria's firstborn.

"But of course," Holden replied. "Just make sure no one sees you come or go," he said as he pushed his body against hers and planted a long, sensuous kiss on her lips, letting it linger as he pressed his throbbing erection up against her belly. "It is never locked. And if you want to meet me out here sometime, we can arrange that as well," he whispered in her ear.

Elizabeth wrapped her arms around his neck, kissing him back firmly, knowing precisely where it would lead if they didn't stop now. "I will be missed if I don't get back soon, so we should go," she said wistfully. Begrudgingly, Holden took her hand and walked with her to the fork in the path, where they parted with one quick kiss.

Elizabeth guzzled her water before reaching the house, passing back through the main doors of the veranda to allow for her return to be noted. When she got back up to her room, she stripped off her clothes, which were damp from the heat and humidity. She took a quick, cool shower and resumed her position on the chaise, again wrapped in only a towel.

October 18, 1857

Well, it is now widely known now that John Clayton of Noble Oak Plantation is with child. Or rather that I am, and I'm sure by now Liam has heard. I hope he's not mad at me for not telling him directly, and for letting him take me on a blanket and smother me with kisses while I knew I was carrying his master's baby.

The announcement party went exactly as planned. The food was scrumptious and perfectly prepared, the guests were courteous, and again we had a small band playing on the patio just as we had for the gala. When the big moment came, John tapped his knife on his champagne glass as expected, and I got up from my chair and stood beside him. He put his arm around my waist and waited for the room to quiet. He raised his champagne glass and told the room he had grand news to deliver, then looked down at my belly. The crowd erupted with murmurs when he did that, knowing exactly what the signal told them. He stated loudly that an heir to the Noble Oak Plantation was about to enter the world, and the room erupted in cheers and clapping.

It pains me that these men in the world of high stature can announce to a crowd of people, some strangers, that a boy is about to be born. How in the world do they know and what do they then say if that baby is a girl? That it was a mistake, that a boy was supposed to be born first? How in the world do you apologize for a girl who will become a woman will then be expected herself to produce a future heir at some point? It makes no sense to me, but they need to play their silly games, and I'm expected to play along as well.

So, I stood at the head of the table with my husband, one who spits in his hand (as he may have done before with a common whore) before taking me just a few nights ago, and I smiled at our guests. As the lady of the house, I'm expected to take everything he says in stride and take no offense at anything he does or says. Those are the rules, and they are the rules I shall be expected to pass down if the baby is a girl.

Elizabeth remained in her room, anticipating that Charles would come home for dinner as he said he would tonight. She could smell the freshly baked bread, and it stirred her hunger. She'd skipped lunch as usual, instead spending the lunch hour in Holden's embrace in their new secret space. She'd drawn looks from Gwendolyn and Faye when she returned, though nothing but a large grin from Nettie when she'd passed through the kitchen for lemonade on the way to her room, watching as Nettie put the bread into the oven.

She closed the diary and locked it in the safe, then slipped on slacks and a top that Dehlia would have approved of as dinner attire, should she join her husband at the big table. She wandered downstairs, noting the table settings for two and the bottle of white wine that sat chilling in a large silver ice bucket in the center. Someone must have spoken to Charles as he would have ordered that ahead.

Elizabeth walked through the kitchen doors as Nettie was pulling out two perfectly browned loaves of bread. She set them on wire racks, then she turned to close the oven door, spotting Elizabeth.

"Well, well, glad you come out to join us!" Nettie said with a large grin, wiping her hands on her apron. "Nettie have a treat fo you tonight. Mr. Freeman called and ordered his favorite roasted leg o lamb, with dem tiny red potatoes and steamed greens with my secret sauce. Must gon' be a special night!"

Elizabeth looked at Nettie curiously, as she was aware of no special event, no birthday or other celebration that she'd been made aware of, so she just shook her head. "I have no idea what that might be," she said.

"Well, Miss Elizabeth, I guess we'll soon find out. I hear him comin' now," she said with a glance toward the doors that led to the foyer.

Elizabeth walked out in time to see Charles as he burst in through the front door, all smiles and throwing his topcoat and briefcase onto the entry bench. When he saw Elizabeth, he walked to her, bringing her in for a close embrace, shocking her somewhat.

"I have amazing news," he said excitedly, causing Elizabeth to cock her head to one side, hiding a smile.

"Do tell," she said.

"I've just finalized the purchase of my childhood home, a neighboring plantation, one that was not available when I bought this place but that came on the market unexpectedly a few weeks ago. I made an offer to buy it, to place it back into the Freeman family, and my offer was accepted today." Charles was gleeful and in a state that she'd never seen.

"I'm so happy for you, Charles," she said, trying to pretend that she cared. She was confused as to his desire to include her in such a celebration; however, she now understood the reason for his return at a reasonable hour, the special menu, and the wine that sat chilling for their meal together. Something warned her, though, as to his motives about buying another plantation.

Charles noted her lack of enthusiasm but was unphased. "I'll go change for dinner and see you down here in ten minutes."

Elizabeth nodded and returned to the kitchen, where Nettie was setting a giant leg of lamb on a board to rest while dishing out heaping mounds of potatoes, carrots, and broccoli onto a large porcelain platter. Faye stood beside her, waiting for instructions.

"Cover dat so it stay hot, girl," Nettie said, shaking her head and wondering why Faye had to be told everything. *No common sense in that child.*

Faye, the traitor, the spy, Elizabeth thought, remembering Holden's words, watching her out of the corner of her eye. Faye refused to engage her looks, pretending to be interested in the way Nettie was carving the lamb now that it had rested. Nettie nestled the slices of lamb amongst the vegetables then covered the platter. Dinner was almost ready to be served.

"Well, I guess I will take my seat in the dining room," Elizabeth said, feigning excitement. "Faye, you may open that bottle of wine now. I'll wait for Charles there at the table."

With that, Faye followed Elizabeth into the dining room. Elizabeth sat and watched while Faye uncorked the wine, returning it to the ice bucket then checking that the place settings were in order. She returned to the kitchen as Charles came bounding down the hallway, taking his seat.

"Oh dear, let's let them set the food on the table, and I will pour the wine!" Charles was exuberant, jumping back up to take the bottle of wine out of the bucket and to Elizabeth's end of the table, filling her glass and kissing her lightly on the top of her head. He then moved down to his seat, filled his glass, and returned to set the bottle into the ice.

Faye entered the dining room with the very large platter that displayed a large leg of lamb, partially carved and surrounded by a melody of potatoes, carrots, and broccoli. It was more than a dinner platter; it was art. Nettie had outdone herself.

Faye took Elizabeth's plate from in front of her and placed a reasonable helping of meat and vegetables on her plate, then set it in front of her, and then she did the same with Charles's plate after which she excused herself.

"If there is anything more you all need, please let me know." Faye directed her comment to Charles, not Elizabeth, and left the room hastily.

Charles raised his glass and said loudly, "To the acquisition of the Freeman family plantation, Whispering Pines." He took a large sip of his wine, watching as Elizabeth smiled and obligingly drank from her glass.

"Tell me more," she said, pretending to be interested. After setting down her glass and picking up her knife and fork, she prepared to dig into the lamb.

Charles began with the story of when the plantation was built by his great-, great-grandfather and then went on about the war and a fire and talked of slave trading, none of which interested Elizabeth in the least. She was still thinking about the secret cottage and how she might return in the coming days to hide away and read—and perhaps even to receive Holden in that historic bed, where apparently a bastard heir had been conceived that Charles would never mention even if he knew about it.

When Charles finished his lamb and his story, after bragging about the rich history of the place and how he would restore it to its former glory, Elizabeth mentioned that she had a slight headache and wanted to return to her room, hoping that her feeling weary would dissuade him from creeping into her bed that night. It worked.

Elizabeth was able to excuse herself to her room, taking one last glass of wine up with her and bidding her husband good night without as much as a smile. He hardly noticed as he served himself another helping of the lamb and refilled his glass with wine.

The next morning as soon as Charles left for work, Elizabeth donned a hat and a light dress, put the diary in a cloth shoulder bag, and stopped by the kitchen to take a fresh cinnamon roll.

"Where you think you goin' at this hour, missus?"

"I'm going for a stroll early today; it feels as though it is going to be a hot one," Elizabeth replied as she wrapped the cinnamon roll in a towel and filled her bottle with water.

"No tea for you today? You okay?" Nettie asked.

Elizabeth smiled. "I'm good, Nettie, thank you. I just realized that I've been taking my walks so late that I come back drenched with sweat."

"Suit yoself, Miss Elizabeth. But if I was you, I wouldn't be gone long. Folks will talk."

Elizabeth's smile turned to a frown. Did that mean people were already talking? Likely so, but she couldn't care less.

December 15, 1857

Due to the coming child, the preparation of the nursery, and the impending winter, I've not written in quite some time. My belly is rounding, there are no more trips to town, and my midwife checks in on me daily. John doesn't visit me for sex any longer, which I'm relieved to report. He pretty much leaves me alone these days. I wonder how he satisfies himself now given all that he used to need from me. When I see him having those fits of anger, I remember the way he used me to relieve his stress and I wonder.

There are dozens of negro ladies, slaves who live on the plantation, and if he was in need, he could surely go visit one of them. If he does, I just don't want to ever know about it. I've heard tell there are all sorts of little cabins out there in the woods where slaves live, but I am not brave enough to venture out there to verify that.

Well, I don't have to think about any of this until next year. The baby will come sometime near the end of April, according to my midwife. That seems so far away and yet so close at the same time. I don't know if I'm ready to be a mother! I have so much help, and I realize that I need to be grateful for all of that as there are so many other women who are not rich and don't live on plantations and don't have husbands who provide for them and care for them as I am cared for.

I had the house decorated for Christmas and am happy to see the candles when they are lit on the fresh tree. I worry about the possibility of fire, but the light from the real candles is about as special as it gets. Someone is always standing near with a bucket of water in case something happens, as we sing carols and enjoy it all safely.

I only see Liam from a distance these days. He's busy because the cold has come upon us and the horses need more care and feed, and truthfully, I think he's doing everything he can to avoid me. We ran into each other a couple of weeks ago when John and I were discussing a Christmas hayride with the family. He insisted we go out to the stables and talk to Liam. I resisted, but John insisted, and there I found myself face-to-face with the man who put the biggest smile on my face that I will likely ever experience in my lifetime, while standing arm-in-arm with my husband. I can still feel Liam's hands on my waist as he helped me down from the buggy out at the lake and the way he snuck a kiss on my lips while he lifted me down.

The men got the hayride planned, and all the while I avoided looking at Liam, instead pretending to play with the barn cats. The men discussed details of which horses to use, what time the wagon should be ready, and that the hay would have to be fresh and without any mold, something hard to come by this time of year.

I was never so glad to leave that barn, but I admit I snuck a quick look at Liam on the way out. He was raking one of the horse stalls, but he looked up and caught my glance. He smiled, which gives me hope.

Elizabeth closed the diary and rolled over to see Holden coming through the door of the cabin. She had watched from an upstairs window as Charles left the house that morning after having his breakfast, his driver holding the door for him as he exited with his briefcase, headed to the city.

She'd walked directly down to the cabin with the diary, wrapped herself up in the quilt, and lost track of time. She hadn't arranged a meeting with Holden, certainly, but having had an open invitation, she hoped she wasn't violating his space out there. After all, he'd said she could come and read anytime she wished.

"Hi, um. I was just reading. I'm so sorry I didn't let you know or ask permission," she said.

Holden walked across the room and jumped on the edge of the bed, laughing. "You of all people do not need to ask me for permission, for anything on this property," he said. "However, I hold you in contempt, m'lady, and for that you must pay." Smiling, he took the diary out of her hands and set it on the nightstand next to the bed, pushing her hands to the headboard while lowering himself only slightly over her and kissing her on the lips. He refrained from letting his full weight cover her, and he felt her body arching up to meet him. He kissed her hard on the lips.

"What are you reading?" Holden asked, looking over at the old, leather-bound book.

"Oh, just something I found in the house," Elizabeth said truthfully. "I pulled a number of books out of the library when I arrived." She smiled and attempted to distract him from the book that had no title, reached up, and tweaked him on the nose with her fingers.

Holden reacted by biting her fingers playfully. They both stopped abruptly when they heard rustling outside. He jumped up and went to the door, looking through the windowpanes. He burst out laughing as he saw a wild boar stomping about on the porch and rooting around the bushes, looking for anything edible.

"Ha! I thought I was going to have to draw a saber to defend the lady of the house," Holden said playfully before returning to the bed.

This time he lowered himself fully on top of Elizabeth, covering her mouth with kisses and letting his hands roam freely when she did not resist. Once he had fully explored her breasts, one hand traveled down and more quickly than she would have imagined unbuttoned her pants. His fingers were suddenly exploring places they'd not yet traveled. She found herself in a state of arousal with which she was unfamiliar, and her breaths came quickly and rhythmically. He waited for a sign that he needed to back off, but she only encouraged him by grabbing him and pulling him in tight.

Their clothes came off hastily, and once they were lying on fresh sheets and covered with the old quilt, their lovemaking took a new, slower pace. He pushed himself up on his elbows and looked into her eyes as he rhythmically thrust all his being into her in such a loving way that she found herself almost in tears—tears of joy for having the experience and tears of sadness for what she would never experience with her husband. When their climax erupted simultaneously, it was slow, driven, powerful, and then over, leaving them both shuddering and holding each other tenderly.

~~*~~

Elizabeth strolled into the kitchen a little after eleven in the morning, having stopped in her room first to hide the diary.

"Hmmm, something here smells awful good," she cried cheerfully, eyeing the shortbread cookies that Nettie was putting into the oven.

"You missed breakfast, Miss Elizabeth," Nettie said softly. "And they noticed. "

Elizabeth looked at Nettie with a blank stare, as if having to answer to the senior member of the staff—although the oldest—was not on the table.

"Alright then, here I am. What did I miss?" she asked, trying to remain calm. She had checked her hair and applied a touch of lipstick while she was in her room, so she knew she didn't look as though she'd just had a delightful romp under an old quilt.

"Just a lot o' prying from Faye and questions from Gwendolyn 'bout food. They both don went to town together and wanted your list. I told 'em I had no earthly idea where you might be, except you left with a bottle o water and a book, and they should jus leave you to your walkin' and your readin' and to git on out toward the city and git the shopping done." Nettie looked at Elizabeth, and a certain knowing crossed her face. Elizabeth saw it—it was unmistakable—and she noted that it was clearly without judgment.

"I'm sure they can handle one trip to the store without my input," Elizabeth said, grabbing a cookie that sat warming on the rack and popping it into her mouth. She was suddenly ravenous but wanted to return to her room for some uninterrupted time before Gwendolyn and Faye returned from town.

~~*~~

January 2, 1858

John Clayton was having a bad day. One slave had run off, and he'd had to sic dogs and a posse after him. Another had gotten into a fight with one of his best tobacco pickers and nearly killed him, and the price of tobacco dropped sharply for some unexplained reason. The markets fluctuated, and he knew the price would come back up by the time it was picked and dried. He hoped, anyway. He knew himself to be in need of a release and could not visit Adria, for the baby was in there, and he was truthfully worried about injury. He'd heard that it posed no danger at all to the unborn as long as one took it easy.

That was the problem. He didn't feel like being gentle. There was one of the slaves; she was young and very pretty as far as negroes could be attractive to him, but he'd seen her watching him and knew that if he sent for her, she probably wouldn't mind. He pulled Atticus aside and told him to bring her to the old cabin deep in the woods.

John grabbed a walking staff and pretended to go out for a survey of the property, as he often did. He turned off the lake path and walked along a narrow, overgrown trail. He soon came to the one-room cabin. The door was ajar, the windows had been cleaned recently, and the bed was freshly made. He had ordered it to be kept neat and tidy in the event he might need to use it as he would today.

He noted that the quilt sat on the old bed, pulled tightly without a wrinkle, and the pillows had fresh pillowcases that looked as though they'd been left out in the sun for a good bit of time. He leaned his staff up against the wall, went to the wash basin, poured a little water into his hands, splashed his face, then dried with the towel that hung on a hook. He went to the bed, sat down, and took off his boots, then pushed himself up against the iron headboard and waited.

Within fifteen minutes, the woman appeared. She was a girl, really, but old enough that he didn't feel guilty asking for her. Her name was Grace, and she had been named for the intense rays of sunlight that shown through the window onto her glistening body as she had her first bath. The women in attendance at the birth told her mother that it was God's grace shining on her like that, so they named her Grace.

John instructed Grace to undress and watched while she did, dropping pieces of clothing on the floor one at a time, never looking at him. He then told her to come and undress him. She obliged, never looking at his face and trying not to look at his hard, red, writhing manhood. Negro men didn't look anything like that. They were brown, just like the rest of their bodies. She'd never seen anything so ugly.

He ordered her onto the bed then climbed on top of her. He took her gently at first, testing to make sure that she was not a virgin. When he was sure that she was not, he began taking out his day's frustrations on her—not in an awful way, just not in the same gentle way he would have had to have been with Adria. Once he was finished, he rolled over and told her to get dressed and go outside, where Atticus was waiting to take her back to her quarters.

Once Grace was gone, John went back to the basin of water and found a washcloth, then he washed himself and dressed. He took his walking stick and headed back to the plantation house. In the months following, he would meet her there regularly, unbeknownst to anyone but Atticus.

The month before Adria gave birth to a son, Grace discovered that she, too, was pregnant. She did not tell the master, although John would find out some time later.

Once Adria had given birth and after a short time had passed, enough that she had healed down there according to her midwife, John would resume his visits to Adria's room and leave the negro woman to birth his baby in the slaves' quarters, surrounded by other women, with Grace refusing to tell anyone who's baby it was—although they all knew it was a white man, as the boy was more white than black, and there was only one white man they knew of who would dare bed one of the master's slave women, and that was the master himself.

A few months after John's first-born was beginning to crawl, he got word through Atticus that there was a rumor the baby boy who had been born to the girl slave, Grace, might have been sired by the master himself. Late one evening, John paid Atticus a visit at the bunkhouse down the path from the servant's entrance to the kitchen, where Atticus lived alone. His instructions were to take Grace and the baby to a neighboring plantation, where he had made arrangements to trade her for a woman slave close to her age.

The neighbor agreed because the deal was a good one, a baby boy who he could start working in just a few years, and the mother who was a good cook and had once served in John's kitchen. Atticus was to take them the next morning and make the trade, with the story that the white liverymen had sired the bastard child.

Chapter Twelve: Adria

Charles walked into the dining room at exactly seven o'clock, surprised to see Elizabeth sitting there with a teacup, a soft-boiled egg, and toast in front of her. She was just beginning to pull the top off the egg and had a tiny spoon in her hand that would delicately scoop down inside the egg and pull out the warm, still-runny yolk. She paused with the spoon above the egg when she saw Charles come through the doorway. He was shocked to see her up so early.

"Well, well," Charles said. "You are up early. What is the occasion?" He tried not to show the tinge of anger he was feeling. She had not allowed him to come to her room for the past two nights, and he felt his window of opportunity closing. He planned to find a way to her bed tonight, which meant he would have to be nice.

"I'm going to town today with Gwendolyn to do the shopping, and I thought I would have breakfast and take a walk before we leave at ten," she said. He looked at her sharply, and she added, "With your permission, of course." She said this with a twinge of disgust on her tongue but knew she would have to clear it with him now, or Branson would have to call him at the office later.

"That is fine, of course, darling. Why don't you pick up something yummy for dinner?" He took a sip of his tea that had been steeping prior to his arrival. It was thankfully still hot. "Is there anything you've been craving?" Small talk was painful for him.

"Nothing, really. Nettie has already given us her list, and I just want to go to the library." She was set on trying to establish more of the details of what she'd been reading in Adria's diary. After Holden said that so much of the history that he had shared with her was common knowledge, she presumed all of this must be in print somewhere, so she would start at the library. She knew there was so much that Charles was hiding from her, and she was going to figure it all out—whether he liked it or not.

"The library?" he started, buttering a piece of toast. "What in the world would you want to find there when our library here is so extensive?"

"I just like libraries, Charles. Is that alright?" she replied, her eyes narrowing. She would not be pulled into another discussion with him about books on the history of the place, when he would again insist that all she need do was ask him, and he would tell her everything she wanted to know. Charles suddenly felt the need to change the subject if he was to stay in her good graces.

"Elizabeth, I have an idea." He sipped his tea, looking at her and trying to gauge her mood. "How about we throw a party?"

Elizabeth raised an eyebrow but didn't respond.

"Now that most of the remodeling is done on the interior, and you and Gwendolyn did such an amazing job on the living room, we could host a party and show off the place. What do you think?" A genuine smile appeared on Charles's face. He waited for her response.

Elizabeth thought of the grand gala that Adria had been in charge of planning.

"Where will they park the buggies?" She meant it as a throwback to the grand parties that were held at the plantation house in the past. At first, Charles missed the reference, then he understood what she was trying to say.

"I'm sure there were some amazing parties thrown here throughout its history," Charles said. "But it is unlikely anyone is going to want to drive a buggy out here from downtown like they used to do. That said, I'm sure Holden could handle that part."

At the mention of Holden, Elizabeth grew weak, remembering his delicate but passionate kisses. "What do you have in mind then, and when?" she asked. The guest list would likely include a number of his extremely boring colleagues, which made her dread the party in advance.

"Oh, I don't know, probably just a dinner invitation with the intention of showing off the new spaces and the cottage, a general housewarming for those who haven't yet seen the place."

Recalling the number of guests at the wedding, none of whom ventured into the house past the back hall with the bathroom that the staff used, the number might include everyone who attended their wedding, none of whom Elizabeth had known before—or cared to see since.

"Sounds lovely," she lied. "Just decide when and give the guest list to Gwendolyn, and I can get to work." With that she pushed her chair back. "I think I'll go see if Gwendolyn is in yet. Will you let Branson know that we'd like to leave at ten?" She walked into the kitchen and straight out the back door.

Faye stood in the living room, pulling back the great curtains and tying them open as instructed by Elizabeth to do daily, so as to let in the early light. When Faye saw Elizabeth heading down the path, she froze. She was half tempted to follow her, but knowing that Charles still sat in the dining room finishing his breakfast and might need something from her, she opted to stay. Faye decided to take more notice of the direction Elizabeth went each time she stated she was going out on one of her walks and to note the time of her departure and when she came back. It was her duty, her promise to Charles upon her hiring, that she would be his eyes and ears, and she knew that her job depended on it.

Elizabeth heard light tapping when she neared the bunkhouse. She entered to find Holden holding a chair upside-down, nails in his mouth and a hammer in his hand. She laughed.

"Nails for breakfast? That's a new one," she said, smiling.

Holden set down the chair, spit the nails into his hand, and laid the hammer on the counter.

"Just fixing a rickety chair, and no, I had eggs for breakfast," he said, laughing. He walked to the door and pulled Elizabeth into a tight embrace, inclined to smother her with kisses but opting to take it easy. He was well aware that Charles had not yet left for the day, and Branson would be getting the car ready for Elizabeth's trip to town. And then there was Faye to watch out for. He pulled back after a swift kiss on her lips.

"Good morning, beautiful, so good to see you up and around this early." Holden noted the way the sun's early rays raked low through the windows and hit the highlights in Elizabeth's hair. Her lips shimmered from his kiss, and she looked radiant. He wished he could lay her down and make love to her right at that moment.

"I will be gone most of the day, as you probably know. There are no secrets here, it appears." She smiled at him but with a look of concern, then continued. "I'm going to go to the library, although Charles thinks the idea is foolish. I want to find more that has been written about the history of this place and about neighboring plantations." She was again on the verge of telling him about Adria's diary but managed to refrain. "Listen, Holden, I know this sounds crazy, but with everything you've told me, and the very little that Nettie has mentioned, this place has a rich, convoluted history, and for some reason Charles does not want me to be informed. But I live here now, and I want to know more. There are ghosts here, Holden. And I don't mean that in the sense that there is anything to be afraid of. It's just that the walls are speaking to me in a way. I need to know more of what transpired here from the beginning, when slaves lived here and people with names like Atticus and Adria roamed these paths and slept in these beds." Elizabeth was animated, and Holden found it incredibly sexy.

"Go to the library, Elizabeth. You will find everything there. Just ask someone." And with that, he planted a kiss on her forehead and a pat on her ass and sent her toward the door. "Now go, before we find our little spy peeking through the glass. And don't forget to ask the librarian for information about the old Freeman plantation."

Elizabeth stopped at the door and turned. "What do you mean?"

"The *old* Freeman plantation, not this one. It was just over the hill. Charles's grandfather lost it when the price of cotton was down a few years in a row, and after slaves had been set free and his trading income was in ruins. There is a lot to discover there about your new husband's family."

Elizabeth was shocked to know that Holden was so keenly aware of the plantation owned by Charles's family so many years ago—*Whispering Pines*. She wondered if he also knew that Charles had just purchased it to bring it back into the family and that he intended to take the crew from their work on the old slaves' quarters and send them over to the old family property as soon as they'd finished preparing the cottage for his mother's arrival.

~~*~~

Elizabeth and Gwendolyn rode in silence in the back of the sedan as it moved down the wooded back roads, the curves rocking them in unison back and forth. The trunk was filled with groceries and other supplies, and at Elizabeth's feet lay a large cotton bag filled with books. Gwendolyn had not asked her the reason for her visit to the library, and she certainly didn't need help shopping, so they had spent the day separately caring for their respective reasons for going to town. They rode silently, taking in the landscape, the neighboring plantations, and the large iron gates that cloaked each of them in stately significance.

Elizabeth's mind was racing as they passed certain plantations that she now knew the names of from the books she'd scanned during the day. The history was not only rich, it was now *her* history, that of her husband and his family, and that of Adria. She could not wait to get home and lock herself in her bedroom and read.

Now there was the issue of Charles wanting to throw a party. How boring it would be, ultimately, and how awful in a sense because Dehlia would have to be present. Charles's brother, Bryce, and his wife and children would come, which would mean they would need to prepare an additional guest suite to accommodate the family as well as a room for Dehlia. Not that they didn't have the room, but it was an incredible amount of work on top of what would surely be a guest list nearly as extensive as that of their wedding.

And for what? Elizabeth thought as they pulled up to their gate, which opened with the push of a button that was mounted on the dash of the sedan. To show the world something that they were already well aware of: The Freeman family had enough money to buy not one but apparently now two plantation homes.

Branson pulled under the portico and stopped the sedan. Gwendolyn opened her own door and climbed out while Branson came around and opened Elizabeth's door, which always annoyed her but was something she was trying to become accustomed to, although it was difficult. She was perfectly capable of opening her own damn door. And for the record, she knew how to drive. She vowed in that moment that she would push Charles to give her a car and that she would someday soon be free to come and go as she pleased.

Once the supplies were unloaded, Elizabeth hauled her books up the staircase to her room and set the bag in the corner. It had been a long but productive day, and she was starved. She ran back down the stairs to check with Nettie, who had already unloaded the day's haul of groceries and much to her surprise, found Charles sitting in the kitchen. He was home early and chatting eagerly with Nettie about the party, the food, and that night's dinner. He had a beer in his hand—Elizabeth seldom found him to be a beer drinker—and for a change, he was in a pleasant mood.

"Join me?" he asked, raising his glass. Elizabeth hated beer, and he knew it, but she appreciated the gesture.

"No beer for me, but I would be happy if there was a bottle of white wine already chilled and open," she replied, looking at the refrigerator. At that, Charles jumped up and opened the fridge door, and there sat a bottle of her favorite, just corked according to Nettie. Charles pulled it out and set it on the counter, pulling a glass from the wine glass rack above and setting it down in front of Elizabeth.

"Please, allow me," Charles said with a grin as he uncorked the bottle and poured, causing Nettie to turn around and give him a look that Elizabeth caught, almost bringing on a giggle.

Nettie turned to the stove, shaking her head. *Must be baby-makin' time,* she thought. *Whatever it takes. Let's get this gon' since that be why we all here.* She turned back to the giddy couple, noting that Charles was really the only giddy one, and Elizabeth just sat taking it all in, smiling and sipping her wine.

"Alright, you two lovebirds. What you say we talk 'bout what time dinner be ready so that I kin make sho it's on the table, hot and on time."

Charles looked at Elizabeth and then back to Nettie. "Let's say two hours. Does that work for you, Elizabeth?" Charles watched for her response.

"Sure," Elizabeth started. "That will be fine, but since we skipped lunch, I'd like to take a little snack to my room. Can I make myself a plate of cheese and crackers?"

With that, Nettie slapped a laugh and let out a howl. "Child," she said, the "d" almost silent, "you the lady of the house. You put whatever you want on a plate and take whatever you want to you' room. I'll see you back down here in two hours."

With that, Elizabeth pulled a couple of nice cheeses that they'd brought from town, cut a chunk from each one, then wrapped up the remainder and returned them to the refrigerator. She added crackers from a box that was already open in the pantry and then a small knife, covering it all with a cloth napkin.

"Perfect," she said, gathering the plate in one hand and her wine in the other. "I'll go get ready for dinner." She walked out the doors of the kitchen, leaving Charles and Nettie standing in the middle of the kitchen staring at each other.

"Mr. Freeman, I do believe that was an invitation," said Nettie, knowing it was likely not, but wanting to get him out of her kitchen so she could prepare the evening meal.

As soon as Elizabeth set down her plate and wine glass, there was a light knock at her door. Charles didn't wait for her to open it but came walking in with a full beer in his hand. He stood with his arms open as if waiting for her to come to him. When she didn't, he ignored the rebuke and went to her, setting down his beer and gathering her in his arms.

"We have two hours," he whispered in her ear. She was shocked. He'd never been so amorous with her, and she was slightly excited but leery as well. He wrapped his arms around her waist and after kissing her lightly on the lips, quickly pulled the loose cotton shirt she was wearing up and over her head.

Elizabeth stood there in her bra and slacks. Having had a long day of travel, she felt sweaty and not in the mood to be mauled—and certainly not in the mood for sex.

"I really need to take a shower. It was so hot in town. I'm starving, and I'm hot." Elizabeth watched as Charles's gaze landed and stayed on the lace rim of her bra.

"Then make it quick," he said. "I'll wait in your bed."

Elizabeth was shocked and taken aback by the suggestion that Charles was proposing they have sex right here and right now before dinner, in broad daylight. Not that she was opposed to the idea—it was just unusual for her, and certainly out of their normal pattern thus far.

She took a cracker off the plate, topped it with a large slice of cheese, walked to the bathroom, and shut the door. Noting that Charles had begun to undress, she stripped off her remaining clothes and turned on the shower knobs, waiting for the hot water to steam the shower doors before stepping inside. She quickly rinsed her hair—shampoo could wait—then soaped up the rest of her body and rinsed, stepping back out of the shower in under five minutes. She turned off the water and grabbed a towel.

"You done in there?" Charles asked, tempted to barge in and pull her naked body to the bed.

Elizabeth elected not to get dressed again because what would be the point. It was obvious that Charles had the intention of having sex before dinner, so that would be happening. She was just trying to make it less awkward than it needed to be by walking through the door to the bedroom in two towels. She quickly towel-dried her hair, then grabbed a dry towel and wrapped it around her body. She opened the bathroom door to see Charles sprawled naked on the bed. He had an erection—either from thinking of her, anticipating what was about to come, or from physical manipulation—it mattered not. He let out a low whistle when he saw her standing in the doorway.

"Drop the towels," he commanded.

~~*~~

The next morning found Elizabeth and Gwendolyn at the dining table huddled over lists of names scrawled on papers left over from the wedding. Charles had not prepared a new list for the suggested party, but he simply told them to find the list from the wedding and send an invitation to all because it encompassed everyone in his circle, then and now. The two of them sat with tea, discussing logistics, which although were simple compared with the wedding, had changed due to deaths, births, marriages and divorces.

They managed to whittle the list down to a manageable event, one that would not exclude any influential people in the Freeman's inner circle nor offend any perspective clients nor aged friends of Dehlia. Again, Elizabeth's friends from her life before were not included, and she dare not ask. When they were finished, Gwendolyn handed her a final list, which Elizabeth folded and tucked into her pocket. She would review it later and would begin planning for seating arrangements.

Gwendolyn made a call to a printer in town to ask if he could print the invitations later that day, which he said could be done. Elizabeth instructed Gwendolyn to hand-address each envelope in her simple but attractive cursive, then drop them at the post office. Each would contain an RSVP card that could be mailed, but likely most would call the number on the card to respond. They opted to leave Charles's secretary to field the calls and compile the RSVP list. Charles shouldn't mind, as it was his party, after all, thought Elizabeth. With that out of the way, they turned to the planning of the food.

Nettie would be given a set of instructions as to the menu, which would be simple but elegant, and according to Charles, the alcohol should be free-flowing, which meant special attention should be paid to those guests who might need to leave their cars and would require transportation home. That meant Branson would be tasked with hiring additional drivers for the evening, just another detail but an important one in order that no one would end up being a casualty of their celebration.

Elizabeth found herself exhausted before noon, and she tasked Gwendolyn with going to town alone and getting the invitations out. She moved to the kitchen to discuss the menu with Nettie, who she found sitting at the counter for perhaps the first time ever.

"Everything alright?" Elizabeth asked as Nettie looked up in surprise.

"All good, Miss Elizabeth, all good," Nettie said as she straightened up, giving Elizabeth a look that belied comfort and conceded pain.

Elizabeth came around beside Nettie and pulled up a stool, put an arm around her large frame, and held her tight. "Okay now, time to come clean, Nettie. I'm here for you. What's up?"

Nettie held herself together, struggling to voice the words. "Remember the night my daughter was in the accident an' I couldn't come to work for a whole day?"

Elizabeth nodded, remembering the time. "Yes, Nettie. Is she alright?"

"Well," she started slowly, "She was fine for a few days, then things started happenin'. With her belly and such. Turns out when she had that accident, she was pregnant, and as a result, she been strugglin' this whole time, and today she lost dat baby." Nettie put her head back into her hands and began to weep silently.

Elizabeth held her grip on Nettie, then began rocking her back and forth as one would a child, she supposed, although she'd never had the experience. They sat in this embrace for a long time, until Nettie finally regained her composure somewhat.

"Nettie," Elizabeth began. "I want you to go home to her now, and we will see you tomorrow, or the next day or the next. However long your daughter needs you is how much time you need to spend with her." She continued to hold Nettie as she sobbed silently. "Please, as our gift to you, you need to take the time with her—for her and for you. We'll manage, okay?" She gave Nettie a big squeeze. "We can all make tea and peanut butter-and-jelly sandwiches, and no one here is going to starve."

Elizabeth turned to face Nettie, putting her hands on either side of her large face. "We care so very much about you, and I want you to know that. Now go. You take the time you need to heal your daughter, and to heal yourself. When I see you walk through this door again, I will know that everything is better."

"Thank you, Miss Elizabeth, thank you. I'll go now, but I'll see you real soon." With that Nettie took off her apron after drying her tears on one corner, then set it on the counter and walked out the back door.

Elizabeth left the kitchen and headed for her room, taking a sandwich that she'd just made, along with a bottle of lemonade that she found in the refrigerator. She didn't know how long Nettie would be gone, and at that point it didn't matter. It was more important that Nettie take care of her daughter, and no one in the household should care, really. Faye and Gwendolyn could fill in. The party was scheduled for two weeks from that day, and Elizabeth did not doubt that Nettie would be off no more than a day or two.

When Elizabeth returned to her room, she set her plate and lemonade on the table, pulled the list out of her pocket, and sat down to give it one last review. She scanned the names, most of whom she did not recognize. Her eyes froze on the name Clayton-Johnston, then *Lillian*. How had she missed this in putting together the list? Gwendolyn had done the writing while she'd sifted through names. Gwendolyn must have written it down without realizing the significance.

If the name Lillian Clayton-Johnston had been on one of those lists, then she had been in attendance at her wedding! Elizabeth had to get to the bottom of this without asking Charles. Elizabeth decided to make some time later that day to go through the books from the library and figure out how the name Johnston came to be attached to Clayton—who this mysterious woman was and where she was from—and if perhaps she was of the same lineage as the author of the diary. Elizabeth took a bite of her sandwich and sat back, opening the diary to read while she ate.

January 14, 1858

Christmas was real nice this year. John arranged for the hay rides, we had lots of family here, the tree was a big one cut from out on the land somewhere, and the food seemed never to stop coming! Seems I'm getting hungrier by the day, but I know the importance of being careful with my weight so I don't end up twice as big as I was before I got pregnant.

Rae and I have been working on the baby's clothing. I'm learning to crochet and how to add embroidery to the blankets and other things like hats and booties. The winter here is mild compared to what I hear it is farther north, but still we have cold nights, and thankfully we have a lot of wood and a lot of slaves to make sure it is cut and stacked and that our fireplaces and woodstoves are always stoked.

I hope the slaves are staying warm. Rae says they're alright, and her mother lives out in the quarters so she checks in over there every day. She tells me all the time how lucky she feels and how grateful she is to have a little room of her own downstairs off the kitchen. It's the least I can do for her, as I call on her several times a day to help me with things, and I certainly couldn't go sending someone over to the quarters to fetch her every time I need something.

I don't talk to Liam much right now because it just doesn't seem appropriate as I continue to grow larger and larger with John's baby. I wonder what he is thinking and if he wishes sometimes that it was his. Someone made a joke the other day about me having a watermelon in there, but I had to remind him that watermelons get ripe in the summer, and I would be darned if I was going to hold out with this baby until August!

I don't see much of John these days. He is busy on the plantation and out in the tobacco fields, and there is a lot of talk about unrest, as he says, not just here but all over the country, including out West where the Indians are upset about all of the land we have taken from them. Here in the South, the slaves are constantly talking about a rebellion, so I hear.

John says it is always a worry and has been happening for decades here and there. But not our slaves, I don't think. I don't hear any gossip about this from Rae, although she shares other things with me, but I doubt she would breathe a word about anything they talk about outside of this house. I'm sure nothing like that would ever happen, but the people in the North all the way up to Washington D.C. and beyond, they don't like it a bit that down here in the South we keep people as slaves. We're certainly divided as a country over this issue. Yes, I'm sure with the help of the army, we could put down any rebellion, but it would be a tragedy no matter what if fighting of any kind broke out.

I'm so torn about the whole thing, as I really wish we could just have these people employed like we do Atticus and Liam. I don't know why we have to own them and work them as hard as they work, but it is not my place to speak about this. I do my best though, through Rae mostly, to send things over to the quarters, like extra food and blankets when it is cold like it is now, even though Rae says they are fine.

When I hear that one of them is ill, I send for the doctor. John hates getting the bill, but I dare him to take up this issue with me. I tell him if someone lives on this property and they are sickly, they will get the help they need.

At some point, I know Rae is going to come to me and tell me she's sweet on someone. She's fifteen, soon to be sixteen, so it is bound to happen. The slaves do get married out there, and a few have had babies. John says that's a good thing, that it increases our stock. When he says it that way, it sounds like we're letting them breed as if they are cattle, and it makes me sick to my stomach.

At least we treat them well. I would have it no other way, and John knows this. Also he's a good man at heart, and very rarely does he order one of them to receive a beating. There are so many horrible stories about the mistreatment of slaves. I hear them even when I don't want to. I don't see it because mostly things like that don't happen here, but it I know it happens. No one can deny this.

I just don't know what I would do without Rae. Surely, if she married someone, she would want to move out to the quarters to be with him. I can't imagine, really, trading living in this beautiful home for living out there. I have never seen the quarters, and I don't want to, but love does funny things sometimes—just look at the chances I've taken with Liam.

Elizabeth closed the leather-bound book and put it down in her lap. She ran her fingers around the edge of the stitching, remembering the late-afternoon lovemaking with her husband the previous day, if you could call it that. She recalled seeing him lying naked on her bed and being repulsed. Compared to Holden's body, Charles was already shriveled and weak-looking at thirty-five. She could not imagine how he would appear at sixty-five. She knew Charles didn't love her, and she suspected that yesterday's orgasm would be his last for a while as he sat back and waited to see if she started her next period.

She pulled the list off the table, again looking at the name Lillian Clayton-Johnston. On a blank sheet of paper, she began arranging names in groups, according to the proximity of the table where she and John would be seated. She made sure that Lillian Clayton-Johnston would be at her table—seated right next to her.

Chapter Thirteen: The Party

Two weeks had flown by. RSVPs had been received, but not many by mail. Charles's secretary, however, had taken more than forty responses by phone. Amongst those received by mail was one written in the most flowery cursive Elizabeth had ever seen. The way that she'd written her name "Lillian Clayton-Johnston" in almost a Victorian cursive had thrown Elizabeth into a daydream about a very pregnant Adria in the diary, wondering where in the lineage Lillian came from. If she didn't find it in her books, she'd find out in a couple of days at their party, she was sure.

Elizabeth needed to make a last-minute trip to town to find something to wear for the party. After combing through her entire wardrobe, Elizabeth realized that the clothes she owned were either from when she worked in an office before meeting Charles or gowns that Charles had purchased for her for much more formal events. She wanted to make a statement. She wanted to wear something sexy and not over the top—something that certainly would never be taken as business attire but wholly appropriate for the event.

Elizabeth asked Branson to plan to take her that afternoon, but he said that Charles needed him in Atlanta, suggesting instead that Holden drive her. Branson said he'd make the call to Charles, then arrange it, and that her car would be ready just after lunch. Elizabeth's heart skipped not one beat but several. She went to her room and pulled her hair into a bun, slipped on nice pants and flat, sensible shoes—making a note to find some tall sexy heels for the party—after which she found a purse and light sweater for the outing and before going downstairs applied mascara and a hint of lipstick.

She went to the kitchen, announcing to Nettie that she would be back in a few hours. Nettie gave Elizabeth one look and knew that something was different about her. Then she noted the mascara, and when Elizabeth told her that Holden would be driving her, not Branson, she began to worry. She'd hold her tongue, but she would worry.

"Is there anything more you need in the way of food?" Elizabeth asked Nettie.

"No, Miss Elizabeth. I'm all set. Thank you for asking." Nettie looked her up and down again. "If you don' mind me asking, why is Holden driving you?"

Elizabeth flushed, revealing a nervous smile that she tried desperately to conceal, to no avail. "I'm not sure. Branson said he was unavailable and that he would have Holden drive me in. I need a dress for the party, as I realized I've got nothing appropriate. I must make an impression on Charles's colleagues, and I'm sure there will be influential people here. I don't recognize the names and don't really know who's who. Gwendolyn knew a few of the names when we were making the guest list, and maybe when I get back from town, I can run the list by you to see if you recognize any names that I should know."

She wouldn't mention it to Nettie, but she had the guest list tucked away in her purse, intending to ask Holden the very same thing. With all that he knew of the area, she was hoping he could answer a few questions for her, possibly saving her embarrassment the night of the party.

The front door opened, and Holden entered with his hat in his hand. Elizabeth came through the kitchen doors at the same time to see him standing there. She froze, smiled nervously, and turned around to see if Nettie had seen anything before the doors swung closed, but she was engaged in kneading dough that she would freeze for the fresh bread she would be baking the day of the party.

"Holden," she said quietly. "You're early."

"Yes, ma'am. I am. Is that alright?" he looked over her shoulder to see if they were being watched, but apparently, they were quite alone in the foyer. He too noted the mascara, admired the color of lipstick, and for just an instant allowed his eyes to rove from her lips downward to her shoes and back to her face, lingering on her waistband and one lonely button.

Elizabeth smiled, happy actually to have the extra time with him. She picked up her purse and sweater. "Let's go then. I'm ready."

They were halfway to town before Holden looked in the rearview mirror to catch her looking at him. "Yes?" he questioned, smiling.

"I was just thinking about my situation, about you, about everything." She looked away.

"And what are you thinking about everything?"

She shook her head slowly. "I don't know how I got myself into this, and I don't know how long I can last."

"But you only became Mrs. Freeman a few weeks ago," he replied, looking into the rearview, checking her profile as she looked out the window. "You want out already?"

"Six to be exact. Weeks," she said then continued. "Holden." A tear rolled down her cheek. "I'm quite sure that I'm property, much like the slaves who lived at the plantation at one time. Charles doesn't love me. Dehlia can barely tolerate me, yet everyone is waiting with bated breath for me to produce a child."

Holden wanted desperately to pull over the car, to take her out of her seat, wrap his arms around her, and kiss her deeply. He knew this to be true. He'd known it long before she realized it, and he hated Charles for putting her into this mess. "Everything will work out, Elizabeth. You will see."

She looked at him in the mirror.

He returned a terse, concerned look, while trying to force the edges of his lips into a smile.

The shopping took much less time than Elizabeth thought it would. She knew which department store would likely have what she wanted, and she managed to get everything there—the dress and shoes, a new bra and panties, because why not! She had Charles's credit card and no money of her own any longer, so she didn't even look at the tags. It was a small price for Charles to pay for having someone sire his offspring who he don't have to eat with, sleep with, nor even talk to if he wasn't inclined or actively trying to breed.

Holden had waited outside for Elizabeth. As she left the store, the thought occurred to her to take Holden out for a late lunch. Surely, he would know of a place where they could get something to eat, and it would give her time to pull out the list and run the names by him.

He was delighted at the suggestion, and very soon he swung into a swanky diner on the outside of the downtown area. It was just enough down-home to keep the likes of Charles and his colleagues from entering, yet just upscale enough that the clientele was decent. Holden assured Elizabeth the food was amazing, and he recommended the seafood étouffée.

Once they were seated and lunch was ordered, Elizabeth pulled the guest list out of her purse.

"Holden, I have a favor to ask," she started. "This is the guest list for the party this weekend. Many of these people were at the wedding, most of them I believe, but I can't say that I recognize a single name except one. Would you mind going through the list with me and enlightening me as to who exactly some of these people are, if you know?"

"I have no problem trying, Elizabeth, but I'm doubtful that I will be well-endowed with information as to Charles's colleagues, and I wasn't at your wedding." He took the list from her. She watched as his eyes scrolled down the page, stopping here and there, nodding once or twice.

"Well?" she asked when he seemed to have finished scanning the names.

"There are a few people here who I do know, but mostly not," he said. "I'm sorry that I can't be more help, but I can point out those that I know of and what their stories are." He moved around the table to sit next to her in order to look at the list together. The long length of his leg against hers grew warm with the contact. His right hand held the paper on the table, and the left slid down underneath to rest on her leg. His hand burned her thigh, her heart raced, and she turned to look him in the eyes. He smiled and gave a light peck to her lips. His gaze returned to the paper.

Holden began by picking the first name and telling a story, then moving on to the next. She retrieved a small pad that she'd tucked into her purse and made notes while he talked. He went through each that he knew, stopping at one and letting out a low whistle.

"This guy, William Stapleton, you want to know him. He is the owner of the plantation next door that I told you about. He has all the answers that you are looking for with regard to this place. Seat him close to you, and he'll talk your ear off about the history. You won't regret it."

Elizabeth remembered the name, and she also recalled that his RSVP did not include the plus-one guest option checked on the card. She made this note about him as the waitress showed up with their entrées. When she left, he slid out and around to the other side of the table. Elizabeth's thigh was still warm where they'd been touching. He picked up his fork and looked at her sincerely.

"I can tell you one thing," he said as he curled fettuccini noodles onto his fork. "If I'd been at the wedding, I might have had to stand up and object, you know, when they got to that part in the ceremony about *does anyone have a problem with this marriage?*" He paused before putting the noodles into his mouth, letting them dangle on the fork. "I'm sure I would not have been the only one at the wedding who knew what your situation would soon be—that you would be basically a hostage and used like a heifer. I wouldn't have been the only person who would have known that Charles Freeman will never love anyone but himself." He took the bite into his mouth, chewing slowly while watching Elizabeth's reaction.

"Holden, thank you for caring. It means so much to me." She noted the genuine look of affection on his face, something that Charles never expressed toward her.

They ate the rest of the meal in relative silence, barely making small talk. She thought about his words, spoken from the heart and so true.

Elizabeth took the check when it was presented and laid the C.F. Freeman Visa down on the bill, not bothering to look at the total. When they were ready to leave, Holden came around to her side, took her hand, and helped her out of the booth, still holding her hand as they walked to the car. He put her in the backseat as he was saddened to have to do, preferring instead that she ride home tucked close next to him, but respecting the fact that at this time it was not possible.

When they pulled in under the portico, Holden got out, opened her door, and professionally lent his hand to help her out, reaching back in to retrieve her purse that still sat on the seat. He handed it to her, struggling not to let his glance linger on her face. She took the purse from him, thanking him, then turned and walked in the front door, letting him follow her in with the dress box and bags containing her shoes and other items.

Elizabeth stopped abruptly when she saw Charles walking toward her. He was sporting a smile that questioned sincerity.

He gave her a light peck on the cheek, eyeing Holden as he did so, then taking the box and bags from him.

"Thank you, Holden, for escorting my wife to town," Charles said curtly. "Now, I need to ask you to take the car around and ask Branson to give it a wash and wax. Tell him to park it under the portico until the party in case it rains." He dismissed Holden with a flick of his chin. His eyes narrowed, but his grin remained. Charles could sense the air between Holden and his wife, without a doubt, and he didn't like it one bit. He would ask Faye to keep a closer eye on both of them.

~~*~~

The night of the party, guests began arriving a little after five, the time indicated on the invitation should they want to spend time mingling before dinner, which was scheduled to be served at six. Elizabeth heard tires on the gravel below and looked out her window to see Branson speaking with the guests, pointing to where Holden stood ready to park them. She checked herself in the mirror one last time.

Faye had helped with Elizabeth's hair, pulling it back into a tight bun at her neck but leaving a few dark strands to frame her face. Elizabeth applied her own makeup, lightly but enough to make a statement, finishing the look with a red lipstick that the woman who sold her the dress also suggested, saying it would make her lips the highlight of the outfit. She puckered in the mirror. It was true.

Elizabeth wore a simple diamond necklace, one that Charles had given her as a wedding present, and small silver earrings that dangled just enough that the sparkle would draw attention when she turned her head. Elizabeth stepped back and took in the dress and heels, turning in the full-length mirror to note how the fit accentuated her thin waistline. The dress had a raised pattern of blues tinged with red on the edges, the hem hitting conservatively just below the knee. The heels were deeper than navy but not black. The low back would turn heads, without a doubt. Elizabeth's toes peeked out of the shoes revealing red, freshly painted nails, and the height of the heels would bring her up more closely to seeing eye-to-eye with Charles, which she doubted he would appreciate.

Elizabeth had picked out a delicate deep red shawl, the color meant to accentuate the tinges of red in the dress, which she draped around her shoulders before opening her bedroom door. Faye stood outside ready to knock. She stopped, wide-eyed, taking in the lady of the house and how the dress and makeup had transformed her. Faye smiled, curtsied a bit, and pointed toward the stairs with her eyes.

"The guests are arriving, and Mr. Freeman is asking for you."

"Thank you, Faye," Elizabeth said as she stepped back into her bedroom. "Tell him I'll be right down."

Faye turned and quickly walked down the stairs, while back in her room Elizabeth took her time. She had planned her entrance—a vision that did not include trailing behind her assistant into the grand dining room.

Charles spotted Elizabeth as she entered, and he was stunned. He'd never seen her look so beautiful, not even at their wedding. He crossed the room where guests were milling about, sipping cocktails, some who noticed her right away and others who had no idea that she was the lady of the house. He took her arm, kissed her on the cheek, and whispered to her as he led her into the center of the room. "You look incredible, darling."

Elizabeth turned, accepting champagne from a waiter who stood with a glass upon a tray for her. She scanned the room, honestly not recognizing a soul, but she was not intimidated. She had already made it clear who was the lady of the house, including her mother-in-law, who had arrived shortly before she made her entrance.

Dehlia looked somewhat frumpy, even with the stylish hat she wore, and Elizabeth could see a twinge of envy as she tried not to admire Elizabeth's choice of wardrobe for the evening. Dehlia again delivered *the look* that she'd perfected as of late when Elizabeth was in her presence. Elizabeth smiled at her, let Charles take her by the elbow, and as he did, let her shawl droop just a little so as to reveal more of the back of the dress. He began introducing her to their guests, intentionally steering her away from his mother.

Charles took Elizabeth from one person to the next, some who she vaguely recalled from the wedding, others who were not in attendance but were colleagues of Charles or whom he did business with who he'd added to tonight's list. Soon it was close to time to ask everyone to take their seats so that dinner could be served. Elizabeth excused herself to check on Nettie. She pushed through the double doors of the kitchen, champagne glass in hand, and came face-to-face with Holden.

He sucked in his breath, threatening to let out a whistle, but refrained. "Elizabeth," was all he could say in what was almost a whisper.

"Holden," she said cordially, a twinkle in her eye. She knew that he liked what he saw. She noted Nettie standing behind him, hands on her hips, and changed her tone. "Thank you for taking me shopping; otherwise, I might be standing here in sweatpants and a T-shirt!" She laughed a little and pushed past him, daring his eyes to follow.

"I...I...just snuck in to grab one of Nettie's shrimp puff appetizers," Holden said as he turned to follow her through the kitchen with his eyes, noting her deliciously bare back only partially obscured by the shawl. "I'll get back to parking cars!" He smiled and tipped his hat to Elizabeth, grabbed another puff off a tray, winking at Nettie, and just like that he was out the back door.

"Nettie, are we ready to go?" Elizabeth asked.

Faye, who had been watching the entire interaction from the end of the kitchen, nervously fiddled with a strand of her coarse, black curly hair that peeked out from underneath the bonnet Nettie had instructed her to wear tonight. Faye would not be seen in the kitchen and serving in the dining room with loose hair, Nettie had commanded. Faye watched Elizabeth take in the food laid out in the kitchen, from entrées to desserts—as well as the way she looked at Holden. She didn't really understand what she was seeing, but she knew that there was something different about Elizabeth when she was around Holden, something she didn't quite understand.

"Faye!" cried Nettie, "Stop fiddlin' wit yo' hair and take a tray of those shrimp puffs out and mingle in dat crowd. An' don' foget to hand everyone a napkin who takes a puff from you." Nettie rolled her eyes. "And smile!"

Faye leapt to attention, rearranging the puffs where those that Holden took created a little hole, and gave Elizabeth a sideways glance as she pushed through the kitchen doors.

"That girl, sometimes..." Nettie said. "Yes, Miss Elizabeth. We ready. Everythin' is ready. My daughter jus left a minute ago. She helped me git all the main course finished and will be back in a few minutes to help serve. Everythin' is waitin' in the oven, warm and ready for you to give the command. Salads are already plated and in the refrigerators. We'll have those hot plates dished and out to the tables faster than you can shake a stick. Now go enjoy your company, and then jus give Faye a nod when it's time to start bringin' out the food."

Elizabeth returned to the dining room, noting Faye walking amongst the remaining guests who were still standing, those who had not yet found their place cards. The shrimp puffs were a hit, and her tray was nearly empty again. Seeing that it would just be moments before everyone was seated, Elizabeth went to the head table where Charles pulled out her chair for her to take a seat. Still standing, he instructed Gwendolyn to have the bar waiters begin circling the tables with the wine selections, then he tapped his glass with a knife.

The room stilled to a hush, and Charles smiled broadly. "I'd like to thank all of you for coming tonight. Purchasing and restoring this old house, this great plantation, an icon of the South and the original Clayton family home, has been quite an undertaking, and we are happy to share the progress with you tonight. After dinner, you are welcome to stroll through the ground-level rooms, which include the master suite that has just undergone an extensive renovation. You are welcome to view it all. Let me know if you have any questions." Then he looked at the woman seated to Elizabeth's left.

"And ladies and gentlemen, I would be remiss if I did not introduce you to Lady Lillian Clayton-Johnston, the great-great-granddaughter of Sir John Clayton, who built this fine place. He and his wife are pictured in the painting in the main hallway. Please take a look, should you be inclined. Dinner will be served promptly." With that Charles strode across the room, spoke in whispered tones to Gwendolyn, accepting a refill of champagne from a waiter as he passed by. Servers came from the kitchen pushing carts loaded with salads on chilled plates.

Lillian, her beautiful gray hair swirled into a knot at the back of her neck, sat next to Elizabeth, feebly fumbling with a ring on her finger, seemingly embarrassed and shy. She looked at Elizabeth with slightly damp hazel eyes and smiled. It was then that Elizabeth felt she was looking directly into the eyes of Adria, *her Adria*, the woman who loved Liam. This woman likely looked as Adria did when she was old and gray.

The twinkle in Lillian's eyes revealed stories of her life and experiences in this old home as a young child—not long after its days as a slave plantation. As Elizabeth studied Lillian, she hoped she was looking at a reflection of her great-grandmother Adria, and she wanted to take her into her arms and hug her. Instead, Elizabeth picked up her fork, began eating her salad, and returned the smile warmly.

"So very nice to meet you, Mrs. Clayton," Elizabeth said. "You must have so many stories about this place."

"Oh yes, many, for certain. But it was my great-uncle John who owned the place when I was little." She accepted a pour from the waiter who offered her wine, cutting him off at half-glass. "They tried to keep the place up. The slave trade originally kept the plantation running, and when that was no more, it was tobacco and cotton, then the big Wall Street crash sent tobacco prices falling. My uncle John just couldn't keep up and nearly had to sell. Then he and my aunt died in a terrible car crash, and this place nearly went into ruin. They had no children, and no other family members could afford to take it over." Lillian took small bites of her salad as she spoke.

"My husband and I lived in a neighboring county. He passed some time ago, but we were here often, and yes, I spent time here as a little girl, most definitely. It was magical!"

Charles dismissed Gwendolyn and stood watching Elizabeth and Lillian from across the room as they engaged each other, smiling and laughing. He wondered what was being said, how much was being revealed to Elizabeth, and if Lillian was making any sense at all. It was said that she might have dementia, so part or most of what she was saying could be completely made up. He could only hope.

As Lillian shared, Elizabeth wanted to hug her again, to take her to her room and show her the diary, to hear everything—all of the history she could recall before it was lost forever. But all she could do was sit and stoically entertain this descendant of the original first lady of the house. "Well, we are certainly blessed that you accepted our offer to come to dinner tonight, and I would like to have you come again if you would receive my invitation," Elizabeth said to her.

"That would be lovely, my dear," Lillian replied.

At that moment, the first course arrived, the waiters in their white tuxedos performing perfectly as they danced around the room whisking away salad plates and delivering everyone's food in time to assure that all was still hot when it landed on the tables. As the guests finished their first courses and then those dishes were whisked away, the main course landed, as choreographed as the first. In Elizabeth's mind, she was giving Nettie and Gwendolyn praises with every bite. They had pulled off this night's meal and the delivery, perfectly.

The dinner wound down with desserts, with some guests accepting and others instead opting for a tour. The first to ask to see the renovations was William Stapleton. He came to the head table when Charles was away speaking with guests. He offered his hand to Elizabeth, introduced himself as the owner of the adjacent plantation, Stately Oaks, and asked if he could get a tour.

Elizabeth blushed but rose, taking his hand after turning to glance at Lillian, who gave her an encouraging nod and smile. Then Elizabeth set off with William down the great hallway toward the painting and the master bedroom, him guiding her by the elbow.

They stopped in front of the painting. "Oh, yes," William said. "The first John Clayton and his lovely wife. We have a lot of literature about them, more pictures and such, over at our plantation next door, should you want to come and explore some time."

"I'd like that," Elizabeth said. "I have heard that it is now a museum. Is that true?"

"Yes," William replied. "It is an honor as the descendant of the original owners of the property to be able to share the rich history of the plantation—the good and the bad—some very, very bad, but it must be told." He stood in front of the painting, still holding Elizabeth's elbow. He was very tall and *stately*, just like the name of his plantation, and Elizabeth noticed not wearing a wedding ring.

"Will you show me the newly renovated master bedroom that Charles alluded to?" he asked.

Elizabeth led him to Charles's room. She'd hardly been in since the renovation was complete and wasn't sure what to say. As they stood in the middle of the room, looking about, Elizabeth eyed the place where behind the loosened baseboard she had found the diary of Adria Clayton. William spoke in a whisper. "This isn't your room, is it?" He turned to look at her, realizing his transgression. "I'm so sorry, none of my business."

Elizabeth didn't know how to respond. No, it wasn't her room and never had been, and she was extremely uncomfortable standing in Charles's bedroom with this tall, handsome man who she knew nothing about.

"I'd love to visit your museum," she replied. "Next week. I'll have Branson drive me over, but I'll call first."

William's lips formed a smile that was somewhat seductive but that he was obviously trying to conceal. "I'll look forward to it," he said, letting go of her elbow.

A noise in the hallway alerted them to a presence, and they parted. Charles was standing in the doorway.

"Ah, there you are, darling," Charles said, scooping up his wife with a swift arm around her waist. "So nice to see that you are enjoying your tour, Mr. Stapleton. I hope Elizabeth was able to show you what changes we've made and that you approve of our keeping to the historical confines as is fit for a renovation such as this."

He sure knows how to turn on the Southern charm and bullshit, Elizabeth thought as she stood watching William sip his wine while Charles maintained his grasp around her waist.

"Yes, you've done an excellent job. The Clayton family should be proud," William replied, locking eyes with Charles. "And I've just invited your wife over for a tour of the museum sometime next week. It seems as though she knows little of the history of these two plantations, and it would befit her to have a better understanding so that she can pass down the history to your children."

Elizabeth cringed. He was smooth, throwing in that bit about her needing to know in order to pass down the information, but it worked.

"Of course, Mr. Stapleton," Charles replied. "That should be fine. I'll send her over with Branson one day next week, and you can give her the tour." He looked at Elizabeth questioningly. "In the meantime, I think I shall take my wife back to the dining room where dessert is being served." He glanced over his shoulder as he escorted Elizabeth out of his bedroom, where she had never laid on the bed nor made love to him, to lock eyes with a younger, taller version of himself.

They left William standing in the middle of Charles's bedroom and walked down the hall toward the dining room, noting when William came out of the bedroom and into the hallway, stopping to study another painting just outside the bedroom door. Elizabeth paused in front of the painting of Sir John and his wife.

"Why is she not listed on the title plate?" she asked. "Earlier you said something about her perhaps not being that important. Was that what you said?" she asked Charles.

"Oh, darling, I doubt that I put it that way," Charles replied. "But back in those days, the man of the house was the master—over the slaves, the property, and yes, sometimes the wife. Paintings such as this often listed the husband, the landowner as the significant…"

"And what? The lady was so insignificant that she not be named?" Elizabeth interrupted. She was broiling. She got it. The tradition that began in this house 120 years ago continued to this day. She knew that Charles must have been the one who had added Lillian's name to the guest list, knowing full well that she was a descendant. And of course, he knew much more of the family history than he would admit to her, and yes, he'd known all along who the unnamed woman was in the painting—even though he'd said that she might have been unnamed because she was unimportant.

What, like all of the women in the Freeman and Clayton families? Elizabeth wondered.

Charles and Elizabeth returned to their table, where Lillian sat eating a chocolate mousse, scraping the sides of the ramekin, enjoying it to the last bite. She looked up with a bright smile when she saw Elizabeth standing over her.

"Delightful party, my dear, definitely in the ranks of a Clayton family gathering." Lillian licked the small spoon, smiling between bites. "My great-grandmother would be proud."

The comment sent chills through Elizabeth—chills of gratitude for the recognition that she might be succeeding in her newfound role. She knew that while her happiness might remain elusive, her responsibility to the family would continue to escalate. Then suddenly thoughts of Holden swept through her head, and she imagined the danger she could be placing herself into—as if she stepped out of line, things might go very badly for her.

"Why, thank you, Mrs. Clayton," Elizabeth replied, looking over at Charles, smiling. He returned her gaze with an icy stare. Lillian caught the interaction as Elizabeth cringed, sinking back into herself as Charles had intended. Lillian noted that the men of the Freeman family had passed down two things through the generations: *manipulation and control over their wives*.

Chapter Fourteen: The Heir

Elizabeth sat on her bed, counting the days since Charles had been in her room. Her period had not come. She wasn't concerned yet, but she was not ready to be pregnant. They had only just consummated the marriage and to what extent? She felt hollow, unloved, and unsure that she would even be able to remain in the marriage, no matter what the cost. Elizabeth sat with the diary in her lap, wanting to skip breakfast and read all day, a sign that all was not exactly normal.

Faye knocked on her door.

"Come in," Elizabeth said.

Faye opened the door, where she stood holding a tray with her tea and a biscuit.

Elizabeth nodded. "Please set it on the table, Faye. I'm going to read for a bit," she said.

"Yes, ma'am," Faye said, setting down the tray then walking to the foot of Elizabeth's bed.

"Is everything alright, Miss Elizabeth?" she asked. Faye had also counted the days since her last monthly and had been keeping a sharp eye out for any sign of its arrival, but nothing yet. She was hopeful.

"Yes, Faye. I'm just feeling like reading a bit, then I'll be down to attend to business, alright?" she asked, extending a bit more authority than she'd intended.

Faye stopped short of asking Elizabeth if her *feeling* might be related to the possibility of a certain condition, deciding that she would simply wait to see that Elizabeth ate her biscuit and that she wasn't displaying any signs of nausea and would keep her mouth shut for now.

"Yes, ma'am. I'll be up for your tray when you are finished. Call for me if you need anything more." With that, Faye turned to leave the room, glancing back to see Elizabeth open a leather-bound book and wondering where she found that one because she didn't recognize it as having come from the library downstairs.

February 21, 1858

The baby is kicking and stirring now. It is the craziest feeling, but I love it. He, or she (I must consider this), is in there, having such a good time. When I want to sleep, the baby is running like a dog having a dream, and sometimes the baby sleeps while I go about my day.

It is such a joy, and at the same time, I am so afraid. After all, it is my first. So many women I talk to laugh off my concerns since they've given birth to four, six, (ten!), and they reassure me that this is just part of becoming a mother and there is nothing to worry about.

Only two months to go, maybe less depending on who is giving me advice, and I will be holding this little one in my arms, watching as my breasts deliver the milk that will continue to give this baby nourishment. I am overjoyed at the thought!

I hear John and others in the dining room late at night, discussing the issues of the day, the slaves who are acting out, and the rumblings still coming from the North. We are so divided, and it makes me sad. President Buchanan seems to side with us and our right to own slaves, but rumor has it that he also tries to favor the North, to the extent that he bought his sister's two slaves and then set them free by bringing them into his own household as servants, but no longer enslaved.

Now we have this fellow Abraham Lincoln, who I hear the men talking about with great fervor. Seems like he's going to stir things up, and he plans to run for the presidency. Now I don't know how this is all going to play out in the long run, but I hear them talking about the country becoming "like a stick of dynamite" and one of them said, "The fuse is running short, and everything is about to blow."

It pains me to think of what could happen, with my baby coming and all, if war breaks out soon because I am certain they would call John to serve. Then what? Would it just be me and Atticus running the household? What about Liam? Would they take him away too? I must not think of all this impending doom as I don't know if babies read our thoughts, and I only want to think good things for all our peace and happiness.

The baby's room is ready, and we have the layette made up so beautifully. The blankets and baby clothes are all knitted or sewn cotton with a crochet finish, and all are ready to receive the little one. Rae has been such a big help. My midwife still checks in on me daily, and Hattie has made it clear that she will be right here with me to support the midwife. The women around me are so incredible. It seems like it was more than childbirth that has made each of them into the strong women they are, all of them having very different lives.

Yesterday, I saw Liam outside as I watched from the upstairs window. He was actually riding one of the horses; it looked like maybe just for fun. He trotted the mare around the field and then headed out down the path that went around the lake. I watched for a short while, missing him, missing the feeling of his arms around my waist when he lifted me down from the buggy, his lips on mine sometimes as he did so. I wonder if this is the end, if he will find another woman to romance, and if someday right in front of my very eyes he will fall in love and marry. Would he leave us if this happened, get another job maybe in the city? Or would she move into the apartment down by the livery stable and join him here on the plantation? I truly hope not. I don't know if I could bear it.

I have written this before, I know, and I'll put it in words again: I'm surely going to have to burn this diary someday. But the truth has to be written in order to preserve my sanity. It must. I cannot contain it any longer, and I certainly cannot say it aloud to anyone: I am in love with Liam!

There. I said it—or rather I wrote it. I feel better, but I also feel scared. Many things could happen if this should be known, the least of which would be Liam losing his job here and leaving the county forever. That would break my heart.

The worst that could happen, however, would be that John would challenge him in some way. Duels are not a thing of the past in the West, so I hear, but here in the South, we are too sophisticated for such a thing. If we were not, I could not be sure that John wouldn't put himself above such a challenge, should he know the extent of Liam's love for me, and mine for him.

Elizabeth closed her eyes. She was tired, but she wanted to read on. However, instead of returning to the diary, she decided that it was time to comb through the books she'd found downstairs in the library. She rose, found the cloth bag and brought it back to where she'd been reading, then quickly slid all of the books out onto the shiny table.

She picked one titled *Clayton County Historic Plantations*. It was a coffee table–style book with a color photograph of a large plantation home with two enormous pillars holding up the roof of an overhang. The front dripped with moss that nearly covered the entrance. She flipped to the table of contents and scrolled through the list of featured plantations, her eyes landing on the *Nobel Oak Plantation*, underneath listing Sir John Clayton as the original owner.

Elizabeth excitedly flipped to page twelve, seeing for the first time an image of her house—the house belonging to Charles and Dehlia she reminded herself—as it was when it was first built. She noted that in the image it did not have a portico. The front was starkly bare, although still quite stately. She also recognized what were then saplings, which were now trees that stood more than a hundred feet tall, and the one freshly planted oak tree that stood alone in the front yard that Adria referred to in her diary. No vines covered the front as they did now. A couple stood on the porch, unsmiling as was customary in the day. The title under the image read, "Sir John Clayton and his wife, Helen. 1850."

Elizabeth thought of the picture in the hallway downstairs, the same couple as in the image that she was studying now, although the picture that hung downstairs showed John and his wife—*Helen*—much later in their years. Elizabeth found it curious that Adria also never mentioned her mother-in-law by name. Was she really that insignificant, as Charles had said the first day they stood together in front of the painting? It wasn't merely the chauvinistic nature of the times because her husband seemed to enjoy the custom still. *Well, at least now she has a name,* Elizabeth thought. She flipped the page, wishing for more information on the house in which she was sitting. But this was a picture book, meant to showcase the homes, nothing more. Merely a paragraph described the materials and the time it took to build. *No mention that it was built mainly with slave labor.*

Elizabeth went back to the stack of books and picked out another. Just then, there was another knock at her door. "What is it?" she asked with more volume than she intended, somewhat irritated. "Come in, already!" She presumed that it was Faye, returning to get her tray. But when the door opened, it was Gwendolyn.

"I'm sorry, Mrs. Freeman, but there is a Mr. Stapleton in the foyer, asking for you."

Elizabeth jumped up from the chair and gasped, wondering, *Why is he here? What should I be wearing besides a nightgown?* She regained her composure, putting the books down on the table and trying not to panic. She noted Gwendolyn was still standing in the doorway and said, "Please tell him I'll be right there."

She pulled a casual outfit—slacks and a long-sleeved top—out from the closet and dressed quickly, remembering how Mr. Stapleton had held her elbow, guiding her through her own house, and how when Charles discovered them alone in his bedroom—standing far too close together, she now realized—she'd seen more than a flicker of jealousy in his eyes. She checked her face and hair in the mirror, applied a quick coat of pearl pink lipstick, then went down the stairs to greet her guest in the foyer.

William Stapleton stood with his hat in his hands, smiling as he watched Elizabeth descend the stairway, recalling how beautiful she'd looked the night of the party. "I do hope you will forgive me for calling without advance notice," William started. "But after our conversation the other night, I couldn't wait to show you the neighboring plantation. If now is not a good time, I understand." He looked nervously at Gwendolyn and then Faye as she stepped from the shadows of the hallway. "Your husband agreed that it would be alright for me to show you through the plantation museum, if you recall, so I wasn't sure if an advance phone call would be mandatory." He extended his gaze to Gwendolyn, who shrugged, deferring to Elizabeth.

"Why, that is lovely, Mr. Stapleton, and thank you." Elizabeth looked at Gwendolyn, then back to William. "Will you first have some tea on the patio? Nettie made the most delicious sweet biscuits this morning."

"I'd love that, Mrs. Freeman," William replied, taking a step farther into the foyer.

"This way, then," Elizabeth replied, turning to show William out to the veranda, calling to Faye over her shoulder. "Faye, please bring tea and warm biscuits," then to Gwendolyn as she took William's hat, "Please let Mr. Freeman know that I will be taking an outing to the Stately Oaks Plantation."

The two settled into patio chairs. It was a lovely morning, the sun throwing sparkles onto the lake where the wind rippled the water. The swans were again circling the lake in a group, each one separately taking the lead with each lap. Elizabeth and William gazed out at the view, Elizabeth finally breaking the awkward silence. She knew exactly why William Stapleton had come in the middle of the day, when he knew Charles was in the city. It was the way Charles had whisked her away from William in the master bedroom while she was giving him the tour—so rudely. He had certainly shown up as a rebuke to that act.

"I never got to finish giving you the tour," Elizabeth started.

"We can certainly finish that another day," William replied then adding, "when your husband is home, of course."

Faye appeared with tea and biscuits, setting the tray in front of them. She placed a cup in front of William along with a silver box containing a selection of teas. She set Elizabeth's cup in front of her, which already held her teabag, then poured hot water over the bag while William looked through the selection of tea. When he made his choice, Faye did the same for him, then set the hot pot on a trivet, covering it with a quilted tea cozy. She nodded to Elizabeth and stood back from the table awaiting further instructions. Truthfully, she wanted to hear what they would be discussing, but Elizabeth sent her back into the house.

"Thank you, Faye. We'll just be a few minutes here," Elizabeth said, dismissing her with a nod toward the patio doors. "Please shut those doors and pull the curtains in the living room to keep the sun from heating up the room." She smiled at Faye, who was watching William with an air of distrust.

Faye did as she was told, lingering to watch Elizabeth and William having a good laugh over something, a little too friendly she thought for two people who had just met. Elizabeth could hear Gwendolyn in the hallway speaking into the telephone, standing with the phone in one hand, looking out the patio doors at Elizabeth and William.

"Yes, I understand, Mr. Freeman. Yes, I'll tell him. Thank you, we'll see you this afternoon." Gwendolyn set the phone in the cradle and went through the living room, slightly cracking the patio door to address Elizabeth and William.

"Sorry to interrupt. I just spoke with Mr. Freeman. Mr. Stapleton, he said to tell you that today is not a good day to visit. He will give you a call to discuss a time when he and Mrs. Freeman can come and tour the plantation together."

Elizabeth turned red. William, midway through a biscuit, looked at Elizabeth, then cleared his throat. "Thank you for letting me know. I shall be taking my leave," he said, then moved to stand.

"Oh please, Mr. Stapleton, William. Please stay and let's finish our tea," Elizabeth said.

William looked from Elizabeth to Gwendolyn and nodded. Gwendolyn shut the patio doors, giving them privacy once again. William sat back down. There was so much he wanted to share with Elizabeth, but this was clearly not the time.

Once Elizabeth knew that their conversation would be safely private, she spoke again. "Mr. Stapleton, Please accept my apologies for my husband's behavior. He can be quite controlling." She tried to smile sweetly at William. "He means well."

"This place has a history of housing men like him, Mrs. Freeman," William said, "going all the way back to the first John Clayton. You might have wondered why the woman in the photo hanging in your hallway is not named." He watched as Elizabeth looked toward the patio doors, fearing that Faye might be trying to eavesdrop. "Her name was Helen, Helen Barrington before John Clayton took her as a bride. It was a great scandal at the time, as the Claytons and Barringtons were huge rivals in the slave trade business. Lord Barrington, as he called himself—I think the family descended from some royalty in Britain—at first refused to let Helen marry Sir John. But the two, having met at a gala thrown by the governor at the time, would sneak off together to meet whenever possible. Once word got out that the two had been in each other's company without a chaperone present, Lord Barrington, fearing the worst, allowed the marriage to proceed swiftly. Not eight months after the wedding, Helen gave birth to her first son, John the second."

William took a sip of his tea, then continued. "Helen was shunned from most social gatherings and political events where the same governor and all his cronies, including her husband and especially Lord Barrington, were together in one place, so as to keep the gossip at bay. It was known that John Clayton threatened to beat her like a slave at times if she didn't bend to his will. She had no power as the lady of the house. They did not have parties, and they did not attend any social functions together. It has also been said that the slaves and servants would hear her wailing in her room and that sometimes he would lock her door and take the key with him when he went to town.

After pausing to gauge Elizabeth's reaction to that story, William went on. "After giving birth to her last of four children, a daughter, it is said that Helen went mad and was committed to an asylum, where she died at forty-five. Afterward, Sir John was assisted by his son for some time, showing him how to manage the household, slaves, and servants. As soon as John junior turned eighteen, he married a girl named Adria—I don't recall her maiden name—and the two took over this plantation. Sir John took his younger children and moved to Mississippi. It is told that the father and son continued in business together and would occasionally meet in New Orleans to acquire slaves as new ships came in, although the younger John was forever angered over the way that his father had treated his mother, blaming his father until his death for his mother's illness and premature death.

Elizabeth sat mesmerized by all that William knew about the history of the Clayton family and of the other families who inhabited the county over a century prior.

"I'd love to know more," she said. "Where can I find more information?"

He laughed. "There's so much more I could tell you, and some things that might shock you, but apparently your husband would rather tell you himself."

"What do you mean? He professes to know very little of the history, only what he's read in books and what the real estate agent told him." She was watching William for a reaction that found him raising one eyebrow at the last remark.

"I have everything written in a book in the museum, including the family tree back to the first John Clayton. When your husband gives you permission to visit, with or without him, I will show you." With that, William set his teacup back on the saucer and stood. "I guess I really should be going now, lest your servants begin to gossip amongst themselves," he said.

Elizabeth rose and turned as Gwendolyn opened the patio door for them. Of course, she and Faye had been watching their every move, looking for any sign of impropriety, which they would report back to Charles. Gwendolyn handed William his hat as he walked through the foyer toward the open door to his car. He paused to address her. "Thank you for your hospitality. I hope to see you again sometime."

Gwendolyn stood glaring, obviously annoyed by the intrusion. She simply nodded her head.

Elizabeth went back up to her room, furious that Charles had declined the invitation from William on her behalf, how embarrassing—and after he'd told him in the master bedroom that it would be fine for her to tour the plantation museum, before he'd whisked her away. *What was he thinking?* That she couldn't be trusted to tour a public museum with a man who he himself had invited to their party? Or that she might find out some secret that he sought to keep from her? She guessed it had to be the latter.

Elizabeth picked up the book that was on top when Gwendolyn had interrupted her earlier and started to read, but she was still quite angry and so decided instead to try and find Holden. She changed her shoes and took a hat off the peg by her door, turning to doublecheck that she'd hidden the diary.

Faye watched from the kitchen window as Elizabeth rounded the house and headed out toward the bunkhouse. She thought she could follow her and not be missed, but just as her hand touched the knob of the door, she heard Nettie's voice behind her. "Jus where you think you be gon', young lady?"

Faye stammered something inaudible and closed the door. Nettie opened the kitchen door wide for some air, then invited Faye back into the center of the kitchen with a sweep of her hand. "I need some help in here. Promised Mr. Freeman chicken an' dumplings tonight, an' I have a chicken dat has been boiled and needs cuttin' up. Grab yoself a knife an' start by gettin' the skin off." Nettie turned to look out the window in the direction that she, too, had seen Elizabeth take off walking. She felt sorry for that one.

Jus like the previous ladies of the houses, Nettie thought, *jus as my mama and grandmama had known them to do, whether it be a Clayton or a Freeman, they was always takin' off after one fella or another, cuz o the nature o the men they married. They drove their women to act out dat way. Din' make it right, but they don it themselves fo' sho. This Mr. Freeman, he was no different.* So far Miss Elizabeth seemed to be holding up, but Nettie didn't give her more than a year.

~~*~~

Elizabeth pushed open the door of the bunkhouse. It was unlocked, but quiet, dark, and empty. She left and walked around the lake path, taking the farthest path to the cabin in the woods where she'd first made love to Holden.

She found him there, fussing over a table that was turned upside-down, screwing a metal plate in where the table leg had come apart from the tabletop. She entered quietly and snuck up on him, causing him to jump, let out a little *ahh,* and drop his screwdriver. He turned and grinned, grabbing her around the waist and pulling her in tightly. He began smothering her with kisses, his hands roving between her breasts and the button of her slacks. He knew why she'd come. It was clear. She had no book in her hand.

Elizabeth didn't resist and quickly undid the buttons of his shirt one at a time, until within moments, they breathlessly stood naked in front of each other for the first time. Holden took a step back, eyeing her from head to toe, then brought her in to him and kissed her delicately.

"You are so beautiful, Elizabeth," he whispered in her ear. "I can't stand it. I must make love to you this very moment." He pulled her to the bed and gently laid her down on the fresh quilt that he'd recently brought to the cabin. The next thing they knew, it was more than an hour later. They both fell into a gentle sleep and awakened to find the sun lower than either of them were comfortable with.

Elizabeth sat up quickly and dressed while Holden watched from the bed. She glanced over at him, admiring his sleek, tan muscular body, noting his chest hair had matted a bit after the sweat dried. She smiled, went to the bed, leaned over, and kissed him.

"I'd better hurry. I'm likely in trouble." She rolled her eyes. "I'll think of something to tell them, and it won't include you." She smiled, leaned over, and looked him in the eyes, kissing him delicately on the lips.

"Take the lake path. I'll take the path back to the old slaves' quarters in about fifteen minutes, so if they are looking for both of us by chance, we'll come from different directions."

Elizabeth turned at the door to see him slowly getting up to pull on his jeans. "Holden," she called to him.

"Yes, Elizabeth?" he replied.

"I don't know what I'm going to do. I don't belong here." She was near tears.

"Don't worry. Like I said: It will all work out." He blew her a kiss before she walked out onto the porch.

~~*~~

When Elizabeth came through the door of the kitchen, Nettie was dishing chicken and dumplings into a bowl, and Faye was pulling cornbread out of the oven. They both turned when they saw her, surprised at the way she looked. Her hair was windblown, or something of that sort, and her clothing was all askew.

"Mr. Freeman is at the dinner table. He wanted to know where you were, and he's not happy," Nettie said quietly. Faye watched Elizabeth straighten her hair and her blouse and walk into the dining room.

"Where have you been, Elizabeth?" Charles asked sternly without any other greeting.

Elizabeth sat at the other end of the table, taking the chair at her place. "If you must know, Charles, I got lost." She watched as Faye came in and set a bowl in front of him, waiting until Faye went back to the kitchen to continue.

"Thank you for your concern, though, and it's nice to see you as well." "How was your day?" she asked with such a blatant lack of concern that it angered him even farther.

"You do know that you are not to leave the house without someone accompanying you—not even to take those walks of yours." He picked up a spoon and sampled the soup. "There are wild boars roaming in some parts of these woods. If you cross their path, you could be killed."

"Oh, so you *do* care," Elizabeth said with a facetious look, accepting the glass of wine that Faye put in front of her. Nettie had ordered it for her, knowing she'd need it, and a glass of scotch for Charles. At that point, Elizabeth didn't care what Faye heard because it appeared she and Charles were about to have their first fight.

Charles took a drink of his scotch, setting the glass down too firmly.

Elizabeth continued, "And what in the world caused you to rebuke the neighbor and decline a tour of the museum on my behalf?"

"It is not the appropriate thing for a married woman to do, to run off with another man to tour his home alone." Charles wouldn't look at her now, just down at his soup.

"It is not his home. It is a museum, open to the public. He just happens to be a descendant. What do you think you are doing, controlling me in such a way?"

"You will do as you are told," Charles said, giving her a steely, unsmiling look down the long table. With that, he pushed back his soup, picked up his scotch, and started toward his suite.

"Charles!" Elizabeth exclaimed and watched as Charles stopped, turning to look at her. "I will not be treated this way. I will not."

Charles took several healthy strides to reach Elizabeth's end of the table. He leaned over her and took a fistful of her hair in his hand, pulling tight, causing her head to be cocked to one side, and holding her there. "Did you hear me, Elizabeth? You will obey me, for better or for worse." He jerked her head straight back to an upright position and released her hair.

"Fuck you, Charles," she said.

Charles turned and left the room. Faye entered the dining room with a bowl of chicken and dumplings for Elizabeth and the bottle of wine from which to refill her glass.

Elizabeth stood, picked up her glass and took the bottle from Faye, stepped away from the table, then stopped and turned. "Faye, please bring a hot bowl of chicken and dumplings to my room in about an hour. I'm going to take a bath."

She had planned to skip dinner and just drink wine but thought better of it. She was ravenous after the lovemaking with Holden, and the thought of not eating anything at all made her nauseated. When Elizabeth got into her room, she turned and locked the door. Then she turned the bathtub hot water on full blast.

The bathwater was steaming and just what Elizabeth needed to wash away the pain of the way Charles treated her, although she would have preferred to leave the scent of Holden on her body for as long as possible. Once the water cooled, she stood, took a towel from the rack and all a sudden had the urge to throw up. Elizabeth ran over to the toilet and heaved, although she had nothing but wine in her stomach. She brushed her teeth, filled a glass with water, and retired to the chaise where she promptly fell asleep.

Elizabeth woke to the sound of Faye's knocking. "Come in," she said, sleepily.

"I can't, ma'am. It's locked," Faye replied.

Elizabeth got up and crossed the room, opening the door just long enough for Faye to enter, then closing it behind her. Faye was carrying a bowl of chicken and dumplings on a tray, the smell of which made Elizabeth nauseated again, but she held it in check.

"Thank you, Faye. Leave it here. I'll eat it in a minute. I'm in for the night. There is no need to come back for the tray. Please tell Nettie goodnight, and you have a good evening. I'll see you tomorrow." She wanted to dismiss Faye quickly in the event that she had to run to the bathroom again. But the feeling passed, and she was suddenly quite hungry. She managed to eat half of the chicken and at least one of the dumplings, and they were delicious.

Elizabeth was quite sure now that she must be pregnant. Not very pregnant, of course, no more than four weeks. She was shocked at how quickly that happened. She'd heard of people trying for months, years sometimes. She brushed her teeth again and went to bed, falling fast asleep and not waking until after eight in the morning.

When Elizabeth came down to the dining room for breakfast, she noticed Charles had eaten, but his dishes had not yet been cleared. Faye entered immediately, and upon seeing Elizabeth knew something was different. She looked peaked, ill.

"Are you alright, ma'am?" Faye asked, a glimmer in her eye suggesting maybe she knew better.

"I'm fine, Faye. Thank you. I just had an exhausting day yesterday, getting lost on the trail and all. It took a lot out of me. I'm good now—and hungry! Can you please ask Nettie to make me pancakes? I haven't had pancakes in so long I can't remember."

"Yes, Miss Elizabeth. I'll do that, and I'll be right back with your tea." Faye exited the dining room, entering the kitchen with a smirk.

"Miss Elizabeth is not feeling well, Nettie. But she's asking for pancakes."

"Well then, she'll get pancakes," Nettie said. "Now here, take her tea out there before it gets cold." Nettie had Elizabeth's breakfast tea, hot water, and milk on a platter.

"Do you think she's… ," Faye asked, but Nettie cut her off.

"Ain't none our business right now, none yours especially. Jus do your job, Faye."

Faye left the kitchen doors swinging as she exited the room. *I am doing exactly what I've been asked to do,* she thought.

Chapter Fifteen: Sequestered

Charles sat with his feet on his desk with a glass of scotch in his hand, something he would never do in the company of others, but he had no more appointments for the day, and his assistant had gone home. His investment firm was flourishing to the point he'd been thinking about taking on a partner. Suddenly, there was a knock on his door, and before Charles could bring his feet down, his brother, Bryce, walked in.

"Hey, big brother, I see you're kicking back! About time!" Bryce sat down in the chair opposite Charles, who did not bother moving his feet. "What? You're not going to offer me a drink? It's five o'clock!"

"Since you know where it is and I am kicking back, as you said, feel free to help yourself." Charles watched as his brother took in the skyline behind him, wondering if it would be possible for the two of them to work together. *Likely not,* he concluded.

"Hey, I'm sorry we missed your party," Bryce said then went to the drink cart and poured a measure of scotch, not bothering to find the ice. "Since we're pregnant again, we don't get out much." He swished the drink as if it needed a stir and took a sip. "Plus, I understood it mainly to be a tour of the property, and I've seen it many times already. I figured you wouldn't miss us. How did it go?"

"Boring, actually, pretty boring. But the people who needed to be there showed up. Mother was there, and that guy from the development project in midtown showed up with his wife. I think he was impressed. He wants me to finance the deal."

"I heard Elizabeth was a real knockout," Bryce said over the rim of his glass, eyeing Charles and giving him a half smirk.

"Yes, she looked lovely," Charles replied. "I heard it from every man in the house, eligible or not," Charles said reluctantly. "Apparently you did as well."

"Mother said that Lillian was there. Did Elizabeth talk to her?" Bryce asked.

"They engaged in small talk from what I could tell, only enough to spark Elizabeth's curiosity, nothing more. They talked about getting together again soon, which of course will not happen unless one of us is present." Charles handed his brother his own, now-empty glass, indicating the need for a refill. Bryce turned, picked the scotch bottle off the cart, which was within reach, and refilled his brother's glass, topping off his own and setting the bottle down on the desk.

"Lucky for us, she has dementia," Bryce said.

"Yes, lucky for us," Charles replied, raising his glass in a toast.

~~*~~

Charles pulled up to Marigold's townhouse at about seven, with three healthy drinks under his belt. Branson opened his door and, although knowing the drill, reminded Charles that he would wait across the street. One tap on the door revealed a woman who was open for business. Her full-length lace gown was not see-through, but it might as well have been. She ushered Charles through the door and showed him to his favorite chair, handing him a glass of his favorite scotch, which she kept on the table for him.

Once Charles was seated, Marigold knelt at his feet, removing his shoes and giving his feet a rub with his socks still on, then moved her hands up underneath his pants to massage his calves. She brought her hands out and placed them on top of his pants to massage Charles's thighs and kept it going as she crept closer to the target. When he visibly showed signs of relaxing to her touch and leaned his head back in the chair, she unzipped his pants and brought him out into the open, something he would never imagine Elizabeth doing, but then he'd never given her the chance. Her expert touch, skilled tongue, and lack of inhibition brought him quickly to a climax.

As tired, spent, and angry as Charles was, he still had it in him to follow Marigold to her bedroom, something that he made a habit of doing at least weekly for almost the past ten years. There she could take every bit of anger out of his system, to the extent he never remembered it had been there. It was her specialty. She had no desire for more from him and neither did he from her. It wasn't until his mother insisted that he sire an heir or else cede control of the family business to his younger brother did he even consider marrying or giving over his orgasms to any other woman, ever again.

Once Charles was released and replenished, he dressed and went outside, where Branson was waiting. He thought about Elizabeth all the way home and how he'd treated her so badly. The truth was he just didn't care for her. As beautiful as she looked at their party—and he didn't want to know what that dress cost him—the fact that every other man there wanted her badly whether they would admit it or not didn't make him want her any more.

He remembered what she'd said after he'd pulled her hair. He'd never heard a woman talk like that—not outside of the movies. He would wait the six months he'd promised his mother, and if Elizabeth didn't get pregnant, he was off to Monaco, and Bryce could have the family business—*and* the plantation houses. If she had a girl, *God forbid*, he would give it one more chance, and then he would be out.

Charles's car pulled into the plantation driveway a little after nine. He noticed that Elizabeth's light was out. *Good thing,* he thought. He was going to have a talk with her in the morning. Not that he suspected her of anything, but he was going to make sure that she didn't roam as much as she tended to do. He felt the need to tighten the reins—not for any other reason than to increase control. She would not be going to town anytime soon, no matter the supposedly urgent need, and as far as William Stapleton was concerned, an outing to his plantation-turned-museum was not in the cards. There was too much information there, things that would cause Elizabeth to wonder and possibly ask too many questions, questions that begged answers that he wasn't prepared to give. Elizabeth needed to shut up, be a good girl, have a baby boy, and then get the fuck out of his life.

Branson let Charles off at the door, then he pulled the car into the garage. Charles entered, finding the house quiet, which was to his liking. However, as soon as he shut the door, Faye appeared, startling him.

"Faye!" he shouted in a whisper. "You scared the shit out of me. What are you doing? You should be home by now. You have to be back here early tomorrow. Could you not get a ride home with Gwendolyn?"

"No, sir," Faye responded. "Mrs. Freeman took her dinner in her room, and I waited for her to call to retrieve her dishes and run her bath, and before I knew it, Gwendolyn was gone, Nettie was gone, and Branson was with you. There's a cot in the old kitchen servant's room. I'll sleep in there. Don't you worry."

"Fine," Charles said. "I'll see you in the morning." He turned to go up to his room when Faye called to him.

"Mr. Freeman," she said.

"Yes, Faye. What is it?"

"I think she's gon' have a baby." She was proud of herself for being the one to deliver the news, although she was far from sure. "Sir, it's just that I'm real good at counting the days, and Elizabeth's monthly is now far overdue. And she's been actin' weird about food and looked sick when I brought her food last night and again this morning when she came down for breakfast. Then she said she was cravin' pancakes. All those things are usually indications that somethin' is gon' on in there."

Faye shifted from one foot to the other, her anxiety causing her English to break, nervous about confronting Charles, but trying to show him that she was doing what she was hired to do. She just wished she had proof that those walks of hers were ending up with Elizabeth being in someone else's bed. *Like Holden's,* she thought. But she would not go as far as to speculate; she would just keep a better eye on her.

Charles was silent for a moment, recalling how he'd mistreated Elizabeth that morning, trying to push back the guilt that was now creeping into his belly. If his heir was in *her* belly, then it wasn't right. He'd have to keep his emotions in check—at least for now, until he knew for sure.

"Thank you, Faye, for letting me know. Please keep an eye out for any sign that she might be, or might not be. I will be waiting either way." He turned and walked down the hallway to his bedroom.

Faye was feeling both proud of herself and somewhat guilty at the same time. She knew how far back Nettie's family went with the Freemans and that her grandmother had worked in this very house for the Claytons. They had always been faithful to the owners, or back then, the *masters,* of the houses. Betraying the lady of the house was not part of the occupation. She knew that when was hired and thought it was strange at the time, but it was what Charles wanted when he interviewed her. She was to watch Elizabeth and to tell him everything, every detail about her daily life that she could remember, and she was to write it down if she didn't think she could remember.

Faye had never told anyone, not Nettie, nor Gwendolyn, not even her own mother or sister, what her agreement was with Mr. Freeman. As far as everyone knew, she was just part of the help. She was assigned to help Elizabeth mainly, but when she wasn't taking care of her needs then she was supposed to help in the kitchen, and if Gwendolyn needed her, she would help her too.

So far, Faye hadn't been able to tell Mr. Freeman very much because there wasn't much to tell—until today. She did tell him when Elizabeth had her monthly and made sure he got up there to see her when she was probably going to drop one of her eggs. Faye told Charles about the walks and that Elizabeth went this way and that, starting out in a different direction nearly every day. Elizabeth told Faye she was exploring the woods, which Faye relayed to Charles. She didn't think anything was funny about those walks, so she stopped telling him about them. Faye had not been past the edge of the lawn, never on any of those trails; she was too afraid. She'd heard stories about the wild animals that roamed out there. She'd even heard tell from Nettie that an alligator found its way into the lake one time. Lord knows how far it had to travel to get to the plantation, but she didn't want to find out, especially if there was a swamp close.

Luckily for Elizabeth, Faye had no knowledge of the bunkhouse or the old cabin farther out in the woods, not even the old slaves' quarters, although she saw the edge of the building from the very top floor once when she looked out the window and the light was just right. Faye had mentioned it to Nettie, who brushed it off as a painful memory of the captive humans who at one time lived cramped in there like rats.

~~*~~

Elizabeth was at the table again when Charles came down for breakfast. She wouldn't look at him, instead focusing on one of the books she'd brought back from town. She had been deep into the history of the county, and she even found Charles's great-grandfather mentioned somewhere. She certainly didn't want to discuss any of it, preferring to bury herself in it and continue reading.

Her breakfast sat cold, though, as her tummy had been rumbling a little. She was on her second cup of tea when Faye came back to ask if she wanted something different to eat.

"Maybe some oatmeal, if you don't mind, and please tell Nettie I'm sorry. The eggs just aren't agreeing with me this morning." Elizabeth looked up at Faye, still ignoring the fact that her husband sat at the other end of the table. "I'll keep the toast, though, thank you."

Charles raised an eyebrow, looking down the table at her, wondering if the change in her breakfast craving might be associated with pregnancy. She loved eggs and had them almost daily, either sunny-side up, soft boiled, or in an omelet with cheese.

Elizabeth went back to flipping through the book pages, making mental notes about historical facts related to both the Claytons and the Freemans, how and when the county was named after the Clayton family, and looking for history of the place next door, the Stapleton's plantation.

Charles cleared his throat after a few minutes in an attempt to get Elizabeth's attention. She ignored him.

"Elizabeth," he said sternly. She looked up from her book, expressionless.

"Yes, Charles," she replied.

"What are you reading?" His attempt at small talk died before the words reached her. She shrugged and turned her attention back to the book.

Charles stood, pushing his chair back, causing it to scrape loudly on the wood floor. "I'm talking to you, Elizabeth." He increased both the volume and the intensity of his voice.

"I hear you, Charles. What is it that you need?" Elizabeth would parry. She had nothing to lose at this point.

"I asked you what you are reading. Is it too much to answer me?" he asked.

"Is it too much to say good morning, Charles? And perhaps to apologize for the way you were rough with me last night?" Elizabeth now stared at him, still standing in front of his chair, his knuckles turning white due to the pressure he applied to the table.

Charles was torn between an apology and an insult, choosing to stay calm. "I am sorry for getting angry and for the way I touched you," Charles said slowly. "But we are going to change the rules a little. Starting today, no more trips to town and no more phone calls to your sister or to anyone for that matter. We are not going to tour the plantation next door, and you will not receive Mr. Stapleton for tea again alone. If he wishes to come calling, he can do it when I am here."

"Or what? What exactly are you afraid of, Charles? That I might hop on a train and leave you if I get a chance to go to town? That I might call my sister and ask her to come get me? Or that I might run off with Mr. Stapleton, who I must admit is quite becoming." Elizabeth smiled then, causing Charles to clench his fists in an attempt to hide his rage.

"You don't want to know, Elizabeth. Don't test me."

She stood with her book, taking the long way around the table to avoid passing close to Charles, walked through the foyer to the hallway, and went up to her room. Once there, she locked the door. She had taken to locking it now whenever she was alone in the room—partially because she didn't want anyone walking in on her while she was reading the diary and also that she was becoming somewhat afraid of her husband.

Charles walked into the kitchen where Gwendolyn, Nettie, and Faye stood at the counter, discussing the couple and their spats both the previous night and just then. Nettie was speaking when he walked through the doors, and she abruptly shut her mouth, sure that he'd not heard what she had just said about feeling sorry for Elizabeth.

He turned his anger with his wife toward the staff as they stood together, unsure what to do or say.

"She will not leave this house today!" he said. "I want you all to make sure of that. I will talk to her tonight again about what she can and cannot do, where she can and cannot go— like on those silly walks of hers. There is no reason for her to be out in the woods like that! Is that clear?"

Nettie immediately thought of Holden. She knew about both the bunkhouse and the cabin where the first Sir John Clayton had sired a baby with one of the slaves. That had been talked about all the way down through her family, and they all knew that Mr. Henry, the direct descendent of John Clayton who built this house, was traded along with his mother as a baby to deflect gossip and grew up on the plantation that belonged to Charles's great-grandfather. She was pretty sure that Charles didn't know about any of this, and she had no desire to make him any smarter.

The three staff members said not a word; they just stood still huddled together, Nettie holding Faye's hand under the counter, all nodding in unison. Charles turned and walked out of the kitchen, banging his fist on the swinging door as he pushed through.

From upstairs in her room, Elizabeth could hear Charles addressing the staff loudly and heard him rip the telephone cord out of the wall and throw the phone on the floor, although at the time she had no idea what has just happened; it was merely a loud commotion. She sunk down into the chaise, drew a blanket over her lap, and picked up the diary.

March 21, 1858

I think the baby will be here any day. The way he kicks in there, you would think he is a jockey training for a race, but instead of kicking the horse, it is my insides that are taking a beating. I'm not feeling the rocking motions they say will overtake me—contractions they are called—just before the birth, so I guess I have some time to go, but one never knows!

John has been out a lot more lately, and when I say "out" I mean not coming home on time or not coming home at all. I heard the servants talking about it quietly in the hall, but I couldn't quite make out what they were saying—something again about trouble brewing, about him going to meetings with officers from the Confederate army, about possible fighting over keeping slaves. I think they want to be free, and I don't blame them. But who are we going to be fighting? Every person in the North?

Our president, James Buchanan, is of a mind that we can keep our slaves if we want, which I hear has a lot of people in the North very upset with him. John told me something about Georgia seceding from the Union, but I'm not sure what that means other than that we would no longer be a part of the group of northern states. We have an army called the Confederate, and I hear the

Union of states that we just left has been building up their army in case they must fight against us. Oh Lord, I just want to live my life here on this plantation and have children and stay out of John's way when he is mad. Let's please not go to war. Some of us have family on both sides of the line!

Every day now, my midwife comes and checks me. She says I'm dilating, which means I'm starting to open up so that the baby will have an easier time coming through. Hattie has been busy boiling sheets and drying them out in the sun, and they're stacked in my room beside big wash basins and some tools the likes of which I've never seen.

I sure hope John is home when this baby decides to come. I don't want to do this without the comfort of knowing he is downstairs in case there is trouble, but from what I hear I will be surrounded by women who will come to help. My midwife, Hattie, Rae, and Hattie's sister, Elsa, will be here. They've all helped babies be born, so I guess I'll be in good hands.

I really miss seeing Liam and our trips to town in the buggy. His lips are so soft, and when he looks at me with those blue eyes, my heart melts. I love the way the sun shows the tiniest bit of red in his brown hair when it hits just right. He says his grandmother had completely red hair and that others in his family do as well. I've seen one or two people with completely red hair like that and freckles, and I'm glad Liam doesn't look like that. He's perfect just the way he is.

Oh, just now as I write, I feel one of those contractions. I've never felt anything like it! I wonder if I should call down to Hattie and have her send for the midwife. She did tell me that some women have contractions days before the baby is born. She mentioned something about the time in between them. Maybe I'll just keep track of the minutes in between so that I can let her know. The baby is coming! He will be John Clayton the third. My precious firstborn.

The noise downstairs had stopped, and Elizabeth presumed Charles had left for his office. She decided to go downstairs and get a cup of hot water with some fresh ginger to calm her tummy. After the outburst from Charles, she'd left her oatmeal sitting, but she would ask Nettie to warm it back up and add some apple slices and cinnamon. She unlocked her door, poked her head out, and looked both ways, then slipped out into the hall, tiptoeing quietly down the stairs carrying her tray. Before Elizabeth rounded the corner to the dining room, she heard Nettie and Holden in the foyer. Nettie was telling Holden about Charles's behavior and that the staff was afraid.

"Can you fix this?" Elizabeth heard Nettie ask Holden.

"Yes Nettie, that is an easy fix. I'll have the phone back and working and will install it before lunch," Holden said.

Elizabeth rounded the corner to see Nettie hand Holden the phone. The two stopped talking and looked at Elizabeth.

"What happened?" she asked, looking at the telephone in Holden's hands.

Nettie looked at Holden and back to Elizabeth. "Yo' husband had a temper tantrum and done ripped it right out the wall."

"I'll be back in a couple hours and will reinstall it," Holden said, tipping his fingers to the edge of his beret. He turned to leave.

"Holden, wait," Elizabeth said, then she turned to Nettie. "Nettie, will you give us a moment? I need to speak with Holden."

Nettie nodded, turned, and went to the kitchen, where Faye was working on a pudding recipe that Nettie had given her to keep her busy and out of the business of the household.

Previously, Gwendolyn had gone into town with Charles and Branson, although she rode in the front to avoid sitting next to Charles. Charles had told Gwendolyn that if she wanted to do her shopping, she'd better hurry. He said he would have Branson drop him at the office and then Branson could take her around town to run her errands. Privately, Charles told Branson that he would not be coming home and that he would take a taxi from his office, handing him an overnight bag and instructing him to put it in the trunk. Branson knew where Charles's taxi would land. He nodded and placed the bag in the trunk without a word.

When Nettie had seen them drive away, she'd gone down the hall to survey the damage, noting that the box where the phone cord had been attached was hanging loosely from the wall. The shelf that the phone sat upon inside the cubby was scratched but intact. She had walked straight out the door and over to Holden's place, summoning him to follow her back to the house, which was where Elizabeth found them.

Now back in the kitchen, Nettie went about her business, trying to pretend nothing was wrong. Faye eyed her carefully, afraid to start a conversation because Nettie looked distraught, possibly angry. She thought it best to keep her mouth shut and make the pudding.

"Holden," Elizabeth said, walking into his arms. He held her tightly, looking nervously around and toward the kitchen. "I need you to hug me."

"Elizabeth," he whispered in her ear. "Nettie told me everything. I'm so sorry." He figured he would take the chance that no one would come upon them.

"Holden," she said again.

"Yes, Elizabeth," he replied.

"I think I'm pregnant."

Chapter Sixteen: The Ultimatum

A few minutes later back in her room, Elizabeth finished the oatmeal that Nettie had fixed for her. It was still warm. Nettie had added a little cream with the apples and cinnamon, and it was just what Elizabeth needed. After eating that and drinking the ginger tea, she felt like herself again.

She took a quick bath, then dressed, knowing that she'd be seeing Holden soon when he came back to repair the telephone. She took extra time with her hair, adding a quick base of foundation as well since she'd been looking a bit peaked as of late. After applying a quick touch of shiny lip gloss, she was ready to receive Holden when he came to fix the telephone, looking much better than she had that morning after fighting with Charles.

Elizabeth was angry about the stunt her husband had just pulled. Really, just jerking the phone out of the wall in such a way? What exactly was he trying to prove? She knew Charles had a temper, and she'd heard that it ran in the family, but couldn't something like that play itself out over generations and be over and done?

In particular, to think that Charles would dictate that she should suddenly be cut off from her sister drove shivers down Elizabeth's spine. She knew that the first thing she would do once the phone repair was made would be to call Penny and ask her to come for a visit. Their previous discussion around this had ended in her sister making an excuse that had something to do with one of her children being sick.

But Penny would come if Elizabeth needed her; she knew that. Yes, her sister was busy with the kids and all, but if Elizabeth put enough of that serious tone in her voice, Penny would understand, and she would come. Elizabeth suspected that her conversation would be overheard because Faye would be lurking somewhere and pick up a telephone extension somewhere in the house once she realized Elizabeth was on the phone. She would have to speak in code, more or less, to make small talk but insert phrases that would alert Penny to the situation.

Screw Charles if he would dare deny her a visit from her sister. She'd already given up her best friend, who probably wouldn't speak to her even if she could contact her. She refused to be held captive in this way and decided right then that if this continued, she would formulate a plan to escape.

Elizabeth cleared her own dishes, trying to stay away of Faye's prying eyes, and walked down the stairway with her tray in hand. Gwendolyn met her at the bottom of the stairs, taking the tray from her, concerned. Elizabeth noted that Gwendolyn was back from town already. That had been a short trip.

"Miss Elizabeth, is everything alright?" Gwendolyn asked. "You don't need to be bringing dirty dishes down; you need to make us work for our wages."

Elizabeth tried to muster a smile around the comment, knowing full well that it was Faye who she was trying to avoid by bussing her own dishes.

Elizabeth handed the dishes to Gwendolyn with a smile and turned toward the patio. "I think I'll take some sun outside. Don't worry. I won't run away," she said with a half-smile,

Gwendolyn watched her go, wondering why she'd not let Faye come and get her dishes, but she thought she knew the answer. She had suspected for a while that Faye was in on something with Mr. Freeman. The way Faye sat seemingly aloof yet on guard the previous evening as Gwendolyn spoke to Nettie about Miss Elizabeth—Mrs. Free*man*—needing to be able to live as a free *woman* did not go unnoticed by either of the two. Nettie wouldn't say much back, and Gwendolyn noted the way she glanced at Faye instead of answering. She recalled seeing Faye about to follow Elizabeth out the door as she went out for one of her walks. Nettie had stopped her, intentionally giving her a random job to do instead of prying.

As far as Gwendolyn was concerned, it was not up to them to keep an eye on Elizabeth, although she had no idea about Faye's orders from Charles. It was bad enough that Miss Elizabeth was more or less a prisoner in her own house, now even more so since Mr. Freeman lost his mind and pulled the phone out of the wall. He'd probably be upset if he knew Holden was down at his place fixing it right this minute.

Faye was still in the kitchen, helping Nettie because Elizabeth hadn't called her to draw a bath nor help her fold her clean laundry. Faye reflected that it certainly wasn't her place to reveal to Charles that Gwendolyn and Nettie were talking like that. More importantly, her allegiance to each of their families was strong. The chance that Faye could be the cause of either or both of them losing their jobs would be devastating to her own reputation. Should that happen, she would *never* be hired as anyone's house manager in the future.

Faye sat peeling potatoes and keeping an eye on the pudding that was slowly cooking on the stove, pretending to be uninterested in the conversation between the two women. She was thinking, too, that she had to find a way into Elizabeth's room. She had to confirm somehow that Elizabeth still had not started her monthly. Elizabeth had what she needed in her room if she had started bleeding, and all she'd have to do would be to take out her own trash the way she was now bringing down her own dishes, and Faye would never know.

The front door opened, the bells on the handle chiming as Holden swung it open wide, holding a toolbox in one hand and the telephone under his arm. He stood grinning, proud that he'd been able to make the repair. Gwendolyn greeted him and walked with him to the phone cubby.

From out on the patio, Elizabeth heard their voices and then a light tapping as Holden worked to reattach the phone box to the wooden frame of the cubby. She waited until the voices subsided, then she got up from the lounge chair, stretched, and walked quietly through the dining room to where Holden was working.

He heard her approaching and turned to smile sweetly at her. The look in his eyes told her that he hoped the baby was his. The look in hers told another story.

"Good morning, Elizabeth," he said softly as she stood looking over his shoulder at the kitchen doors, sure that prying eyes were peeking through the small cracks.

"Good morning," she started. "And what a morning it has been." She kept her voice low enough that only he could hear her.

"Do you think it will work now?" she asked, looking at the phone, noting that it had a small crack running horizontally across one side.

"I think so. Let's give it a try." Holden pushed the wires through the slot in the phone box and reconnected them to the terminals, then replaced the cover with a screw. He picked up the receiver and was delighted to hear a dial tone. He pressed the numbers, dialing the phone out in his room. It rang and was soon followed by his voice on the other end with the message that he wasn't in at the moment.

"Who did you just call?" Elizabeth asked.

"I called myself," he said, smiling. "I'm not home."

"You have a phone out there?" she asked, her eyes widening.

"Of course, yes, I do. It was a request of mine when I was hired," he responded, taking in her troubled eyes and wishing he could hold her. He lowered his voice even more. "What are the chances you could get away this afternoon and meet me out at the cabin?"

Elizabeth looked over his shoulder again and then around into the dining room, to make sure the comment was not overheard by anyone. "What are the chances I could use your phone?" she asked. "I need to call my sister—to speak to her privately."

Holden smiled and nodded. "Do you think you can make it over without being seen?"

"Of course," Elizabeth said. "I pretty much know where everyone is at all times. Branson is in the garage waxing Charles's car, Nettie and Faye are cooking, and Gwendolyn is moving books in the library to dust the shelves. Branson will go into town just before five to pick Charles up at his office, and they will return by six, unless Charles has another of his famous last-minute meetings that go until late into the night."

Holden recalled seeing Charles cut his lights the last time he came home late, sure by the overnight bag he carried that he had not been out attending to business, unless one took a shave kit and change of clothes to such a meeting and then felt the need to sneak back into his own house afterward.

"Fine, then, come between four and five. I'll wait for you. I'll keep an eye out as well to see who among the staff leaves, if anyone. I look forward to wrapping you in my arms, Elizabeth."

The comment unnerved Elizabeth as she was sure Faye had secrets spots in the house, now quite sure that Charles had charged her with the task of spying.

Elizabeth touched her fingers to her lips and kissed them, blowing the kiss his way off the tips, then she turned and went up the stairs to her room. She was suddenly overcome with exhaustion, although she'd done nothing so far, all day. She sat down on the chaise, covered up with a throw, and holding the diary under her arm, fell fast asleep. She dreamed of making love to Holden. In her dream, he stood up after making love to her, turning his back briefly while he dressed. He zipped up his trousers and turned back around to look at her, glaring now. It was Charles! Elizabeth awoke with a start, sweating, and tossed off the throw. She reached for a glass of water that sat on the table, drank it all, then opened the diary.

May 16, 1858

I cannot believe that it has taken me so long to sit down and write again. Having a newborn is so much work! Little John was born on March 21, just a few hours after I last put my pen down. Those contractions quickly started coming closer and closer together. Hattie called the midwife and put kettles of water on the stove to boil. She sterilized a bunch of things, and I just laid in bed watching the little guy writhe around inside, pushing from the inside so hard that it caused great ripples on the skin of my belly. He seemed ready to push himself out, which is pretty much what he did!

John made it home just a few hours before the baby was born. The men got word to him that I was ready to give birth, and I heard tell he jumped into his buggy and kept his horses at a gallop for most of the way home. He didn't need to do that as he actually had plenty of time, but being his firstborn, he was nervous too. Plenty of women die in childbirth, so I think he may have been a bit concerned about that as well.

When the contractions were coming hard and fast, the women let John see me one last time, then shooed him out of the room so they could take over. And boy did they: Hattie bringing the hot towels, and the midwife moving her hands all over my stomach, massaging that baby into place to make sure his head stayed down while telling me to keep pushing. Then Little John gave one big kick, and I gave one last push, and he shot out into the midwife's waiting arms.

It was exhausting, but they said it was quick, compared to some. While the midwife cleaned me up, Hattie gave the baby a little sponge bath, and within a few hours of holding him, he was already suckling at my breast. We both fell asleep just like that, and Hattie stayed by my side throughout the night while John came in now and then to check on us both.

He's a proud papa, and from the smell of whiskey on his breath when he came in late, the men had been getting him juiced up, celebrating the birth of his heir. He'll probably be a little nicer to me now, for a while I hope anyway, after all I just gave him a son.

Little John is almost two months old already, and he changes every day. His hair is thick and dark, and his eyes are exactly the color of his daddy's. He smiles a lot, but Hattie says it is probably just gas. I think he's looking at me when he does smile, and I am more in love with him than I am my husband.

I don't do much around the house right now, mostly just nurse the baby and try to take care of easy things, like making sure this place gets a good spring cleaning. The weather is perfect now, and it is time to take the rugs out and beat them and wash all the floors in the entire house. It will take at least a week just to get that done. But before we can do that, we have to dust everything up high so that all the dirt that comes down will get carried out with the rugs. I'm so glad we have people to do all of that. I know that not everyone has servants or slaves, and they have to do that themselves. I think I'd go mad if I had to tend to this baby and try to do all the cleaning while he slept.

Elizabeth put the diary down under a pillow on the chaise and laid back, looking down at her own belly. She pushed it out as far as she could, trying to imagine what it would be like when it expanded. She'd never known anyone who was pregnant other than her sister, and she lived so far away that Elizabeth only saw her once with her first child and a couple of times during holidays with her second. Penny hadn't told her a lot of details about the birthing process, so Elizabeth planned to ask her lots of questions when she came. *If* she came. She was sure that Penny would find a way, especially when she told her she was pregnant.

She looked at the time. It was nearly four o'clock. Elizabeth ran to the bathroom, splashed cold water on her face, and straightened her hair. She walked down the stairs into the kitchen. Nettie was there, stirring a pot of soup, and there was no sign of Faye nor Gwendolyn.

"Good afternoon, Nettie," Elizabeth said. Nettie jumped, startled a little as she often went into her zone while she was cooking. "Where is everyone else?"

"Oh, Miss Gwendolyn don left already. Her son is sick. Faye is outside waitin' for Branson. She gon' catch a ride home with him in his own car. I guess Mr. Freeman called him to say he din need a ride."

Elizabeth flinched. "So my husband isn't coming home tonight?" she asked tersely, but she was happy inside to hear this news. It would make her excursion over to Holden's an easy one. "Well, Nettie, just leave me a bowl of that soup then, and you can go home early as well. That will be enough for me. I will see you tomorrow."

Elizabeth walked down the hall to the library, where she could see the progress that Gwendolyn had made that day. From that room, she could see Branson outside as he readied his car to leave for the day, and she saw Faye climb into the front passenger's seat. Within minutes, the two drove away. That left Nettie. Elizabeth knew she shouldn't try to sneak over to Holden's with Nettie still in the house. She looked around the library at the newly dusted and reorganized bookshelves, then at the perfect sitting spaces for one who would want to relax and read right there. But she preferred to read in her room and had plenty of books still to go through before bringing any more up—and she was only halfway through the diary. So she elected to sit by the window in the late afternoon sunshine and wait until she saw Nettie's large frame wandering from the rear kitchen door and around the back of the garage where her car sat parked in the shade.

As soon as Nettie pulled out and drove down the long driveway, Elizabeth jumped up and walked straight out the front door over to Holden's. With everyone gone now and Charles apparently not coming home—so he told Branson—a twinge of jealousy sparked in her alongside the feeling of being free for the night. She was able to go anywhere she wanted—and that was straight into Holden's waiting arms.

Once Elizabeth arrived at the cabin, Holden brought her into his embrace, kissed her, led her slowly but deliberately to his bed, laid her back gently, and began to undress her.

"Wait," said Elizabeth somewhat breathlessly. "I need to call my sister. I can't do it tomorrow once everyone is back in the house, and I don't want to call her too late. She'll be putting her kids to bed."

Holden leaned back and let her roll over and off the bed, pointing in the direction of the telephone on a little desk by the window. "I can give you two some privacy," he said. "I'll wait on the porch." He watched as Elizabeth rose and made her way to the telephone, sat down at the desk, and began to dial the number that she knew by heart.

Elizabeth kissed Holden when he paused on his way out and bent down to put his face next to hers.

I think I'm more in love with him than with my husband. Elizabeth recalled Adria's words as she watched Holden walk out to the porch and shut the door quietly.

She picked up the telephone, checking to see that the cord was long enough, and moved to an overstuffed chair in Holden's living room. Penny picked up on the third ring, somewhat breathless and not recognizing the number on caller ID.

"Hello? Hello?" Penny asked as she answered, wondering who would be calling her from this number that she did not recognize.

"Penny, it's me," Elizabeth started. "Do you have a minute?"

"Elizabeth!" Penny nearly screamed into the phone. "I'm so happy to hear your voice! What is going on with you? I've been worried!"

"It's okay," Elizabeth said, and then she began to cry. "It's not okay."

Penny grew immediately concerned. "Are you hurt? Are you safe? Where are you? This is not your number."

"I'm at a friend's," Elizabeth answered, not caring to go into detail. "I have to make this quick, but I need to let you know what is going on, and please, please, Penny, I need you to come."

Elizabeth proceeded to tell Penny about Charles's outbursts of anger, the way he basically raped her when she was fertile, and how he had banned her from future outings, confining her to the house. She described the rage that morning that had driven him to pull the phone out of the wall. She told her sister all of this as quickly as she could, keeping her voice low so that Holden would not overhear the details. Then she got to the point of the call.

"Penny, I'm afraid. And I'm pretty sure I'm pregnant. My period is almost two weeks overdue, which has never happened in my lifetime. I need you to come."

"Oh, my darling sister, Elizabeth," Penny replied. "Of course, I will come. Let me figure some things out. How can I get back to you?"

That question Elizabeth was not ready to answer. She couldn't give her Holden's number because then she would have to give up more details.

"I'll call you back as soon as I can. Charles can't know. You'll just have to show up."

"Done. I'll wait for your call, and I will have a date for you when you call back," Penny replied. "Elizabeth, please be careful. I will see you soon. I love you."

"I love you too, sister," Elizabeth replied. "Goodbye. I can't wait to see you."

Elizabeth put the phone back in the cradle and opened the front door. Holden was sitting, shirtless, in the rocking chair on the porch, gazing out at the lake. He looked up when he heard her come out. "All good?" he asked, getting up and wrapping his arms around her, walking her backward through the doorway all the way to the bed, lying her down gently, kissing he as he did so. "Where were we?" He began by pulling her shirt over her head, exposing her lacy bra, and moved his hand quickly down to tug at the button on her jeans.

Elizabeth grabbed a handful of Holden's hair as he kissed her belly, and his lips wandered south from there.

It was dark in Holden's cabin when they finally gave in to the exhaustion, soaked in sweat and satiated. Elizabeth rolled over and looked at his bedside clock. Eight o'clock, and no headlights, no chance that Charles would return because his car was right here in the garage. She was alone with Holden, her lover, her friend, and she wanted to sleep with him. She'd be safe out here even if anyone arrived before Nettie, who was usually the first. Anyone else, including Charles if by some chance he might show up that night, would presume she was in her room sleeping and would not bother to look for her.

Elizabeth had not eaten, however, and she was starving. She got up, wrapped herself in Holden's large flannel shirt, and pulled on her underwear. She knew Nettie would have left the soup on warm in the kitchen, so she decided to walk across the lawn into the back door of the kitchen and bring back dinner for the two of them. She returned with two bowls on a tray and one of the small crusty loaves of bread that had come out of the oven just before Nettie left.

Holden had set the table while she was gone, opened a bottle of wine, and poured himself a hearty glass, hers less than half. *In the event that she truly is pregnant*, he thought, *a few sips will be safe, but no more than that.* He'd even lit a candle that sat flickering in the middle of the table. Elizabeth put the bowls of soup and bread on the table, leaving the tray on his counter. She sat down, eyeing the wine.

"Cheers," she said, holding up her glass to the candlelight, seeing his face on the other side of the table.

"Cheers to you, lover," Holden said, clinking her glass, taking a sip, then leaning over to touch her on the lips with a long, lingering kiss.

Once they'd eaten and cleared the table, Holden took her hand and led her back to the bed. "Round two?" he asked.

~~*~~

Sunlight streamed in the window as Elizabeth woke to the sound of tires on the gravel driveway. She sat up with a start, realizing that it was late, later than she wanted it to be. She peeked out the window to see Branson arriving in his car, again with Faye in the front seat. Faye climbed out and went through the front door while Branson pulled the car around to the side of the garage.

Elizabeth had to figure out a way to get back into the house without Faye seeing her leaving Holden's place. She was frantic but trying not to panic, realizing that Faye would soon be knocking on her bedroom door.

"What am I going to do?" she asked Holden, who was still lying in his bed naked, the sheet only covering half of his body, showing her that he could initiate round three in a heartbeat. He smiled, jumped up, and pushed his erection down into his jeans while he pulled them on. Tugging a T-shirt over his head, he laughed. "Let me handle this," he said as he gathered her in his arms again, giving her a strong lingering hug and a firm kiss on her lips. "I will go to the front door and ring, and Faye will answer. As soon as she opens the door, you walk out and around to the back patio and enter through those doors. From there, you can get to the stairway and to your room while I keep Faye busy in the foyer. Branson will be in the garage fiddling with the car, so don't worry about him. He doesn't pay much attention to anything."

Holden's plan was brilliant and worked perfectly. Elizabeth was up in her room when Faye knocked, asking if she wanted tea. She answered through the door, still wearing last night's clothes and without having had time to brush her hair. She was a mess, but a happy one.

"Yes, Faye. I'd love tea. I'm not dressed yet, so give me a few minutes, and I'll be down for breakfast." Elizabeth undressed and took a quick shower, not washing her hair but feeling refreshed as she arrived downstairs, taking her place at the table. Nettie had arrived while she was showering, and Elizabeth could smell bacon frying in the kitchen, which made her ravenous.

Faye brought Elizabeth tea and milk, and she could feel Faye's eyes taking in every inch of her. Was it obvious that she was pregnant? Was it apparent that she'd spent the night making mad, passionate love? Were her cheeks pink and glowing for some reason that Faye would not understand? She wondered what excuse Holden had used for bothering Faye at that time of the morning. He was brilliant and oh, so lovely.

"Would you like breakfast now, Miss Elizabeth?" Faye asked.

"Yes, Faye. I would love some of that bacon I smell frying and two eggs over easy with grits, please. And toast with strawberry jam." It was a big breakfast, for sure, double what she would normally eat, but last night's lovemaking had left her spent and starving again. Faye would make a note of her enormous breakfast, taking it as a sign that she was already eating for two.

Chapter Seventeen: Marigold

Charles arrived at Marigold's apartment a little after seven. He'd called from his office to let her know that he'd be spending the night then hailed a taxi. He ordered food from a restaurant close to her place, requesting that it be delivered shortly after his arrival.

He set his overnight bag down in the hallway after she let him in the tall front door and walked to the kitchen, pulling the bottle of scotch out of her cabinet and pouring himself a healthy shot. He then went to her living room and sat on the couch, gesturing to her to join him. As she got close to him, he reached out and drew her down onto his lap, causing her to let out a huge belly laugh. She was used to his strict commands, but he wasn't usually frisky, and this was fun. It was unusual, though, because this time Charles had let her know in advance that he planned to spend the night, which rarely happened.

Marigold had no idea how out of control Charles had been earlier in the day and what a fit he'd thrown. She was used to him bringing his anger to her to be tamed, but tonight was different. He was softer. She wouldn't know it, but his guilt over the fact that Elizabeth was likely pregnant and that he was here with Marigold made things different. It felt odd to him, and he didn't know why.

Marigold sat in his lap feeling his erection grow, kissing him as he sipped his scotch, watching him melt a little and relax, putting her hands on him to make sure he would be hard enough when she was ready. His jaw was still clenched, indicating his anger hadn't fully subsided, but Marigold took the chance and straddled him, lifting up her dress as she did so, revealing that she wore no underwear and was ready to receive him even though he'd done little to help her get there.

His head rolled back on the couch, and he set his glass on the end table, giving in to her relentless pumping up and down, almost relinquishing himself fully to her, then finally grabbing her waist firmly, commanding her to stop. She hovered over him, her great breasts coddling his face, but doing as she was told.

"What's wrong, Charles?" she asked. He'd never failed to enjoy her advances before.

"I just can't right now," was all he could say.

Marigold climbed off Charles, pulled her dress down, then turned and went to the bedroom. To say she was unhappy was an understatement. Her agreement with him was that she could have no other lovers as long as he took care of everything: her apartment, food, utilities. She was also sworn to secrecy about their affair and had been for ten years. Being of mixed race, although only one fifth negro as far as she could calculate—her descendants had all been slaves. Many children had been sired by white slave owners—any relationship with anyone of mixed race in the seventies was strictly forbidden in the social circles where Charles lived and worked. Marigold didn't mind being his dirty little secret, but only if she got what she needed, and sex was part of their agreement.

Charles finished his drink and called a taxi. It would cost him a fortune to get home, so he had the taxi driver drop him off at a hotel on the main highway where it would be easy for Branson to come get him in the morning. He first had the driver take him by a liquor store and then through a fast-food drive-through. He didn't want to drink any more without eating something, and the food he'd ordered hadn't been delivered by the time his taxi arrived. He hated fast food as much as anything, but he wouldn't drink on an empty stomach. He had important meetings the next day and did not want to come in to the office hungover.

Charles needed to sleep. He didn't want to go home and perhaps have to see and speak with Elizabeth after the scene he'd created that morning, yet he couldn't find it in himself to spend the night in Marigold's arms. She was good for taking the edge off, but recalling the few times in ten years that he'd opened his eyes to see her lying next to him repulsed him. He knew he'd made the right decision. Tonight, however, he couldn't even unload his anger into her. It wouldn't come, and he had to stop short of embarrassing himself by losing his erection.

Charles poured a shot of scotch into the hotel glass and tore into the fast-food bag, devouring the sandwich and his drink within minutes. He refilled his glass, turned on the television, and climbed into bed after pulling his clothes off and throwing them into a pile on the floor. He thought about Elizabeth, about how soon it would be evident to all that his seed had been planted. The pressure would be off. His mother would leave him alone—for a while—at least until the baby was born. If it was a girl, he was screwed.

He downed his scotch, turned off the TV and the lights, and finished what Marigold had started. It wasn't as delightful as what she could have done for him, but it did the trick, and he was asleep within minutes.

The next morning, Charles surprised everyone by walking through the front door at seven-thirty. He had called Branson early, who had returned to pick him up at the hotel after dropping Faye at the plantation. Elizabeth was finishing her breakfast, Gwendolyn was back in the library taking note of what still needed to be cleaned, and Nettie was watching Faye as she rolled out dough for cookies. Nettie noted that one of the loaves of bread was missing but didn't see any dishes in the sink, so she wondered what exactly Elizabeth had fixed herself for dinner.

Charles walked to the dining table and sat down as if nothing was unusual. He did not intend to explain his absence the prior evening nor where he'd just come from. Branson was the only one who knew, or so he thought. One day a few months back, Branson had spilled to Holden that Charles had a lover in town while the two men were working together on the engine of the tractor. Branson knew the woman too and that she was about a quarter black and descended from staff of the old Clayton family. Wouldn't be good for that kind of information to get out, not with Mr. Freeman's clients anyway, so Branson kept his secret safe, except for that one slip, one that would later come to haunt the entire family.

Elizabeth was horrified by her husband's presence, after how he'd behaved the day before. That combined with her sneaking a call to her sister and spending the night with Holden, she was way off her center and could not look at him. She had finished the bacon, toyed with the eggs, eaten half the grits, and was dunking toast in her tea, a habit that completely annoyed Charles. She looked up to catch him staring at her as she lifted the soaked bread to her mouth. She locked eyes with him, took another bite, then pushed her bread back into her teacup. There was something about Earl Grey and milk on toast, and she liked it.

Faye brought Charles his tea, then she stood back, waiting for him to give her a breakfast order. He pulled out the morning paper and opened it, shielding himself from Elizabeth and giving Faye his request from behind the pages. He rustled the newspaper, trying to read but unnerved by knowing his possibly pregnant wife was staring a hole through the pages from the other end of the table. He put down the paper, stirred his tea, and looked up at Elizabeth.

"I was horrible yesterday, and I regret my actions," he said after taking a sip.

"Apology accepted," Elizabeth replied, knowing full well that he was not authentically apologizing in any way.

He stopped short of asking if she was pregnant, knowing that it would uncover his covert plan to have Faye keep track of her monthly.

"You did not come home last night," she said calmly.

"I had a late meeting and took a hotel room in town," he replied. It was the truth, after all. He just didn't have to tell her who his meeting was with.

Memories flooded back of making love to Holden, waking up in his arms, and how she would very much like to repeat that. "I would politely request that going forward, that if one's husband plans not to return home to sleep in his bed, that he inform his wife ahead of time." Elizabeth used the third person deliberately because she certainly did not feel like his wife, and knowing ahead of time would enable her to plan time with Holden.

"I will try to remember to do that," he said as Faye set a plate in front of him.

Elizabeth excused herself and walked out the patio door, rounding the corner of the house and nearly running into Holden as he approached the kitchen entrance with clean dishes from their dinner the night before.

"I'm going for a walk. I hope you have a good excuse as to why you are returning two bowls to the kitchen," she said with a sparkle in her eye. "I might head over to the barn."

"Got it," he said, smiling. He gave her a wink as he held the door open with his foot, then walked into the kitchen.

Elizabeth walked through the door of the stables to greet the horses, *her horses*. Today was the day she was going to ask for riding lessons. The horses needed to exercise, and she needed an excuse to spend time with Holden. She knew that he was the one who cared for them and the only person who knew how to ride—Branson only helped care of the tack. So it would seem a reasonable request for someone sequestered on the property to be able to take lessons and to be able to ride as long as she stayed on the property. Holden could also be seen as the chaperone, and she would convince Charles that if not, she would ride on her own, just as she took walks alone. Although she was now quite familiar with most of the closer-in trails on the property, there were others farther out where she'd not yet ventured, those that would be more easily accessible by horseback.

Elizabeth was feeling emboldened although still very much a captive while growing alarmingly fearful of her husband's violent outbursts. She did not imagine that he would consider Holden a threat for one moment. Yet she could also hear in her mind the talk that Charles would have with Holden while discussing riding lessons and about his expected conduct when alone with his wife. Charles would have that threatening glint in his eyes, the one that he had shown her now on more than one occasion.

Elizabeth stood looking through the slats of the stall at a gorgeous brown mare and felt sorry for her. The horse didn't get a lot of exercise, and Elizabeth, knowing how much she liked her own walks, knew that girl would surely appreciate getting out of the stall and the fenced-in area to which she was normally confined—much like she herself had been for months—and out on a trail.

Elizabeth was startled by hands that suddenly wrapped around her waist. She turned to face Holden, a flush of excitement coming over her. Stifling a squeal, she put her arms around his neck and stood up on her toes to reach his lips.

"Where is Branson?" he asked.

"Took Gwendolyn to town," she said. "Then he'll likely come back to take Charles to his office once he's finished his breakfast and showered."

"What are your plans for the day?" Holden asked after kissing her deeply one more time on the lips, growing hard.

"I'm taking riding lessons."

He looked down at Elizabeth, over at the mare, then back at her. "Oh, you are, are you? And who is going to do the teaching?"

"That would be you," she replied. "I'll meet you back here in two hours. I just have to let my husband know."

"You mean ask for permission," Holden said with a scowl.

"I will demand this," Elizabeth said. "If he expects me to remain sequestered until I produce an heir, the least he can do is give me the run of the property, and for that he says I need a chaperone."

She kissed him one last time as he released his grip on her waist. "Leave it to me. I have a plan."

Elizabeth returned to her room and dressed in jeans and boots, adding a long-sleeved shirt. Although the day would be hot, the clothing would protect her from the sun. She found a hat that would cover her face and shoulders and picked up a light pair of leather gloves. She'd ridden horses when she was little, although never had lessons. Her experiences had always been limited to rides on docile horses that knew to follow each other around on the same familiar trails, only to return to the barn to be brushed and fed then repeat the same ride the next day.

She needed to give Charles the chance to finish his breakfast and get ready for the office, deciding she would catch him off-guard as he was walking out the door, so she had some time to kill. She picked up the diary and opened the patio door, finding a chair on the balcony and settling in to read.

Meanwhile, Holden set about pulling down saddles and the tack needed for a lesson. He would include a special harness as well as a second lead so he could hold Elizabeth's reins until she was more comfortable with the mare.

Although Holden was delighted at being able to make Elizabeth happy and give her respite from her embittered marriage, he was troubled by the idea of riding lessons. It made him nervous. Although nearly everyone in Charles's inner circle knew of the affair he'd been having for a decade, Charles would not tolerate even a suggestion of the same regarding his wife. Holden was sure that the staff had their suspicions about him and Elizabeth, but it was nothing that anyone would ever discuss with him. He didn't trust that little spy Faye one bit and knew that they would have to conduct their rides in the open so that Faye could report back to Charles that this was nothing more than a harmless riding lesson.

August 21, 1858

Little John is crawling around like a sand crab. He is so funny to watch. He'll go straight full speed until he bumps into something, then he turns and crawls in another direction. He's the sweetest boy.

I've pretty much returned to overseeing the household and starting to make plans for another gala. My milk dried up when I went back to working, so Hattie arranged for a wet nurse to come in. We gave her a little room off the back of the kitchen, where she can bring her own baby, so she nurses one and then the other. I don't envy her!

I make sure Hattie is feeding the nurse well so that her milk is plentiful and nutritious. When both our babies are sleeping, she helps Hattie in the kitchen. It sure is busy around here these days. John's business is booming, so he comes and goes. When he is here, he has taken to wanting to come to my room at night, but the last thing I need is another child so soon. My body is just starting to return to normal.

John says the drums of war, as he calls them, are beginning to beat a little more loudly. He says he doesn't know how long we will live peacefully, but he says we should take advantage of it because he sees war coming. Our slaves are happy, I think, and I don't hear any rumors of them joining this cause or threatening to revolt. It is really more about the people in the North than it is about the slaves, although I'm sure a good many of them would rather be free to roam outside the confines of this plantation.

Liam and I have started to see each other again privately, although just as much as I don't want to have John's baby right now, I don't want to have Liam's either, so we keep our affections to a minimum. A few kisses and cuddling on a blanket by the lake is good enough for me, although I can tell he wants to go back to the old ways, lift my dress up, and go further.

John is talking about taking a trip to New Orleans. He needs to meet a ship that is coming in and purchase more slaves to sell here in Georgia. I'll have to run the household then by myself, which will be fine with me because not having him try to visit my room will be a relief.

I know John loves me in some ways as a married couple should. I can't say I feel the same, and it is awful to put this into words. We disagree about more than we agree on. I can't tell him how I feel about the slave trade, and all I can do is make sure he doesn't go off on any of his rampages and order a slave to be beaten for a minor infraction. I've intervened more than once and will always do so.

Elizabeth closed the diary and sat on the patio, taking in the mid-morning sun. It would be very hot soon, but at that moment, it was breezy and delightful. Charles should be ready to head out soon, so she returned to her room and put the diary in the safe. If she was going to be out riding for any length of time, she was sure that Faye would snoop. She stood up, straightened her clothing, picked up her gloves, and prepared to confront her husband about a riding lesson.

She walked back down the stairs, where Faye had just cleared the table completely. Faye turned and looked at her, noticing the high boots with the pants tucked in, wondering what in the world Elizabeth was up to now.

"Has Charles come down?" Elizabeth asked.

"He done left already, Miss Elizabeth. Said somethin' about being late for a meeting shend dashed out of here."

"Fine, then. I was going to tell him I'm having a riding lesson today, but he'll have to find out after the fact." Elizabeth watched Faye for a response.

"If you like, ma'am, I can call and ask for you," Faye offered.

"That might be a good idea," Elizabeth replied. "But I tell you what. You tell him I'm just going to be in the main pasture today. I'm not going off riding on a trail. Today, I will learn the basics of riding." She turned to go out the door toward the barn then looked back at Faye. "Please also tell him if he has a problem with it, he needs to come home and tell me himself. And please tell him Holden will be giving me the lesson. He's the only one who rides. Otherwise, it would be Branson, and I don't think he knows a thing about four-legged horses, only beasts with four cylinders."

Elizabeth thought that might satisfy Faye's curiosity as to why Holden and not Branson, who Charles assigned to all things related to transportation. Elizabeth guessed that would include horses if in fact Branson knew how to ride. She knew that Nettie was a bit suspicious of her and Holden now, but she was sure Nettie would never share anything like that with Faye.

Elizabeth walked into the barn as Holden was saddling the mare. His horse was already saddled and waiting by the barn door.

"Perfect timing," he said, noting how absolutely stunning Elizabeth looked in her slim pants and boots—and although they weren't actual riding boots, they would pass for now. He cinched the saddle tightly, took the reins, and led the mare to the barn door, tying her to a post.

"Her name is Bella, and she knows her name, so she'll like hearing it from you. As you get to know each other, say it often." He stroked Bella's mane, then took Elizabeth's hand and led her around to Bella's left side so that he could get Elizabeth up into the saddle. Elizabeth deftly put her left foot into the stirrup and swung her right leg up and around. It had been a while, but she did this unassisted.

"Like riding a bike, I guess," Elizabeth said, a big but slightly nervous smile on her face.

"Not exactly," Holden said, untying Bella and handing Elizabeth the reins. "Bikes don't have the personalities that these two do. Just don't take her out without me," he said, swinging up onto Jack's back, the horse he rode the most. "And this is Jack," he told Elizabeth. "Since I mostly ride him, Bella doesn't get as much exercise, so this will be good for her."

Holden pulled Jack around in front of Bella. "Just follow me, slowly. We're not going to go faster than a walk today. As long as you don't urge her on, she'll stay right behind Jack."

"Just like the trail rides I remember," Elizabeth said glumly.

"Exactly," Holden replied. "Once you get familiar with her and I see that you can handle her, we'll take the trail around the lake. They know it, so it will be an easy ride." He nudged Jack with his knees, who started forward.

"But not today," Elizabeth said. "I don't want Charles to get angry. He left before I could tell him—ask him—about riding lessons."

"He's always angry, Elizabeth," Holden replied. "I don't think that will ever change."

Holden led Jack along the fence line at a slow walk, looking back at Elizabeth, who was holding Bella's reins loosely and seemed to be enjoying herself immensely.

When they got to the far end of the pasture, where Holden was sure no one could see them, he stopped Jack and turned to Elizabeth. "Bring her up beside me."

Elizabeth did so, and when she was even with Holden, he leaned way out of his saddle and planted a kiss on Elizabeth's cheek. She was nervous about anyone seeing this and that Bella might spook, but Bella was comfortable with Jack and Holden, so she didn't budge.

Elizabeth sat smiling, but the smile quickly turned to a frown. "I'm so worried, Holden, that Charles might find out about us and divorce me. And fire you."

Holden sat thinking for a moment, deciding that it was time she knew the truth.

"Elizabeth, if you think there is a chance you will leave this relationship anytime soon, and something tells me that will be the case, you need to build your war chest. I'll give you something to add to it."

Elizabeth's smile turned genuine. "Tell me," she said. "Is it awful?"

"Unbelievably," Holden replied.

"Go on," she said, waiting, her eyes widening.

"I know it is not my place to tell you this, Elizabeth, but I care about you. I don't like the way he is treating you, and I don't like it that you have to fear him, fear a potential divorce or worse." He paused, as she sat waiting. "Okay." Holden sat for a moment gathering the courage to say what he needed to say. He could see Elizabeth growing impatient. "Charles has a mistress in town, has for ten years. Those nights he is very late or doesn't come home at all..." He let the sentence dangle.

Elizabeth sat, stunned. So that was it. She actually wouldn't have guessed. She thought Charles had more integrity than that, but it made perfect sense. And it was probably the answer as to why during all that time she waited for him to come to consummate their marriage, although it was an issue for her, he was satisfying his needs elsewhere. Therefore, he felt no rush to come to her. And indeed he didn't come to her until Faye reported that she was fertile.

She was angry, and she was sad. But she was glad that Holden had shared the information with her, as it did indeed give her one more thing to add to her so-called war chest—the biggest gun so far. She appreciated knowing because it answered a lot of questions that she had. "Well, well," she started. "This changes everything, doesn't it?"

"Yes and no," he replied. "You're still pregnant. He doesn't know it yet, I presume, or you would have told me. Once he knows, he'll likely spend more time in town with her as his objective will have been met."

"Only if I have a boy," she said. "His objective is to have a son." She paused. "What's her name?"

"Marigold," Holden replied. "Her name is Marigold. And there is one more thing that you should know. She is descended from slaves. Although she could pass for white, so says Branson, she has a tawny brown skin that one could perhaps take for Italian or Greek, but that's not the case. Her great-great-grandfather was a slave."

"That doesn't add a gun to my war chest," she said. "That's a cannon."

"But your lips are sealed, yes? For now anyway?" Holden asked. "Promise me. Otherwise, I'm gone, Branson is gone, and Gwendolyn will have to walk to town." His wide grin revealed his dimples as he looked forward, nudging Jack along the fence line once again.

They circled the pasture twice, keeping a reasonable distance in case prying eyes were recording the event that would be relayed back to Charles. Once back at the barn, they rode inside, stopping at Bella's stall. Holden jumped down, tied Jack's reins to a post, and came around to help Elizabeth out of the saddle. He looked around first, then wrapped his arms around her and kissed her deeply as her feet touched the ground. "I hope it is my baby," he whispered.

Chapter Eighteen: Bryce

Charles once again sat at his overly large desk, his feet up on the edge and a scotch in his hand. The door opened, and his brother entered.

"We must stop meeting like this," Charles said. "Mother might worry."

"Don't be concerned about it. She is already in bed, I'm guessing," he said as he poured himself a scotch. "After all, it is just after five. Her shows will start, the scotch will have kicked in, maybe a sleeping pill, and it is lights out." He was there to talk business, discuss one serious issue, and wasn't going to engage in much small talk.

Bryce advanced toward Charles's desk, sitting on the corner, pouring a healthy measure of the scotch taking a gulp, and looking his brother squarely. "The good stuff, as always," Bryce started.

"Yep, wouldn't have it any other way," Charles replied, taking a sip of his own. "So, tell me, brother, why exactly are you here?"

"Time is running out," Bryce said. "Mother gave you six months from our last meeting. You pissed away three of them interviewing, throwing parties, and trying to decide who the fuck was going to birth your heir. Now here we are with less than two months left, and she's not pregnant yet."

"We don't know that now, do we?" Charles answered, locking eyes with his little brother.

Bryce raised an eyebrow, took another sip, then refilled his glass.

"Do tell?" replied Bryce. "Are you holding something back from the family?"

"Not holding anything back, just not one hundred percent sure in this moment. But I am fairly certain that she is with child." Charles took another sip and looked coldly at his brother, an ominous grin forming on his lips. "That resets the clock, doesn't it, dear brother?"

Bryce bristled. He set his glass down on the edge of Charles's desk. "As soon as it is confirmed, the clock will reset, but not until then." Bryce left his glass on the desk and walked toward the door.

"Oh, brother," Charles called out. "That doesn't solve our other little problem in any case, does it? If I should have a son this year, the trust will have an heir, but the largest liability that the Freeman family has right now may be hurtling down the dark road of dementia."

Bryce stopped and turned. "Lillian? What is her state of health?"

"It waxes and wanes from what I hear," Charles said. "One minute, she is completely lucid, but at other times she doesn't know who she is or where she grew up." Charles took a bigger drink, nearly draining the glass and handing it to Bryce.

Bryce took the glass from his brother and filled it from the crystal bottle on the cart, handing it back to him, still angry but listening. "How much longer do we think she might live? Are we in contact with her doctor? What about the nursing home?"

"It is anyone's guess," Charles said. "But rest assured, she has likely never seen the will nor the trust that was created before her uncle and his wife died in that crash back in the '20s. So at this point, she would have no idea that she, in fact, is the only rightful owner of the Noble Oak Plantation, regardless of the fact that it has sold twice since they died."

Bryce reclaimed his glass and filled it again, pacing across Charles's office. "What if, by some chance, she finds out?" Bryce looked at his brother coldly again. "And why in God's name did you invite her to that party?"

"Keep your enemies closer," Charles said with a grin. "And by watching her throughout nights like that, we can firmly assess her state of mind. There is no other way."

Little did the brothers know, though, that William Stapleton had also been watching Lillian throughout the evening. She seemed pretty clear-headed to him, as she sat and talked with Elizabeth and others at their table. She recited names of other relatives and spoke of growing up at the plantation, although she "understood that it had been sold when her great aunt and uncle perished," he heard her tell Elizabeth.

Sitting at an adjacent table, William was able to listen for any signs of declining mental health, and he knew that if the documents he held at his estate were authentic, the woman dining at the table next to him should in fact be the lady of the plantation at this very moment, lucid or not.

One of the reasons that William had approached Elizabeth the night of the party was that he wanted to test the waters, to see what she knew, which he calculated amounted to nothing by the end of the evening. By the look Charles gave him as he whisked Elizabeth out of the room and away from him, there was a good chance that he knew everything. William found his wife quite attractive and knew that a life with Charles would be a life like many other women in the Freeman and the Clayton lineage suffered, some who had gone mad after years of abuse, others who were quite possibly murdered.

Bryce stopped pacing and stood in front of his brother's desk, shoulders back, delivering an ultimatum. "If that grand old dame is the key to our family's future, we need to do something to put her out of her misery and take her out of the picture." Bryce's lips were pursed in a tight, thin line.

"I don't know exactly what you are suggesting, but I am not prepared to go that far to insure the family fortune," Charles replied. "If you are, then go for it. Meanwhile, I intend to have Lillian over again soon to measure her state of mental health in closer proximity. Elizabeth rather liked her for some odd reason and said to her that they should get together again, so I will suggest it, and Elizabeth can invite her over for dinner." He tipped his glass to his brother. "You are welcome to join us, but you must promise me that she makes it from my house back to the nursing home alive."

Bryce walked out the door and straight to the elevator, fuming. It was bad enough that they had discovered through a set of documents delivered to them by their banker, found in an old box locked in a vault that had remained there since the automobile crash of 1929, that the plantation did not actually belong to Charles. Nor did it belong to the family despite the fact their shared funds were used for the purchase—as long as Lillian Clayton Johnston was alive. She had no children and no assigned heirs that they knew of, so as long as she died quietly and quickly it would not affect their investment. It was not good that Charles and Elizabeth were entertaining her. What if being in the house brings her to a lucid moment, and she suddenly has the idea that she might just possibly be an heir to the estate? The brothers were not sure, but she might have actually known that to be the case at one time.

It was clearly written in Lillian's uncle's trust that preceded their families' interests by almost fifty years. The fact that they'd come upon the documents and had been able to lock them back up without anyone else reviewing them was a miracle in itself. No one in the family but the two of them was aware that Lillian, being the only direct descendant of John Clayton, was fully entitled to the house should she present herself to the court. Millions of dollars would fly out of the family's coffers should that be revealed.

Bryce knew that any sudden turn of health, or worse the disappearance of an old descendent of the county's namesake, the original John Clayton, would cause quite a stir and would not be worth the risk. But the fact that his entire inheritance I don't understand this rested in two places was unnerving. The control of the family fortune would go to Charles's firstborn boy, should he be lucky enough to have a boy with this pregnancy or the next. If that didn't happen, per the trust, Bryce's own son would be next in line, giving him more power from that day forward.

If Elizabeth gave birth to a boy, Charles would remain in full control until his son turned twenty-five. That would not eliminate Bryce's inheritance entirely, but knowing Bryce would ultimately lose control to his nephew would rattle him. Not that Bryce had control now because Charles made all final business decisions, but Bryce was graciously allowed to participate to a great extent in the day-to-day operations of the family business. Charles's son might not be so kind. Bryce would have to watch for twenty-five years as Charles slowly relinquished control of the trust to his son, at which time he would be close to the age that his own father had passed, albeit early in life.

And if somehow old lady Lillian came around—she wasn't that old but dementia had taken its toll—they could lose the plantation entirely. There was apparently no legal way to appeal that, none that they'd been able to find without consulting an attorney, which might in itself set off an investigation.

Bryce slammed shut the car door, nearly catching his fingers in the latch. He started the engine and squealed out of their office tower parking lot, turning heads, not caring that some could recognize him. The news channels would interview witnesses who saw him burning rubber out of the lot and down Broadway just hours before the old lady went missing. Wasn't worth the risk, but boy was he hot. Instead of going home, he went straight to the club that he and Charles frequented, sat down at the bar, and ordered a double.

~~*~~

Back in his office, Charles called home, and Gwendolyn answered. "How did the shopping go today?" he asked. "Clean out my bank account yet?" He rarely tried to be funny, so Gwendolyn made sure to laugh.

"Got the new sofa for the library. It will be delivered on Friday." She held the phone, wondering why he'd called.

"And Elizabeth? Is she there?"

Gwendolyn wondered why in the world he would ask such a thing. "Of course, she is. Where else would she be?" Gwendolyn replied.

"I heard she went for a horseback ride this morning. Please tell her I will be home in one hour, and I would like to see her in the library." He hung up and left his office, heading for the parking garage.

Charles often left the office early. Today; however, it had been much later – he'd in fact been the last to leave—and in a much more controlled fashion than his brother. He had driven himself in that morning because Branson had told him he'd be ferrying Gwendolyn around town for an extended shopping trip. Charles kept an old Volvo in the garage for the days he drove himself. It was one of the classics, a head-turner, and fun to drive.

One hour would give him time to stop by and apologize to Marigold. He felt he owed her an explanation for abruptly stopping sex with her the other night, which sent her to her room in tears, and he hadn't talked to her since. He thought that an apology in person would rubber than a phone call.

Elizabeth showered after her ride, changing into a light dress and sandals. Although the heat typically quelled her hunger, she was ravenous. She went to the kitchen and asked Nettie to make her a big salad and a tuna sandwich, turning to Faye, who had been sitting at the counter talking to Nettie. She had just said something to Nettie about Elizabeth being out in the pasture riding with Holden, and Nettie had told her to mind her damn business. She didn't usually cuss, but she was growing weary of Faye's prying and spying, and she knew everything that Elizabeth did was getting back to Charles. In Nettie's opinion, it wouldn't bode well for Faye to have this reputation when she went looking for her next job. You didn't betray the lady of the household unless the man of the house was secretly padding your bank account or making other promises he wouldn't keep.

"Faye, would you please bring my lunch up to my room when it is ready, with a tall glass of lemonade and an extra glass of ice? I'm going to be reading in my room." Elizabeth looked from Nettie to Faye, understanding that she had just interrupted a conversation that would not be shared with her. She walked through the large hallway, stopping in front of the painting of John *and Helen,* wishing she could add Helen's name to the plate underneath. She thought about Adria and the life she described living here, walking the same halls, throwing grand parties—and taking a lover, *just as she had done with Holden.* The parallels were beginning to intrigue her.

The information that Holden shared with her about Marigold that morning had changed everything. The fact that Charles had a lover—even now—was incredulous. Of course, she couldn't get angry, not after her own behavior put her in the same ranks regarding infidelity, but a Black woman? Not that Elizabeth had a racist bone in her body, but it was the South, and the rules were the rules. Only a few years prior, coloreds and whites couldn't even use the same bathrooms. Things were progressing, but interracial relationships were not accepted in social circles such as those of the Freeman family. Elizabeth was sure that she had just been availed of a secret that as she told Holden put a cannon firmly in her war chest.

Elizabeth pulled the diary out of the safe and carried it to the chaise. She pulled a fan out from the corner of the room and turned it on so that it would face her while she read. She laid back to get comfortable until her lunch arrived.

November 15, 1858

Little John is eight months old today. It is hard to believe, as watching him trying to walk and almost getting a word or two out of his mouth is like watching my husband as he must have been at this age. This boy is the spitting image of his father, makes the same faces, and has the same temper already! I wonder if it runs in the family or if all Southern men are wired this way.

My father had a bit of a temper, not nearly as bad as my husband's, but I've learned that as long as I stay out of his way for the most part, I don't have to experience it. He doesn't show it so much in front of other people, so I keep company as much as possible. Even in my room, I have Rae around or someone cleaning, and in the kitchen or dining room someone is always there, so when he addresses me within earshot of others, he is cordial.

It makes me wonder what would happen if he ever found out about me and Liam. He would want to have him beat like a slave I'm sure, or worse. I don't know if John is capable of murder, but I guess any man is if he is riled up enough. Or if they have to fight in a war.

Some men came again to talk to John. He told me later to keep quiet about it, that they were gentlemen from the Confederacy, which I assume is connected to the fact that John says we will soon have a separate army, the Confederate Army. He says they traveled over from South Carolina and that within the next year some organization would take place regarding Georgia and some other states that want to leave the Union. I try to understand, but John doesn't want to tell me much as apparently this is a big secret at this point. Some man named Jefferson Davis was with them, and apparently he is leading this movement to break off from the North. They talked about a man named Abraham Lincoln too, who they say is going to run for president next year and that this is not a good thing because he wants to free all of the slaves. All of them! Can you imagine? Where in the world would they all go? This talk makes me weary, and I'm happy in a way that it is men's business as I have enough to tend to on a daily basis.

Elizabeth closed the diary, imagining life before the war, with slaves attending to every need. She had that herself really, but they were free Black people and paid well, she thought. *She hoped*. Although she really had no idea what Charles paid them, she never heard them complain. Nettie had her own car and a home somewhere not too far away, and so did Gwendolyn. Faye didn't have a car, but she was still young. She said she was saving up for one.

Faye knocked on Elizabeth's door, which was already partially opened, and entered with her lunch on a tray. Elizabeth quickly put the diary under a pillow as Faye came around and set the tray on her table, picking up another book that she'd found in the library.

"What are you reading?" Faye asked.

"I pulled a number of books from the library the other day again, Faye. I read one, then finish it, and then go get another. You should try reading more. It broadens your perspective on things." She did not intend to share anything more than Faye needed to know at this point, least of all that she'd found a 120-year-old diary from a previous lady of the house that she now lived in.

"Yes, ma'am. I should do that," Faye said, eyeing the stack of books on the table but looking at the pillow, under which she'd clearly seen Elizabeth put the book that she'd just been reading. Surely nothing in the library was so off-limits that she'd have to hide it—unless she didn't really get it from there.

Elizabeth caught Faye eyeing the ribbon that stuck out from underneath the pillow, the ribbon that Adria had carefully sewed into her diary as a bookmark. "I'll see you down in the kitchen when I'm finished with my lunch, Faye," Elizabeth said, dismissing her. She locked the door after Faye closed it, retrieved the diary, and started reading where she'd left off while she ate her lunch.

January 5, 1859

Christmas was delightful this year, little John's first, and although I don't think he truly understood why he was presented with so many packages to unwrap, he delighted in the candles placed everywhere that lit up every room. I swear we go through as many candles at Christmas as we do the rest of the year long.

John cut a pine from out in the forest and made a wooden stand for it. I put a basin underneath the tree as I always do and filled it with water to keep it from drying out so fast. We made strings of cranberries and wrapped them all around the tree from top to bottom. We put little clips on the tree that hold candles, and for the first night and then only again on Christmas Eve did we light them all, while the tree was still fresh and the needles weren't too dry. We sang a few carols, and then we blew them out. Little John loved this part the most, I think. He puckered up his little cheeks and blew and blew, barely able to blow out just one, but he had so much fun!

We just took the tree down a few days ago, and boy what a mess it made. The housemaids will be sweeping needles out of the living room for weeks! We put the strings of cranberries out in a tree in the backyard, and we can look out there and watch the birds enjoying them.

January is a dreary month for me. I don't suffer from the depression that many people talk about in the dark days, and I'm glad of that.

This house is hard to heat, and we practically have to have one person going from room to room all day long just keeping the fires going. That back door opens every five minutes, I swear, as someone comes through with another armload of wood. It's hard to keep a house warm when the door is open and closed so many times a day.

We keep our room extra warm for the baby. His crib is next to the bed, and we have extra quilts on all of the beds for the winter, but some nights it gets real cold, and I bring Little John into bed with us to make sure he doesn't get the pneumonia. It is going around bad this year, and people are dying. It is sad to see.

Even a couple of our slaves got it and died. John was mad about that, as that is a lot of money buried out there, he says, but I don't see it that way at all. Those were people, they had families, and they will be missed. We can replace them, but their families can't.

I talked to Atticus yesterday about making sure there was enough wood out there in the slaves' quarters. He says it's important because there is no insulation. I told him to put an oil stove out there, and he said it would be expensive, but I said I don't care, do it anyway.

John has to take a trip way over to Texas soon—something about politics again. I swear this is getting old, but if he likes it, I can't say a word. Texas is going to join us if we go to war, he says, as they don't like this Abraham Lincoln. They've all taken to calling him Abe for short. This Abe Lincoln is real trouble, John says, and he must go to Texas to have a meeting with their governor about joining the rest of us states that are going to form a new country.

I look forward to John being gone for a couple of weeks. I will find a way to escape to town with Liam, with the excuse of buying more backing for the quilts I'm working on. I see a twinkle in Hattie's eye when I tell her why we're going, but she knows better than to say a word. She packs us a lunch so that we can stop somewhere in a park to eat. That is if we can find a place warm enough, I say to her.

We always find a place, though, and we will pick a warm day, and Liam will pack a couple of extra blankets. Cold temperatures will not keep us from finding a way to wrap ourselves together under the quilts and kiss and touch each other under our clothes. Liam has talked me into touching him, stroking him, down there. No one ever asked me to do that before. John always takes care of that part before he asks me to open my legs. Liam opens my legs with his kisses, something else I doubt John would ever consider! We still haven't actually made it all the way, and I stop Liam before we get there. I know he gets frustrated, and sometimes he turns away from me and finishes what we've started, cleaning himself up with a towel he brought.

I'm just not ready for another baby, and God forbid I get pregnant and the baby comes out looking like Liam. It would be obvious with that red hair of his, I imagine. I keep counting the days after my monthly though, and soon enough, I'll find a way to let him in, when enough time has passed after this baby and when I'm sure that it is not my fertile time.

I know I keep saying I have to burn this book, but I won't. I'll keep writing and writing until it is full, then I'll find a place to hide it where no one will find it until we're all long dead and gone and nothing in here that I say will matter any longer.

Oh, you have no idea, thought Elizabeth as she closed the diary, *no idea how much your words matter right now.* She put the diary back in the safe. Now that Faye had caught on to the fact that she was hiding something, her snooping would increase. Elizabeth was sure of this. No more sticking it under a pillow. It would have to go into the safe every day, whether she was in the house or not. It would be disastrous if Faye took it to Charles. Elizabeth had to finish it before anyone else could know about it, if ever.

Elizabeth thought about something William Stapleton had said during his last visit. He'd alluded to knowing secrets about the Clayton family as well as the Freemans, but he said it so quietly, as he obviously didn't want anyone within earshot to hear him say this. She knew he was trying to get her to the museum alone, so it must be something that he did not wish to show Charles. She made up her mind that the next opportunity she had she would sneak over and see what it was he wanted to show her. Hell, she could ride a horse as it was only the next plantation down the road.

Elizabeth finished the last of her lemonade and picked up her tray. When she opened the door, Gwendolyn was there poised to knock. Elizabeth startled. "What is it?" she asked.

"Mr. Freeman called. He said he would be home in an hour, and he wishes to see you in the library." Gwendolyn took the tray from Elizabeth and gave her a knowing smile, wishing she wasn't the messenger in this case, then she turned and walked back down the hall.

Elizabeth stood, contemplating the message. *"He wishes to see you in his library." What in the world could that mean,* she wondered. Had he found out about Holden? Was it serious, or did he simply feel the need for a formal meeting with his wife? So weird.

Elizabeth took a look in the mirror, deciding to put on a little makeup and change her shoes to something nicer, something other than house flats. She should look more like she was attending a meeting, if that was the case. She decided to go to the library at that moment and wait for him there. She could pass another forty-five minutes in there reading, no problem, and she was tired of staying in her room.

~~*~~

Charles pulled up in front of Marigold's apartment, parked, and took out his keys. He hadn't called in advance as their arrangement was that he didn't need to. He turned the key in the lock and opened the door to see Marigold standing in the hallway in a robe and slippers.

"Why have you come?" she asked Charles, unsmiling. "If you're here for sex, I would have to eat something and shower. I skipped lunch and haven't showered since yesterday morning."

"I'm here to apologize, Marigold." Charles shifted uncomfortably. He was not used to apologizing to anyone. But given their history, he felt he owed her this one. "For the other day. Do you have a moment?"

She motioned him in wordlessly, then turned toward the kitchen. "I'll bring tea."

"No need, really, not for me," he said. "I'm headed home."

"Home for the day? So early? Is everything alright?" she asked.

"Everything is fine. I just need to talk to Elizabeth about some things. She's been overstepping her boundaries, and I plan to give her a warning."

Marigold nodded, listening to words that she herself had heard before. She'd been given ultimatums and warnings over the years. She usually conceded as she'd grown used to the lifestyle, not having to work, all of it in exchange for sex and staying quiet about it. She had stepped out of line a couple of times. She tried secretly dating another man once, a Black man, and Charles found out. He blew his top. Marigold promised she wouldn't try anything like that ever again. She was curious as to his wife's infractions. She also wondered if he had ever put his hands on her.

Charles stood there, his hat in his hands, trying to comprehend his situation. Elizabeth was pregnant by all accounts, yet she'd been out horseback riding with Holden, and he was concerned that this might affect the pregnancy. He wasn't sure if Marigold was the one to ask about such things, but he felt he could trust her enough to run it by her.

"Elizabeth has been horseback riding," he started. "With Holden, our groundskeeper. I'm not worried about Holden. I'm worried about the baby."

With that, Marigold turned and came to stand in front of him with her hands on her hips. "Baby? What baby?" she asked. "Is Elizabeth pregnant already?"

"I believe she is," he said. "I've asked Faye to keep an eye out, and she is now two weeks past the time when she should have…"

Marigold interrupted him. "She missed her period." Marigold eyed him carefully and could tell he was worried. "So what? You need an heir for the family. That is why you married her, right?"

"But the horseback riding," he started.

She let out a laugh. "Oh, really, Charles! You are worried about a little romp on the back of a pony? That baby isn't going to be bothered by any such thing, don't you worry. You can even have sex with her while she's pregnant, right up to the last month or so if you're comfortable with that. A lot of men find it sexy. You should try it." She was shaking her head in disbelief. He really had no clue about women, about pregnancy. His only skills were in business; he knew how to manipulate and control people and that was about it.

"I must be going," Charles said, giving her a light kiss on the cheek—another thing he rarely did. "Again, I'm sorry."

Marigold thought this baby thing might have actually softened him. But she would soon come to doubt that.

~~*~~

Elizabeth was sitting in the library, curled in an overstuffed chair, when she heard Charles's voice in the hallway.

"She's in the library, waiting for you," she heard Gwendolyn say.

The door opened, and Charles stood still for a minute, eyeing the layout of the room snd deciding where he wanted to sit to address his wife. He chose a stiff-backed chair next to a walnut table that held a Tiffany lamp. He lowered himself slowly into the chair, noting that Gwendolyn was in the doorway.

"May I bring tea?" she asked.

"I think we're good," Charles answered for both of them.

Elizabeth was hungry again and thought that tea and biscuits would be nice. She started to say something, then closed her mouth, deciding not to override his decision. Gwendolyn looked at her, waiting, but she shook her head, indicating that she would forego her request. Gwendolyn nodded, backed out the door, and closed it gently behind her.

"Well?" Elizabeth thought she would get the conversation started. "You wanted to see me?"

"Yes, I did. I do. We need to talk," Charles said. He shifted in his seat. He wasn't angry, but he needed to put her in her place. And he needed her to be honest with him. "You're pregnant, aren't you," he said not as a question but rather a statement of fact.

Elizabeth felt her face grow hot. *It had to be Faye.* But then again, she saw Nettie giving her a side-eye the other day when she placed a very large lunch order. But Nettie would *never.* Would she? "What makes you think that?" she asked.

"You haven't had your monthly," he replied.

"How would you know?" she asked. "Oh wait, I know. It's your little spy, Faye. She's in charge, isn't she? She sent you to my room after she counted the days following my period, told you when I would be fertile. Told you how many times to fuck me to make sure the timing was right, and then just like that, you're gone and haven't been back. Now she's telling you I haven't started my period yet because that is part of her job." She paused. "Unbelievable."

Charles flinched when Elizabeth used the word "fuck." Women in his world didn't talk like that. She also didn't answer him, which was also unacceptable.

"Answer me," he said, glaring at her now.

"Maybe," she said.

"Maybe what? Maybe you are pregnant?"

"That's what I said. Maybe. Because I do not know. Why don't you ask your little spy to schedule a doctor's appointment for me. I need to get out of the house." She was angry, but not wanting to taunt him any further. She remembered what happened the last time she did that. Although, if he thought she was pregnant, maybe he would refrain from any physical abuse.

"You were out of the house today already," he said. "Riding horses, so I hear."

"Yes. So?" she asked. "Last I heard, those are my horses too."

"But you didn't request a riding lesson from me first," he said, sternly.

"Now I have to make a request for every little thing I do?" She got up. "If that is the case, I request to be dismissed."

"Fine," he said, standing to face her. She walked around him and out the door, avoiding him as he reached out to touch her, possibly kiss her, neither of them could be sure.

Chapter Nineteen: William and Lillian

Back in her room, Elizabeth fumed. She thought of ways to deceive Faye into thinking she started her period. She needed a little more time before admitting to Charles that yes, she was undoubtedly pregnant. She knew it, after all. No period, the nausea, the hunger. She thought back to that week when both Charles and Holden had made love to her—well suffice it to say Charles fucked her and Holden made love to her. In any case, she wished she'd waited with Holden so that she would have no doubt.

She picked up another one of the books that she had pulled from their library. This one was on influential people in Georgia in the nineteenth century. She scrolled through the index and found two John Claytons listed. The first, born in 1805, was cited as building the Noble Oak Plantation in 1850. She turned to the second, born in 1827. There he was: Adria's husband. In the photo, he was dressed in the uniform of the Confederate Army. He had a mustache and stood holding a rifle. Farther on down the page, it mentioned that he married Adria Coleman in 1857, and there below the paragraph was a picture much smaller than that of John, but it was her.

Elizabeth got chills, seeing Adria's picture in the book and reading about her from someone else's perspective, the woman who had become an obsession for her as she followed her footprints through the dining room and down hallways, bathing in the same room she guessed and quite possibly becoming pregnant in the same bed. There had been many new mattresses on her bed, but John said that the frame was from the original house. Most of the furniture was also original, which meant that she was lying on some of the same couches and eating at the same tables as Adria had. It was exhilarating to say the least, and now here she was looking at her face in a book.

Elizabeth put a bookmark on the page and looked for the paper she had with William Stapleton's number on it. He'd given it to her on his way out when he came for tea. She knew that William had much more information, and she intended to contact him and arrange a meeting.

She fully expected the knock at the door when Faye came around later that afternoon with a home pregnancy test. Faye had actually bought one at a store on the way home, at Charles's request, the day after she first told him she thought Elizabeth was pregnant. She got two, actually, planning on holding on to the second one in case the first was negative. She handed it to Elizabeth with a smile, which was met with the door being closed in her face.

Elizabeth put the test on the bathroom sink. She would deal with it later, when she was ready to read the result without crying out. Maybe she'd have a glass of wine first to settle her nerves. She heard a car down below and saw Gwendolyn and Faye driving away together. Nettie's car was still there, but Branson's was also missing, which meant he'd gone home for the day. It was just Elizabeth and Charles in the house, as well as Nettie.

Elizabeth opened the kitchen door slowly, glad to see Nettie alone. "Where's Charles?" she asked. "Not that it is up to you to keep track," she added, smiling warmly at Nettie.

"He mentioned headin' over to Holden's cabin," Nettie said.

Elizabeth froze. *Why in the world would he need to talk to Holden?* "Is everything okay?" Elizabeth asked, her mouth still open.

"I believe so. I know'd he was worried about you, said somethin' about the horses and that he needed to talk to Holden, but he wasn't upset." Nettie was making crawfish cakes, patting the round shapes and putting them on a baking sheet. "Said he'd be back in jus a bit and is lookin' fo'ward to dinner. He loves crawfish so he gon' be excited."

"Nettie, I need to tell you something," Elizabeth started.

"If you gon' tell me you wit child, I already know it," Nettie said, turning to show Elizabeth a huge smile, her teeth lined up in perfect order, displaying a large gap between the two in front.

"But how..." she started.

"Miss Elizabeth, with all respect, I been 'round the block, and I been watchin' you when you was sick, you was almost green for a few mornings. Now you doublin' your order for breakfast and lunch. Make no mistake, I don' need to see no test; you pregnant." Nettie was still smiling and still patting out crabcake circles.

"I've got a test in my bathroom. I guess I should go take it so I know for sure," Elizabeth said.

"You go do that. It will make Mr. Freeman a lot happier, if anythin' can do that, and we'll fix on gettin' ready to have a baby in the house!" Nettie was obviously happier than Elizabeth was about it, and Elizabeth knew that she should adjust her attitude. After reading Adria's notes about pregnancy and birth, she knew she had a lot of catching up to do.

"Nettie, is it okay to ride horses when you're pregnant?" Elizabeth asked.

"Oh, child, you can do anythin' you want right up to the day you drop dat baby. Jus be careful." Nettie was still shaking her head as Elizabeth left the kitchen. "But you gotta know Mr. Freeman ain't gon' take too kindly to you runnin' around on horseback with young Mr. Holden, so watch out," she said under her breath after Elizabeth was well out of earshot.

After peeing on the stick and watching the clock, the two lines that appeared gave Elizabeth the positive result she knew the test would show. She tossed the test into the wastebasket and went to lie down.

~~*~~

Charles knocked on Holden's cabin door. Holden had been lying down on his bed with his boots still on but dangling off the edge. He had been thinking about Elizabeth actually and had grown hard. When the knock came, he thought there was a chance that it would be her. When he saw the top of Charles's head through the glass pane at the top of the door, he pushed his erection down and pulled his shirt out of his pants in the front to further cover himself. He opened the door to Charles, who stood not wishing to come in, but signaling that they sit on the porch.

"Holden, I'd like to talk to you," he said.

"Sure, Charles. How can I help you?" Holden asked.

"It's about Elizabeth," he said. Holden could have guessed that. "I hear she went riding with you today."

"Yes, sir. She came out to the barn and demanded that I saddle a horse for her, told me it was time she learned to ride *her* horses." He expressed "her" as if Elizabeth had said it just like that, which of course she had not.

"Well, I don't want to make a big deal out of this, and I don't mind her learning to ride, but she must stay in the pasture. I don't want her out on the trails. And she must never ride by herself. She could get hurt." Charles was looking out at the forest as he talked to Holden. Holden was grateful for this because he didn't want to have to look Charles in the eyes.

"I understand, sir. I will make sure that someone accompanies her at all times. I guess that will be me since Branson doesn't ride. Will you be letting her know that she cannot ride the trail around the lake? She brought that up after our lesson today." Holden did not want to be the bearer of bad news, hoping Charles would tell her.

"I will let her know tonight at dinner," Charles said. "Just make sure she is safe." Charles got up to leave. "And Holden," he started.

"Yes, sir?" Holden responded, waiting for Charles to finish.

"Do not, under any circumstances, let her go out on the road. Do you understand?" With that, Charles stepped off the porch, then turned to look up at Holden. He noted Holden's firm physique, wishing for a moment he took more time to work out. He hoped he didn't have to worry about this fellow.

"I understand, sir." Holden leaned against the post holding the porch roof, looking very much like one of those guys in the cigarette commercials, Charles thought.

"Do you have a girlfriend?" Charles asked him.

"I do, sir. I just don't have the opportunity to see her very often." Holden thought of Elizabeth and how sweetly she arched her back and came when he pushed into her and how he wished he could have more of that.

"Well, if you ever need to take time off to spend with her, you let Branson know." Charles turned and walked around the corner to the front door. Holden went back into his cabin and shut the door, looking over at the telephone and wondering when Elizabeth's sister was going to come visit. He *wished* he could take time off to spend with Elizabeth; he wanted her so badly. But things were going to play out as they would, and he didn't think that he would have much control over the outcome. He was happy that the conversation with Charles went how it did. It could have gone either way. He shivered, tucked his shirt back in, and went out to the bunkhouse to work on a piece of furniture that was in need of repair.

~~*~~

The table was set nicely when Elizabeth came down for dinner. She saw Nettie's daughter, Twyla, set a vase of flowers in the middle and return to the kitchen. Twyla looked very much like Nettie in the face—sans the big gap between her front teeth—but that was where it ended. She was tall and lanky with somewhat knobby knees. She had her black hair pulled back into a tight bun. *Practicing to be a house manager takes so much work,* she thought. Gwendolyn, realizing Elizabeth's discomfort with Faye, had given her the night off and instead brought Nettie's daughter in to help with dinner.

The plates were set on chargers, and the fine China was out. Crystal glasses sat next to a wine decanter, and a bottle of the good stuff sat next to it, waiting to be opened.

Elizabeth went into the kitchen, greeting Nettie's daughter. "Hello, Twyla. It's nice to see you," Elizabeth said warmly.

"It's nice to see you, ma'am," Twyla said with a slight curtsy.

"Thank you for setting the table so beautifully," Elizabeth continued.

"You're welcome," Twyla replied. "I enjoy doing it, and I love arranging flowers."

"It shows. You do an amazing job." She turned to look at Nettie, who was beaming. "I'm starving," Elizabeth said.

"I bet you are," Nettie said with a grin. "Mr. Freeman said he was goin' to his room but he'd be comin' back in a few minutes, so if you wan' wait at the table, I'll have Twyla bring you a little cheese and crackers to put down your hunger."

Elizabeth sat at the table, noting the appearance of a celebration, wondering what Charles was up to now. As Twyla set a plate in front of her and poured water into her glass, she heard his footsteps in the hall. She took a quick bite of cheese and waited for him to come and take his place.

Charles sat down, and while looking down the table at Elizabeth, he signaled to Twyla that she could pour the wine. She had already opened it and put it in the decanter to breathe and was happy to have been given the responsibility to assist with serving. Twyla poured Elizabeth's glass half full as instructed by Charles, then she filled his to double. Elizabeth realized that this was in accordance with pregnancy protocol and she did not fault him for giving the instruction—especially having just seen the two solid lines on the test.

Once Twyla set down the decanter and returned to the kitchen, Charles raised his glass.

Elizabeth did the same, to which Charles proclaimed the toast, "To Charles Freeman the third." He then took a sip while Elizabeth still held her glass in the air. She lowered it slowly to her mouth, took a drink, and set it down quickly.

"Yes," was all she could mutter. She took another bite of cheese as Charles watched her from his seat, elbows on the table and hands folded. He almost dared a smile. "When?" he asked.

"When what?" she replied.

"What is the due date?" He was asking when the baby would be born, to which she had no reliable answer. She could only commit to giving a doctor the first day of her last period and letting the doctor tell her. "I have no idea," she said. "I'll find a doctor and make an appointment."

"It is already done," he replied. "You have an appointment tomorrow at ten in the morning. Branson will take me to the office, return for you, take you to your appointment, and wait."

This did not surprise Elizabeth, although she would have liked to have been included in the search for a doctor and discussion. Was it a man? Woman? What credentials were presented? The full scope of what she'd given up when she said the words "I do" was beginning to weigh heavy on her heart right now. And her on mind. She had to remind herself though, that had she not moved into this house, she never would have met Holden.

"I met with Holden today," Charles said, snapping Elizabeth out of her thoughts with his name.

"And?" she replied, tingling with fear, trying to appear aloof.

"We talked about your riding lessons," he said.

"Oh, yes, that. I know now that I hadn't forgotten that much. I haven't ridden since I was a child, but it was like getting back onto a bicycle." She was trying hard not to wear her thoughts as facial expressions.

"I wasn't happy to hear that you'd gone out with Holden, without my permission, but after our discussion, I think you will be safe to take lessons from him." Charles took another sip of wine, nodding at Twyla, who had re-entered the dining room and was waiting for his signal to bring the first course.

Safe with him is an understatement, Elizabeth thought, taking another small drink, knowing Charles would likely limit her to one half-glass for the evening.

She looked up at him, catching the incredulous look on his face—as if he'd just watched a street beggar devour a handout. *Yes, okay, she was pregnant and hungry. Was that alright?*

"Good and thank you. I like Bella; she's a good horse." Elizabeth nibbled on another piece of cheese. She was ravenous now.

"I instructed Holden that you are to stay in the pasture. You will not ride on the trails into the forest or around the lake."

Elizabeth tossed a piece of cheese onto her plate with such force that it bounced, which was quite unbecoming in a setting that was so elegant, but she couldn't care less. There he was again. First, he wasn't happy that she was riding, but now he was okay with it, but only if she stayed in a very small confined space. The control was driving her mad. She hoped that Holden had not agreed with his demands.

"Why?" was the only word she could muster, lest she spit out the rest of the cheese that still rolled around in her mouth. She was trying hard not to get angry. She was making progress. Baby steps, yes, but he had agreed to let her ride with Holden, for which she was grateful.

"Because I don't want you to get hurt. If you are on a trail and an animal crosses your path, a horse can spook and rear up, and you could be seriously injured. The baby…"

"Oh please, Charles. That only happens in the movies. I've walked that trail morning, noon, and late afternoon and have never seen anything but ants." She drained her glass. "And yes I shall take very good care of the baby, but right now that little one is but the size of a plum pit floating in an ocean. There is no need for this level of concern."

Twyla came with salads on chilled plates that had been dressed with a light balsamic vinaigrette, Elizabeth's favorite. Silently, she accepted her plate and picked up her salad fork, and before Charles was halfway through his, she was finished.

She looked up at him, watching him watch her destroying the salad. Yes, okay she was pregnant and hungry, was that alright? She refused to talk to him now.

"I told Holden if he needs some time off to see his girlfriend, he just needs to ask Branson, so you'll have to work out your riding schedule around that," Charles said as he scooped the last bits of lettuce leaves onto his fork.

Elizabeth was shocked. "Why does he need time off? How far away does she live?" Elizabeth asked, trying to remain calm and nonchalant.

"He didn't say, just that he doesn't have the opportunity to see her very often, which I presume is because of his work schedule. He would probably feel that it would be awkward to bring her out here, so I told him he could take time off to be with her if that is what he needed." He looked at Elizabeth. "That is fair, don't you think?"

"Yes, Charles. That is perfectly fine. I'll talk to him about it and about scheduling my lessons tomorrow around that if need be."

Twyla then came from the kitchen with a cart that held their entrées. She first went to Elizabeth, took her salad plate and exchanged it for an entrée, then repeated the effort at the other end of the table.

Once they were both served and began eating, Charles kept watching Elizabeth as if he had something more he wanted to say.

"What? What is it?" she asked.

He took a bite of his crawfish cake, nodding approvingly toward the kitchen door.

"I've been thinking about inviting Lillian Clayton out for dinner. I wanted to run it by you first."

What an odd thing, Elizabeth thought, although she just nodded.

"Well, what do you think?" he asked.

"I guess it would be fine," Elizabeth said, although inwardly she was excited for a chance to spend the evening with Lillian and perhaps pick through her memories—what was left of them—for anything she could still remember, especially now that Elizabeth had more details about the family. It would be a great opportunity. "When?"

"I think next week. Let me get through this workweek and reach out to the nursing home. I will have to arrange transportation, which means someone will have to go to the nursing home with Branson to pick her up."

"I can do that," Elizabeth replied, still trying to hide her excitement.

"That would be great. Bryce and Aimee might come."

Elizabeth flinched. She had only met them once at the wedding and hadn't seen them since. Charles talked about his brother but always with an indication of competition. Elizabeth knew that if she didn't have a son, Bryce would be one step closer to taking control of the family's trust. Apparently, they would have one more shot if this baby were a girl. If their second was not a boy, Bryce would take control, and his son, Devon, would be named to take over at age twenty-five. But no pressure.

"What interest do they have in Lillian?" Elizabeth had to ask.

"I think it is more nostalgic than anything. They're curious. Given that she grew up in this house until a certain age—no one is sure just when and neither is she—we're guessing it was right up to the time her uncle John Clayton died along with his wife in the car crash." Charles was acting as if he had few details although Elizabeth knew he was hiding something. "It was then that the house was sold to pay off back debts."

Elizabeth winced. That fiery crash she'd been told about on more than one occasion … the John Clayton III that perished then was the same who Adria referred to in her diary as 'Little John III'. Adria would have also been dead by the time of the event, for which Elizabeth was glad.

"What a horrid way that would be of losing your son" she thought, her hands sliding gently down to her belly.

~~*~~

The next morning Elizabeth woke up, a wave of nausea rolling across her brain and down to her belly. She pushed back the covers and threw up in the trash can by her bed. That was close and quite unexpected. Maybe the second glass of wine that she snuck up to her room after Charles retired for the evening was not agreeing with her embryo. But fine, whatever. Now that the cat was entirely out of the bag, she would leave it for Faye to clean up. She was happy about being pregnant, unsure that this morning sickness was something she was prepared to contend with, and she was ostensibly very angry about Faye and her confirmed role in monitoring her every move, down to her periods and controlling when she had sex. *Or so they thought.*

Elizabeth needed to make a phone call. She put long pajama bottoms on under her nightgown and went downstairs to see that Gwendolyn and Faye were not there yet. Branson had already taken Charles to the office, and Nettie was humming around the kitchen. Elizabeth opened the front door quietly and quite literally ran over to Holden's cabin.

Although Elizabeth now had permission to talk to Holden, ostensibly about riding lessons, she planned to keep the noted encounters to a minimum. She knocked quietly on the door. He opened it, his hair looking like someone had just given him one of those swirlies that they used to do to each other as kids. He was shirtless, causing her breath to catch.

"Yes, ma'am. Have you come to talk about riding?" He looked out the door, then in both directions, pulling her inside. "Because I've got a pony that would love you to hop on and take him for a quick gallop." He wrapped his arms around her and kissed her deeply, not stopping until she put her hands on his chest and pushed back.

"Holden, please. Gwendolyn and Faye will arrive any minute, and Branson could come back any time to take me to my doctor's appointment. I need to call my sister back." She gave him a quick kiss on the lips and batted her eyes.

"Okay, alright, the pony ride can wait," he said jokingly, handing her the phone.

Elizabeth took the phone and sat down in the overstuffed chair, dialed the number and waited for Penny to pick up, who was out of breath again when she finally answered.

"Hey, sis. It's me," Elizabeth said.

"Oh, I was on the treadmill," Penny replied, still panting.

"Can you make it?" Elizabeth asked while Holden traced her breast with his finger, watching her nipple grow hard.

"Yes, I can!" Penny squealed. "We've made arrangements with my in-laws to take the kids so Harold can focus on work without having to be the single parent, and I can book my ticket. Just say when!"

Elizabeth thought that probably after the dinner with Lillian would be best, so as not to complicate things, so they agreed on the following weekend. There, it was done, and no, she had not received Charles's permission. As soon as she hung up the phone, Holden pulled her onto the bed. "Just a quick one," he said, teasingly, knowing the answer.

"Later," she said.

"As in later today?" he asked, giving her a puppy-dog look, his bottom lip furled, pleading.

"As in later," she said, giving him a quick kiss on the lips and skipping out the door. She was happy that her sister had been able to work things out with the kids. Now if none of them got sick in the next ten days, she would soon be driving to the airport with Branson to pick her up. She ran quickly across the lawn and up to the door as she heard a car coming up the driveway. She was still in her nightgown. She quickly ducked in the door, hoping Gwendolyn and Faye had not seen her nor where she came from.

They had not, but Nettie, who had just thrown a bucket of soapy water out the back door onto the gravel, saw someone leave Holden's cabin and run around the corner toward the front lawn just as the chimes on the door tinkled. That someone was unmistakably Elizabeth who undoubtedly had been wearing only a nightgown. She shook her head, "That girl in fo' some trouble, I'm afraid," she muttered to herself, although vowing never to say a word. She wasn't like Faye; she would never betray the lady of the house, no matter what happened.

Elizabeth ran to her room and showered quickly, knowing that Branson would be back soon to take her to her appointment. While the hot water ran down her back, the thought came that she'd not asked Holden about *the girlfriend*. That one threw her for a loop. She couldn't imagine Holden to be the type who would cheat. She would ask him about it as soon as they were alone again. She dressed casually, taking note that whatever she wore she would have to remove entirely as soon as she got there. She went down to the dining room even before Faye could bring her tea, surprising her as she walked out of the kitchen.

Their eyes met, and neither moved for a minute.

"I think I'll have breakfast now, Faye," Elizabeth said, changing directions and going to her place at the table. She wasn't going to be mean to her, the little spy that she was, but she was no longer going to let her into her world, not in any sense. She was a servant, end of story. "Can you ask Nettie to make me some oatmeal like she did the other day and two soft-boiled eggs?"

"Yes, ma'am," Faye said, turning back to the kitchen.

"Oh, Faye," Elizabeth called after her. "And toast, please."

Faye rolled her eyes. This woman was going to weigh 200 pounds if she didn't watch what she was eating.

Branson entered through the front door. Upon seeing Elizabeth, he went to the dining room, removing his hat. "Ma'am, we'll be leaving in forty-five minutes. Will that give you enough time?"

"I guess it has to, doesn't it?" Elizabeth said, smiling. "I'll be ready. I will see you out front."

Her breakfast came fast, as Nettie was aware she needed to leave. She ate quickly, returned to her room to grab her purse—*when was the last time I needed a purse?*—then looked in the mirror and ran a brush through her hair. She would have time to put on a little makeup during the ride into town, so she grabbed her makeup bag at the last minute and walked down the stairs through the foyer and out onto the porch just as Branson was pulling the car up to the front door.

The doctor was a woman, thank God. Elizabeth had been dreading the thought of opening her legs to a strange man. She'd always preferred a woman gynecologist and had hoped that Charles would want the same for her with an obstetrician. The doctor was friendly, asked her a host of questions, took notes on a form that she placed into her chart file, then gave her a brief exam. This involved putting a couple of gloved fingers inside her vagina and pushing around on her belly. Surprisingly, the doctor didn't need to look inside as Elizabeth had thought would be the case. But as there was nothing to see at this point and it was too early for an ultrasound, what more was necessary at this time other than determining a due date based on last period and sexual interaction?

The last question Elizabeth had answered but only half truthfully. Her responses were correct except the one day when she had sex with Holden, after the first two days with Charles and before the last. She felt terrible about the whole thing— and exhilarated at the same time. What woman had sex with the groundskeeper while she was in the middle of delivering the promised heir to a family fortune?

When Elizabeth and Branson returned to the plantation, it was lunchtime. Nettie already had a huge vat of soup cooking, and Elizabeth could smell the bread baking when she walked through the door. She could see Gwendolyn in the living room, pulling the curtains closed against the midday sun. There was no sign of Faye, but she supposed she could be close. She waived at Gwendolyn, pointing up the stairs to indicate she was going to be in her room. She was exhausted by the trip to town and yet ecstatic that her sister was coming in just ten days. She had to figure out a way to tell Charles. But first, there was something more pressing that she had to work on: finding a way to make contact with William Stapleton.

Elizabeth imagined another trip to Holden's cabin to use the phone was what would need to happen but thought she should take her lunch first. Gwendolyn knocked on her door as she was pulling a shirt over her head. She'd dressed up for the appointment and was now trying to slip into something more comfortable.

"Come in," she said from inside her cardigan.

Gwendolyn entered and waited for Elizabeth to smooth her sweater, smiling. Elizabeth noted how all of a sudden everyone had taken to looking at her belly first before her face.

"Nettie would like to know if you are ready for lunch and if you would like to take it in your room or in the dining hall." Gwendolyn was so proper, sweet, and efficient, and Elizabeth so appreciated those qualities about her.

"Please let her know I will have lunch in my room today, Gwendolyn, and thank you. The trip wore me out a bit." Elizabeth moved toward the closet that held the safe with the diary as Gwendolyn retreated, closing the door slightly but not all the way. Elizabeth walked to the door and shut it completely before returning to spin the dial on the safe and retrieve the diary. She wasn't taking any chances. Faye could be lurking, could peek through a crack in the door and see her in the closet opening the door of the safe. She was not happy about having to be so guarded in her own home—*in her own room*—but she was content to do what she had to do to keep her secret safe.

March 15, 1859

It is Little John's birthday, and Abraham Lincoln has officially announced that he will be running for president. My husband says it will take some time before the Republican party decides to get behind him and push him as a candidate, which will give the Confederacy time to put up the perfect candidate for the South. Lincoln is a fool to think anyone in any of the southern states will be voting for him, but anyone has the right to run, I guess.

Those men have been coming around more regularly talking to John about things that are to come, and it doesn't look good. When they talk about us splitting off from the Union states and forming a separate country and a government of our own, it makes me nervous that John is going to be involved. I don't want him in any sort of conflict. Why can't we just keep doing what we are doing, and if war comes, as they say may be inevitable, the army can protect us, and they can take the fight up north. I cannot dream of fighting in my fields, of people dying on my land. The safety of my entire family could be be at stake.

And by then my family will have increased. I told John today at Little John's first birthday party that I am again with child, and he was so happy! He danced around the parlor while our friend Natalie played the piano. Little John just beamed in his papa's arms, and everyone in the room was elated. I want it to stay that way forever. This baby will likely be a Thanksgiving baby as I think it happened around the first of February. That would make me six weeks along, and the doctor agreed.

Liam is not so happy with the news. I mean, he's happy for me, but he so wishes it could be him dancing in the parlor. He would be a good husband as much as he is a good lover. When John was in Texas, Liam and I took several trips to town in the buggy. We've decided that while picnics on the grass wrapped in quilts are fun, we are adults and need to find a safe place to continue our adulterous relationship. There. I had to use that word. I needed to see it in my own handwriting. I am an adulterer. A sinner in the eyes of God. But I also hear that God is a loving God who does not judge. It is all confusing, but one thing is clear: My love for Liam will assure that we are never to be apart, no matter what happens.

Elizabeth closed the diary when a knock at the door signaled her lunch had come. She once again tucked the precious diary under the pillow on the chaise and went to open the door. It was Gwendolyn this time delivering her lunch, not Faye. She was curious about that but not in the mood to inquire as to Faye's whereabouts. It was likely due to the fact she was finding it increasingly difficult to hide her disdain for the girl.

"Hello, Gwendolyn. Please come in," Elizabeth said, holding the door open. "You can set it on the table, thank you."

Gwendolyn left the tray and went to the door. "Mr. Freeman said something about arranging a dinner with Lady Lillian Clayton. Are you prepared to discuss the menu?" she asked.

"I'll give it some thought. Thank you for asking. After my lunch and a nap, I'll be down."

"Yes, ma'am," Gwendolyn said, shutting the door quietly.

Elizabeth took the diary from under the pillow and sat looking at the cover, the picture depicting the plantation house where she now sat eating, her food resting on Adria's table, the sinner, the adulterous lady of the house. She wondered if someday people might call her *Lady Elizabeth. Doubtful,* she thought, as the term "Lady" applied in Adria's time and up until the turn of the century. Although it had been mostly applicable to wealthy white women in the South, initially it was used to set the lady of the house well apart from the slave mistress and any other women of lower social standing.

Elizabeth thought about the upcoming dinner with Lillian and Charles's brother, wondering why their mother had not been invited. Was it a business dinner or was there more to the evening? Perhaps Dehlia was just too much of a distraction sometimes. She had no idea what to serve them, surprised that Gwendolyn had asked her. That was surely a question for Charles.

After Elizabeth finished eating, she laid down on her bed, surprised to realize that it was nearly two o'clock when she woke up. She sat up and looked around the room at all the finery: the embroidered cushions, the beaded edges of the chaise, the silk tassles on the lampshades. It was all very lovely. It wasn't a bad life, really. If she could only live here amongst all this but with someone she loved, and not be held captive, it would be a dream come true.

Elizabeth felt great after her nap. She went downstairs to find Gwendolyn, calling out her name. Faye appeared from somewhere in the living room as Elizabeth walked toward the open patio doors to say Gwendolyn had gone to town for a quick trip for supplies. Elizabeth nodded in her direction, noting the dusting cloth in her hand. She was a good worker by all accounts, she guessed. Elizabeth just wished Charles didn't have her in his back pocket.

"I'll be back, Faye. I'm going to walk the trail around the lake."

Faye watched her go, wishing she was that brave. She knew Mr. Freeman didn't want his wife out there in the woods alone, especially now that she was going to have his baby. She felt proud about that, having been the one who sent him to her room at just the right time.

Elizabeth headed down toward the bunkhouse, thinking she would first check there for Holden. The door was locked, so she continued down the path toward the lake trail. She turned right, walked the long way around to the bench, and sat down. She gazed toward the plantation house, noting the shimmering reflection of the place in the lake. Had she not just taken a nap, she thought she could fall asleep right there. She heard a rustling in the bushes. Recalling the last time that she sat on the same bench and Holden had come out of the woods, she called his name.

"Holden? Is that you?" she asked, hearing no reply, just more rustling sounds. Her skin prickled. She saw a big branch next to the bench, sort of a walking stick that someone might have left there. She picked it up, looking toward the sound coming from under the canopy of trees.

Suddenly, a wild boar emerged from the dense forest. Elizabeth screamed loud enough that someone would hear her, if anyone was listening, even over in the yard of the house, but no one was within earshot. She screamed again and jumped up onto the bench, holding the stick in her hand. The boar walked out onto the trail and stopped, looking up at her.

"Go! Go away!" Elizabeth screamed at the creature.

The boar looked up and down the trail and then back into the dark of the forest. More scurrying could be heard. Elizabeth was in a panic, trying to figure out what she would do if there was a pack of them. She'd heard about them attacking and killing dogs in packs. She noted the tusks that grew up from the bottom jaw of the animal. She gripped the stick firmly, ready to fight.

Suddenly from out of the forest came a little one, a baby boar, then another and another, until six of the little guys emerged, running up to their mama and huddling. The mama boar looked up at Elizabeth––what a sight she must have been––then turned and trundled down the path back toward the bunkhouse with the babies following her in a straight line.

Elizabeth let out a sigh then a gasp and a giggle, all at once. What she thought was going to be a fight for her life turned into a sighting of a darling little boar family. The babies were cute, she thought, with their tiny little tusks and the black wiry hair that sprung out everywhere from pink skin. The mama boar was not so cute and would have put up a fight had Elizabeth been truly threatening. She climbed down off the bench and continued along the path away from the boars, turning off at the path that veered away from the lake toward the old cabin, keeping the stick with her as a weapon. It might be feeble against wild boars, but it would have to suffice.

She heard banging as she neared the cabin and was relieved to see Holden on the front porch holding a hammer, bent over an upside-down table. He turned when he heard her coming, smiling broadly and setting down the hammer, coming down the stairs to greet her.

"Elizabeth, what happened?" he asked, noting the way her face was flushed red and how she was still gripping the stick as if a weapon, her knuckles white.

"I'm okay. I'm okay," she said as if trying to convince herself. "I just came across a wild boar on the path. I jumped up on the bench and was prepared to fight. But then out of the woods came a gaggle of little ones. Is that what you call them? A gaggle? A flock? Anyway, once the little ones were all with the mother boar, she took off down the path in the other direction, and I came running down here to find you."

Holden took her in his arms, smiling behind her head. She buried her face in his shirt, gripping him tightly.

"Wild boar encounter, scary," he said. Finally, her grip lightened, and he brought her away from him, looking into her face, noting that she had shed a few tears onto his shirt. "Come on, let's get you some water." He took her hand and led her up onto the porch, pointing to the rocking chair. "Why don't you sit here in the shade, and I'll bring you a glass. I keep water out here for when I'm working."

Elizabeth was relieved and sat looking out at the view from the cabin. Not much could be seen from here besides woods, and the cabin couldn't be seen from the main house. That was probably why the original John Clayton built this place out here, for privacy, a place he could escape to, and now she knew he would sleep with slaves out here—at least one that she knew of anyway. She looked forward to meeting with William and picking his brain for more details, which is why she'd come to find Holden in the first place.

When Holden returned with her water, she drank nearly the entire glass without stopping. She'd have to remember to bring water with her from now on. She'd been told by the doctor that extra water was important during pregnancy, but she'd left the house empty-handed.

"There, that's better," Holden said, taking the glass from her. "Are you alright to walk back alone or would you like me to come with you?"

"That wouldn't look good now, would it? Escorting me through the woods, just the two of us," she laughed, feeling better now and deciding that absolutely no one would hear of this encounter, lest she never be let out of the house until the baby was born. "Holden, I need to get in touch with William Stapleton. I need your help."

"Why old Bill?" he asked. "You sweet on him?" He was teasing her.

"When he was here for tea, the one and only time that will ever happen since Charles threw such a fit afterward, he told me he had some things he wanted to show me, some information he wanted to share with me. And I want to know what it is before Thursday. We're having Lillian Clayton-Johnston, the only living descendent that I'm aware of from the original Clayton family, over for dinner, and I have some questions for him about her. Do you think you could at least call him for me?" She pulled a scrap of paper from her pocket where she'd scribbled his number but with no name. She was so paranoid about being caught with things like this. If someone were to discover this, she would be questioned. Without a name on it, she could easily plead her innocence. She handed Holden the paper.

"Here's his number. Can you please tell him we're having Lillian over again? He knows her. She was here for the big dinner party, as was he, and it was because of her appearance I believe that he pulled me aside and started telling me there are things I need to know. Charles whisked me away when he found the two of us talking, then later forbid me to have him back at the house without him being present. He got angry when he found that I'd been invited to the museum and made Gwendolyn promise to tell him if I made plans to visit, he would have to join me."

Elizabeth believed that William had intended to tell her much more over tea that day on the veranda, but with Faye hovering and Gwendolyn standing guard at the patio doors at the time, it quickly became apparent that it couldn't happen.

Holden took the paper and put it in his pocket. "Yes, of course, I'll call him for you. And I think I might know part of what he wants to tell you, but I'll let it come from him."

Elizabeth was surprised. How much did Holden know and why had he not shared everything with her already? He was most likely afraid to rock the boat, she guessed. Now her curiosity was at a higher level than ever.

"Thank you, Holden. I appreciate you. Now, I will take my leave. I may have some wild boars to contend with." She picked up the stick, which she decided now would accompany her at all times on the forest trails, and headed down the path after giving him a light peck on the cheek.

Elizabeth walked back to the house, recalling the conversation when she'd told Charles she had never seen anything on these trails but ants. My how that had changed in an instant.

Chapter Twenty: The Dinner Party

Holden did as he promised and called William, relaying all of what Elizabeth requested, then sat waiting for a reply. There was a pause and William, not knowing how much information he could trust Holden with, simply replied, "So very interesting that they are having Lady Lillian over again. Hmmm…"

"Is there something you want me to tell Elizabeth?" Holden asked.

"No, but there is a book I can get to you, if you can make sure you deliver it to her without anyone else's knowledge. Can I trust you with this?" William presumed that if Elizabeth asked Holden to call, he was trustworthy, but he couldn't take any chances with the information.

"Of course," Holden replied. "The Clayton family secrets are safe with me. Trust me on that." He presumed the book was regarding the Clayton family, having just mentioned the upcoming dinner with Lillian.

They made arrangements for Holden to go over to the museum that afternoon. He met William in the lobby, and after a very brief tour, which William was not aware he'd already taken, they went into William's office. There on his desk sat a very old book, a ledger of sorts. It was leather-bound, and the edges were frayed, as if it had seen a lot of wear. He handed it to Holden.

"I've put markers on certain pages that Elizabeth might want to study. Please tell her to lock it up. I will make arrangements to get it back from her within three days. There is so much more she needs to see, and not only about the Claytons but about the Freeman family over the same time in history."

Holden took the book home and placed it in a trunk under his bed. Other than Elizabeth, no one ever came in his cabin, not that he was aware of anyway, so it would be safe there. He would find Elizabeth somehow and get it to her.

It didn't take long to track her down. She was in the kitchen having Nettie prepare her lunch. Holden walked in the back door, stopping when he saw Elizabeth. "Excuse me," he said, catching himself looking down at her belly. He took off his hat and addressed Nettie first.

"Good morning, Nettie. How are you?" then to Elizabeth "And you, Mrs. Freeman, good morning to you. Am I interrupting?"

"No, not interrupting, this mama-to-be is just gettin' hungry," Nettie said, looking at Elizabeth with a broad smile. She was sure by now that Holden knew, but she wanted to make sure. After seeing her sneak out of Holden's place, she wanted to confirm everyone was clear on everything. As clear as she was, anyway, about the fact that there was something going on between these two. She looked at Holden and then back to Elizabeth. "What can we do for you?" Nettie asked him.

"Charles and I had a meeting yesterday, and he said that we could schedule regular riding lessons as long as we stay in the nearby pasture for now. I was coming up to see when Mrs. Freeman would like to schedule her next lesson, but I was going to stop in first to steal one of your cinnamon rolls. I could smell them all the way down at my place."

Nettie grinned and gestured to the pan sitting on the counter. "Help yourself, chile'," she said, turning back to work at the stove, where a grilled cheese on fresh homemade bread was just about ready.

He sure knows how to butter her up, Elizabeth thought to herself as she watched Holden working Nettie. She studied his face, his bright blue eyes and dimples the first things that always caught her eye. The locks of hair that fell around the edges of his face curled in the steamy kitchen. She found him so incredibly sexy. She knew she might blush hard if she took in any more.

"How about this afternoon?" Elizabeth asked. "After I've had lunch and a nap, after it cools down just a bit, can we say four o'clock?"

"That will work. I'll have the horses saddled." He put his hat back on, picked up a cinnamon roll from the tray, and without hesitation took a bite. "Oh Nettie, I don't know how you do it."

"Go on, git outta my kitchen," she said with a chuckle.

"See you at four, ma'am," Holden said looking over at Elizabeth, and with Nettie's back to him, he gave her a wink before walking out the door.

~~*~~

Elizabeth showed up promptly at four, knowing that Charles would likely be home in a couple of hours. Unless he had one of those *unexpected client meetings*, she would have at least two hours alone with Holden. She found him in the barn with the horses saddled and tethered. She was ready to go and excited to get back up on Bella and to hear that hopefully Holden had made contact with William.

Before helping Elizabeth up onto her mare, Holden produced the book that William had given him, briefly explaining what William had said regarding bookmarks and things that she needed to know or might find interesting.

"Let's hide it right here," he said, pointing to a pile of saddle blankets. "When we come back from the ride, you can take it with you. William is expecting me to return it within three days or so, definitely before your dinner with Lillian."

Elizabeth took the book in her hands, feeling the weight of it and, more importantly, the history. She opened it briefly to reveal that it was a ledger of sorts, containing notes signed by John Clayton, and that it was obviously a journal as well, describing and cataloguing the purchases and sale of slaves, where he bought them, when he sold them, and to whom. The leather cover was worn, and the pages had been stained with John Clayton's sweat as he laid his arms upon the paper to write. This was pure gold. A yellowed Bill of Sale fell from the pages as she started to hand the book back to Holden. He knelt and retrieved the paper, carefully holding it with two hands as he read to Elizabeth:

"For the sum of $1,000, one negro man, a Prime Field Hand.

For the sum of $800, one negro man.

For the sum of $400, one negro woman, good breed stock."

Elizabeth shook her head, noting that these people remained nameless, uncited in history. "Where did William get this? Did he say?" Elizabeth asked as Holden took the book from her. He carefully placed the paper back into the center of the ledger.

"He only said that you might need to pay special attention to the pages that he marked. He told me that this is just the beginning of a trove of information that he has regarding the Claytons. He mentioned having similar documents relating to the Freeman family as well, but apparently this is what he wanted you to see first."

With that, Holden buried the ledger under the stack of blankets, then led Elizabeth back to Bella and helped her up onto the mare, handing her Bella's reins. He quickly hopped up on Jack's saddle and led the way out of the barn.

They took the same route as before, stopping in the very same place that he knew was shielded from the house, but this time Holden suggested they dismount for a moment. He helped Elizabeth down, although with her insisting that she was fine dismounting Bella by herself. He dropped the reins because he knew neither of the horses would care to go anywhere when they were standing in a field of tall, delicious grass.

"Come, I want to show you something," Holden said, taking Elizabeth's hand. He led her through the grass, up to the fence line, where a small brook wound back and forth between the small pines, hosting a huge array of wildflowers. He bent down, picked a small purple flower, and handed it to her.

Elizabeth took it, sniffed, and noted no discernable scent, but it was beautiful. She loved that it had small, heart-shaped green leaves on the stem as well.

"It is a blue violet," Holden said, happy that she was enjoying the moment. "It is also edible, as are the leaves, so if you ever get in a pinch, lost in the forest amongst wild boars, you can survive on this," he said, stifling a laugh. "But we should get going."

"Thank you, Holden," Elizabeth said, holding the flower and his gaze. "Thank you for showing me things like this. Thank you for being my friend and my lover and for giving me hope in this crazy situation."

He took her in his arms, wrapping her tightly and kissing her with such passion that she could hardly breathe. She pulled back.

"We should make an appearance in case anyone is watching," she said.

"You're right. We will be missed. Let's get back on these ponies." Holden smiled, taking her hand and leading her back to their horses that had not moved.

They moved through their *lesson*, which was really no more than a comfortable stroll around a small pasture. Elizabeth was now feeling quite capable with Bella, however knowing that she had a long way to go to be deemed a proficient rider. She wondered what Bella would do if she encountered a wild boar on the trail, hoping she would never have to find out.

Once back in the barn, Holden took off the saddles and tethered the horses to a stall, intending to brush them as soon as Elizabeth returned to the house. He pulled the book from under the blankets. "You're going to have to get this back into the house with you somehow and not let anyone see it." He handed her the book.

Elizabeth took one of the smallest blankets off the stack and wrapped up the book, then put it underneath her arm. If anyone saw her and had a question, she would think of something. She headed to the door then stopped.

"Holden, thank you for everything." She smiled at him, almost in tears. She was not a crier, but being pregnant was bringing all her emotions to the surface. "I mean it."

Holden walked to Elizabeth and again gathered her in his arms, kissing her for the longest time. "I know I've said this before, but everything will work out. I want you to trust this and know that I am here for you and only you, no matter what."

"Are you saying you don't have a girlfriend? Charles told me you needed time off to see your girlfriend." Elizabeth hadn't intended to bring it up and didn't want to come off as being jealous—as a married woman she had no right—but she was feeling raw all of a sudden.

"Elizabeth, there is no other woman in my life. I promise you." He kissed her again and led her to the door of the stable. "I was talking about you when I told him I didn't get to spend that much time with my girlfriend." He squeezed her hand before letting go. "Now don't get caught with that book and tell me what you find out."

~~*~~

The doorbell rang downstairs. Elizabeth had finished dressing, twisted her hair into a bun, and applying a bit of lipstick. She heard Lillian's voice in the foyer. She quickly left her bedroom, closing the door behind her, and hurried down the stairs to greet her.

Lillian stood looking a little bewildered, clutching a handbag that looked to be from the 1950s if not earlier, wearing a little pillbox hat that spoke to the same decade. Instead of having Elizabeth go to pick her up, Charles had decided that he and Gwendolyn would go together to get her so Elizabeth could make sure the house was in order and dinner organized. Of course, that was absolutely Gwendolyn's job, and Elizabeth surely could have accompanied him, but Charles was not inclined to want to show Elizabeth where Lillian currently lived.

Elizabeth hoped Lillian was having a good day and in a good place for conversation, and she hoped that Lillian remembered her!

"Lillian, how nice that you could come!" Elizabeth said, taking her outstretched hand and holding it for a minute as they locked eyes. Elizabeth now saw the resemblance between this woman and that of the woman in the picture down the hall, Lillian's great-great aunt Helen. "Please, come, let's sit down. Dinner will be ready soon."

Charles entered the door behind her with a small overnight bag, surprising Elizabeth. They had not talked about Lillian spending the night, but she was thrilled. He handed the bag to Gwendolyn, who took it upstairs where unbeknownst to Elizabeth a room had already been prepared.

Earlier in the day, Gwendolyn had received a call from Charles while Elizabeth was out riding, letting her know that she would come with him to the nursing home to fetch Lillian. Elizabeth's lessons were daily now and beginning to raise concerns amongst the staff—Gwendolyn being no exception. She'd looked out the window from time to time as she'd prepared the room upstairs next to Elizabeth's. From what she could see, Elizabeth and Holden were simply riding around, talking, Holden gesturing for Elizabeth to sit more forward or to hold the reigns just so to get the horse to maneuver one way or the other, occasionally turning in complete circles. She didn't *see* anything of concern; it was more of a *feeling* that she was having.

Elizabeth led Lillian to an area in the living room where there was just one small couch and one chair, an intimate setting where the two of them could sit close together. Lillian placed her handbag on the end table, choosing the chair. Elizabeth sat on the couch, mesmerized by the fact that she was sitting with the great-great-granddaughter of the woman who ran the household and lived in the plantation house for nearly fifty years. She didn't know where to start.

Lillian looked out at the lake, where the setting sun cast shadows on the water. "I miss this place," she said. "My aunt Rose used to let us swim in the lake." She trailed off, reviving memories. "My brother, Michael, got a spanking once for chasing the swans." Then out of the blue, "I wonder what really happened to Juliet."

Elizabeth turned white, looking over Lillian's shoulder to see if anyone heard the last comment. They were still alone, and she was quite sure everyone was out of earshot. "What did they say happened to her?" Elizabeth dared to ask.

"They say she committed suicide, but I don't know. I doubt it. That husband of hers…" Lillian lowered her voice to a whisper and cupped her hand to her mouth. "I think he would have been your husband's great-grandfather."

"Yes," Elizabeth said, still watching to see if Charles or anyone else could have overheard the comment.

"Some say he killed her. He was a bad man."

Just then, they heard footsteps and the doorbell ring. Gwendolyn opened the door just as the bell rang, letting Bryce and Aimee inside while telling them Charles would be right down. A light rain had begun to fall. Sensing incoming weather, Branson had moved Charles's car to the garage so that they could leave their car under the portico. The hot, humid air wafted in behind them. Gwendolyn ushered them into the living room, where Elizabeth nervously stood to greet them. Luckily, Charles walked into the living room at that very moment.

"Dear, brother, welcome!" he said to Bryce then to his wife, "Aimee, how lovely to see you." He kissed her on the cheek and grabbed his brother's hand. They shook firmly but somewhat awkwardly, as the last time they'd met in Charles's office hadn't gone too well. Still, Bryce and Aimee had accepted the dinner invitation. They had to; they needed to check Lillian's level of lucidity.

Aimee walked up to Elizabeth and gave her a warm embrace. "How are you settling in?" she asked.

"Good, good, thank you," Elizabeth replied, turning to Lillian. "You remember Lillian, yes? From the wedding?"

Lillian had been sitting in her chair, letting the family have a moment. She was staring out at the lake again anyway, enjoying a vision that had surfaced from long ago of cousins running across the expansive lawn in the bright sunlight, boys chasing girls, dogs barking, geese honking. They had swans back then, but they also had geese. Their cook would rob an egg now and then from the nest that was not far from the kitchen door and scramble it up for the children to show them that it was just like a chicken egg but bigger. Lillian came back to the present at the mention of her name. She looked up at the four, giving them a weak smile.

"Hello, everyone. I'm Lillian. It won't bother you if I don't stand, I hope?" She sat up taller in the chair and stretched out her hand to Aimee, who leaned over her and took it, noting how incredibly soft her skin was—*paper-thin, she noted*—then bent down and kissed her cheek.

"Nice to see you again, Lillian," Aimee said as Bryce came around her and did the same.

Elizabeth walked over and rested a hand on the back of Lillian's chair. "We were just visiting, waiting for you to arrive. I do believe we could move to the dining room whenever we're ready, as Nettie has an incredible meal waiting for us!"

Elizabeth's eyes sparkled, yet Bryce noticed something that hadn't been there before—a distant, cautious wariness. He also noted that Charles hadn't addressed her, kissed her, nor touched her since he entered the room. He then looked down at her belly, which was still firm and seemingly flat.

"Yes, let's," replied Charles, looking toward the dining room, studying the seating arrangement. Their main table was too large to comfortably entertain a party of five, so he had the workers bring in a smaller wooden table from under the veranda outside and oil it earlier in the day. Gwendolyn had arranged the chairs comfortably spaced. He and Bryce would head each end, Elizabeth and Lillian could sit on one side together, with Aimee seated across from them. Charles took Lillian's hand, helping her to stand, and motioned for Elizabeth to follow, which she did, giving Bryce and Aimee a gentle nod as she passed them.

Sometime during the second course, Lillian began to reminisce about her childhood. The vision she'd had earlier of running across the lawn had sparked other memories, and suddenly she was babbling happily about this event and that—and with amazing accuracy—causing Bryce to give Charles an alarmed look.

"My father, William, married my mother, Eliza, in nineteen hundred, right here on the plantation. There were two weddings that year in this house. John Clayton the fourth married his sweetheart, Rose, here on the lawn, just like you two," she said, looking at Elizabeth fondly. "I was born the next year in nineteen o' one. John and Rose had three children, of course one of them being the last John Clayton, who died in that terrible accident. I was just eight. It was the same year that the stock market crashed, sending everyone into a panic. Cotton prices fell, and tobacco prices went to the bottom—even though people were smoking like fools to calm themselves."

Silence enveloped the table, as everyone sat shocked at the amount of detail Lillian was able to remember, given she supposedly had dementia. Bryce and Charles exchanged another concerned glance, which Elizabeth caught out of the corner of her eye. Whatever was going on between these two was worth figuring out, if she could.

Charles spoke first. "Lady Lillian, what do you remember of your great-aunt Juliet?"

The question shocked Elizabeth, who had just read in the journal that William had loaned her that Juliet was John Clayton's sixth child, and that she'd been born with red hair. Bryce looked over at Aimee, who sat waiting for an answer, curious but unaware of the significance of the question.

"Not much," Lillian responded, looking at Charles. She knew full well what he was asking, and she wasn't going to get into any detail, but oh, yes, she remembered her. She knew that Juliet was born just before Lillian's great-great-grandfather passed from injuries he'd received in the war. She had heard the scuttlebutt about Juliet being the child of a romance between her great-great-grandmother Adria and their liveryman, who was Irish. She had heard many rumors about the affair lasting for years, that it started before and continued on during the war while her husband fought with the Confederate Army. And she heard this from Juliet herself, when she was very young, too young to have been apprised of such information, but she'd taken it all in with awe as she sat at Juliet's feet. As Juliet grew older, she would muse about who her real father had been to anyone who would listen, while also expounding about her marriage to that monster husband of hers, Charles Freeman the third. When Juliet died, the notices all said that she had hanged herself, but her husband had her in a sealed coffin faster than anyone else could get to the undertaker to see the bruises.

Lillian remembered that it was Juliet who taught her to knit. Her red hair had begun to reveal coarse streaks of white, and she would let Lillian brush it when she came to visit. Lillian loved telling Juliet that she had never seen anyone with such beautiful eyes and that no one else in the Clayton family had blue eyes. Innocently, Lillian had pried about this. Juliet had a way of staring at her blue eyes reflected in the mirror as Lillian brushed her hair, knowing in her heart that Liam was indeed her real father.

"She had beautiful blue eyes," Lillian finally said, after drifting off for what was an uncomfortable amount of time for Charles and Bryce. "And red hair. And I'm quite sure everyone knew."

Charles hid his shock at what she'd just said, looking at Elizabeth, who was feigning an aloof curiosity, although her stomach was turning and her skin was crawling. Charles was completely aware that although his great-grandmother Juliet was the *recorded* daughter of John Clayton the second, rumors were that he had not been the father. When Charles's great-grandfather married Juliet, it caused quite a stir, kicking up the rumors again about the affair between her mother, Adria, and the liveryman. Charles's father shut him down on more than one occasion when he'd asked, telling him that they were rumors, nothing more. The rumor that Juliet had been murdered by her husband also loomed large in their family, but it officially remained a mystery.

Charles had kept all this from Elizabeth. Of those at the table, only he and Bryce, and now apparently Lillian in a lucid state, were aware of their connection to the Clayton family and the murder—or so they believed. Their mother, Dehlia, had no idea about the papers in the safety deposit box nor the trust that was drawn up more than a hundred years ago. No one else knew that this woman sitting at his table was the rightful heir to his house—the house purchased with funds from the Freeman family trust—at least he hoped. Charles played dumb when working with his real estate agent, and again when he showed Elizabeth around the property. Yet he wanted so badly to purchase the Noble Oaks Plantation house that he paid well over the asking price, causing many to wonder why—most notably William Stapleton.

Faye and Gwendolyn tended to the dinner, coming out with courses as Nettie had them ready and clearing away dirty plates promptly. When they brought out dessert, ice cream covered with fresh strawberries drizzled with chocolate sauce, Elizabeth was stuffed. It was so delicious, though, that she finished every bite. She looked over to see Lillian's eyes somewhat droopy and cleared her throat, looking at Charles.

"Well, Lady Lillian, can we have Gwendolyn show you to your room?" Charles caught Gwendolyn's attention, nodding to Lillian.

Elizabeth stood up. "I'll help her too," Elizabeth said, taking Lillian's hand. They retrieved her pocketbook from the living room and ascended the stairs, Elizabeth holding her elbow firmly and Gwendolyn following. They passed Elizabeth's door, which she noted sat slightly ajar from where she'd left it, causing her to pause briefly. She continued, however, figuring someone had been in there for some reason. Faye would have certainly taken the opportunity to snoop, no doubt, while everyone was engrossed in conversation. She would check on things later to see if anything was amiss.

The door to Lillian's room stood open. The bed had been neatly made and turned down, and a footstool had been placed where she could easily step up onto the high mattress. Lillian's overnight bag had been placed on a chair in the sitting area.

"Lady Lillian," Gwendolyn started, "there are fresh towels in the bathroom for you and a pitcher of water on the stand along with a glass. Should you find yourself in need of anything more, please don't hesitate to ring the bell." She pointed to a porcelain knob on the end of a long, thin braided rope that stretched up to a pulley near the ceiling. The line went across to another attachment and disappeared into a pipe that went down the corner of the room and through the floor.

Elizabeth couldn't hide her surprise. "What in the..." she began as a question. She had no idea what she was looking at.

"Oh, my dear!" Lillian laughed. "I remember when that was installed! We are over the kitchen. When my aunt Helen took ill with the typhoid, they put her in this room until she recovered. They installed this so that she could ring for tea, a hot water bottle, or someone to come up and tend to getting her to the bathroom. My, oh my." She was shaking her head, smiling.

"I'm just next door too, so if you need anything in the night, don't hesitate to call my name. I'm a light sleeper, and I'll leave my door open," Elizabeth said, turning to Gwendolyn.

"And I'll be down in the kitchen for another hour or so cleaning up, otherwise I'll see you in the morning." With that, Gwendolyn left the room, leaving the two of them alone.

"How do you like living here?" Lillian asked.

"I like it," Elizabeth responded, yet with a sadness that was palpable.

"And Charles? How is he treating you?"

"He's a good husband."

"Anger and abusiveness run in this family, my dear. Please just be careful." Lillian reached out her hands, inviting Elizabeth into her arms. "When are you due?"

They hadn't spoken about the baby, not a word about Elizabeth being pregnant. "March," she replied.

"That's nice, the same month I was born. I'll be eighty then. Maybe I'll still be around when the baby is born." With that, Lillian gave Elizabeth a gentle hug, causing her to stifle her tears.

"I'll see you at breakfast, Lillian. Sleep well."

Elizabeth returned to the dining room to find it empty; Bryce and Aimee had gone home. Faye was clearing the last plate, and Gwendolyn was in the kitchen by the sounds of things. Charles was also nowhere to be found.

"They said to tell you they were sorry they couldn't wait to tell you goodnight," Faye said of Bryce and Aimee. "They had to get back to the children." She started to the kitchen, offering no mention of Charles.

That night, Elizabeth slept fitfully. She dreamt of Holden becoming Liam and she as Adria. And of her baby being born with red hair. She woke drenched in sweat and went to the bathroom to shower quickly before breakfast. When she arrived downstairs, Lillian was sitting looking out at the lake again, a teacup in her hand. Oh, how Elizabeth wished she could crawl into that mind and live the experiences that Lillian was daydreaming right then. She wore a beautiful smile, and the sunlight shone gently on the silver curls that framed her face.

"Good morning, Lillian," Elizabeth said as she walked up behind her. She didn't want to startle her. Two places were set, causing Elizabeth to wonder if Charles had already gone to town.

Faye appeared with her tea and a plate of biscuits. "Good morning, Miss Elizabeth," Faye said. "Mr. Freeman said to tell you he has an early meeting, but he'll be home by noon to take Lady Lillian back home."

Elizabeth was pleased to hear this. She wanted more time alone with Lillian. When Holden returned the journal to William, he was given another to pass to Elizabeth. This one held much more detail about the Freeman family and what Lillian had alluded to the previous evening. Indeed, this book, written by "Author Unknown," detailed how Charles Freeman the first had been in direct competition with the first John Clayton with regard to the slave trade and tobacco. The Freemans grew cotton as well, giving them another angle at the markets, and it was said that although the two were not enemies, the competition kept them apart at great lengths. Charles Freeman avoided going into battle, claiming a defect in his bones that prevented him from marching long distances or carrying heavy munitions. He gained the upper hand as his business prospered even during wartime, while on the other side of the country Adria was single-handedly trying to run the Noble Oak Plantation and manage the slaves while her husband fought. After the war ended and John Clayton returned, the two men never spoke again.

The book ended with the death of Juliet. The author speculated as to it being a murder, not a suicide. The author detailed Juliet's looks, just as Lillian had described her the previous evening. It went on to tell how she'd birthed three children, the first being Elizabeth's husband's great-grandfather, Charles the third. After her last of three children was born, Juliet fell into a depression that lasted an entire year, made worse by Charles's misdeeds in business and his fondness for other women. In 1915, they were forced into bankruptcy and lost the Freeman plantation. Elizabeth stowed this book upstairs beside Adria's diary in the safe. She hadn't finished it yet, and she wondered if William knew who the author was. Something told her that he did.

Elizabeth looked at Lillian. Lillian would have been fifteen years old when the plantation house was sold, yet she stopped short of giving up any further details.

Who was it sold to? In whose hands had it been since? Elizabeth wasn't sure if Lillian didn't remember, or if there hadn't been a time where it was appropriate to bring it up.

"Did you sleep well?" Elizabeth asked, watching Lillian as she sat gazing peacefully out at the water.

"So well, my dear. It was amazing. I've slept in that room many times. I dreamt of my husband." Elizabeth noticed Lillian's eyes welling up a bit, causing her to dab the corners of her eyes with her napkin. "He was such a good man. Died way too young. The cancer took him."

Elizabeth had heard this. "I'm so sorry."

"Everyone has to go sometime. We just have to live our lives in whatever way we can and make sure we do what we have to in order to find happiness." Lillian looked at her. "You're not happy, Elizabeth, are you?" Then adding, "I'm sorry. That's none of my business."

Elizabeth looked around and toward the kitchen where Nettie was preparing breakfast and Faye was readying another tray to bring out to them. She lowered her voice. "Charles can be difficult. And to tell you the truth, I think he married me just so that he could have a baby."

Lillian took her hand across the table. "You will find your happiness, trust me. The Freemans are a difficult family, and you'll never truly be a part of it, just like Juliet never was. But make it work as best you can. You only have this life, you know." Lillian pulled her hand back as Faye approached with breakfast.

Once they finished and the dishes were cleared, Elizabeth suggested they take a little walk around. They wouldn't venture all the way out to the bunkhouse, maybe just down to the dock and over to see the horses. It was a little windy on the lawn, so they stood and looked out over the water.

"Let's go see those horses of yours," Lillian said.

Elizabeth led the way around past Holden's cabin to where the stables sat on the other side. Lillian stopped at the porch and whispered something to Elizabeth, which she didn't hear, so Lillian said it just a little louder. "That's where he lived," she said.

"Who?"

"The liveryman," Lillian said with a wink. "The father of Juliet."

Elizabeth looked over at the porch and at the front door, fond thoughts of Holden warming her belly. She took Lillian's hand and walked toward the stables. They heard whinnying as they entered through the large door and saw Holden with Bella's foot in the air, cleaning out her hoof. She was taking it in stride, then whinnied even louder when she saw Elizabeth. Holden turned, giving her a smile, his dimples showing, causing her heart to flutter as always.

"She sure is happy to see you!" Holden said, putting Bella's foot down and walking over to the two women who stood hand in hand, still in the doorway. He reached out his hand to Lillian. "Hello, ma'am. I'm Holden." He looked at the way she studied him then over at Elizabeth.

"This the fellow you've been riding with?" Lillian asked, looking back at Holden. "You know what you're doing? Are you a liveryman?"

Holden laughed. "No, ma'am. I'm the groundskeeper, but I know horses. I mainly fix things. But Elizabeth here wanted to learn how to ride again, and Charles gave me permission to give her lessons. Mainly we just ride the fence line around this pasture." He pointed out the door with a glove.

"Oh, he gave you *permission,* did he? That was generous of him," Lillian said, not hiding her distaste for Elizabeth's husband.

Elizabeth cleared her throat, looking wide-eyed at Holden.

"Let me introduce you to Bella," he said, offering his hand to Lillian. She was charmed by the action, took hold of his arm just above his glove and let him lead her to the mare, who stood patiently, chewing on a mouthful of hay.

Elizabeth followed, coming around to stroke Bella's forehead. Bella threw her head back and whinnied, then nuzzled Elizabeth's face.

"She really likes you, Elizabeth." Lillian smiled. "That's a good sign. Horses know good people when they meet them." She turned to Holden. "Where's the other one? I'm guessing he's a little bigger and friskier, which is why you put her on Bella."

"How did you know?" Holden asked, winking at Elizabeth as Lillian took his arm again and let him lead her over to Jack's stall. Jack leaned his head out and over the gate, prompting Lillian to give him a pat on the nose.

"Good boy," she said to Jack. "Good looking horses, and you're taking care of them, I can tell," Lillian said to Holden, then she turned to Elizabeth. "Shall we? We have one more building to see. I would like to see the old slaves' quarters."

Elizabeth was surprised at this but nodded. She took Lillian's arm and walked her out the other end of the barn, turning to wave good-bye to Holden, who blew the two of them kisses and bowed. The two continued arm-in-arm around and down a wide path, Lillian pausing briefly to look back at the barn.

"He's a nice man. I can see why you like him." Lillian looked up at Elizabeth and smiled warmly. Elizabeth returned her smile but was guarded. This woman had a knack for extorting secrets and then generously returning them to the owner. She hoped she could trust her, but at this time she couldn't take any chances.

Once the old slaves' quarters was within sight, Lillian stopped. "Oh yes, I remember this building well. What is happening to it? Is it being remodeled?"

"Yes, Charles is fixing it up for his mother, Dehlia. She'll be moving in late summer, early fall, as soon as it is ready."

"I'm so sorry to hear that. Sorry for you, that is." Lillian turned to face Elizabeth, certain that there was no one within earshot. "The entire family is dreadful. I heard all about it growing up, trust me. As soon as Juliet married a Freeman, our two families were forever linked, so I know a lot—a lot more than I can admit. Or remember!" She chuckled, then continued. "Yes, I have my good days and my bad days, and what I can't remember I can *feel*. Most people think it is worse than it is, but I can tell you there is something strange going on between your husband and his brother—something to do with this place. I can't put my finger on it, though."

Elizabeth thought about the second book that William had loaned her. She was barely into it and had already learned more than she could have imagined about the things Lillian was saying.

"This place," Lillian pointed ahead with a stick that she'd found on the trail, "housed at least four families at a time, in only three rooms. And no plumbing! Just awful. My family was good to the slaves, don't get me wrong, but just imagine. Have you been in there?"

Elizabeth nodded her head, and Lillian continued. "After the war, when all the slaves in Georgia were officially free people, about half of them stayed on here. They had no place else to go, and if they stayed and worked, they got fed, and they got paid. Not a lot, but Adria was always fair with them, and when her son, John, took over after his father died, there were still probably ten people living in there."

She took a pause and a deep breath. "Then Henry showed up around 1872. He was probably about fourteen at the time. His mama, Grace, she was John Clayton's mistress, died before the war ended, so once he was free, he couldn't think of any other place to go except back to where he was born. He came here to Noble Oak."

Elizabeth froze on the path. Holden had told her that Adria's husband had sired a Black baby with a slave woman and that they were traded together to a slave owner at a nearby plantation when the baby was just six months old. It was also recorded in the ledger, the first book that William Stapleton sent home with Holden for her to read.

Lillian was not finished. "Henry showed up as soon as he was a free man, though still a boy really, to ask for a place to live. John Clayton was, of course, in denial, pretending not to know Henry or of this slave named Grace—his mama—and turned him away. Well, he came back a few years later after his daddy John Clayton had died from his war injuries, and Adria let him stay because she knew Henry was telling the truth."

Elizabeth continued walking beside Lillian, realizing that all of what she was saying now was exactly everything she'd been reading about in the books that sat in her safe.

"I don't know what to say," Elizabeth said. "This is all so overwhelming."

"Don't worry about it, honey. You just keep riding horses with that handsome young fella out there in the stables, and everything in your life will work out just fine. I guarantee it." Lillian let out a little chuckle, turning to head up toward the house, where Charles was likely waiting to take her back to the nursing home. Lillian started to take a step, then paused, nodding toward the stable. "You two would make some fine-looking babies."

With that, Lillian turned and walked away, leaving Elizabeth standing—temporarily frozen where she stood, and in time—watching this beautiful old woman who'd just confirmed so much history, take the path with quick, agile steps, swinging her walking stick back and forth because she didn't need it, not really.

~~*~~

Elizabeth stood in the doorway, watching the car drive away that carried Lillian in the back, Branson driving, and Charles seated next to her, thinking about how much history Lillian had just shared with her. Elizabeth was reeling from it all. Gwendolyn came out behind her, watching the sedan as it pulled down the drive through the tall gates.

"She's really something," Gwendolyn said.

"That is an understatement," Elizabeth replied. "I need to lie down."

Elizabeth went to her room and immediately retrieved the latest of William's loaned books. She quickly turned to the pages that described Henry's return to the plantation after first being rejected by his father, how Adria accepted him, and how he met his half-brother, John Clayton the third, finding out that they were born in the same year, eight months apart.

Henry knew better than to make it known that the master John Clayton had sired him. Adria had long suspected it though, and she thought it best that they should both take that secret to their graves, although it was said that on her death bed Adria admitted it to someone—and it was confirmed in the book authored by "Unknown." Elizabeth would ask William who he believed may have written that book.

Adria had taken Henry in and let him stay in the old slaves' quarters because by then the number of inhabitants had dwindled to only five or six, and they were either paid field workers or house servants. A number of the freed slaves had finally journied to other parts of the country since they'd been able to work and save a little money, either looking for relatives or simply new lives. Henry later married, and Adria moved him and his wife into the bunkhouse where they went on to have two children. His children grew up, and eventually his wife passed, then he died there sometime after Adria passed, happy and at home.

Elizabeth laid on her bed, trying to take a nap, but the events of the day were too stimulating, and she could not even close her eyes. Unbeknownst to Charles or Bryce, Lillian was completely lucid at times, and to the extent that she knew more of their own family history than they likely did. They'd made her out to be a dawdling old lady with dementia, and although Elizabeth had seen glimpses of that both at the dinner party and over the past twenty-four hours, her moments of lucidity far outweighed those of any implied dementia. Elizabeth could not wait to have Lillian back out to the house, to talk to her about the history of the place, as well as that of the Clayton and Freeman families. She wished she could arrange that when Charles was away but he kept his schedule to himself, including his disappearances into the arms of his mistress.

Elizabeth could not help but acknowledge the great detail with which Lillian explained the events of the days back then. It was uncanny how the history that Lillian offered completely lined up with what Elizabeth had just read in the book from William. She wondered if Lillian might have even read the book herself at some point in time.

Elizabeth was angry at how Charles continually conspired to cut her off from this rich conduit of historical facts, not only of the Clayton family but his own. She could not let him know the extent of Lillian's mental acuity, however, because Lillian had expressed to Elizabeth earlier in the day that she thought there was something going on between her husband and his brother that made her extremely uncomfortable. She'd said she could not put her finger on it and now neither could Elizabeth.

When Elizabeth requested another visit from Lillian, Charles firmly shut her down. His excuse was that they had just been trying to coddle her, to entertain her as one of the last remaining Clayton family members who had grown up exploring the grounds. And as he said to Elizabeth, because they owned the house now, there was no reason to let her roam and relive memories. There was simply no point to it at all, he'd said, although his denial for the visit was purely his way of making sure Elizabeth and Lillian did not develop a friendship. Keeping the two of them at arm's length was in his best interest.

Chapter Twenty-One: Elizabeth and William

Holden had finished saddling Bella and thrown Jack's saddle up onto his back when Elizabeth came through the door into the barn. God how she loved seeing his back muscles bulge under the weight of a saddle and how his tight blue jeans fit, giving him the look of a real cowboy.

"Howdy, pardner," she said with a drawl.

He turned and laughed, pointing to Bella. "She's ready for you. She let me know she's been bored, and she is ready to get out into the pasture. You've been busy and neglecting her, she told me."

"I've had company," Elizabeth responded, taking Bella's reins off a post. "And what interesting company it has been. I hardly have words."

"I don't doubt that," Holden said. "She's a peach, that's for sure. A purebred Georgia peach."

"And she can remember far more than anyone I know around here has perhaps ever known about this place." Elizabeth stood holding Bella's lead, perplexed.

"What is it? You okay?" Holden asked.

"Yes, I'm doing fine—except for the fact that while a lot of things are making perfect sense and lining up, other things remain a mystery, and Charles seems to want me to stay where I am—without information, without company—and is restricting access to the one person who can avail me of the true history of this place." Elizabeth walked over to Holden, waiting as he tightened the stirrups and prepared Jack for their ride.

"Why do you think that is?" he asked.

"Lillian made a very interesting comment: she feels there is something unsettling between Charles and Bryce, something that somehow involves her but that she can't put her finger on it. Pretty astute for an old lady with dementia, I'd say." Elizabeth stood, watching Holden as he pulled Jack around beside Bella, ready for their outing.

"I'm sure she has good reason for her gut feelings. She's been around a long time. She's seen some stuff go down here that we cannot imagine, I'm sure." Holden turned to face Elizabeth, touching her chin with his finger and leaning in to kiss her. He heard footsteps and stopped. Branson entered through the far door of the barn.

"Hello, Branson," Elizabeth said, startled but relieved they'd not been caught. "We were just going out for our ride. I've been meaning to ask: How was it getting Lillian back to the facility the other day?"

Branson shuffled into the barn head down, obviously bothered about something. He still wore the chauffeur's cap that he'd worn when driving Charles to town and back earlier in the day. He was a stocky man with overly large, worn hands, showing years of working on equipment and vehicles. His face bore similar lines, perhaps indicating a life of hardship. "Well, it was interesting," he said.

"What happened?" Elizabeth asked.

"I don't know. She and Mr. Freeman started talking about something, and Mr. Freeman became agitated. Then she got upset. As he was helping her out of the car, she made some remark about him regretting his decision." Branson shifted uncomfortably, feeling that perhaps he shouldn't be sharing so much information with Elizabeth, and in front of Holden no less. "He grew very angry afterward. I could see him in the rearview mirror as I drove him to back to his office. Something she said had him boiling, and he hasn't been the same since."

"Thank you, Branson, for taking her home. She seemed to have had a lovely time." Elizabeth was trying to deflect what it was that Branson was trying to relay, having no idea what Lillian and Charles may have had a disagreement about. What might be one decision that Charles had made that he would regret, according to Lillian? It seemed things were getting more mysterious by the day.

It also seemed that it was time to plan a visit with William, whatever that might take. Her sister was coming in a week, and visiting the museum next door would be the perfect outing for the two of them. Elizabeth had broken the news to Charles just the day before that her sister was coming. They had still been fighting, days later, as to why Elizabeth could not entertain Lillian on a regular basis.

"Well, then I'll entertain my sister, and you will not deny me *her* company. She will be here in eight days," Elizabeth had thrown out, shocking Charles completely.

"What in the world are you thinking, Elizabeth?"

"I'm thinking that I am pregnant, and I need some time with my sister, who has safely delivered two children. I will take the time to ask her questions that I cannot ask anyone else, and we will spend some time seeing the area." It was cut and dried, just like that, Elizabeth insisting that Charles relinquish control of these daily arguments in favor of giving his wife a couple of days with her sister. Then she dropped a bombshell. "She'll be renting a car."

After a minor verbal skirmish, Charles said he just hoped that they wouldn't plan any outings that would compromise the staff nor the order of the household. He had things so neatly dialed in, he'd said that rocking the boat would be a bad thing, and he would not stand for it at all.

Rocking what boat? she'd thought, *Other than his tight level of control?*

Charles had still not given her a reason for refusing a continued relationship with Lillian. He felt he didn't need to, he'd added, saying that it simply wasn't necessary. In reality, Lillian's visit had scared him. He'd been told by others, including the nursing home staff, that she had dementia to the point that many days she had no idea where she was, which was just where they needed her. She had been quite subdued at their wedding and then although somewhat less at the dinner party they'd hosted a few weeks back, he generally expected her to be worse.

However, the Lillian who'd just showed up and spent the night was a lively old lady, although she drifted off a few times while pulling out childhood memories of life on the plantation likely sparked by ripples on the water outside or the flock of swans that floated past the window. She recounted not only the names of past relatives but the year they were married. He later heard that when he left for his meeting, Elizabeth gave Lillian a tour of the plantation that included the barn and the old slaves' quarters. Who knows what they talked about on that walk.

Charles had Branson drive them to take Lillian home to the facility and had ridden in back with her so that he could ask her a few questions in private. She looked out the window for most of the drive, remembering some of the families who owned certain homes along the route, trying to stay lost in those memories and avoid small talk with Charles.

She gave him short, one-word answers for the most part, understanding that her animation threatened him in some way. She'd seen the looks that passed between the two brothers during dinner when she happily recounted brushing Juliet's hair as a small girl.

Juliet's death was a dirty family secret that they were trying to keep buried, just as they were burying Elizabeth before she gave birth, as they buried nearly every woman in the Freeman family before their time. Juliet did not suffer from postpartum depression as her husband tried so hard to convince the family. She suffered as Elizabeth would suffer, although wishing it would not be so.

Lillian saw Elizabeth for the prisoner that she was, noting that in the twenty-four hours she was with them not once had Charles said a kind word to Elizabeth, touched her, kissed her, nothing. Elizabeth was there for one thing only: to give this man a male child so that this horrible family could continue to produce a lineage of Charles Freemans.

But Lillian had a feeling that Charles had not chosen as wisely as he thought. This girl was as spirited as Bella, as strong as any woman she'd ever met, and would not be subdued as easily as Charles hoped. She'd seen the other side of Elizabeth: the one who lit up when they encountered Holden in the barn, the one who was taking riding lessons, the one who shared with her that her sister was coming and she hadn't told Charles yet, and more importantly the one who told her she had a very special book that she would share with her next time they met in private. She would wonder about that book until they met again.

Charles was forcing Elizabeth's hand, and Lillian knew it. Had he given her a fairytale existence and pretended to care for her, she might be one to stick it out, but it was obvious from Lillian's visit that things could go very badly for Charles and likely for the family. The fellow in the barn—she'd forgotten his name already—would have something to do with it.

Lillian knew a few family secrets that she'd not yet shared with Elizabeth that weren't in the book, but she would somehow find a way to help her out of the madness that Charles would slowly instill in her if he followed in the footsteps of his father and grandfathers. Lillian wondered how his mother, Dehlia, had somehow escaped that fate. Lillian planned to help Elizabeth escape it as well. Charles would soon see. Lillian left him with a few words that she hoped would plant doubts regarding his behavior, but only time would tell.

The day was warm, and the light that fell across the long blades of grass gave the pasture a relaxing glow. Elizabeth and Holden rode side-by-side; she was deep in thought about the life she'd unwittingly chosen, about this man beside her, and about the husband who clearly did not love her. She looked over at Holden. "You've been quiet," she said.

"So have you," he said, smiling, clenching a blade of grass in his teeth.

"Branson seemed upset," she said, looking back at the barn to see if he was still moving tack around to the outside wall. He had Holden build a shed attached to the barn with a large overhang for protection, telling him that Charles had discussed getting another horse, which came as a surprise to everyone, and that he needed more space inside the barn. Elizabeth could see a tiny figure moving from the barn door to the shed. When they were clearly out of sight, Elizabeth pulled Bella to a stop. "Holden, I'm going to see William when my sister gets here. And I'm going to find a way to see Lillian. Can you find out where she lives? Branson knows since he took her home. Can you find out, in some way that won't arouse suspicion?"

"I can do that for you," Holden replied, pulling Jack up closely beside Bella and leaning over to give Elizabeth a kiss.

He pulled back and sat quietly. "I haven't had a chance to tell you this, but when I last saw William, he told me to tell you there's more. Lots more. Let me know when you finish the book you have now, or maybe you want to take it back to him yourself."

"I'll take it to him. I will have finished it before my sister gets here."

"Good idea," Holden said, then he continued, "Hey, I have an idea."

Elizabeth looked at him without replying, arching her eyebrows.

"Why don't you meet me out at the cabin tomorrow sometime. Or better yet we pack a lunch and ride out there."

"Charles said he doesn't want me riding the lake trail. He's too worried about animals scaring the horses and me getting bucked off."

"These horses don't buck. Not at a swamp pig, that's for sure. Jack here is familiar with them. He'll balk and snort and stomp and send those pigs running. I'll ride ahead anyway and can always take a rifle for protection." Holden looked over at her as she contemplated the idea. As long as they weren't gone too long, it could work. Charles would find out, of course, Faye would see to that. They would be noticed heading out that way on the trail from about any room in the house. The thought of being wrapped in Holden's arms, of resting her head on his bare chest, was more than she could manage to contain. She let out a huge sigh, causing him to turn back to look at her.

"Let's do it," she said, knowing she would later face the wrath of Charles. She would cover for Holden, insisting that it was her idea and that Holden was merely obeying her wishes.

"I'll pack the lunch." He turned Jack around to face Elizabeth. "There's one more thing."

"Yes?" she asked curiously.

"William told me he knows who wrote that book."

~~*~~

A cherry red sedan pulled into the driveway at a little past four o'clock. Charles was not home yet. This delighted Elizabeth, as she would have some time alone with her sister before he arrived for dinner. She threw open the door and ran down the steps as Penny was getting out of the rental car, nearly tackling her.

"Woah! Hold on!" Penny said, laughing. The two embraced as though they'd not seen each other for years, although the wedding had just been four months prior. "Let me get my bag," she said. "It's in the trunk."

"Branson will get it," Elizabeth said, taking Penny's hand, leading her into the house. Gwendolyn and Faye stood waiting to be introduced, which Elizabeth did briefly, then she led Penny into the kitchen.

"My, it smells amazing in here!" Penny said.

Nettie greeted her with a smile and open arms. "Well, if you ain't the spittin' image o Miss Elizabeth," Nettie said, giving Penny a heartfelt squeeze. It was her trademark greeting. If Nettie liked you right off the bat, you could count on a "big ole hug" as she called them. Nettie brought out an appetizer tray from the refrigerator and produced a chilled bottle of white wine.

"Elizabeth said you like white wine, so here you go," she said, pouring a half-glass of wine for Penny and sparkling soda with lemon for Elizabeth, who had promised Charles she would stop drinking until after the baby was born, even though her doctor told her a glass here and there would not affect the baby one bit.

"You girls go on outside," Nettie said. "I'll have Faye come along behind you with some food."

Elizabeth showed Penny to the veranda, the doors to which Gwendolyn had opened wide while they were in the kitchen. Penny followed and took a seat on one of the chaise lounges after reclining it slightly. It had been a long travel day, and she was beat. Elizabeth sat beside her, close enough that they could talk without being overheard from the dining room. She waited for Faye to leave the tray and return to the kitchen.

"Boy, do I have a lot to tell you," Elizabeth said, looking over at her sister, so very happy that she had come.

Penny smiled at her. "You look good," then looked down at her belly. "Not showing yet," she said.

"Any day now," Elizabeth replied. "I'm just at seven weeks." They both dove in to the platter that was lined with crackers and cheeses, olives, veggies, and a dip that appeared to have fresh dill sprinkled on top.

"Just what the doctor ordered," Penny said, munching on a carrot. Then she lowered her voice. "How is Charles treating you?" she asked, knowing the answer. She could hear in Elizabeth's voice when she called that she was fraught with anxiety.

"He's an angry man," Elizabeth replied, looking over Penny's shoulder toward the house. "I wouldn't have done it if I'd known."

"I'll bet not," her sister replied. "What are you going to do about it?"

"I don't know yet," Elizabeth said, thinking of Holden. "I guess after the baby comes, we'll know more. If it is a girl…" Her voice trailed off.

"What? This isn't a country where the girl babies are cast out, sis. If it is a girl, you'll likely be asked to try again."

"Forced would be more like it," Elizabeth replied.

"And if another girl comes?"

"Then his brother, Bryce, is appointed head of the family trust, and his son, now six, would be next in line. It's sort of a two-strikes-and-you're-out situation, per the agreement Charles made with everyone." *Everyone but me,* Elizabeth thought. "If he hadn't waited so long to marry, it might not be such a pressing issue. But it would mean the end of the Charles Freeman lineage. Every other Charles since the first, who was born in 1850, had a duly named successor. He won't handle it well and will blame me, that much I can tell you." Elizabeth eyed her sister's wine, tempted to take just a sip.

"You will love this baby no matter what," Penny said. She sat back looking across the lake, noting the swans on the far side. She envied her sister only as far as she could skip a stone across that water, which she hadn't done since she was a child.

"Can I see where I'm sleeping? I'd like to freshen up before dinner." She drained the last of her wine and was ready to change into something clean. It had been a hot, sweaty flight into Atlanta.

"Of course!" Elizabeth was sorry that she had to ask. She should learn to be a better hostess. "Right this way." They left their empty glasses and half-eaten appetizer platter on the table and headed through the dining room and foyer, up the stairs to the same room Lillian had just occupied. Elizabeth had fun showing Penny the cord that would pull the bell and ring the kitchen below, although knowing she would not.

Penny walked around the room, peeking out the windows and taking in the extravagant furnishings, the four-poster bed and the clawfoot tub in the bathroom. At some point, a shower had been added in one corner of the bathroom, just as in Elizabeth's room. It was quite elegant, and Penny had never stayed anyplace so luxurious. "It is beautiful," she said.

Elizabeth stood with her arms crossed. "Yes, it is. If Charles wasn't such an ogre, I could probably get used to it." She walked across the room to leave. "I'm just down the hall, first door on the left. Just knock when you're ready, and we'll go down together." Elizabeth also needed to change and get ready for dinner. She would keep it casual as she knew Penny would.

Dinner was uneventful. Charles was polite but angry underneath his smile. He was most upset at the fact that Penny had rented a car rather than letting him have her picked up. With Penny and Elizabeth having a vehicle, he couldn't control where they went or who they visited. It was unnerving. As soon as the dinner dishes were cleared, he wiped his mouth with one of the good napkins that Elizabeth had insisted they use, pushed back his chair with a scrape on the wood floor that echoed loudly in the expansive room, and bid them goodnight. It was early, but he insisted that he had some work to finish up in his room, then an early morning meeting. He apologized insincerely to Penny for not being able to show her around during her visit.

Charles knew that even if he was available, he would not be welcome or invited on their outings, wishing now that he'd made some kind of plan to have them followed. Oh well, it was just three days. They wouldn't get much done in that short amount of time.

~~*~~

The next morning, Elizabeth sat at the big table finishing her eggs when Penny shuffled sleepily into the room.

"Shit, this is the longest table I've ever seen. Where do I sit?"

Faye heard this and jumped to bring a chair over next to Elizabeth on the corner at her end of the table. Penny sat rubbing her eyes.

"Tea, ma'am?" came a voice from behind.

Penny startled, turning to see Faye behind her. "Do you serve coffee here?" Penny asked, hoping that was the case. She really wasn't a tea drinker.

"Yes of course, ma'am. Do you take cream or sugar or both?"

Faye was doing her job, but something about it annoyed Penny. She looked at Elizabeth. "Bring both, please. I'll decide once I taste the coffee. Is that okay?" She smiled at Faye, then turned to Elizabeth. "I haven't slept that hard since before I had Brandon." He was her youngest, now five. "Sorry, I don't mean to seem snotty, but I love my coffee at home so I didn't know how to answer her. And I'm not used to having *servants*."

"Don't worry, sis, the coffee here is good. You'll likely only need cream. She'll be back to ask you for your breakfast order so don't be caught off guard." Elizabeth laughed as she scooped up the last of her soft-boiled egg with a piece of toast.

"But I don't see a menu," Penny said, looking around.

"It is pretty much whatever you desire," Elizabeth said, looking toward the kitchen. "Nettie is usually fully prepared for whatever. Eggs, pancakes, oatmeal, bacon. You name it."

"Damn, Elizabeth, and you aren't prepared to give up your sanity for this life?" Penny was, of course, joking and not fully awake, but Elizabeth raised a finger to her lips. The coffee was set in front of her within minutes, and Faye stood, as Elizabeth told her would be the case, almost at attention, waiting for Penny to let her know what she might want for breakfast.

Penny gave a wave in the air. "Can we just have a moment?" she said over her shoulder to Faye as she poured cream in her coffee. Faye gave a nod and a half-curtsey and returned to the kitchen.

Elizabeth already had a plan for the day, but she couldn't tell Penny the full details just yet. Knowing that she was going to have wheels for the next few days, Elizabeth had set up a heavy schedule for the two of them right out of the gate, hoping Penny wouldn't be offended. It would be anything but a relaxing vacation, that was for sure. Once they got off the property and could talk freely, Elizabeth was sure she could convince Penny that the itinerary was much needed and important for ensuring Elizabeth's well-being during this insane experience she called her marriage. She wanted to talk about it but could not while they were within earshot of Faye.

She'd already let William know that his museum was the first stop. Elizabeth had also phoned the nursing facility. Complements of Holden, she had the name, number, and address of Lillian's current home and had used his telephone to let them know they would be picking Lillian up for lunch. The afternoon was open so far as town was concerned, but as a third horse had arrived just the day before, Elizabeth thought that an afternoon ride in the pasture might be in order.

"Before we leave for the day, we'll stop by the barn and let Holden know we might want to ride this afternoon," Elizabeth said, speaking her thoughts out loud.

"What are you saying, Elizabeth? I am going to ride a horse today?" Penny took a sip of her coffee, clearing the cobwebs, wishing she could speak freely with her sister.

"Yes, um, I'm sorry. I was thinking through the day in my head. Sorry I haven't apprised you of today's schedule. Well, maybe we will ride, if we have time. Have some breakfast, and we'll talk in my room," Elizabeth said quietly as she nodded to Faye, who had just approached the table again. Penny ordered scrambled eggs and bacon with a side of hash browns off the top of her head. Faye nodded and walked away, looking back at the two of them. They were up to something that she was sure she wouldn't be able to report to Mr. Freeman, as softly as they were talking.

"So really, just like that? No menu, you just give your order and don't even have to snap your fingers to make the magic happen?" Penny was smiling now. The caffeine was kicking in, and her sense of humor was returning.

"This is pretty much how it works," Elizabeth replied. "Every once in a while, we're out of something, but then it goes on the list, and Gwendolyn goes to town and stocks up."

"Unreal," Penny said, looking around the home. The long table was ridiculous, but she was sure it had its place at one point in history. She was happy now, though, to be sitting closer to her sister so they could whisper. "So, what are we doing today?"

Elizabeth looked over her shoulder, pointing with her eyes and a nod of her chin toward the kitchen door. "Finish eating, and we'll get out of here."

~~*~~

Elizabeth and Penny came out dressed and ready for the day. The red sedan still sat by the front door—Penny had the keys so Branson couldn't move it—Elizabeth being sure that this had annoyed Charles to no end. She placed a large shopping bag and her purse into the vehicle. Although they had no intention of shopping, really, they'd have to come back with *something* to justify the hours they would spend in town.

"Before we leave, we have to talk to Holden," Elizabeth said. "Come with me."

The two sisters walked over to the barn where Holden had been somewhat expecting them. The new horse was settling in, and her whinnying could be heard from outside the door as they approached. Holden had tied her reins to a post to groom her. He stood talking to her quietly, brushing her gently.

Holden turned when he saw the sisters' shadows moving underneath the mare. Not to upset her, he walked away slowly, signaling to Elizabeth to stand still. He greeted them at the door in almost a whisper. "She's settling in nicely," he said to Elizabeth. Then to Penny, "Hi, welcome to Noble Oak Plantation. I'm so happy that you could come and visit." He reached out his hand, Elizabeth noting that Penny was so enamored with Holden that she put out her hand but forgot to shake.

Holden addressed Elizabeth, "Let me introduce you to Sonnet. She's a three-year-old with pretty good manners. She's hasn't been ridden enough, but you can handle her, Elizabeth. Your sister can ride Bella."

At the mention of her name, Bella whinnied and extended her head over the top of her stall. Elizabeth walked over and scratched Bella's nose, giving her a peck on the cheek. "This is my girl," she said as Penny reached up to stroke her mane.

"And this is Jack," Holden said. Jack would forever be the one in charge in this stable, and he knew it. He stomped his foot when Holden walked to the gate, hoping it was time to be released for a ride. Penny watched Holden stroke him from his brow to his nostrils, calming Jack like he calmed Elizabeth when she was frustrated. He had the touch.

Penny stared at Holden's tight jeans and even tighter knit shirt that outlined his muscles as he stroked his horse, imagining what her sister must have to endure having this oh-so-attractive temptation living on the property.

"Holden, we need to be going," Elizabeth said. "We have an appointment with William, and then we're taking Lillian to lunch."

Holden's eyes widened. Elizabeth knew exactly what she was doing, and he was happy to see that she was taking advantage of the opportunity of having a vehicle at her disposal. "Perfect," he replied. "When you return, come get me if you have time to ride, and I'll saddle the horses up."

~~*~~

Penny pulled into the driveway for the plantation house still known as Stately Oaks but that was now broadly recognized as a museum, nudging the rental car in between two tour buses. She and Elizabeth got out and approached the steps next to the sign that indicated a check-in point. William had been expecting their arrival and came out to greet them.

"Ladies, welcome. Elizabeth, I am so very happy that you've come, finally. I have so much to show you." After introducing himself to Penny, William led them up the steps through a side entry and directly into the grand foyer where governors and a President were once welcomed. "Let's get started."

William took them from room to room, citing the history of each decade and who in his family ruled over the slaves, who ran the plantation, and how they had narrowly escaped ruin when the war ended and they no longer had the income from trading slaves.

For Elizabeth, the purpose of the visit was not as much to entertain Penny but to get the "Author Unknown" book back to William in exchange for another that Holden mentioned was waiting for her. Once the tour was concluded, William led them into his office. Elizabeth withdrew the book she had just finished from her large shopping bag, and—much to the surprise of her sister—handed it to William who set it on his desk then picked up another, larger book, leather bound with frayed edges much like John Clayton's original ledger. He placed it into Elizabeth's outstretched hands. She was ecstatic and could barely contain her excitement. She placed the book into her bag, then folded it carefully and held it close to her chest as if for protection. Penny turned to study the wall of books across the room. Clearly there was something clandestine transpiring here, as there were no words exchanged in the process.

"Just read it. We'll talk soon," William said quietly when Penny was out of hearing. As soon as they were back in the car, Penny questioned her about the interaction. Elizabeth told her a bit of a white lie. "He's helping me with research on our house." In fact, the book that he'd given her was another journal of sorts, passed down within the Freeman family for decades, with each Charles Freeman adding bits about his time living on their plantation. It had been lost—to the family anyway—shortly after Juliet died, but not before her husband added comments that surely would have had him locked away for murder. How it came to be in William's possession was not something he would freely discuss. Only after letting Elizabeth borrow the first two books did William trust her enough to share this one, the most important of all, knowing it could end her marriage should her husband get wind of it being in her possession.

Elizabeth would never be able to admit how it was she came to know the extent to which the Freeman family had been involved in the atrocities of those days so many years ago. She had absolutely no proof that her husband's great-grandfather had murdered Adria's daughter, Juliet, only whispered rumors. William, however, seemed to feel that once she read the book, all that would change. There was more: The abuse didn't end with Juliet, and it wouldn't end with her unless she put a stop to it.

All of this was too much to spring upon her sister at this point, so Elizabeth explained away the exchange as if William ran a lending library of sorts, that he was just helping her with research on the plantation, the Claytons, and the region during slave times. She hadn't decided yet if she was going to show Penny the diary.

On the drive from the museum over to the nursing facility—Penny didn't like to call them "homes" as most were far from *homey* with their bright lights and horrid smells—Penny brought up Holden.

"How do you sleep at night?" Penny started, throwing Elizabeth off guard. She maneuvered the rental car down winding roads, enjoying the view of thick forests and manicured lawns stretching up to mansions perched on hilltops.

"What are you talking about?" Elizabeth asked, following Penny's gaze. "Living in this area amongst all of these rich white people?" Penny had worked as a community organizer in college, fighting against racism, understanding better than Elizabeth how much of a driving factor it remained for so many things in Georgia.

"I'm talking about Holden," Penny said, stifling a giggle. "My God, is he handsome. You ride with him every day?"

Elizabeth's face flushed, revealing feelings that she fought to contain but that burst forth uncontrollably now that Holden's name was mentioned. Penny looked over at her.

She knew her sister well enough to know that something was up. Elizabeth had a habit of making a strange, overt gesture with her mouth when she was trying hard to keep a secret, and Penny just caught it out of the corner of her eye. "Shut up. Don't tell me."

Penny nearly had to stop the car. Elizabeth hadn't answered so they drove on in silence.

Elizabeth couldn't answer. There was too much to tell. She didn't know where to start a conversation such as this, and she would not have time to finish it before they arrived at their destination—and they couldn't be late. Elizabeth pictured Lillian sitting in the lobby by the door with her purse in her lap, waiting.

The image of Lillian reminded Elizabeth of the time she was in Colorado at her grandfather's 100th birthday party. The event was held at the assisted living facility where he'd been for the previous five years. As she was wandering back from the bathroom to the room where the party was being held, she passed through the lobby, where a sweet-looking old lady who looked a lot like Lillian sat by the front door looking down at her hands, which were folded in her lap. Her face was pinched into fraught lines, and she looked as though she might cry.

Elizabeth had stopped to ask the woman if she was alright. The woman looked up at her, her eyes tearing. "My son. I think he forgot about me," she said, looking down at the ancient watch on her wrist, noting that it appeared not to be working, judging by the hands both pointing to twelve o'clock. It was nearly four in the afternoon.

"Why do you think that?" Elizabeth asked, noting the dainty watch face mounted on a faded red leather strap.

"He was supposed to be here over an hour ago. I was here visiting a friend, and he was supposed to come back and give me a ride home." The woman looked out the glass of the front doors, her eyes darting back and forth, scanning for his vehicle.

"I can give you a ride," Elizabeth told her. "Let me get my purse. I'll be right back."

Elizabeth returned to the party, which was winding down, and told an aunt that she'd be right back. The woman was standing by the door clutching her purse when Elizabeth returned. The two walked the short distance to her car, and Elizabeth helped her in, then came around and got into the driver's seat. "What is your address?" she asked the woman.

"It's just right down this road," she replied. "It will be easier for me to show you." Elizabeth started the car and pulled out of the parking lot in the direction of the woman's finger. She continued to guide Elizabeth down the road, telling her when to take a left, then another. And then a right. Soon it became apparent to Elizabeth that the woman was confused. Suddenly, it dawned on her that the woman had no idea where she was. After the woman made a comment about a corner store that didn't used to be there, she knew something was up. She pulled into a gas station, took the keys from the ignition and told the woman she'd be right back. She borrowed their phone and called the facility, reaching a staff nurse. She told her the story, describing the woman and that she had her in the car a few blocks away.

The nurse let out a loud sigh, telling Elizabeth that they had been looking everywhere for her. She told Elizabeth that the woman had dementia and often sat by the door telling the same story to passersby. Elizabeth felt awful. She had just kidnapped a nursing-home patient!

When she pulled up to the nursing home, two male nurses came through the front doors and assisted the old woman out of the car and back inside. Elizabeth parked her car and went back to the party. As she rounded the corner, she saw that the woman had joined her grandfather's birthday party and was now seated at a table with other residents, a piece of cake in front of her and a napkin tucked in her shirt. She smiled and waved as Elizabeth passed by.

"Elizabeth?" Penny looked over at her, worried.

"We're almost there. I'll tell you later. I promise," she replied quietly, looking forward, still deep in thought.

Chapter Twenty-Two: The Journal

August 30, 1859

It is so unbearably hot today. August is usually bad, but for some reason, I just can't stand it. The windows are all open, but there is no breeze. I hardly slept last night. The baby is kicking like crazy, trying to get comfortable I guess but which caused me to change positions hourly. I'm much bigger than I was before at this point. Hattie says she thinks it's a girl, but I don't know why.

I still have three months to go and can't imagine getting any bigger! I don't have much energy for the household, and John says not to worry about it. He says I should rest when I need to, and the help will make sure things get done.

Liam waves to me every morning from the stables when I take my walk around the plantation. John won't let me go far, and someone always has to go with me. His waves mean nothing to the help, other than he is just greeting the lady of the house as she strolls. To me, his waves are a signal that it won't be long, and I'll be in his arms again, just as I was last time after I healed from the birth of Little John.

We won't be calling him that much longer, as he's growing so fast! John sits next to me on the bed and pats my stomach, singing to his future sibling, calling out the name of a boy or a girl depending on his mood and making up stories. He has quite the vocabulary for a boy who only turned two years old just six months ago. So far, he's named the baby either Delilah or Buck, and I have no idea where he heard either of those names, although it had to be from one of the servants or a deliveryman. I think the fellow who delivers our ice is named Buck. John would never go for that!

John had to travel over to Louisiana again. Part of the trip was to greet an incoming ship that is bringing slaves. He'll look them over and decide which ones he wants to keep and which ones he will plan on selling. The other part of this trip is to meet with politicians and army men. The talk of war is everywhere now, and it breaks my heart. Even Rae says she hears the other slaves discussing it out in their quarters.

There is a boy that Rae has been meeting who also lives out there, and it appears he has grown quite sweet on her. I know this because he makes up excuses to run things over to the quarters for her or bring things back up to the house. I have Hattie make them extra food some nights and send it down, especially on days like today when I know they've worked a long day. He shows up at the kitchen door with a tin platter that has been scrubbed clean and will hand it to Rae. I see how he lets his hand linger on the plate just a second too long, just to feel her touch.

The days are lasting over twelve hours right now, but they are getting shorter, and by the time I have this baby, we'll be moving closer to winter. I dread the dark days in this big house. We can't keep enough candles burning to light the hallways and have to keep lighting them and then blowing them out in order to save them. There is always someone walking ahead of me lighting them, and then once I'm in my room, they walk back and blow them all out until they get to their rooms off the kitchen.

I think I hear Little John crying, so I must put this diary away safely now. I think I've found a very good place for it when the book is full. No one will ever find it I'm sure, not until the house is torn down or crumbles.

Elizabeth closed the diary, hearing footsteps in the hall. There was a light knock on her door. It was Penny. She slid the diary under a pillow where she would keep it until it went into the safe.

"Come in," Elizabeth responded.

Penny slowly pushed the door open.

"Good morning. Did you sleep well? Are you ready for breakfast? We can eat in here. It would be nice, actually," Elizabeth said as she moved to embrace her sister.

"Like a rock," Penny responded. "That bed is beyond comfortable. Should I go back and ring for coffee, or do they just know when to bring it?" She glanced at the door just as Faye arrived with a tray. "Unbelievable," she said under her breath.

Faye walked through the open door, pausing to acknowledge the women, noting Elizabeth's nod to the table. She set the tray down.

"We'll be having breakfast here," Elizabeth said to Faye. "If you can give my sister a few more minutes with her coffee, we'll be ready to order. Soon."

Faye nodded and left without saying a word, closing the door behind her.

Penny poured coffee into her cup from a tall silver pitcher, then added cream. She noted that Faye had not brought sugar, now knowing that she didn't use it.

"I must say, it is a different life," Penny said, stirring her coffee. She looked at Elizabeth with a quizzical expression. "Are you going to tell me?"

Elizabeth knew exactly what she meant, and yes, she would. It was time to tell Penny everything and quickly, starting with her first encounter with Holden at the bunkhouse and winding up with their daily horseback rides and kissing down by the stream. She stopped short of telling Penny that the baby might be his. She just couldn't. Not yet. She wasn't even sure herself and wouldn't be until the baby was born. She kept her voice low and the story short, knowing that Faye would be returning, fearing an ear to the door.

When their breakfast arrived, Elizabeth had already switched the subject and was talking about books when Faye knocked. In between bites of eggs and French toast, Elizabeth spoke about the Claytons and the Freemans, including more of the historical aspects and leaving out the bit about Juliet being sired by Liam. Of this she was certain now, as it was even mentioned in the journal she read late into the previous night, the newest loan from William. So far, she was skimming over most of the day-to-day details, looking for the bits that she was most curious about, but this was the history of her husband's family going back over 100 years, so she would keep this one a bit longer and memorize every single page.

In the journal, Charles Freeman III described marrying Juliet Clayton in 1884 and mentions the scandal in more detail than

Elizabeth had ever previously heard. Although Adria Clayton attended their wedding—her husband had passed by then—rumors whispered behind her back echoed loudly in the hallways. Charles described a confrontation between Juliet's soon-to-be mother-in-law and his bride just days before the wedding, asking if the rumors were true. Charles wrote that Juliet, her red hair tied high in a bun and her blue eyes on fire, told his mother to ask Adria herself. "Why not," she said, "she might tell the truth!"

Charles continued, writing that later that night his mother did ask, but Adria did not answer, avoiding the query with a warm smile. Charles admired her ability to deflect the question that he'd heard thrown at her so many times, mostly in passing and in private, but sometimes occasionally in higher-profile situations. He also overheard whispers in hallways at banquets, as ladies did love to gossip. He wrote in the journal that he cared not by then, and that publicly he proclaimed to love Juliet above all else and that none of that mattered. Although as he wrote of his love for her on the following pages, he also admitted torturing her with his words, sometimes bringing her to her knees with false accusations of infidelity, suggesting she'd learned that from her mother, and he confessed to his journal that he would occasionally strike her.

"So, what's in the book that William sent home with you?" Penny asked, perhaps a little too loudly. Elizabeth's eyes darted to the door, which thankfully remained closed. Still, she put a finger to her lips. Elizabeth lowered her voice to just over a whisper.

"The book is a journal of sorts, one that has been passed down through the Freeman family since the mid-1800s," replied Elizabeth. "Each Charles Freeman contributed an entry, up until my husband's great-grandfather's last remarks. I don't know why it stopped there, perhaps William knows." Elizabeth stopped short of telling her sister that he described in detail the way he tortured his wife and that she died after birthing three children. "He mentioned a fire that consumed most of the plantation, the plantation that Charles just bought to rebuild."

Elizabeth would leave it at that. She decided it was time to change the subject and get on with their day. "Is there anything you would like to do today? Can I take you on a walk?" Elizabeth's eyes twinkled, also something Penny had not seen since she'd arrived—except of course when she was close to Holden.

"That would be a fabulous idea," Penny said, beginning to pick up the plates.

"Oh no, we don't have to bus our dishes," Elizabeth said to her sister.

Penny put the plates down, shaking her head.

The bunkhouse door was open when they arrived. Elizabeth correctly guessed that Holden anticipated her giving her sister a tour and had left it unlocked for them. Penny let out a low "wow" as she walked through the door and then across the living room, touching the chairs and the old earthen pottery and running her hands across the quilt, almost exactly as Elizabeth had done the first time she was in the bunkhouse.

"This is pretty amazing," Penny said. "How old is this stuff?"

"If I had to guess, I would say most of it is at least 100 years old but probably older. The quilt is newer, of course. Holden said he found it in a trunk full of bedding that held a few that were in pretty good shape, so he brought this one here and put it on the bed to give the place a cleaner look. The mice had ravaged the last one."

Penny was checking out the kitchen counter, admiring all the old dishes and cast iron, taking the lid off the Dutch oven and peering inside. "This is the real deal, sis, all of it. Like a museum."

"Yes, it is, and we've decided to keep it just this way. No one will live here, and I don't think we plan on turning this place into a museum such as William has, so most likely you are among only a handful of people who may ever see it—as long as Charles owns this place." Elizabeth thought about the generations of Claytons who had lived here and wondered how it was that they'd ever lost the property. The crash was horrible for the family, but surely someone from the family could have come to save it sooner. Lucky for her—and for Charles and their soon-to-be heir—that didn't happen. She thought about Lillian and their lovely lunch just the day before, realizing they'd never spoken about the bunkhouse.

~~*~~

Lillian had been waiting, just as Elizabeth knew she would be. She stood up when she saw the red car arrive at the entrance. An orderly escorted her to the car, leaning in and asking Elizabeth to identify herself—a far cry from the way she'd been able to easily take the woman out of the facility in Colorado. This time, she'd even had to give him a picture ID, which he copied and returned to her. She was actually glad for this because knowing Lillian was safe made her feel better.

Their lunch had been brief. With Penny there Lillian was hesitant to go deep into any conversation that might turn to gossip or accusations about Elizabeth's husband or his family. They could save that for another time. Elizabeth mentioned that she and Penny had toured William's family plantation.

"Oh, I bet he had a lot to say about us Claytons," she'd said jokingly. "I hear tell we were all rivals—our family and his, as well as the Freemans."

"He was very kind," Elizabeth replied, figuring she'd not mention any of the books, not yet. Elizabeth put cash on the check—she did not use the credit card so as not to add the restaurant to the trail of her day in town—noting Lillian was staring out the window deep in thought.

"We should do this again soon," Lillian said wistfully as the waiter returned with the change, her gaze still fixed on something outside. "I like this place." Although she'd not come close to finishing her meal, it was such a step up from what was served where she lived.

"Please, let's do. I'd like that. I'll call you soon. I promise." Elizabeth patted her hand softly, then pushed her chair back, stood, and helped Lillian to her feet. She steadied Lillian while placing her purse on an outstretched arm, then led her outside to the car.

She had wanted to make contact with Lillian so that she knew where she was and would make a plan to see her again, soon, once Penny left. It was easier this time because Penny had a car. It would be more difficult later, but she would find a way. They had dropped Lillian off at the door, where the same orderly welcomed her inside, giving Elizabeth and Penny a wave and a thumbs-up.

~~*~~

Penny had inspected every room of the cabin and was still admiring the old hand-forged curtain rods when Elizabeth spoke. "Ready? So much more to see," she said with a wink. "Let's go."

She led Penny back to the path that circled the lake, past the bench where she and Holden had kissed, then they took the fork that led down to the old cabin. They heard tapping as they walked up on the porch. Opening the door, Elizabeth saw Holden with a hammer in one hand, trying to balance a shelf against the wall with the other, and cursing through a mouthfull of nails. She ran to help him.

"Here, let me help you with that," Elizabeth said as she held the shelf steady, their sides touching. Holden tacked the shelf up enough that it would stay put. He could finish securing it later. He took a step back and noticed Penny standing in the doorway watching them, arms folded across her chest, a curious smile on her face.

"Thank you," he said to Elizabeth, turning to Penny. "Welcome to the old cabin in the woods that no one knows about—except you now too." He smiled and winked at Elizabeth.

Penny's eyes shifted to the wrought iron bed tucked into one corner, another fresh quilt draped across it with pillows on top. *So inviting,* she thought, looking from Elizabeth to Holden. The chemistry was palpable, hot. Elizabeth had already shared bits and pieces about their affair, coming clean when Penny had pried. As much as Penny wanted to scold her about the chances she was taking that could end her marriage—and possibly risk her parental rights once the baby was born—she couldn't deny that the heat these two gave off when they were in the same room together was a blast furnace compared to the small fire that sputtered when Charles was in the room.

Penny walked through the cabin in the same way she'd just explored the bunkhouse, touching everything, marveling over the perfection—the old wood cookstove that also heated the place in the winter, the knives that had been forged by someone long ago, *probably a slave,* she thought, frowning. The wood floors were sturdy, although they creaked just a bit as she walked.

"This place is so cool," Penny said. "I think I like it better than the bunkhouse, probably because it is tucked back here in the woods, so private. Who knows what went on here a hundred years ago, right?"

Elizabeth and Holden exchanged knowing looks. Penny knew she wasn't going to receive an answer.

"Why don't I show you the old slaves' quarters?" Holden asked. "Then after lunch, we can saddle up the ponies and go for a ride."

They'd returned from town the previous day too late for a ride, so the two sisters exchanged a glance, Penny giving him a thumbs-up. "Sounds like a plan," she added.

Elizabeth and Penny followed him down the path, which cut over to the old building that housed so many during the plantation's busy times. Penny could not help but stare at him as they walked—so muscular, the tight jeans, pure perfection.

The workers had completed most of the construction and had just a few cleanup items to check off the list. They'd left the door unlocked, planning to return the next morning to install carpet, which had disgusted Elizabeth. She wanted to go to Charles and make a plea for the old wood-planked flooring to be refinished, until she found out that Dehlia had insisted.

The newly installed bathroom was modern but not so much that it took away from the feel of the old place. The kitchen had running water for the first time since its construction more than 100 years prior. Elizabeth turned on the faucet, which produced a forceful stream.

"Dehlia will love it," Elizabeth said, looking at Holden, who knew that she was dreading her mother-in-law's arrival.

"Wait," Penny said. "Are you talking about Charles's mother, Dehlia, who I met at the wedding?"

"Yes," Elizabeth said, dropping her head. She had not yet mentioned this to her sister. "She's moving in sometime soon, when this place is done."

"I'm sorry," Penny said. "She was sort of a bitch to me at the wedding."

Holden let out a laugh. "I'm glad we're all on the same page about that."

"We should get going," Elizabeth responded, locking eyes with Holden, who returned the look, managing to muster a tight grin. He knew how much Elizabeth was dreading her mother-in-law's arrival and felt for her.

Elizabeth led Penny back to the rear of the house while Holden took the fork in the path that would take him to the stables.

"We'll go in the back door and surprise Nettie," Elizabeth said.

When they entered, Nettie was in her usual mode, stirring something on the stove, humming a tune, deep inside her own world. She startled when she heard the door slam although Elizabeth had tried to catch it.

"Where you two been?" Nettie asked. "Mr. Freeman been askin' 'bout you. He's in the dining room waitin' for his lunch. He don' come home early he said, to visit with Miss Penny here and have some lunch, then he said he gon' go back to town. He has a late meetin'."

I bet he does, Elizabeth thought, wondering if that meant he was not coming home. "We've just been on a walk around the lake," Elizabeth offered, not wanting to mention the bunkhouse tour and certainly not the cabin. "We'll join him then, Nettie. Thank you."

Elizabeth took Penny's hand and led her through the door to the dining room, where their place settings sat waiting. She led Penny to the chair that sat halfway between each end of the long table. It was awkward. Elizabeth wished for a different table but knew that Charles would never part with this one. Penny sat looking at Charles, who smiled a weak smile, his hands clasped together, waiting for his wife to take her seat.

"I take it you two are having a good time exploring the plantation," he said, directing the question to Penny but then looking at Elizabeth with a somewhat threatening air.

"Yes," Penny said. "The place is delightful!" She didn't dare offer anything more, not knowing what she was supposed to say or not mention.

"We're going to ride this afternoon," Elizabeth started. "The new mare is ready. I've seen Holden working her in the pasture." Then she turned to Penny. "I'll let you ride Bella. She's as gentle as they come."

Charles stirred at this remark. "You, Elizabeth, should ride Bella. We don't know how this new mare is going to take to a stranger on her back."

Elizabeth stiffened. She didn't want to fight in front of her sister.

"I just said," she started, "I've seen Holden working with her in the pasture. She is sweet and calm and poses no threat. I'm sure you know that about her because you decided to buy her and bring her here." Elizabeth was challenging Charles in a way that infuriated him since he couldn't continue to banter without appearing to be an asshole.

Penny shifted uncomfortably in her seat. "I'll ride either one of them if it helps. I rode much more than Elizabeth when we were growing up. Heck, put me on Jack!"

The mention of Jack stirred something in Charles. That was the horse that had thrown him when he first brought him home.

"I tell you what, why don't you cancel your ride this afternoon, and I'll talk to Holden first about the new girl's behavior. I forget her name."

"No, Charles, we're not going to cancel our ride, and her name is Sonnet. And she is beautiful." Elizabeth was embarrassed, humiliated, and angry, but she held her composure, smiling at Charles, defying the challenge.

The food came just then, injecting a welcome distraction. They ate the rest of their meal mostly in silence, with Elizabeth starting a conversation here and there that would dwindle and die because talking would involve looking at each other. Penny was embarrassed, Elizabeth was angry, and Charles didn't give a shit. When he finished eating, he wiped his mouth with his napkin and stood, again scraping the chair on the tile, which annoyed Elizabeth and gave her goosebumps.

"So lovely to see you again, Penny. Perhaps before you leave we can take a tour of the plantation next door. They've turned it into a museum so I hear, and I've promised William, one of the descendants of the original family, that we would soon come and visit." He turned to Elizabeth, who was looking at Penny, now shifting uncomfortably at the mention of Charles taking them to visit William.

"I have a late meeting, darling. I'm not sure what time I will be home. Nettie is aware, so you two enjoy your evening!"

With that, he was off; it was like a vacuum sucked the tension out of the air with his departure. Both Elizabeth and Penny inhaled deeply and blew out their breath in unison.

Penny noted the way Charles had called her *'darling'*—so trite and almost condescending—it made her skin crawl.

Faye came to the table and stood waiting for instructions. Elizabeth asked her to bring a bottle of white wine and two glasses, which arrived promptly. Penny picked up her chair and moved it down to be closer to her sister. After following Penny with her lunch plate and silverware, as Penny had eaten only half of her lunch, Faye set a glass in front of Elizabeth, pouring it only half full, then pouring another in front of Penny, filling it nearly to the brim. She'd witnessed the scene and knew that wine was in order for the sisters, although her job was to make sure Elizabeth did not drink much more. She retreated to the kitchen, leaving them to finish their lunch and enjoy their wine.

"Boy, is he ever an asshole," Penny said quietly. "I don't know how you do it." She immediately thought of Holden, wishing he was the guy her sister had married.

"He is difficult," Elizabeth offered apologetically, then changed the subject. "Would you like dessert before we go see the horses?"

Penny declined, and Elizabeth was glad, as she longed to get out to the barn. She felt more comfortable in the stables than she did in what was supposed to be her home. They finished their wine while making small talk about nothing, as everything they wanted to talk about had to be done in private, so it would have to wait.

Elizabeth, eager to get out to the stables, asked Penny, "Do you have any clothes that you can ride in or would you like to borrow some pants and a long shirt?"

"Actually, I think I may need to borrow something. I wasn't anticipating a gallop on a new mare, and my city clothes aren't exactly what I need to be wearing. Do you mind?"

The two stood up in unison, Penny resisting the urge to take her plate to the kitchen, and Elizabeth taking her hand instead.

"C'mon, let's go upstairs."

Once they got into Elizabeth's room and could talk freely, Penny let out a loud moan. "Damnit, Elizabeth. I don't know what to say."

Elizabeth looked at her with a smile. "Then don't say it, or say whatever you wish. It doesn't matter. I've made my bed, as they say."

"Yes, but what about Holden?" Penny asked.

"What about him?" Elizabeth repeated.

"What are you going to do? Once you have a baby, things will get so complicated." Penny knew what she wanted to say but didn't dare. If she was being honest, she would suggest Elizabeth leave right now. Take Holden with her. They could raise the baby somewhere together and live happily, although she knew that would never work. Charles would hunt them down and demand full custody. Instead, Penny thought of her sister having this baby—and maybe a couple more—while living in this prison. It both petrified her and made her sad for Elizabeth.

Penny took the clothes that Elizabeth laid out for her, choices all suitable for riding, and went to her room to change. Elizabeth had given her a pair of boots as well—thank goodness they wore the same size—for which she was glad because her city shoes wouldn't hold up well in stirrups.

~~*~~

The day was hot and humid, but Holden had the horses tied up outside in the shade not far from the barn, saddled and ready to go. Sonnet seemed to be fitting in nicely with the others; they watched as she stood quietly munching on a mouthful of grass, flicking flies away with her tail. They noticed Holden sitting on a stump next to Jack, who kept nuzzling him. Jack was ready to go. Jack knocked off his hat, and when he bent over to pick it up, nudged his butt, causing him to lose his balance and fall off the stump. The girls started laughing. Holden looked up to see them walking across the pasture.

"I guess we know who is the boss around here," Elizabeth said as she approached.

"Yep, we do, don't we," Holden replied, grinning sheepishly, brushing the grass off his hat.

"You look like a real cowboy," Penny said, staring at his blue eyes. "Didn't know they made them here in Georgia."

"Once upon a time, I lived in Montana," Holden replied, surprising Elizabeth. He'd never told her that.

"Well, I'm certainly glad you found your way to the Deep South," Elizabeth said. The two exchanged a tell-all moment that had Penny's heart fluttering. Now that her suspicions had been confirmed and Elizabeth had come clean about their affair, she looked at Holden differently. She wanted the best for her sister, and no matter how much money Charles had, he wasn't the one for her. Now Holden here, he was another story.

Holden helped Penny up onto Bella, still a little concerned that since Sonnet was new to the herd, she might be a little nervous. Elizabeth could handle her though, no problem, he was quite sure, but he held the reins as Elizabeth put her right boot in the stirrup and heaved herself up. He resisted lending a hand to Elizabeth's butt as he normally did. They headed out toward the stream, staying close to the trees for shade with Jack in the lead and Penny in the middle. Elizabeth hung back a little bit, working with Sonnet, turning her left and right, talking to her. So far Elizabeth noted Sonnet had a sweet disposition and a willingness to be reined.

Elizabeth had Sonnet do a complete circle, returning to the trail to follow Bella, when suddenly from out of the brush one of the boars, much larger than the mama she had encountered on the lake trail, sprang from the bushes and crossed the path. Sonnet bolted and reared. Elizabeth, used to Bella's calm nature, was not holding the reins tightly. She lost her grip and slid right off the back, landing with a thud on the ground. Holden heard the commotion and turned to see Elizabeth sitting, stunned, but apparently unharmed. He wheeled around and rode quickly back to her, noting Sonnet standing quietly, head down again seeking a bite of grass, the boar having returned to the bushes.

Elizabeth was wiping herself off as Holden slid off Jack and dropped the reins. He ran to Elizabeth and knelt down.

"Are you hurt?" His first concern was for her, his second for the baby. Charles's words rang in his head. Holden would never be forgiven if something happened to Charles's child.

"I'm alright," she said. "It was one of those damn boars. Sonnet just reared. I should have been paying more attention."

Holden picked her up gently, then brought her in, wrapping his arms around her. She put her head on his chest and began to cry—not because she was hurt, but that she was afraid Charles would find out. She was sure the baby would be fine.

"Please don't let Charles find out. Please."

"Of course not, I won't tell a soul." Holden leaned down and kissed her on the forehead.

Penny sat on Bella, taking in the whole scene, glad her sister wasn't hurt, amazed at the tenderness Holden displayed toward Elizabeth. He was in love with her; there was no doubt. Penny was also sure that the feeling was mutual.

~~*~~

Elizabeth caught Faye's attention as they returned to the house, asking her to go up and draw a lukewarm bath then continuing on to the kitchen to see what was for dinner. Penny raised her eyebrows. This was included in the price of admission, this "draw me a bath thing." Again, unbelievable.

Elizabeth was starving as usual. Nettie poured them both a tall glass of lemonade. Elizabeth downed hers quickly as Nettie stood watching her. "You okay, Miss Elizabeth?" she asked as she refilled her glass.

"Yes, Nettie. I'm fine. It is just so hot out today. I'm going to my room to have a bath and take a nap. What's for dinner?"

"Mr. Freeman asked for roast chicken, so I had Gwendolyn pick up a fresh one from down the road. I'll fix some greens and mashed potatoes. You want anythin' else?" Nettie asked then turned to Penny. "What about you, big sistuh? Is there anything you have a cravin' fo?"

Penny shook her head. "I'm good. I'm just happy to be here."

"Okay, then you two relax. Here's a plate of cookies for each of you. I'll see you around five." Nettie set a plate of homemade peanut butter cookies in front of each of them.

Elizabeth and Penny took their cookies and lemonade and headed up the stairs. Penny turned to look at Elizabeth. She truly hoped she was okay. That was quite a hard landing.

"Are you okay?" she whispered, happily recalling that Charles might not join them for dinner.

"I don't know," Elizabeth replied, standing in front of her bedroom door. "I think so."

Penny gave her a peck on the cheek, turned, and walked down the hallway to her room.

Elizabeth locked her door and stripped off her clothes. She went to the mirror, noting that although everyone said she wasn't showing yet, she could see it. The bulge just below her navel was beginning to appear, only noticeable when she was nude. She rubbed her belly.

"I'm sorry, little one. I should have been more careful. It won't happen again." She noticed a bruise forming on one of her butt cheeks and that she had a scrape on her elbow. Charles would never see the bruise, and she would wear light long sleeves no matter how hot it was until the scrape healed, thinking that she should have a story prepared, though, just in case.

It certainly could have been worse. She was glad that Sonnet had the disposition to just rear and calm, and not take off across the pasture. Holden would have had to race to get her back, and the incident would have been noticed by someone. Elizabeth would be in big trouble right now. Someone would have called Charles, and instead of sliding into the water that had cooled to a perfect temperature, she would surely be taking a verbal beating—quietly of course with Penny here—as Charles knew well enough not to raise his voice to his wife with others in the house. The water felt amazing, and she rested until she felt sleepy. She washed her wound, dunked her head under water to wet her hair, toweled off, then wrapped her head in a second towel and went straight to her bed naked. She crawled under a sheet and laid her head on a pillow, falling fast asleep.

Elizabeth woke to a tapping on her door. "Sis, it's me."

Elizabeth got out of bed, taking the towel off her head and wrapping it around her torso as she walked to the door to unlock it. "Come in," she said as she walked back to her dresser to find clean clothes.

Penny entered and shut the door behind her. "How are you doing? Are you going to tell Charles?"

"Oh, hell no," Elizabeth replied. "I would be locked in my ivory tower for the rest of my pregnancy if he found out."

Elizabeth dressed quickly while Penny watched. She envied Elizabeth's slim body, much like hers had been before having children. She saw the bruise. "You have a bruise," she said.

"I know. I saw it. Also scraped my elbow." Elizabeth held up her arm to show Penny, then put on the lightest long-sleeved shirt that she had. "I'll keep it covered for a few days, then think of a story to tell Charles if he sees it." She rolled up the sleeves as much as she could without letting it show. *I'll have to make sure no one else sees it and rats me out,* she thought. She finished dressing then checked herself in the full-length mirror, noting that her glass of lemonade was still on the table. "How long did I sleep?" Elizabeth asked Penny.

"I don't know. When did you lie down?" Penny responded with a laugh.

Elizabeth sat down with her lemonade. The ice was gone, but the glass was still cold to the touch, so she knew she had not slept that long. "I want to show you something," she said to Penny. She'd decided to show her the diary. The one person she could trust was her sister—well, Penny *and* Holden. She hadn't told him about it either, but she would, soon. She went to the safe and spun the dial back and forth, then opened the door and pulled out the leather-bound book. She handed it to Penny, who studied the cover.

"This is your house," Penny said, noting the image of the plantation house on the cover. "What is this?" she asked as she opened the book to the middle, studying the long cursive writing that filled every page.

"It is the diary of a woman who lived here more than a hundred years ago, Adria Clayton," Elizabeth said. "I found it when Charles was renovating the master bedroom. She had hidden it behind a baseboard after she filled all the pages. She must have pried the board off, hid the diary, then tacked it back up. I'm not sure. But I was up there in his room checking things out after the workers removed the baseboards to install the new carpet, and there it was, stuffed up in the framing."

"Does anyone else know about this?" Penny asked.

"Only you at this point. I'm going to tell Holden."

"Wow," Penny said, running her hands over the leather. "This is so special. What have you learned?"

"Nothing earth-shattering yet. So far it's just been about her daily life and one baby, and she's expecting."

"Like you," Penny said. "Can you read some to me?"

"Sure," Elizabeth said and motioned for Penny to sit down next to her.

November 15, 1859

The baby has come early! I truly thought it would be a couple more weeks, but here she is, Delilah Rose. She is beautiful and has a full head of dark hair like my husband. Little John has my hair, much lighter and wavy. Hers is dark and straight. She is quiet so far, not as demanding as Little John was. She keeps me busy during the day as she likes to eat, but there's no crying unless she needs to be changed.

This birth was much easier, and for that I'm grateful. It is going to take some work, but I will be back to my normal weight soon. With all the chores that need doing around here, it won't be hard. Yes, I have servants for the hard stuff, like boiling the wash and hanging the wet sheets on the line, but I do keep busy, all day sometimes. When I'm not feeding Delilah, I am running up and down the stairs giving orders. Now that it is growing cool again, all the fireplaces need to be stocked with wood, and we're making candles out in the barn. John thinks it is going to be a cold winter and is having me stock up.

Thanksgiving will be here soon. John's brother, his wife Anabelle, and their children will travel over to stay with us for the holiday. They only live a half-day's drive away with a full team pulling the carriage, and his wife is pregnant with their fourth, but they'll come and stay a few days. It will be fun to have the house full, and the children will enjoy Little John and the new baby.

John's brother is nicer than my husband. I don't know if it is because he doesn't have the responsibility of the plantation or what. They live on the other side of Atlanta, in a little town called Marietta. He is a banker, so I imagine it is a fairly easy job, although I would have no idea.

Marietta is a bustling town but not as busy as Atlanta. I was there once. John let me go see my sister-in-law, and he had Liam drive me in the buggy. It was the first time we'd been alone for so long, and it was hard not to want to stop every hour along the way and lie with him in the shade. They had Liam stay in the house with us and gave him a room just down the hall from me. One night real late, he tapped on my door, and when I opened it, he kissed me long and hard, then ran back to his room in his stocking feet. Oh, the trouble we would have been in if we'd been caught!

Elizabeth closed the book, not finishing the entry. "What do you think?" she asked.

"Good stuff," Penny replied. "Reminds me of you."

"How so?" Elizabeth asked.

"You know, pregnant, in love with someone other than her husband, who is also mean."

Elizabeth picked up the book, taking it to the safe. "We should go down for dinner, speaking of mean husbands. He hates it when I'm late to the dinner table."

"Of course, he does." Penny would later muse that Charles hadn't shown up at all.

~~*~~

Once Penny and Elizabeth both returned to their rooms for the night, Elizabeth pulled out the Freeman family journal. She skipped to the end, where in Charles III's own handwriting he described his wife going into a deep depression after their third child. He knew it was common, he wrote, but she was moody, and even after she healed from the birth, she wouldn't let him near her. He described going to town to take a whore now and then, and in his own words described wanting to kill her and the various ways that might take place. So as not to arouse suspicion, he would have to make it look like an accident. Or a suicide, he thought, although not many women did that unless they were really crazy.

Juliet wasn't crazy, he wrote. She was just demanding. She had a bit of a temper that could flair, and it did, often. Some people told him it came along with red hair, and he should be careful. He described sending her to visit her mother at Noble Oak Plantation. He wrote about Adria's passing. Then his notes became cryptic, with angry words filling some pages, ranting and rambling about Juliet's state of mind, admitting that he was probably the cause of her angst. Then his last words, written in a shaky handwriting were: "I think I've killed her."

Chapter Twenty-Three: Penny

Penny stayed almost a week. After assessing Elizabeth's situation and state of mind, she extended her stay another two days. Charles was growing tired of her, and she despised him more than ever. She was torn. She wanted to get back to her children, but she realized how much her sister needed her.

There had been no indication that the fall from the horse harmed the baby. Elizabeth hadn't miscarried, or she would have known, and so they continued to ride every afternoon. Elizabeth rode Bella, and Penny took Sonnet. One day, they went out with the two mares and left Holden behind. He promised not to tell, of course. Penny's last day, she begged off, claiming she wanted to spend some time in their library perusing books. She really wanted to give Elizabeth and Holden some private time.

During the past few days, Elizabeth had opened up to Penny and shared more about the families and the history of both plantations, mostly what she learned from the books that William had loaned her. Elizabeth and Penny read some more of Adria's diary together as well as some parts of the Freeman family journal. Those men had a history of being cruel—not only to their slaves but in business and also to their wives. As Elizabeth and Penny read the things the men admitted, intending their words to be for no one other than the next Charles Freeman, they realized the journal was a how-to manual on how to mistreat people and make lots of money in the process. Elizabeth had not shown Penny the last entry in the journal. She had questions about that entry, why it was the last one, where the journal went after that, as well as how William came to have it in his possession. She would make it her mission to take the book back to William herself, and soon. She had so many questions that she wanted to ask William in private.

There were entries about slaves traded and business deals both successful and sour. The Freeman men journaled quite a bit about the whores they slept with. In a case where sleeping with a particular one of them became a regular thing, the description was changed from "whore" to "mistress."

Every night, Penny called her husband and children from the phone in the hallway. It was inconvenient, standing at the phone kiosk for so long, so Elizabeth asked Faye to bring a chair and leave it there for the duration of her stay. It was the only phone now in the house and by no means private—Charles would have it no other way.

Penny's husband, Harold, was getting a lot done at home, and Penny's in-laws were having a good time with the children, so extending her visit had not been an issue. So far, the children had been to the zoo and the botanical gardens with their grandparents, squealing with delight when they described the elephants and giraffes and how they both fed themselves. They told Penny that they had gone swimming almost every day, and their grandpa had made homemade ice cream. They always said they missed her, but they were always giggling at the same time, which was a good thing.

On the last day of Penny's visit, after Charles had left for the office, Elizabeth snuck into Holden's cabin to call William and then Lillian. Elizabeth needed to take the book back to William, and then she wanted to surprise Lillian with another lunch date while she still had access to a vehicle. The attendant at the nursing home who answered the call thought it would be a great idea and offered to make sure Lillian was ready, using a different excuse for an outing.

While Elizabeth and Penny were in Elizabeth's room planning the day, which she had not asked Charles about in advance—nor did she intend to—Elizabeth came clean with one more thing. They'd been lying on her bed, reading a few more excerpts from the journal.

"Penny, there is something else I want to tell you," Elizabeth said.

Penny looked up from the book. "What is it?" From the look on Elizabeth's face, Penny could tell it was serious.

"Charles has a mistress in town. Her name is Marigold. Marigold MacArthur."

"What kind of a name is that? How did you find out?" Penny asked.

"Holden told me. I was having one of those days where I was feeling guilty about being in a sexual relationship with him. Then he told me everything, I guess to make me feel better. Apparently, Branson takes Charles to see her some days after work and waits, and Charles calls Nettie to say he has a late client meeting and won't be home for dinner." Elizabeth was looking down at her hands. She couldn't look at Penny. She didn't feel that she could be be mad about it, given the situation. "Sometimes he doesn't come home."

"Why does that not surprise me," Penny said. "According to the journal, all the males in the Freeman family have had lovers and mistresses. I wonder how many children they've had with them. Maybe lots, and if so, they probably don't have any idea. There could be dozens of heirs to the Freeman fortune running around with last names like Smith and Barkley." She was trying to add some humor to the situation, but it wasn't working. "Where did the name MacArthur come from?" she added.

"Holden thinks it was from some arranged marriage when she was young—perhaps one that was forced on her through a pregnancy. William might know. He seems to know not only the history, but the current gossip. Let's go see him," Elizabeth said. "I have so many questions."

Penny returned to her room to get the rental car keys while Elizabeth dressed and prepared for a reconnaissance mission disguised as a shopping trip. She stuffed the ledger into a cloth bag and went to the foyer, where she waited for Penny to pull the car around. Penny had never surrendered the car keys to Branson as requested because she didn't like the idea. As strange as it seemed, Penny was somewhat fearful, seeing what a prisoner her sister was.

Gwendolyn found Elizabeth standing there, quite apparently preparing to leave, knowing for certain that Charles had not been informed or asked.

"Gwendolyn, before you say anything, I know. I know you will call Charles as soon as we drive away, as those are your orders. Just tell him that Penny needed to go to town and get some souvenirs for the children. We won't be long."

~*~

Penny parked the rental car in the same spot as before, with William again greeting them and ushering them in through a side door. This time, they went directly to his office. As much as Penny wanted to stay and hear every juicy detail, she also wanted to explore the mansion a little more. She knew that Elizabeth would fill her in later.

"Do you mind if I give myself another little tour?" Penny asked William after Elizabeth stepped inside.

"Not at all!" William replied. "Make yourself at home. There are people around to answer any questions you may have." He turned to Elizabeth, smiling. "This won't take long."

Elizabeth pulled the ledger from the cloth bag that she'd used to smuggle it out of the house and laid it on William's desk.

"I don't know where to start," she said. "There is a lot here."

"I thought the same when I first read it," William said.

"How in the world did you come by this?" Elizabeth asked.

"Long story, but in short, I bought a box of books at an estate sale a while back without going through it first. This journal was in there. It didn't take me long to figure out what it was, and you are the first person other than me to see it. I've hesitated about going to your husband with the book, as there is so much that implicates so many in the family that he'd likely lock it up, and it would never been seen again."

Elizabeth agreed with that completely. Charles was averse— all the Freemans were—to any negative publicity or opinions coming out about them. If they had their way, they would rewrite history.

"The last entry…" Elizabeth trailed off, unable to complete the sentence.

"Yes, I know," William said. "It has been the subject of much speculation for decades, and now we have it here in his own writing."

"Why was his entry the last?" Elizabeth asked, referring to Charles Freeman III.

"I can only guess that it had something to do with the turmoil that surrounded Juliet's death and the fire that occurred shortly after. The upper floor was badly damaged, and Charles didn't have the money to fix it at the time. He took their children and went to live in New Orleans. He left a caretaker in charge, but there was still some looting that occurred.

"He made enough money in New Orleans to start fresh," William continued. "He remarried, as no one there knew of his being implicated in his wife's death, and he could continue to swear her hanging was a suicide. He eventually sold the plantation, and the new owners put a new roof on to protect what was still intact, although I don't believe the top floor, which incurred the most damage, was ever fixed. Your husband will know. I heard he just bought it." William stopped, having brought Elizabeth up to speed and answered her question with a long-winded response.

"Yes, I'm aware, although I've never seen it." She paused, looking directly at William. "What in the world does one do with two mansions?"

"Oh, I don't know. Fix it up and sell it, turn it into a museum, or…"

Elizabeth interrupted. "Or put his mistress in there and start a second family."

William's eyes grew wide.

"So, you know about Marigold?" he asked.

"Yes, I do now, and I'm not surprised that you do as well. Am I the only one who did not?" Elizabeth's eyes flared with anger.

"That, my dear, I cannot answer," William replied. "I only know because Branson is my niece's fiancé." He is quite a bit older than she is, but who am I to judge. Love has no boundaries."

That surprised Elizabeth. "So, you have a direct line into the workings of our household."

"Not everything," William replied. "But I know a lot." He paused, waiting to gauge Elizabeth's level of concern and if she became angry or curious. "I know you are pregnant. I know that Charles is abusive and keeps you locked up like a bird in a gilded cage. I understand that the only reason you are able to be here is because your sister is visiting and she rented a car. Should I go on?" He didn't want to offend her, but there was more she needed to know.

"Please," Elizabeth replied. She wanted to know everything.

"I know Charles had a baby with this mistress of his, Marigold, and that she sent the baby boy to live with her cousin in New York."

Elizabeth sat, stunned. Charles had a son. Therefore, he also already *had* an heir. But a bastard child would never have been welcomed or acknowledged by the Freemans, and likely no one else in the family knew.

"Where does she live, this Marigold?" Elizabeth asked.

"I don't know for sure," William replied. "But I know her apartment is on forty-fifth street by the museum, and that it is on the second floor, and she grows geraniums in window boxes. I know this because Branson told me—as he has spent hours outside her apartment waiting for Charles to finish his business. You're not thinking of contacting her, are you?"

"Of course not. I was just curious," Elizabeth replied, although her plans for the day had just changed.

"Anything more for me?" William asked.

"Anything more for me?" Elizabeth echoed with a smile.

"Yes, there is one more thing you should know," William said, then lowering his voice. "Lillian wrote the book."

Elizabeth shuddered as if a great wind had come and tried to knock her backward. "What did you say?"

"The book, 'Author Unknown,' she wrote it," he replied. But that was not all. He would save the best for another day, after Elizabeth and Lillian became better friends.

"I'm in shock, but I'm not surprised," Elizabeth said. "I've marveled every time we've been together at how much she remembers for someone who has dementia. But now, knowing the details she went into and the depth of information she uncovered while writing the book, if she's forgotten half of what she wrote about, she still likely knows more than anyone left in the Clayton family."

"That's just it, Elizabeth," William paused. "There is no one else—no other living Claytons except very distant relatives." He waited for Elizabeth's reaction. "And likely Charles and his brother—and their mother for that matter—are well aware of that."

"But what difference does it make?" Elizabeth asked, now even more curious about how much more William knew that he wasn't telling.

Just then Penny came to the door, almost out of breath. "Hi there, I'm back!" She walked through the door to William's office and took a seat next to Elizabeth. "Ready to go get Lillian?"

"Yes, I am. We were just finishing up. And, of course, I'm starving, so let's go get her!" Elizabeth turned to William. "It has been such a pleasure, William. I do hope to return soon."

"I'll understand if you do not," he replied with a tight, knowing smile.

~~*~~

Penny pulled the rental car out onto the highway, heading toward downtown, wondering silently about William's last remark. It gave her chills, but she shook it off. The exit to Lillian's care facility was coming up. Elizabeth had been quiet since leaving the museum. Penny pulled into the right lane to prepare for the exit.

"Keep going," Elizabeth said.

"What do you mean 'keep going'?" Penny slowed down.

"Don't take the exit. Keep going."

Penny sped up and got back into the middle lane. "Okay, do you want to tell me what this is about?"

"We're going to find Marigold," Elizabeth said, looking over at Penny, who was driving with fierce determination, both hands on the wheel. Penny wasn't used to driving in this much traffic. Elizabeth could see the strain on her face. "Three more exits—there will be a sign for the natural history museum. Take that one."

Penny drove on, perplexed. Whatever did Elizabeth think she was doing going to find Charles's mistress? Did she want to ruin everything? She was pregnant and needed to stay at the plantation house, get proper care, be surrounded by staff and cooks and...*handsome groundskeepers,* she thought.

"I wouldn't rock the boat if I were you," Penny said, glancing over at Elizabeth before taking the exit.

"You're not me," Elizabeth said, then smiled.

"Thank goodness," Penny said. "Although that cowboy..." She stared straight ahead, grinning, waiting for directions.

"Turn left at the stoplight. This is forty-fifth. It will take us to the street the museum is on, but we're not going to turn in to the parking area. We'll go straight."

Penny followed Elizabeth's directions, passing the museum, noting how Elizabeth's demeanor had grown serious. She'd even ignored the comment about her *cowboy.* "Now what?" Penny asked.

"Just keep driving, slowly. We should be close." Elizabeth was looking up to the second floor of every building, left and right, scanning for geraniums. "There!" she said, seeing a row of flower boxes attached to the side of the building under each of three windows, all carrying a row of red geraniums. "That has to be it." Elizabeth knew she could be wrong, but she had not seen another geranium on the second floor since they turned off the highway.

Penny pulled over to the curb. "Now what?" She waited, watching as Elizabeth got out of the car, staring up at the geraniums as if the window was going to open, and Marigold was going to wave her inside.

"I'll be right back."

"Elizabeth!" Penny said loudly. "You are not going to just knock on the door!"

Elizabeth was already at the stairs and heading up to the intercom. She scrolled down the list of names. There it was: Marigold MacArthur. She raised her finger to the button, then stopped, contemplating what she would say if Marigold answered. What would she do if Marigold didn't answer or worse, if she started screaming at Elizabeth to leave her alone? What if she called Charles? That would be the worst, no doubt. But she pushed the button anyway.

The tone sounded, much like an old-fashioned door chime, although this was electronic, and there was no physical chime. Elizabeth waited a minute, then pushed it again.

A voice came over the intercom. "Whatever you are selling, I don't want any."

"Marigold," Elizabeth spoke into the intercom. "It's me, Elizabeth. Elizabeth Freeman."

"Well, I'll be..." There was a brief pause after Marigold answered. "You can come on up," she said.

Penny watched as her sister spoke into the intercom, seeing the lace curtains of the window part. A woman's face came briefly into view then disappeared as the woman dropped the curtain and turned to push the button that would allow Elizabeth to enter the building.

The buzzer sounded, releasing the door lock. Elizabeth opened the door to the stairwell and went inside. The door closed behind her. She'd forgotten to look at the apartment number, only knowing it was on the second floor. She started up the steps. When she reached the top of the first flight, she heard heels clicking on the wood floors of the hallway. A tall, dark woman appeared. Her hair was pulled back in a bun, and she was wearing an apron over her dress. She walked up to Elizabeth. "How did you find me?" she asked.

"It's a long story," Elizabeth replied.

Marigold looked down the stairs behind Elizabeth and back down the hallway. "You may as well come in."

Elizabeth followed Marigold through an open door into her apartment. It was tidy and clean, and the furniture was not cheap. The dining table was set for two, and a bottle of scotch sat on it. She could smell meat roasting in the oven. She wanted to pinch herself. She was standing in the apartment of her husband's lover. The mother of his child. And she wasn't angry.

"I don't know why I came. I'm sorry," Elizabeth started. "I was curious."

Marigold looked at her, starting at her belly, her gaze then traveling up to her face. She was thin but well built. She was pretty. Not overly pretty, but then Charles never did care for gorgeous women. He wanted "good stock," he'd said. It seemed that he got just that. She'd make pretty babies as well.

Elizabeth noted her wide face, and that she had hazel-green eyes that seemed to change color as she looked into the light and then away. Her nails were neatly manicured, the polish matching the color that she'd applied to her thick, full lips. Elizabeth's feet, just a twinge of jealousy as she stood staring at this perfectly put-together woman who her husband spent undoubtedly much more time with than she.

"It doesn't matter. Here you are. Please have a seat." Marigold offered Elizabeth a chair, and Elizabeth did as she was instructed. She felt like she was moving through a dream— or under water. Everything seemed to move in slow motion. She sat silent, numb.

"My guess is that you want the story," Marigold started. "I'm happy to share it with you as long as you never, ever tell Charles we met. Because if you do…"

"Oh, believe me," Elizabeth interrupted. "I know what would happen. You can rest assured I would not ever breathe a word."

Marigold began with when she and Charles had met—at a party that he'd thrown for his office staff. She'd come with one of his secretaries. She went on to describe how he courted her a bit, then took her on a few dates but always places where no one would recognize him. She told Elizabeth that she knew full well why this was: She was the daughter of a Black woman.

This surprised Elizabeth. She saw Marigold had darker skin, but she did not see the features of a negro. Marigold paused, waiting for that information to fully sink in.

"Go on, please," Elizabeth said.

Marigold continued. She told of a short romance, one that moved from meeting for sex only, to Charles renting her this apartment. Marigold looked around the living room, and suddenly Elizabeth saw it: She saw Charles in everything—the art, the furniture, the rugs. It was all his doing. She *felt* it when she entered, but now she truly *saw* it. It was maddening.

Next Marigold described the arrangement that Charles made with her, that she would not see anyone else, and he could come to the apartment anytime he wished, day or night. If he wanted sex, she would provide that. If he just wanted to spend the night and hold her, she would oblige. He paid for everything, and he gave her a small stipend for spending money on top—something that even Elizabeth did not receive—in exchange for remaining silent. That was it, nothing more, Marigold said, although she added that the arrangement had been in effect for ten years, and it worked for her. It worked for both of them. She wanted nothing more. Marigold promised Elizabeth that she wouldn't wreck their marriage.

Elizabeth sat silently, taking it all in, overwhelmed, but it all made sense now: Charles's late-night client meetings, the excuses when he didn't come home, and how he would up and leave when they fought, not returning for hours. Finally, she spoke. "What about the baby?"

It was Marigold's turn to be shocked. She sat for a moment with her hands folded in her lap, breathing deeply. Elizabeth thought that she saw tears forming. When Marigold regained her composure, she looked at Elizabeth, one mother to another-to-be.

"His name is Daniel," Marigold said. "He is nine. He lives in New York with my cousin Adelle. When he's old enough, I'll send for him. Hopefully by then, you and Charles will have a family, and it won't be a problem for Charles to allow my son to come home."

The two women exchanged knowing looks, sitting quietly together for a moment.

"*Your* son? His son too," Elizabeth said, hoping to elicit a response, though Marigold painfully dodged the opportunity. "I should be going," Elizabeth said. "It's getting late."

"Yes, it is approaching that hour. I never know when he might show up." Marigold smiled. "I'm so glad you came."

They stopped short of hugging. Marigold walked Elizabeth to the door and back to the landing, watching as Elizabeth descended the stairway, holding the railing so as not to take a chance of falling.

When Elizabeth got into the car, she was unable to speak for a moment. Penny sat watching her, giving her time to process whatever had just transpired. Finally, Elizabeth spoke. "She's really nice." She didn't quite know what else to say. "She has a nine-year-old son who lives in New York who she doesn't see because of her arrangement with Charles. It's so unfair."

Just then Elizabeth looked up to see a car pulling up next to them and then in front of the rental car, stopping at the curb. Charles got out, a newspaper in his hand. He leaned back in to say something to Branson, who nodded. Elizabeth slid down in her seat, as did Penny, both of them fully out of sight. Elizabeth peeked up to see her husband walk to the landing, pull his keys out of his pocket, and open the door. When it closed behind him, Elizabeth sat up slowly.

"Let's get out of here," she said.

Penny pulled the car off the curb and around the car where Branson sat with a newspaper open against the steering wheel, waiting while his boss went up and did whatever he did with his mistress.

"That was close," Penny said when she pulled into traffic on the highway. "Are we still going to get Lillian?"

"No, it will have to wait. I couldn't, not right now. This has been too much. It was going to be a surprise anyway, so she won't be disappointed."

They agreed to stop at a mall on the way home and pick up things that would justify a day away from the plantation in the eyes of the staff. Elizabeth had Charles's credit card—maybe Marigold had one too, she thought—and she put it to work.

When they returned to the house, Penny drove up to the front door. Elizabeth began unloading bags, instructing Penny to leave the car in the driveway. She sincerely hoped that Branson hadn't recognize the rental car. Had it not been for

Branson telling William where Marigold's apartment was, she wouldn't have found it, and she did not want to compromise Branson's trust in her or in his soon-to-be father-in-law.

Dinner would soon be ready. Elizabeth and Penny took their shopping bags to their rooms. Elizabeth returned to the kitchen, where Nettie was working, cutting up a chicken, and Faye sat with her head in her hands, telling Nettie her woes. Nettie was shaking her head, giving Faye advice she probably didn't want to hear when Elizabeth came through the kitchen doors.

"Hello, Nettie, Faye."

Faye sat up straight, realizing there was probably something she should be doing besides lounging in the kitchen complaining.

Nettie chopped the last piece of the chicken, slamming her knife down hard and throwing both pieces into the bowl with the rest, where they would be coated with something that would be crispy once fried. It was her secret recipe. Elizabeth had only asked for it once.

"Yum, fried chicken!" Elizabeth said. "I'll let Penny know."

"It will just be the two of you," Nettie said to her, obviously annoyed. Once again, Charles had called to say he wouldn't make it home, and now she knew exactly why.

Elizabeth recalled the smell of roasting meat in Marigold's kitchen, knowing that Charles would have a nice evening, terrified that she'd only missed him by minutes. The feeling washed over her that the visit to Marigold hadn't been just to gain knowledge about her husband's mistress. It was also an attempt to rationalize her own adultrous misdeeds, and she'd succeeded.

"That's alright. I'm looking forward to it already," Elizabeth said, smiling at Nettie. "Penny will be happy too. She mentioned earlier that she's been in the South for a week and has not yet had fried chicken." She turned to Faye. "What did you do today?"

Faye stood up, trying to recall a day that had been filled with mostly nothing.

Nettie spoke for her. "She was lazy today, good fo' nothin'. Gwendolyn was not around cuz her mama don' took sick, so Faye here had nobody to boss her, to keep her busy 'cept me, and she real good at avoidin' the kitchen when she want to. When Branson get home, I'm gon' send her to her mama's."

Nettie was not happy with Faye, obviously, so Elizabeth decided to get her home. The trouble was that Branson was parked in front of Marigold's house, waiting for Charles to eat and "tend to business," and Gwendolyn was not there either with her car.

The thought occurred to Elizabeth then that Holden could drive Faye home. Elizabeth went out the front door and over to Holden's place, walked up the steps of the porch, and knocked on the door. Holden answered in a T-shirt, shorts, and flip-flops. She'd never seen him dressed like that. Although she adored the cowboy look and the carpenter look, here was a beach boy that she'd never met.

"Oh, my," she said, noting Holden's mostly bare feet and tight shirt. "Are you a surfer now?" she asked with a grin. She looked over his shoulder to see a beer on the table and the television playing the nightly news.

"I have a favor to ask," she started.

Holden grabbed her and pulled her in through the door, wrapping his hands in her hair and playfully pushing her against the counter.

"Anything, but you'll have to pay," he said, rubbing his budding erection against her belly.

Elizabeth looked over his shoulder at the house, where she knew that Nettie was preparing to put chicken into hot oil, and Faye was probably perched back on a stool. It would be easy. They had plenty of time, but not now.

"I can't. I need you to take Faye home. Faye is being awful, and Nettie is upset with her. Neither Gwendolyn nor Branson are here."

Holden pulled Elizabeth's head to his lips and kissed her until she stopped talking. He wrapped his arms around her and held her close for a few moments, then released her.

"Anything for you, Elizabeth. Anything. And I mean that. Let me get dressed, and I'll take her."

"Thank you, Holden. I have so much to tell you. Penny leaves early tomorrow morning. Let's meet out at John Clayton's cabin mid-day, before lunch while it's still cool."

"I love that idea." Holden paused, still holding her at arms' length and looked into her eyes. "And I love *you*, Elizabeth."

She folded back into his arms, her head on his chest, and whispered. "I love you too, Holden Grady Harding."

~~*~~

The next morning, Elizabeth and Penny sat at the dining table alone. Charles had gone to the office early. Elizabeth had no idea what time he'd returned the night before, and at this point she didn't care. Penny's flight wasn't until the afternoon, so they had plenty of time for a leisurely breakfast. Faye wasn't in yet because Gwendolyn needed another day with her mom, and the buses were off schedule, causing Faye to have to call and say that she'd be late.

All this was fine with Elizabeth. She enjoyed having the last few hours alone with her sister. Penny knew pretty much everything now. There was very little that she'd not shared with Penny, only the last entry in the journal where Charles III admitted to killing Juliet and the fact that William seemed to take a keen interest in Lillian being the last survivor of the Clayton family. There was a significance there that he'd not explained, and Elizabeth hadn't mentioned it to Penny. She would talk to Holden about it when she met with him.

Elizabeth and Penny could hear Nettie banging around in the kitchen as they finished their grits and eggs, something Penny had requested as a final Southern meal before her departure. They'd gone to the kitchen and served themselves too, something Elizabeth rarely had the opportunity to do, which she enjoyed. As the sisters talked, even though they were alone, they kept their voices low as always, just in case.

"What are you going to do about Marigold?" Penny asked.

"I'm going to help her bring her son home," Elizabeth said, shocking Penny.

"How in the world are you going to do that?" she asked, her eyes widening.

"I don't know yet. First, I have to meet with her again. I just don't know how I can get to her, but I'll figure something out. Holden will have to take me."

Elizabeth was horrified that Marigold had been forced to give up her son in order to keep her home and lifestyle. But she didn't work—Charles insisted—and had no way to take care of herself, much less a child. Charles had been furious at first when she told him she was pregnant. He wanted her to "get rid of it," but she refused. She knew it might be her only chance to have a child. She promised Charles that she didn't care about his money, but she had to keep the baby. He agreed that she could have it, but as soon as the baby weaned, it would go to her cousin in New York. She didn't know then that it was a boy, of course, and Charles hadn't thought this through.

So, Charles did already have an heir of sorts—a partly Black, nine-year-old boy descended from slaves, who was living in New York right now. A boy who was being robbed of his youthful days with his mother because of *her* husband. A boy who likely spent countless days reading his mother's letters and wanting badly to know her, to come home to her. Teachers puzzled over why his homework was turned in frequently with doodles of marigolds at the bottom of the pages. Elizabeth sat staring through her wine glass at the sun's rays that filtered through the large open windows of the adjacent living room.

"And what are you going to do about Lillian?" Penny asked, bringing Elizabeth out of deep thought. "I don't think she has dementia. I think someone put her in that home," she brazenly suggested. "She's old, and she might forget things, as we all will someday. But the suggestion that she has days where she doesn't know who or where she is…I don't see it. Do you think it is possible that the staff are being coerced into issuing these statements and that Lillian is being kept there—like you are here?"

Elizabeth looked shocked. She'd not considered that before. She had been told by Charles and Bryce that Lillian's memory was failing, that the dementia was getting worse. Yes, Elizabeth had seen her drift off a few times, but what eighty-year-old was not entitled to forget a few memories that spanned nearly a century?

The thought that her husband and Bryce had anything to do with Lillian being stuck in that place made Elizabeth cringe. Yet she knew that with the kind of money they had, their ability to crush any threat—real or perceived—was enormous.

"I don't know," Elizabeth replied. "I need to talk to William. There is something that I don't understand, and I think he knows the answer."

Penny was packed and ready to go. Nettie came out of the kitchen, and Holden came over to say goodbye. Branson was in town, and Faye wasn't in yet. Holden took Penny's bags and put them in the trunk of the rental car. He stood back while Penny and Elizabeth held each other, hugging and kissing with Penny promising to return.

Finally, Nettie waved goodbye and turned back into the house. Holden gave Penny a light hug, sending rushes through her body at his touch. Penny knew what her sister was experiencing and didn't fault her one bit for her infidelity, now that she knew what she knew and had seen what Elizabeth was going through. Holden turned and headed back to his cabin.

Elizabeth held her sister at arms' length, looking into Penny's eyes. "Have a nice flight, sis. Call me when you get home."

They had one last big hug, and Penny started to climb into the vehicle.

Elizabeth called to her. "Penny, one last thing."

Penny turned. "Yes?"

Elizabeth lowered her voice, looking out at Holden as he walked away. "There is a chance the baby is his."

Penny stared at her sister, trying to read her face. What she saw was pure joy in the thought that it might be, yet pure terror in that if it was, Charles would come unhinged. She smiled at Elizabeth, knowing that no matter the outcome, everything would work out. She drove away with the intention of returning as soon as she could, and Elizabeth went to her room, changed, and headed to the woods.

Chapter Twenty-Four: The Letters

Charles and Elizabeth sat at the table, waiting for breakfast. The silence that hung in the physical distance between them was like a thick fog. A newspaper sat next to Charles's plate that he would glance down at from time to time, pretending interest, a distraction mainly from the conversation that needed to begin lest he go mad.

Elizabeth had not said a word to him since her sister left. The two women had been inseparable during Penny's stay, unnerving him. He was happy that Penny was gone and would see to it that she did not return—at least not before the baby was born. Where they'd gone on their daily outings remained a mystery. He'd asked Branson, Gwendolyn, Faye, of course, and even Nettie, but none of them had any idea. The two sisters had been so secretive that other than the last day of Penny's visit when they went to town shopping for souvenirs, no one had any idea where they'd been.

Charles doubted that two people would spend days just driving around the county as Elizabeth claimed. What was there to see, really, other than peach orchards, Civil War monuments—*and wait*—museums. Charles was sure that Elizabeth had taken Penny next door and that they'd met with William. He'd bet on it, and he would also bet that Elizabeth would deny it if he asked, so he didn't.

It was no secret that the two families, the Freemans and the Brightons (William's mother had married a Stapleton) had been rivals for a century, even fierce enemies during some periods. If both families were present at parties, insults and veiled threats could be overheard, like arrows shot over bows of ships, though ships sailing not over water but through vast acres of forest that separated their plantations.

Suffice it to say that a century prior, a Freeman coming home to find a Brighton taking tea with his wife without the company of her husband would have been cause for a duel.

Charles had been horrified when Gwendolyn called to tell him William was on his porch with Elizabeth, even inviting her to his home, a museum but nevertheless *his home*, without her husband present. Had Charles been home at the time to come upon this scenario, harsh words would have been exchanged, or worse. Now his wife had likely given herself the freedom to go next door with the excuse of entertaining her sister.

Charles had no doubt that William had enough dirt on his family to sow doubt in Elizabeth's mind—perhaps even regret—about her decision to marry into the Freeman family. Since starting the museum, William had made it his mission to collect every document that he could find relating to the families that ruled this part of the South for hundreds of miles. Word got out, and people would come to him with artifacts, old letters, whatever they found in their attic that was of no interest to them, knowing William would pay to add them to his collection.

Charles knew that the fact that William came calling on Elizabeth at a time that William knew very well Charles would be in the city meant that William had something to share that he did not want Charles to know about. William appeared to be continuing a long tradition of undermining the Freeman family. Charles had to know what was said. He began by clearing his throat, which did not elicit a response from Elizabeth. He did so again, louder. She looked up at him without a word.

"Elizabeth, I want to know how you and Penny spent your time while she was here. It seems you two were out and about quite a lot." Charles sat, waiting for a response, but none came. He slammed his fist down on the table, causing the saucers to jump underneath their teacups.

Elizabeth looked up at him. "We had a lovely time."

Now Charles was angry, but there was nothing he could do. He could not lay a hand on a pregnant woman, and he was sure that Nettie and Faye were standing on the other side of the kitchen door, peeking through any crack they could find to try and catch a glimpse of the fight that they both knew was sure to come once Penny was gone.

"Penny will not come back until you've had the baby. Is that clear?"

Elizabeth didn't respond.

"And the riding lessons—over."

Elizabeth looked at Charles and grinned. She wanted so badly to respond with something that would indicate she knew about Marigold *and about his child*, but she would not reveal her hand, not yet.

Elizabeth knew that she would have to devise a way to get to Lillian. She had so many questions for her now that she knew who had authored the book, but Marigold had taken precedent the day before. That visit was priceless, and the timing was even better. Watching Charles stride up to the door of Marigold's place and open it with his own key was an image she would never forget. And thankfully, she had her sister as a witness.

Elizabeth stood. "I think I'll take my dinner in my room," she said.

Charles ate alone while Elizabeth wrote a letter to William. Faye brought up her food, but surprisingly, she wasn't hungry. She needed Holden to deliver the letter the next day. She pulled out a piece of stationery and a pen and began to write.

She thanked William for trusting her with the ledger from John Clayton, as well as the journal of the Freeman family men. She admitted her shock in finding out that Lillian was the *Author Unknown* of the book that held the greatest significance for her in her current situation, and she let him know that she was trying to befriend Lillian—against her husband's wishes. She also raised the question about there being a connection between Lillian being the only known remaining heir of the Clayton family and the behavior of her husband and his brother around that fact.

Elizabeth asked this last question knowing full well that William knew something more, hoping that when she received a reply, she would understand why Charles had invited Lillian not once but three times to their house, then promptly uninvited her from any future gatherings. She signed the letter *Elizabeth Freeman*, not Mrs. Charles Freeman as would have been expected of a lady of the house—*his house*. Then she added something under her name that she hoped would make William smile when he read the letter.

PS: I went to visit Marigold.

Elizabeth put the letter into an envelope and promptly sealed it, putting it in the safe. She would give it to Holden the next morning to take to William. William held the key to all that she would discover about her husband's family and his estate. She knew that now.

That next morning, Elizabeth stayed in her room until she watched the car pull away with Charles in the backseat, Gwendolyn again in the front, riding along so that Branson could take her shopping after they dropped Charles at his office. Elizabeth ran down the stairs with the letter in her pocket, straight out the door, across the lawn, and around to Holden's cabin. She ran breathlessly to the front door, then knocked loudly.

Holden opened the door, peeking out first to see who it was and what the emergency might be this early in the morning. When he saw Elizabeth, he grinned, throwing the door open wide. "Come in, dear Elizabeth. What's going on?"

She did not come in, but simply pulled the letter from her pocket and held it out to him. She started speaking rapidly about William and Lillian, Marigold and Daniel, and how now that Penny had gone home, she was trapped again and would never know the truth about any of this insanity—and a Freeman had murdered Juliet! She paused but couldn't stop.

"I need you to give this to William and help me get over there to see him. Somehow, I must find a way, without Charles knowing. He knows I'm on to something, and I might end up dead like Juliet."

Holden held a finger to her lips, stopping her. "Wait. Wait, my precious. You're moving way too fast here. I get most of what you're saying, but please come in, and let's sit down and talk about this."

"I can't, Holden. I need to go see William." She looked over her shoulder, imagining Faye at the kitchen window craning her neck to be able to see a piece of Elizabeth on Holden's porch. She continued, keeping a respectable distance in case someone was watching.

"I have an idea. I'm in need of a visit to the doctor in town for a pregnancy checkup. I'll schedule it for when I know Charles will be on his way to the office and we know Branson is busy, and I will insist that you take me. We can make it to the doctor's appointment, but on one side or the other of that, we'll pay a quick visit to William." She waited for a response, but Holden was slow to speak, thinking of the potential repercussion should he get caught.

"Of course, let's figure it out," he said. He had come to realize that he loved Elizabeth more than he could rationalize in his own mind, and to that end, nothing mattered more. What was most important—be it his current employment, his reputation in the county as a property manager, or anything else for that matter—was that she was happy and safe, and he felt in the moment that neither was true.

Holden knew that Elizabeth's mission was dangerous, but imagining that it might be his little one doing somersaults inside Elizabeth's tummy right now gave him cause to be brave. She hopped off the porch and ran back across the lawn and through the tall front doors of the plantation house, which she'd left open, and straight up to her room. She would go back down later, once she had a chance to task Faye with something to keep her busy in another part of the house, then she could use the phone in the hallway to call the doctor to schedule an appointment. She closed her door, retrieved the diary, and sat back on her bed to continue reading the passage from November 15, 1859.

I had a wonderful time in Marietta, staying three nights. It was so very hard to keep myself from sneaking down the hall into Liam's room in the middle of the night. It would have been easy to do, but hard to keep quiet with him, and dangerous as could be. One of us would have been shot if we'd been discovered.

On the way back, Liam surprised me with the news that he had made arrangements, should I agree to the plan, to stay in a room at his cousin's house for the night. It was a small room on the side of the house that his cousin would rent out by the night or longer when there was a need. John was in Texas again with those politicians, doing whatever it is they do while preparing for war, so after Liam and I bid our farewells to John's family, Liam steered the buggy through the heart of Atlanta. He pulled over on a side street that led to a private entrance in the back of the house. It was situated where no one would see us coming or going from the main door. I was shocked and delighted and so very happy to have said yes.

Anabelle had packed some food for our trip back; Liam retrieved the bag and spread the food out on a table, lit candles, and produced a small bottle of whiskey that I'm sure John added to the bag, meant for Liam. He pulled two glasses out of a cupboard, set those along with a pitcher of water on the table, and pulled a chair out for me, beckoning me to join him. I don't really drink alcohol, so the very little bit that Liam poured for me had me growing lightheaded within minutes. We ate in silence, gazing at each other over the candlelight, relishing the moment.

We had barely finished half of the food when Liam pushed back his chair, offered his hand, and took me to bed.

It was the first time we'd been able to spend an entire night together. I never saw his cousin or anyone in the family, and I don't think his cousin would have imagined that it was me who Liam had planned to bring into his house, or he may not have agreed. John has a lot of political power in this region, and anyone who dares cross his path in such a way would be in for a duel, or worse.

Our lovemaking was different, unhurried, and without a time limit as was usually the case. I think we may have had two or three rounds. I cannot recall, but sleep was the least of our concerns. When I woke up in his arms, it was heaven. So peaceful it was. And looking over to see his fair red hair curled around his temple and the way he smiled while he dreamt—I hoped he had been dreaming of me—made me aware of the fact that I've never spent one single evening like that in the arms of my husband. We have separate rooms because he avoids situations of true intimacy. He will do what he has to do to sire another child, but he does not love me in the way I wish to be loved.

Elizabeth closed the diary, thinking of Liam and how uncanny it was that here she was, living in Adria's house, quite possibly sleeping in the same bedroom, and in very much the same situation as Adria had been. Different, yes, but very much the same. She, too, had never spent one single night in the arms of her husband and doubted that she ever would.

There was a tap at her door. It was Faye coming to take her breakfast dishes away. Elizabeth asked her to go up to the third floor, where she knew that in one of the many spare bedrooms there was a trunk with old baby clothes. Two trunks had been found in the attic when Charles had the house inspected by workers to assess the integrity of the roof structure, and Elizabeth had asked that the workers bring them down into a bedroom so that she could see what was in them. Elizabeth had opened one of them briefly and knew that it contained a trove of baby clothes from long ago. Not only was Elizabeth curious as to what else was in the trunks, but now that she was pregnant, she could justify a keener interest in the contents. She told Faye to go up and without rifling entirely through either, find a few outfits and bring them to her. She thought she might press one of the nicest and put it in a frame for the wall of the nursery.

Gwendolyn was still in town with Branson, and Nettie seldom came out of the kitchen, so now that she'd given Faye a chore that would keep her busy for at least fifteen minutes, she went down the stairs over to where the newly repaired phone sat gleaming in the hallway cubby. She looked both ways and across the dining room, then picked up the receiver and dialed the number for her doctor.

The call was answered on the first ring. Elizabeth gave the receptionist her name, then after a brief hold, the receptionist came back on the line. Elizabeth requested a morning appointment during the hours that Branson would be in town, and she got one for the very next day. She quickly went down to Holden's cabin to let him know of her plan.

"Sounds good. I'll be ready," Holden said. He left and drove next door to deliver the letter to William, letting him know that he'd be bringing Elizabeth by the following day.

As Holden drove away, William opened the envelope and skimmed the letter. He was delighted that Elizabeth had found a way to escape briefly to come and meet with him. His goal was to bring the Freeman family's tragedies and secrets to light once and for all, hoping that the knowledge he possessed would free Elizabeth—the latest in a long succession of women held captive by the Charles Freemans of the family—before she went mad as had Juliet, and later Juliet's daughter, driven to destruction via extreme isolation and the occasional beating.

After all, William knew that the current eldest son already had a rightful heir; he just didn't want anyone else to know it. William's curiosity extended to one question, one problem in the equation, and one that he would not solve for some time to come: How had Dehlia escaped being entrapped by her husband, who was also a Charles?

~~*~~

When Charles arrived for breakfast, Elizabeth sat drinking tea. She had already polished off oatmeal, an egg, toast, and a piece of bacon. Although she was eating for two and starting to show, she was being careful. The doctor would weigh her today and measure her against where she should be and let her know his thoughts.

Charles sat down wordlessly, nodding to Faye as she set a teacup and hot water in front of him. He did not look at Elizabeth, just poured steaming water over the teabag, focusing on the bag as it rose to the top and pushing it back down with the force of more hot water. Eventually, he looked up to see Elizabeth staring at him.

"I'm going to the doctor this morning," she said.

"Your next checkup is not for another week," Charles said. He had the schedule on his desk calendar and had just looked at it the day before.

"I know that. But I was having some weird twinges, sort of a pinching sensation down there that concerned me, so I called, and they said they could get me right in. My appointment is at ten."

Charles cleared his throat. "Branson will be dropping me at my meeting at that time," he replied.

"Then Holden can take me."

"Faye should go with you," he said, his eyes narrowing.

"Absolutely not. I have her cleaning out some old trunks on the third floor. There are some things in them that I would like to use to decorate the nursery." Elizabeth knew that any mention of nesting or a nursery would hook him. "Faye's already up there. I showed her what to bring down to the nursery. We'll go through things together when I get back."

"Fine, then. But go straight there and straight back," he said, studying her face for any response.

"Absolutely. I don't need anything else in town." She got up and walked toward the hallway to her room, saying nothing more.

Charles sat smirking, self-absorbed, like a monarch acknowledging a loyal subject rather than a husband treating a woman as his wife, sipping his tea with a pinky raised high over the cup. He didn't turn to watch Elizabeth, although a quick glance revealed her head and eyes lowered as she passed. *Good girl.*

Elizabeth had to contain her excitement. She took the steps two at a time until she reached the third-floor rooms. Faye had already brought down a few things from the first trunk, then earlier that morning Elizabeth had given her instructions to bring the remaining contents of that first trunk to her room while she was at the doctor, and to lay out the things where she could take an inventory. Faye was downstairs serving Charles his breakfast now but would be up as soon as she cleared his dishes.

Elizabeth opened the door to the room, eyeing the trunks, the first one in the corner sitting with the lid still open. She opened the lid of the second trunk. It was stuffed with yellowed papers, books, and a wooden box that sat on top. She noted the old-style clasp that hooked to hold the lid closed. She brought the box out and laid it on the floor, then sat down cross-legged while she lifted the lid to examine the contents. A little drawer that sat on top contained old fountain pens, a few coins, and a pocket watch on a chain. The drawer had a metal handle that she lifted out of the box, revealing a bundle of letters underneath tied with string sitting in the bottom next to a bottle of what used to be ink. Elizabeth looked back at the door, thinking she'd heard footsteps. She quickly grabbed the bundle of letters and stuffed them into the pocket of her sweater just as Faye walked through the door.

Faye startled. "I thought you were in your room. I'm sorry."

"Don't worry," Elizabeth said. "I was just looking through this second trunk to see if there was anything of importance, but it doesn't appear so. Just a bunch of papers and books." She replaced the wooden box back into the trunk. She spotted more below it, much more, but she wanted to come back up when she had privacy and pull everything out. Faye had told her she doesn't read, and now Elizabeth hoped that was true—at least not enough to have any curiosity about the books that lay at the bottom of the trunk. Had Faye found the letters, she might have delivered them to Charles.

Elizabeth turned to Faye. "I tell you what, why don't you get to the bottom of this other trunk and lay out the clothes for me in my room. We'll go through them after my appointment. We'll leave this other trunk for later. Lay out the clothes in piles of what you think might be boy's clothes and girl's clothes, although it seems back then they put dresses on boys until a certain age." She sat smiling at Faye, disingenuously but engaging her, making her feel as though she were an integral part of the completion of this project. Faye sat down next to the trunk beaming, ready to get started.

Elizabeth continued, "The clothes you brought down yesterday were a good start, but now I think I might want to see them all. I will ask Holden to find us a couple of picture frames from the barn storage. We'll press a couple of outfits, one for a baby boy and one for a girl, and we'll attach them to a cloth backdrop with pins and frame them for the nursery."

It was a good excuse and a cover for what she'd already told Charles, so she needed to make it sound important in case Charles questioned Faye at some point so that story lined up.

Elizabeth closed the lid of the second trunk, keeping her hand on the letters in her pocket. Faye set about pulling out clothes while Elizabeth returned to her room. She untied the string, briefly looking through the letters. They were all addressed to Liam, in what could only be Adria's handwriting! It was much more of a flowery script than that of the diary and surely written with a quill pen, but it was Adria's handwriting, Elizabeth had no doubt.

Elizabeth heard Charles talking to Gwendolyn down in the foyer. She quickly spun the dial on the safe, inserting the letters and closing the door in case either of them came to check on her before they left, but not before taking one of them and sliding it deep into her purse. Holden had promised to have a car ready as soon as Charles pulled away, so she quickly dressed but then waited. She would not be able to leave right after Charles, enforcing the theory that Branson could have easily dropped Charles off then taken Elizabeth to her appointment. She thought of Branson and his staid reverence for Charles and the Freeman family. He wasn't dangerous to her, not like

Faye. He was just boring. Anyway, timing was everything, and no one in the house knew the exact time of her appointment. She'd give herself a few minutes.

Elizabeth went to her purse and retrieved the letter, fumbling excitedly to open it without tearing. The flap of the envelope came away easily, and the paper inside slid out to reveal an almost transparent quality. There was writing only on one side, as anything on the back would have bled to the front, rendering the words on both sides illegible.

February 14, 1864
    My Dearest Liam,
    I must start by saying that I miss you terribly. John will be home any day now, and I trust your decision to leave before his arrival. The rumors in these parts have already grown with your departure and that of his impending return. There is hardly a soul around who does not know about us by now, yet we shall soon see if anyone dare tell him. No one remembers his anger the way I do, and surely your decision to leave had everything to do with that.
    The servants also miss you. I overheard Rae and Hattie discussing you while they were peeling potatoes. Everyone here loves you, but none more than I.
    I pray for your return someday, though, as I cannot bear the thought of living the rest of my life without once again being in your arms.
    With all my love,
    Adria

Elizabeth sat holding the letter, staring at the words, trying to put meaning to the fact that Adria had been writing to Liam. Liam had left her! It couldn't be. But it made sense. So far what she'd gleaned from Aria's diary was that John had been preparing for the inevitable—going to war—and that by the sound of things in this letter, he'd done so and was now returning home. From the letter, it was clear that Adria's affair with Liam had intensified during John's absence, to the point that they must not have taken such care to hide it as they once had. It was also clear that Liam knew he had to leave before John returned.

Elizabeth carefully folded the paper and placed it back inside the envelope, then into her purse. She suddenly felt great pain in Adria's words, so different from the last diary entry she'd read after spending the first full night in Liam's arms. She couldn't wait to share the letter with William and ask him what more he might know about their affair and about John and the war. She tiptoed downstairs to find the front door slightly ajar. She heard voices on the porch and opened the door to find Holden speaking with Gwendolyn.

"Yes, ma'am. I understand." Elizabeth caught the last sentence to understand Holden was receiving some sort of instruction from Gwendolyn that had no doubt come from Charles.

"Good morning!" Elizabeth said cheerily to Holden. "Thank you for driving me. I know you have so much to do around here." She looked over at Gwendolyn, who gave her a terse smile in return. She was just the messenger. She watched as the two had a brief discussion, then Holden opened the passenger door and waited for Elizabeth to arrange herself in the front seat. He tipped his hat formally to Elizabeth then to Gwendolyn, took his place in the driver's seat, and pulled out from the portico.

Once they were out the front gates, Holden turned left toward town, then went around a long lake road to William's driveway from the other direction. He'd taken a circuitous route to avoid suspicion should anyone been watching from upstairs, which was likely. They pulled into the property and Elizabeth showed him where William had Penny park her rental car, adjacent to the side door, avoiding tourists and museum-goers.

William noticed their arrival from an upstairs window and came out with his hands in the air, gesturing an animated welcome. He ushered them into his office as before. Holden stood at the doorway, hesitant.

"Oh, please, Holden, come and join us," Elizabeth said, patting the chair beside her. They sat across the very large desk from William, Elizabeth noting stacks of books everywhere, with two prominently centered in front of him.

"I don't have much time," she began.

"Of course not, I understand fully," William said. "I am going to send you home with a couple more books that I came across that might interest you."

"Thank you for helping me piece this life together—my life, the Freemans, and the Claytons. It is all so interesting and overwhelming at the same time."

"Your note stated that you went to see Marigold," William continued. "How did that come about?"

Holden's eyes widened and quickly shifted to Elizabeth. *She went to see her husband's lover?* This shocked him. He suddenly felt responsible for what could have been a disastrous move on her part. Had he not told her about Marigold, she never would have pursued a visit.

"My sister took me over after we left here."

"I shouldn't have told you where she lived," William replied. "But go on, how did it go?"

"It was awkward, as you would imagine, but she was very kind. And yes, she told me about the baby. He's nine now, living in New York with her cousin." Elizabeth looked over at Holden, who still sat staring at her, an incredulous look frozen on his face. "And I saw my husband pull up to her place just as we were leaving." Elizabeth looked back at William. "He has his own key."

William shifted uncomfortably. He and Branson discussed the affair many times when not in the company of his niece. He didn't want to appear to be too interested. But he was fully aware of how much time Charles spent there, that his name was on the lease, that he had been the one who had furnished it, and yes, that he had a key.

Elizabeth decided to change the subject, realizing the time. "There's more. I found a stack of letters in an old trunk that the workers retrieved from the attic." She pulled the letter from her purse and handed it to William.

William put on thin white gloves before carefully removing the paper as she had done gloveless. He carefully removed the letter and read it, then returned it to the envelope. "How many of these do you have?"

"I don't know. There was a stack tied together with string. I just took the one I saw first then hid them in my room. There may be more in the old trunk. I'll go through it when I can find a few moments alone."

"This confirms what was recorded at the time, that her affair with Liam strengthened when John went to war, that they brazenly took more of it into the open, and that Liam felt he had to leave before John returned. As the story goes, John was most angry about his injuries upon his return, one of which included the aspect that he would never sire more children. So, if any others were to come, and one did in fact, it would raise doubt as to whose child it was."

It was Elizabeth's turn to engage a surprised look and hold it with eyes wide. "Juliet?"

"Some say, although there is no proof," William replied.

"We should go, or we won't have an excuse for a delayed return," Holden said.

"You're right," Elizabeth replied, then turning to William. "Are these books for me?" Her eyes rested on the two in the middle of his desk.

"Yes, more of the same. Let me know if you find anything that you didn't already know, or if this material brings up more questions." William walked them down the hallway to the exit. There was still one more very important document that he had yet to share with Elizabeth, one that could seal the fate of the old Clayton family plantation for good. He wanted to share it with Elizabeth in private, so it would have to wait.

Holden pulled the car out and toward the gates, watching William as he waved over his shoulder before returning through the door. "That was interesting," Holden said to Elizabeth, who sat running her hands over the book covers.

"What part did you not already know?" Elizabeth asked.

"That you are daring and maybe a bit crazy." He looked over at her with a smile. "That visit with Marigold could have ended very, very badly."

"Yes, I know, Holden, but I had to go. I had to see her face, look her in the eye."

"Well, hopefully, she will never mention it to your husband."

"She won't. I promise. She has much more to lose than I do."

Holden gave her a sideways glance, pondering that last remark. He steered the car out onto the highway. Within minutes, they were at the clinic, and while Elizabeth was in with the doctor, Holden stayed in the car looking over the books that William had loaned Elizabeth. One was a benign coffee-table book showing more pictures of more plantations. Countless books like that had been written, but there must be a reason William had picked out this particular one. Then the cover photo caught his eye. It was the old Freeman plantation. Elizabeth didn't notice, of course, because she'd never seen it, but he recognized it immediately.

Holden's thoughts went to a few weeks prior when Charles had taken him over to the plantation and asked him to come up with a list of repairs and improvements that would need to take place. Holden had been shocked at the time to find that Charles had purchased his family's old plantation, the one that his great-uncle had lost after the collapse of the tobacco market, after the stock market crash, and after supposedly he'd killed his wife and taken their children to Louisiana.

Holden flipped through the pages to see the mansion in its glory then in complete disrepair, where it pretty much sat now. There were other plantations featured, none that had the same significance, and he made a note to ask to borrow the book for a few days before he next met with Charles about repairs. He might score points if he was able to list renovations that would take it back closer to its original state. It would be worth so much more after restoration. If it weren't for existing circumstances regarding a certain woman that he was madly in love with, he might be up for the challenge of managing that restoration, although at this juncture it seemed unlikely. He then had the thought about how in the letter Adria described Liam's hasty departure, hoping that would not be his fate. He set the book on the seat and picked up the other, but then startled as Elizabeth tapped on the car window before opening the door. Had he seen her coming, he would have come around and opened the door for her.

"Sorry, I didn't see you. That was quick," he said as she slid into the passenger's seat. He placed the books in her lap and started the car.

"I had to make it quick to make up for the time we spent with William." Elizabeth looked at Holden, noting his large hands on the wheel, making it look small, the way she felt in his arms. She thought about the letter—now anxious to read them all—and how it revealed what she would have suspected, that soon Charles's late nights and absences might embolden them as well.

"Holden," she started.

"Yes?" Holden looked over at her, noting the late morning sun as it streamed across her face and how the trees they passed created a strobing effect on her cheeks. It was mesmerizing. She was his Adria of a sort, and he was her Liam. *How uncanny,* he thought.

"What was it that Gwendolyn was telling you when I came out onto the porch?"

"The usual, orders from the master," he said with a growl. "Straight there, straight back. No going to town, no other stops."

"I figured." Elizabeth reached over and put a hand on his leg, causing a stirring that brought warmth through her hands and up into his groin. She left it there until they turned into the driveway. He parked, got out, and came around to let her out of the passenger's seat, noting that she'd left the books on the seat. "I'll get them from you later if that's okay," she said, not to chance taking them into the house while under watchful eyes.

Holden nodded, shut the door behind her, and watched as she walked up the stairs to the porch and disappeared without so much as a goodbye or thank you. She didn't dare, as Gwendolyn came through the door just as her foot touched the top step. Elizabeth did not look back at Holden, lest her eyes reveal what she'd taken such care to avoid revealing.

Holden wanted to talk to her about her visit to Marigold, but he hadn't wanted to bring it up on the ride home—not with her hand on his leg like that. He didn't want to break that spell. It could wait. She wasn't going anywhere.

Chapter Twenty-Five: The Project

Elizabeth went straight to her room, taking the letter from her purse and putting it in the safe next to the others. She removed the diary while doing so and moved to the chaise to lie down. As much as she was curious about the rest of the letters, she needed to catch up with Adria's life and hopefully get to the place where the diary and the letters intersected.

Gwendolyn knocked on her door. "How did it go?" she asked as she entered before Elizabeth invited her in, looking around the room. This unexpected entrance caused Elizabeth to hastily shove the diary beneath her. She flushed bright pink with the realization that although Faye could be easily fooled, Gwendolyn might catch a move like that and have questions. Gwendolyn ignored the flushed face and the quick motion to hide whatever it was that she was reading. She pitied Elizabeth having to spend so much time sequestered in her bedroom, although she understood. She was the lady of the house—but not really. This was the only place she had any privacy, and even so, Gwendolyn had caught Faye snooping in here on more than one occasion while Elizabeth was out. Elizabeth deserved to have a few secrets, and she was no spy, so she cared not.

Gwendolyn admonished Faye each time she caught her near Elizabeth's room when she was out, and Faye would always have some excuse. But she knew that Faye was the reason for Charles's visits to Elizabeth's room during her fertile time. Gwendolyn also passed the library on more than one occasion to find Charles and Faye seated across from each other, speaking in hushed tones. The girl could not be trusted, and Elizabeth had been wise to request that Faye not tend to her laundry or other personal needs any longer. Gwendolyn had suggested searching for a replacement after Elizabeth expressed concerns, but Charles had pushed back on the idea of training someone new when Faye was doing a fine job, so Elizabeth was content to take care of more of those things herself, with the exception of bringing tea. It gave her a new freedom, actually, and she enjoyed it.

"The checkup went fine," Elizabeth replied. "My experience is normal. They said what I was feeling is typical between the first and second trimesters. The baby is just finding a comfortable place to rest now that he is moving more freely and exploring the inside of my womb." She laughed, although it couldn't have been further from the truth. The doctor had asked her a few questions about what she was eating—she'd never mentioned anything about the twinges that she'd told Charles she was the reason for her visit. The nurse simply weighed her, and then she and the doctor talked about vitamins. She told him that she didn't have time for the pelvic exam but promised to return shortly for that. The time she'd been gone from the house fit perfectly with the time required to go to a regular appointment, be examined, and return home with no other stops.

"Ready for lunch?" Gwendolyn asked, Elizabeth knowing full well why it was not Faye who was standing there asking. Anyway, Faye was still upstairs, digging through the trunk as instructed, and it was Gwendolyn who Charles had asked to call and give a full report upon his wife's return.

"Yes, I'd love that. I'm not craving anything right now, so whatever Nettie has prepared will be fine," she added. With that, Gwendolyn left, and Elizabeth followed her to the door, turning the lock. She picked up the diary and returned to the chaise.

February 20, 1860

John is away again. Supposedly, he is on his way to Virginia to meet the man who is said to be running for president, Abraham Lincoln. I don't know why John feels the need to meet him, unless he has some reason that he hasn't shared with me, which is most likely. It will be difficult for Mr. Lincoln to get support from anyone in the South while he continues to push back against slavery, but he has a right to try, I suppose. Mr. Lincoln is apparently mostly worried about our Southern states leaving the Union, more than the concern of slavery so they say. We're pretty divided on this issue, those in the North and us here in the South, and I don't see any way we can remain a part of a union that wants to abolish slavery. John says we will do just fine on our own, and that we'll just have to elect our own president, but he had an opportunity to meet Mr. Lincoln, so he went.

Delilah just turned three months old. She is the spitting image of her father. I see myself in her eyes, but every other feature speaks of John. She is a good baby, and for that I am glad. Hattie is looking for someone to bring in as a wet nurse, and as soon as she does, I plan to take another trip to Atlanta with Liam.

I'll dream up some excuse, of course, as to why we need to stay overnight. I will take a room at a hotel downtown so as to have the receipt, although I will not be staying the night there. Because no one in Atlanta knows me, or Liam, we can safely move about the city together and again stay at his cousin's room. It is so quaint and not at all the type of accommodation I am accustomed to, but it is clean, and I will have the opportunity to spend another night in Liam's arms.

When John finds out I went to the city while he was away, he will be furious, of course. He hasn't laid a hand on me since Delilah was born, and I may have to entice him to get me pregnant again soon to avoid the physical part of his anger, as he would never hit a woman who is with child. Also, if he is thinking about going off to fight, I would like to have one more child, just in case. It's dreadful to have those thoughts, but they do come up when he talks to me about war.

A knock on the door caused Elizabeth to startle. She was deep in Adria's world and still held the diary in her hands when Faye came through the door with a tray. Faye looked down at the leather-bound book, noticing how Elizabeth tried to hide it under the pillow as she approached. She realized she had seen that ribbon peeking out from Elizabeth's pillow before and thought it must be a bookmark of sorts. She didn't dare ask but made a note to look for it the next time she came in snooping. She'd been able to spend a few minutes in her room that morning while Elizabeth was in town with Holden, but her search had revealed nothing new that she could tell Charles about. He would reward her handsomely by putting money into her bank account if she could come up with something interesting, like relaying information about something Elizabeth wasn't supposed to be doing, but *a book*—Faye wasn't sure, but apparently it was something forbidden the way Elizabeth tried to hide it when she entered—that might be worth a deposit that would get her closer to the savings she needed to buy a car.

Faye set down the tray, again eyeing the ribbon poking lazily out from the pillow and draping the corner of the chaise.

Elizabeth caught her glance. "That will be all. Thank you, Faye." She dismissed her with the words while nodding to her door. Once Faye left, she went to the door and locked it again. She put the diary in the safe and pulled out the next letter in the bundle, careful to keep them in order. She returned to her lunch, opening the letter carefully as she had before—she didn't own any white gloves—deciding to read it before touching her sandwich.

April 1, 1864

My Dearest Liam,

I miss you more with each passing day. You have been gone now for over a month, and I am beside myself. With the war raging and now hearing that John has been injured and will be returning home, I cannot bear to think what my life will be like with him home and without you. I understood why you had to leave, as having you here with John back would be difficult for you, perhaps more for me, as once John finds out— and he surely will—it will be challenging, and perhaps dangerous for everyone involved.

After John's brief visit at Christmas, I came to the realization that not only do I no longer love him, but I think about only you. I see you everywhere, in everything. When I see the buggy being pulled around to the front of the house, I imagine you in your jacket sitting tall with your beret tilted to one side, and I hear your voice calling out softly to the horses. I'm sure they miss you as well.

The man I hired to take your place—don't get me wrong, no one will ever take your place—is gruff with them. They do what they are told but do not act the way they do with you. He has to whip them sometimes, which you never had to do.

I have one more piece of news, Liam. I am with child again. Part of me wants to think it happened when John was home for Christmas, but with the way the baby is sitting already I think I'm farther along, which can only mean one thing. I wanted to tell you before you left, as I suspected then, but I knew that you had your heart set on leaving. Once John is home and the rumors get back to him, the sight of you would surely send him into a rage and he'd want to kill us both. It will be less painful for everyone if you are not here, but I dread the very thought of his return and pray that he won't strike me if I am pregnant.

I miss you, darling. I long to wake up in your arms, and I pray that one day I will, once again.

Lovingly yours,

Adria

Elizabeth carefully tucked the letter back into the envelope and returned it to the safe, again pulling out the diary. She didn't care if she stayed in bed all day. She was anxious to close the gap between when John left for the war and when Adria had her last child—rumored to be Liam's in previous writings, including that of the Freeman family journal—but never confirmed until perhaps now. These letters could be the key, yet she wanted to see if Adria may have written about it, confessed the truth in her diary.

She returned to the chaise, looking up to check again that the door was locked. She had promised Faye that sometime that afternoon they would look through the baby clothes together, but that would have to wait.

July 27, 1860

John has been home and gone several times since I wrote last, and Delilah is crawling around like a little crab. She'll soon be walking! Little John runs through the house, sometimes narrowly missing his little sister as she scoots across the carpets. He has a makeshift rifle and has taken to hiding behind furniture, yelling "bang!" and pretending to shoot at people as they come through the front door. All this talk of war has him taking up weapons before the army.

John is gone more than he is present, which leaves me to many more of the household responsibilities than

I care for, as it is exhausting. When John is here, he is quiet and moody, and if I dare ask him what might be troubling him, he says he can't talk about it. But then I hear him talking with those men who come around, about setting up things in South Carolina and about the preparations at Fort Sumter, wherever that is, and I realize that war may be closer than we think. John is in charge of something. I'm not sure yet what that is, but I hear the men calling him "sir." If I dare ask, he tells me to mind the household and the children and let him worry about the fate of the South.

Liam makes himself scarce whenever John is around, then he comes to me when John is away. It is a pattern we've fallen into, and I can't say that it is that bad. When John is here, I am consumed with keeping the children quiet and out of his way. His anger has increased with the tension of the coming war, as has his drinking, and he visited my room twice in the last week, causing me to fear I may be getting pregnant again sooner than I wished. However, I know I've said this before, but it is true. If he is to go off to war and never return, a third child would be a blessing, but I'm so conflicted.

There is much talk about the coming presidential election. Many say that if Mr. Lincoln wins, it will surely usher in a path to war, and at this point he seems to be the favorite, so anything is possible. John tells me that if Lincoln wins, the war will begin shortly thereafter. We will secede from the Union along with several other states, and both sides will begin gearing up for a fight.

It frightens me to know that my husband and thousands of other good Southern men will be ordered onto the battlefield to fight. They all have mothers and sisters and little brothers and don't deserve to die. Why can't these men just find a way to sit down, talk it through, and come up with a solution other than war? John says there are other issues, more than just slavery, that it is about politics, culture, and keeping the federal government out of our business. All of this is too much for me to think about, so I just keep praying that it doesn't happen.

Elizabeth decided it was time to look at baby clothes and put the diary back in the safe, remembering her lunch and realizing she was hungry. She was spinning the lock when Faye again knocked on her door. She quickly pushed her clothes together to hide the safe and exited her closet, then moved to unlock the door, opening it to Faye who had her arms loaded with clothes.

"I thought I would just bring the best ones to you," Faye said, beaming. Her eyes roved to the closet, where clothes still swung on hangers, then to Elizabeth's lunch that sat untouched.

"Oh, dear, please set them down on the bed," Elizabeth said, following Faye to where she dropped the folded clothes somewhat neatly into a stack.

"There are more. I'll be right back."

Elizabeth watched Faye go, disappointed that they were going to use her bed as a staging area for this project, but declined to say anything. She took a moment to eat her lunch, realizing the time and that she would be called to dinner soon.

Faye returned shortly with another armload and set the clothes next to the others. "There," she said. "That's all the good ones. The others are too worn or torn or have moth holes."

Elizabeth started taking clothes off the pile, trying to determine what might be considered boy clothes versus girl clothes. There were subtle differences, which she was soon able to discern, and finally she had a few of each to pick from. Once they had decided on their two favorites, Faye ran to retrieve an iron and a board, returning promptly and plugging in the iron. Elizabeth was amazed at the effort Faye was putting into this project. Once the iron was warm, Faye took the two gowns and carefully ironed each of them, noting that with the age of the fabric, they would be brittle. Then she ironed the fabric that she retrieved from the sewing room and showed it to Elizabeth. It was nice and sturdy and would make an excellent backing for the two pieces.

Once they were finished and ready to put together their project, Elizabeth asked Faye to return the rest of the clothes to the trunk, letting her know that she was going to go down to the cabin to ask Holden to find two old frames for her. She'd seen a lot of them in various places around the property and knew more or less what she wanted. Elizabeth told Faye she would return in an hour and asked her to bring straight pins from the sewing room—not regular straight pins, but sturdier ones, like hatpins. She had seen some just the week before, so she knew they were there. Faye nodded and left the room. Elizabeth followed, turning to close the door, and went down the stairs and outside to find Holden, hoping he was at least in the vicinity.

When Elizabeth turned the corner and walked toward his cabin, she saw the door slightly ajar. She walked onto the porch, knocked, and called Holden's name. The door swung open at her touch, but there was no answer. She peeked in. His bed was neatly made, and the place was tidy as usual. She called his name again, but there was no answer. She pulled the door partially shut as it had been, then turned and headed to the barn.

Bella let out a low whinny when Elizabeth entered. She heard rustling in the corner near Jack's stall and moved farther inside, finding Holden bent over, preparing to pick up a saddle. She snuck up behind him, giving him a firm whack on his ass. He screamed and turned, his eyes wide at first and his mouth still open. He softened and a smile claimed his entire face.

"You!" Holden exclaimed as he spun his entire body around and picked Elizabeth up off her feet in a warm embrace. Without thinking who else might be around, he began planting kisses on her face and neck. "What are you doing out here? Wanting to take Sorrel out for another spin around the pasture? You know if the master found out about your fall, he'd say no more riding." He held her at arm's length now, taking in her face first, his eyes traveling down to where he could just barely discern the way her tummy was beginning to show signs of expanding. Holden had taken to calling Charles "the master" when the dictates came down.

"Yes, I know, no more riding, no more walks alone, no more trips to town. One should start calling me Rapunzel," Elizabeth said, leaning back to invite more of his kisses. He pecked lightly on both sides of her neck, dropping down toward her breasts, then stopped abruptly, remembering that Branson had been outside in the tack shed just a few minutes before.

"To what do I owe the honor of this visit?" Holden asked, pulling away and still sporting a wide smile.

"I need frames, picture frames. I remember seeing some stored. I just can't remember where."

"I know where there are some old dusty ones, no pictures in them. They might be a hundred years old," Holden said. "I could clean them up."

"Oh, goodie!" she squealed. "Even better because what I'm putting in them is over a hundred years old."

He raised an eyebrow. "Oh? What would that be?"

"I found a couple of old trunks that had been brought down from the attic. There are tons of old baby clothes in there. I'm going to frame a couple of gowns for the nursery." She watched him as he cocked his head. "One boy and one girl dress. They used to put the boys in gowns until they were older, but I noticed differences and will frame one of each. Cover the bases," she said, giggling. Holden looked down at her belly again, then leaned down and kissed here there.

"Let's go to the shed," he said as he stood up, taking her hand, and leading her toward the open barn door. He dropped it when he saw Branson coming around the corner, carrying a pitchfork. *That was close,* they thought in unison.

"Hello, Branson," Elizabeth said as Branson looked between the two of them, eyebrows cocked with interest. "Holden is going to help me find some picture frames. I'm decorating the nursery."

Branson sighed with relief. Of course, nothing would be going on between them. She was pregnant with Charles's baby. He smiled, setting the pitchfork down. "I was just going to clean the stalls. I saw some old frames out in the shed. They're dusty, but you could probably clean them up."

"Yep, that's what I recall. We'll head over and dig through them." Holden smiled at Branson as they passed, Elizabeth looking down to avoid his gaze, as if taking care where to place her feet. Branson smiled and looked back at them with a thoughtful expression on his face. Elizabeth looked flushed, and a little too happy given her current state of imprisonment. Nettie told him that Elizabeth was pouty lately, beside herself with all of the restrictions, and that they had all begun to worry if she might try to take off. Now she was talking about decorating the nursery and looked pretty happy. So did Holden for that matter. Branson was still shaking his head as he entered Bella's stall.

Elizabeth walked back to the house carrying two small frames—both just the right size. Holden had taken them around to the water spigot and hosed them off, then leaned them up against the shed to dry. As they dried, he cut a plywood backing for her as she instructed, tacking it onto the back of each frame, then handed her a bottle of glue. She planned to adhere the fabric backing then tack the pressed gowns on with the hatpins. As she came to her door, she found it not as she left it, but closed shut. Someone had been in her room.

Elizabeth turned the knob, went in, and looked around. Nothing was apparently disturbed at first sight, so she set down the frames, shutting the door behind her. She walked to her chaise. The pillow had been turned over, the pillow where she often hid the diary when she was interrupted while reading. She went to her closet. She had come out of the closet earlier when Faye had knocked, and Faye had seen her doing so. Her clothes were parted on the rack, revealing the safe—not at all as she'd left things. The dial sat in a random position wherever it landed after she spun it like she always did after closing the door, careful not to reveal even the last number of the code, so it may or may not have been touched.

So, Faye *had* been snooping, and likely not for the first time. But now that Elizabeth's senses were more tuned to the possibility, she'd begun doing little things like leaving her door in a certain position as she had earlier. Then she noted her curtains. They'd been closed when she left, but now they were open. Elizabeth walked to the window, noting that from the edge of the window, if one were to crane their neck, they would be able to see the shed where she and Holden had spent the past hour working on the frames. Snooping *and* spying, Elizabeth guessed, pulling the curtains back even farther to let in the afternoon light.

Elizabeth had been so cautious, but given the situation, she would be even more careful going forward. Faye was suspicious, no doubt. Elizabeth's every move was being reported to Charles, and there was nothing she could do about any of it. All of this angered her, but she would continue to clandestinely correspond with William and not get caught, finish Adria's journal and read through her letters, and find a few moments when she could go through the second trunk upstairs again, hoping to find more treasures. She prayed that if she was diligent and patient, she might be able to gather enough ammunition to free herself from the prison of a marriage she'd found herself in, by way of accumulating information that would reveal the Freeman family for who they really were, who they always had been. She hoped to barter for her freedom, but she knew that the one point that may never be negotiated was the fate of her unborn child.

Charles was powerful; his brother was less so. Elizabeth had no doubt that Dehlia was still the driving force in the family. She thought again about Dehlia's cottage. Surely it must be near completion. She'd seen workers coming and going, but she hadn't been out there in some time to check the progress. She made a mental note to go out there within the next few days to check in. When Dehlia came to stay, Elizabeth's daily routine was going to change even more. She had a lot to accomplish before that happened.

Elizabeth knew she needed to contact Lillian again. She had so many questions for her after reading the *Author Unknown* book. From all the details and facts that Lillian unwittingly revealed during her visits, those that still roamed freely in her memory—not at all lost to dementia as Charles and Bryce had hoped—Elizabeth put two and two together and with all that William told her, she now knew that *of course* Lillian was the author. Who else would have all the history, *almost verbatum,* that Lillian imparted during their meetings. She was sure that the book was meant to be both entertaining and enlightening to the people who now lived in her family home.

Elizabeth also needed to pay another visit to Marigold. She had her telephone number and would have to use Holden's phone, which would require him to make sure the coast was completely clear. It would be best to make the call one of the afternoons when Charles was late and the staff had gone home. But if Charles was late…she stopped with the thought of him walking through Marigold's door, knowing that if he was late, she might call at a time when he was there drinking his favorite scotch out of the bottle she'd seen sitting on Marigold's table in front of one of the two place settings. The smell of the roast in the oven came back to her. Her thoughts turned to Marigold's tawny brown skin, wondering what Daniel looked like. She would ask to see a picture when she went back to visit.

Just then, Faye came through the door without knocking, no doubt hoping to catch Elizabeth with the diary or the safe open. Elizabeth startled.

"Oh, sorry, Miss Elizabeth, truly." Faye held out a box full of the hatpins she had requested. Faye looked over at the curtains, open wider than she'd left them, the window now slightly cracked. A light breeze came through, causing the curtains to billow slightly. Elizabeth watched Faye's face for the guilt that surfaced, knowing on some level that Elizabeth knew. Faye remained stoic, turning Elizabeth's attention to the project at hand.

"Can we start?" Faye asked. "This is going to be fun." If anything she embarked upon in this household could be considered *fun*.

Faye cut the fabric just big enough to cover the backing where the edges would be concealed behind the frame. Elizabeth took the smoothly ironed fabric, applied a healthy amount of glue to the wood backing, then used her fingers and a piece of cardboard to smooth it out so that as she applied the fabric, no wrinkles would appear. Once she was satisfied, she finished the second, placing them both on the floor where the sun streamed through the windows. She wasn't sure if the sun would help the glue dry faster underneath the fabric, but she figured it couldn't hurt.

"Let's give that glue time to dry," Elizabeth said. "I think I need a nap." She liked using the excuse of pregnancy fatigue, giving her more alone time to read when she was sure not to be disturbed.

Faye nodded, picked up all the supplies except the pins and gowns, and turned to leave.

"I'll come down when I wake up," Elizabeth said as Faye walked out the door, closing it behind her.

Elizabeth listened for footsteps, noting that Faye was going downstairs. She quietly went to her door and opened it, poking her head out. She could hear Faye and Gwendolyn talking softly at the bottom of the stairs. Gwendolyn said something about going to town, asking Faye to come with her. *Perfect*, Elizabeth thought. *Those two will leave, thinking I'm down for a nap.* She quickly went out her bedroom door and closed it behind her, turning right, slipping up the stairs to the third floor, and tiptoeing down the hall to the room where the trunks still sat, both open. She hadn't left the second trunk open. She walked across the room, noting the wooden box still on top of the books as she'd left it, but the wooden drawer sat slightly askew, indicating that Faye had opened the box. Thank goodness she had taken the letters with her. The books were still stacked inside as they had been.

Elizabeth quickly removed the wooden box and set it on the floor. She began removing books from the trunk one at a time, noting the aged dusty covers, some slightly frayed, some pages showing a slight bit of water damage. One book clearly showed signs that it had been exposed to mold at one time. She continued to stack them beside the trunk, noting the titles. They were mostly literary books of the time, including more than one that spoke about warfare, causing Elizabeth to think that this trunk contained things that may have at one time belonged to Adria's husband. Everything in the trunk was masculine, except for the letters in the wooden box, causing her to wonder why and how they got there.

Elizabeth had almost everything out of the trunk when she noticed a large satchel on the bottom. It must have been intentionally placed on the bottom to hide it, as the weight of the books would normally have caused concern for whomever packed them on top of it, but there it was. It was old and brown, with the leather cracked in some places. The well-worn handles were still firmly attached, and the flap was buckled in place with what appeared to be a sterling clasp. The letters *JHC* were embossed just above the clasp.

She removed the satchel, then put the books back into the trunk, followed by the wooden box. She was not sure exactly how much time she would have before Gwendolyn and Faye returned, deciding to take the satchel to her room. It was certainly too big to hide in the safe, so she would have to find another hiding place. She left the lid of the trunk open as she'd found it and returned to her room, again locking the door behind her.

Elizabeth put the satchel on the table, then took a seat. She gently put pressure on the clasp, which opened freely, allowing her to open the flap wide, then she peered down inside. The satchel was filled with all sorts of things. At first glance, she noted the medals—all sorts of medals, which could be nothing other than those that Adria's husband had earned in the war.

Elizabeth pulled them out one at a time, laying them on the table, noting that they remained polished and in somewhat pristine condition.

Next, she found a small journal, such as one might keep in a coat pocket. She opened it to the first page, which was dated March 1861. *The month before the start of the Civil War,* Elizabeth thought. She would put that in the safe for sure along with the medals. Out came a pocket watch, quite obviously gold as was the chain that extended at least twelve inches. Then a locket, also gold. Elizabeth opened the locket, and there were pictures of each of them: John on one side, and Adria on the other. It was worn as if someone had perhaps carried it in their pocket and fondled it as one would a worry stone. The inscription bore the initials *AMC.* Elizabeth wondered what the M stood for; she didn't know Adria's middle name. *Marie* perhaps? She continued pulling things out of the satchel. It was a gold mine by all accounts.

There was a knock at the door.

"Yes? Who is it?" Elizabeth tried to make her voice sound sleepy, yawning while she spoke.

Faye's voice came from the other side of the locked door, so Elizabeth didn't have to worry about the contents of the satchel strewn across the table. "We're back. Are you ready to finish our project?"

"Give me a minute. I'm just getting up," Elizabeth lied. "I'll come down for some tea first and then we can come back up and get this done. Thank you, Faye," she said, dismissing her.

Elizabeth gathered the treasures from the table that would fit into the safe and stashed them in with the diary and letters, clicking the door shut. It was getting full, but there was still room for more. She would finish looking through the contents of the satchel later, but first she had to find a place to hide it. She looked around, her eyes finally resting on the top of the very tall dressing bureau that she used to hold bed linens, one that would require a chair to access. She picked up an embroidered chair so as not to drag it across the floor, setting in quietly in front of the bureau, then climbed up and placed the satchel on top and slid it back toward the wall. She climbed back down and circled the room, confirming that the lip of the bureau concealed the satchel from every direction. Satisfied, she returned the chair and went downstairs for tea.

Elizabeth walked out to the patio. It was such a beautiful afternoon; she thought that she could recline on the patio and perhaps get in the nap that she feigned taking while everyone was out. She was asleep before her tea came. Faye sat the tray down quietly, taking care not to wake her, but wondering why she was so tired if she'd just had a nap.

When Elizabeth woke, the tea water was cold. Faye saw her stir and brought a fresh pot of hot water, pouring it over the teabag in her cup, then taking the pot of cool water away.

Elizabeth sat up, smiling, and looked around. "My, I guess what the doctor said was true. I'm going to be the most tired from now through the next three months." Elizabeth hoped Faye would buy her excuse for a second nap, although the doctor said nothing of the sort. She'd heard it somewhere, so she used the excuse. Faye had no children, so she'd hopefully have no idea if it was true. Elizabeth finished her tea quickly and rose. She walked through the open doors and crossed the dining room, calling to Faye as she came out of the kitchen.

"I'll meet you in my room. We can finish this project before dinner." With that, Elizabeth walked down the hallway and climbed the stairs to her room. Again, she noted that things were disturbed. She was growing impatient with the heightened level of snooping. What was Faye after? Something specific? Or was she just growing impatient, knowing that she was overlooking the find. Elizabeth didn't know how long she'd slept on the patio, but apparently long enough for someone to make a quick run through the room. Faye appeared in the doorway behind her.

"Faye, has someone been in my room?" Elizabeth asked, turning to note the expression on Faye's face change from one of excitement around the project to furtive glances around the room, giving up all of the places with her eyes that she'd searched just minutes before.

"No, ma'am, not that I know of," Faye lied, locking eyes with her.

"Hmmm…okay, well, it seems so," Elizabeth said as she turned, pretending to let it go for a moment but then adding, "I will ask Holden to have a lock installed on the outside so that I can secure it when I leave." She paused. "My privacy is all that I have left. You do know that, don't you?"

Faye looked down at her feet, nodding. "I understand, Miss Elizabeth."

Elizabeth picked up the two frames from the floor and set them up on the table where she'd just rummaged through the contents of the satchel. The glue was set, and the fabric was ready for mounting.

Faye brought the gowns and pins over, and within minutes, they had the gowns pinned into place. They each sat centered in the middle of their frame, but woefully alone. They needed something more to turn each one into more of an assemblage, boy- and girl-themed, and make them more appealing. Elizabeth needed baby things…combs, ribbons or rattles, but they would all have to be as aged as the gowns. She would make it a point to look through both trunks again for anything more that she could add.

"There," she said. "They are finished." She would not mention what more she wanted to add nor that she intended to go through both trunks again when she had time alone. "I'll get nails and a hammer from Holden and maybe even have him help me hang them later." Later *when* she would not say, allowing for the possibility that they could sneak a few minutes alone.

"I think I'd like a few minutes alone now, Faye. Would you mind calling me when dinner is ready?" Elizabeth wasn't hungry in the least, having finished her lunch late, but she had some reading to do and was anxious to bridge the gap between the diary and the letters. And now there was John Clayton's private journal to read, one that he might have taken to war.

Chapter Twenty-Six: The Coming Storm

Charles arrived at his office just before ten. Dehlia was already in the waiting room, making small talk with his assistant, Rose, who eyed him wearily as he entered.

Rose hated trying to entertain the elder Mrs. Freeman, always feeling her questions to be surreptitiously prying. She sat stoically behind her desk, an electric typewriter on one side and a vase of fresh flowers on the other. Rose's hair was turned up in a conservative bun, her makeup spoke of responsibility and service to clients with just the slightest hint of sexy, and her red lipstick matched her jacket perfectly. She couldn't type any memos or notes for Charles or Dehlia would become irritated even though she'd be doing her job. How Rose wished she could at least file her nails while they waited. She watched the hands of the clock move too slowly around the dial, only half listening to Dehlia's ramblings about the pitiful way the interior decorating was being handled, then another rant about Elizabeth and how ill-suited she was to be the lady of such as grand estate.

Rose's allegiance was to Charles; his mother was an exhausted matriarch whose days were numbered, but nonetheless she was required to sit and make small talk until her boss arrived. Some days it was brutal. Today was one of those days, as Dehlia just wanted to go on and on about her coming move out to the plantation house. Rose knew all about it, of course, as she'd had to field calls from contractors for months, and she was well aware that the old slaves' quarters was going to be her new home. She wondered—as everyone did—how Charles's new bride was going to handle that.

Rose knew that Charles was in power and that Bryce sat hungrily in the wings—not wishing ill on his brother but prepared to take over at a moment's notice. She knew perhaps too much about the dynamics of the family. She knew that Charles had a bride sequestered somewhere south of town who had never stepped foot in the office. She'd never met Elizabeth as she'd not attended the wedding. Her father had been in town for only a brief visit and dragging him to the wedding of her boss seemed quite unfair at the time. Charles promised to bring Elizabeth into town one day and that the three of them would go out to lunch but as with many things Charles promised, she'd learned not to hold her breath. Rose also knew that he had a mistress, a mixed-race woman uptown, and that he'd been visiting for many years. She was sworn to secrecy on that one. She looked up when Charles entered, smiling.

Dehlia stood and pointed toward his office door with a painted nail. Charles gave Rose a nod while raising his eyebrows; a gesture she knew all too well. She rolled her eyes toward Dehlia, still smiling, yet said nothing. Charles opened the door for his mother, allowing her to pass. She strode over to her usual chair and sat, first tossing her handbag on the adjacent couch.

"So, tell me, Charles," she began. "What in the hell is going on over there?"

"I have no idea what you're talking about, Mother," he replied.

"My cottage still isn't ready, your wife is out riding horses with the stable boy, and you've once again had Lillian Clayton over for dinner without inviting me." Dehlia got up and walked to the bar cart, picked up a glass, and poured herself a liberal shot of scotch. "And don't tell me what time it is. It is noon somewhere," she said, throwing down half the shot in the first gulp. She returned to her seat, stifling the urge to belch.

Dehlia had just covered a range of topics that led Charles to believe her information came from several different sources. He decided to pick the easy one first.

"Elizabeth will be forbidden from riding until after the baby is born." He waited.

Dehlia sat watching him with her head tilted. "Go on," she said.

"The contractors swear to me that they are very close to putting the finishing touches on the cottage. They were waiting on flooring, last I heard. Then the curtains will be hung, and then furniture will arrive."

"And the place will get a good cleaning, I hope," Dehlia added. "It was absolutely filthy the last time I was in there." She drained the glass, got up, and returned to the cart.

"Dehlia, the last time you were in the cottage, it was under construction." Charles seldom called her by her name, and only when he was annoyed. The rest of the time it was *Mother*.

"I realize that, Charles. I met the foreman. He seemed slow and doddling," she added. "No wonder it's not ready. And what about Elizabeth? Is she behaving? I want to know what she and Lillian talked about at your recent dinner." She dropped a couple of ice cubes into her glass, added another splash of whiskey, and turned to face him squarely. "And please explain why I wasn't invited, Charles."

"Mother," he tried softening his voice. "I thought that the fewer people around Lillian, the easier it would be to get her to possibly open up. There's a lot banging around in that head of hers, and I thought that perhaps Elizabeth and Aimee could extract more information from her if you were not present. I felt she might be, you know, intimidated by yet another Freeman. She and Elizabeth hit it off the last time she was over, so I thought perhaps if left to her own persuasion, Elizabeth might pull more out of her."

"Well, isn't that just dandy," Dehlia said. "Presuming your wife can do a better job at anything is a stretch, unless it is producing a son for you, which remains to be seen. How is that going, by the way? Is she seeing the doctor? Are we still on track for the due date?"

His mother was on a roll. Charles considered pouring himself a drink, but he had work to do. He had not invited Dehlia to his office and hated it when she just popped in like this. It was going to be nothing short of awful when Dehlia was in his face every day. He imagined he'd be spending much more time at Marigold's. But part of his agreement with Bryce was that although Noble Oaks was in the family trust and not entirely his, he would live there and bring up his son while together they would renovate their own family's plantation. Both had been purchased with money from the trust, and the two brothers owned equal shares in both plantations. At the time he purchased Nobel Oak, he was living in a downtown apartment, one not suitable for raising a family. Charles was allowed to move into the Noble Oak Plantation upon agreeing that Dehlia could move into the cottage once it was remodeled. They would then sell her house and put that money into the trust.

"Are we finished?" Charles asked her. "I have a client due in at eleven, and I have to prepare."

Dehlia considered this her dismissal, setting her drink back on the tray. "I'll see myself out."

Charles let out an audible exhale as the door closed behind his mother. He had no such meeting planned, and he would have said anything to get rid of her. He knew for a fact that the cottage would not be completed for at least another two months. There had been multiple complications, none of which compared to the fact that because there had been no plumbing before, they'd had to jump through all sorts of hoops to get the county to agree to adding another dwelling to the septic system. But all this was too much to try and explain to his mother. Best to keep the details at bay. Suffice it to say she would be there soon enough. Bryce let him know that there were multiple offers on the table for their mother's house. Aimee was holding them in order of the highest bid, so once they had a date, a sale there would be imminent.

Elizabeth would hate Dehlia living there. This much Charles already knew. The two were like oil and water, and he wasn't sure who was which some days. He just knew that his life would be upended either way once they were living on the same property. He hoped that it was closer to the birth because Elizabeth would be preoccupied with the baby, and Dehlia might soften just a bit having another grandbaby to dote on.

Having his mother bust in like that always upset him, angered him to the point that he couldn't focus, couldn't work. Knowing it was futile to try and concentrate, he decided to go over to Marigold's for lunch, or whatever it was that she might be serving mid-day.

Charles arrived at Marigold's in a taxi at noon, walking to the door and entering with his key. He called her name, but not loud, waiting for a reply. None came. He walked to the table where his bottle of scotch lived. After first looking at his watch, he poured a shot into a small glass, then decided to take a stroll around her apartment—his apartment really, if one considered who paid for everything—which he loved doing when she wasn't there. It wasn't snooping, not really, as it was just as much his place. He would look through the mail, then through her refrigerator, rifling through her drawers of underwear, taking a salacious interest in the lacy ones, wondering if she'd bought them herself or if they were those that he'd asked Branson to go buy on his behalf, snickering to himself at the comments Branson sometimes made when he returned from the lingerie store.

Marigold had a nice stipend, enough that she didn't have to work and yet still not enough to be able to save, Charles hoped. The last thing he wanted was for her tell him one day that she was leaving. He knew that someday she might want to find her boy, *their son*—although he would deny it to the day he died. Charles was sure that she knew where he was living, although every time he confronted her about it, she swore they'd lost contact.

Well, it hardly mattered now. Elizabeth was going to bear a son for him, and his troubles would be over. The family would get off his back, he would let Elizabeth bear another child or two if she wished, and he would allow her to stay in the house if Dehlia didn't drive her mad. He had made her sign a prenuptial agreement that was so airtight there was little she could do to get any part of the family fortune should she decide to leave. In turn, if he divorced her, she would get a little more, but only enough to send her on her way. Their children, of course, would stay with him.

Charles wandered around Marigold's bedroom, picking up gifts that he'd given her, standing to stare at the art on the walls that he had purchased. He was still angry about his mother's intrusion and frustrated at how she could wreck his entire day just by showing up.

He heard a key in the lock and shut Marigold's drawer, walking out of her bedroom as she came through the front door. She had a grocery bag in her hands and was dressed up a little too much for shopping, he thought, but she looked nice. He walked to her, taking the bag and setting it on the table as she removed her sweater and set her handbag on a chair.

"Charles, what a surprise!" Marigold stood in the hallway with her arms crossed. "To what do I owe this visit in the middle of the day?" She worried about the scotch in his hand at this hour. This signaled his day had likely gotten off to a rough start. He wasn't usually a day-drinker, and when he was, it was rarely a good thing.

"What's in the bag?" Charles asked, choosing not to answer her question.

"Food, Charles, just food. I hope you don't object."

The last thing Charles needed was smart talk from Marigold after the tongue-lashing his mother had just delivered. "I paid for it, Marigold. I can ask what is in the fucking bag." He slammed his glass down on the table and walked to her, wrapping her hair in one of his hands. He seldom kissed her when all he wanted was sex, which was the case again this day. He rarely kissed her at all, actually. One hand held her hair tightly behind her head while his other reached down to unbutton her skirt, letting it drop to the floor.

She knew the drill. And she knew better than to fight it when he was in one of his moods. She began unbuttoning her blouse, slowly at first.

"Hurry up," he commanded.

She pulled her blouse over her head and then her bra, dropping her clothes on the floor and let him lead her nearly naked down the hall to her bedroom, where he pulled her forcefully down on the bed, his free hand unzipping his trousers and releasing himself from his boxers for the act that would take less than five minutes. When he gasped and let out a moan, signaling his finish, he loosened his grasp on her hair and rolled over next to her but just briefly. She didn't so much as look at him, lest her eyes betray her resentment. He got up, turned, and went to the bathroom to put himself back together, leaving her disheveled and half naked on the bed.

~~*~~

Elizabeth had so much in front of her, she didn't know where to start. She had Adria's diary, the stack of letters from the trunk, and now John Clayton's war diary. At least she supposed that he took it to war with him, from the date and the first couple of entries. She was more interested in what was happening in Adria's world with children and the coming war and with Liam, so she started with Adria's diary.

November 7, 1860

I can't believe I haven't written in so long. Having two children is so much more demanding than it was with just one! But I wanted to write today as I'm so distraught. I know that John will be leaving soon, and for how long I do not know.

Abraham Lincoln was elected as the president yesterday. It is a sad day for all of us here in the South, as it indicates we'll undoubtedly be marching into war in the coming months. I hope we get through the winter first, as I cannot imagine those young boys—and my husband for God's sake—being subjected to fighting in the through the winter while the temperatures are low and the snow is everywhere.

John assures me that he will never, ever have to carry a weapon other than a revolver for self-protection, and that he will not be on the front lines. His position has already been established as a strategic one, something high up enough that he will be telling the others what to do and when. His leadership in the community and in the state assures him of this, he says. Oh, I know nothing of war, and I don't want to understand it. I hate everything about this situation! Men can be so awful.

Just like John has to assert dominance over me, the household, and the slaves, men in power have to assert dominance over each other. And none of us, neither John and I nor the people in the North and South, are willing to sit down and talk anything out. One always has to be right, and the other has to back down, or there is conflict, period, and it so often leads to violence. I have seen it in my own household. If John does not get his way, he's ready to go to war with everyone, and to avoid this we all just run to our rooms until he calms.

Anyway, John says he'll try to stay through Christmas, although it won't be a happy one as in years past, in that he will have to leave very shortly afterward to assist the troops in taking up positions somewhere near Virginia, he thinks. He can't tell me a lot, as everything strategic must be kept secret. Even discussing such things in one's own home can be dangerous, he says, as some of the negro slaves have been enlisted as spies to help the North. I can't imagine this, of course, but then I can't imagine a lot of what is happening right now.

Liam is the one who keeps me strong these days. He is always there, whether it is to run me to town in the buggy, where we maintain the tradition of stopping halfway to lie together on a blanket and kiss until our lips are sore, or to meet me at the cabin in the woods to make love in a hasty fashion if John is in town. I swear if John made me feel like Liam makes me feel, I would have ten children for him and love him forever! Liam is always so happy, the opposite of John's disposition. I just hope Little John does not take up his father's moodiness. It would be unbearable having two of them in the house at one time.

Elizabeth rolled over and closed the diary, picking up the letters. It was obvious between the diary, the letters, and the book written by Lillian that Adria and Liam had a longstanding relationship. *Putting the pieces together will be so fulfilling,* she imagined. She wondered about the pieces of her own puzzle as she laid there with another letter in her hand. Between Charles, Holden, and the baby growing inside her, what will become of her in this situation with no war to take Charles away?

May 1, 1864
    Dearest Liam,
    It is May Day! The children are wrapping the May pole with flowers and ribbons, and we are all trying so desperately to pretend that things are normal, although carriages come through daily with wounded soldiers, stopping to ask for food and water, bandages, for any help at all. We are barely maintaining ourselves at this point with the war going on now for three years. The crops are barely tended to, the tobacco fields are fallow, and suffice it to say the slave trade is nonexistent with John and his brothers off fighting this terrible war instead of tending to business. There is little money to buy anything from the traders who pass by with goods, although I reserved enough money to continue to buy sugar and flour from them. We still have livestock, although they have also dwindled as we've had to take them for food. But we have lard and are still able to bake breads and pies.
    Luckily, we had enough in reserves before the war started to continue to feed ourselves. The slaves have been able to maintain enough of a garden for the household and the families in the quarters, but outside

of that, we have little to spare for the injured and the soldiers who are carrying them home. Charles said this time would come long ago, so we prepared our cellars and put up our preserved vegetables and fruits and dried beef and pork before the war started.

We are among the lucky ones to be sure as many are hungry. Sometimes a weary traveler comes by us, but we don't know if he is a soldier who has defected or a Northerner who might want to harm us, so we must run him off even if he is starving. It all feels so wrong, and I just want it to be over.

I wake up every day thinking about you, not my husband wherever he is, and I feel ashamed, but I cannot help myself. I don't fault you for traveling North to your family to avoid the war, as it is senseless. I know we share the same feelings about keeping slaves, and your not wishing to fight for the cause is admirable in my eyes.

I love you dearly, and I hope my letters are finding you. We will be together again soon, God willing.

Yours always,
Adria

Elizabeth startled when Faye knocked on the door.

"Dinner is ready, Miss Elizabeth," came Faye's words from the other side.

"I'll be right down, thank you," Elizabeth replied. She put the letter back in the envelope, noting Liam's address as a place in Colorado, thinking at first Adria's reference to "up north" meaning much farther away from the fighting, but to the best of her recollection, Colorado volunteers had indeed played a role in fighting Confederate Texans, so he had not been completely isolated from the conflict, just on the other side. She gathered the diary, letters, and John's journal and stuffed everything into the safe again—wishing wholeheartedly that she had enough privacy in her own home that this wasn't necessary—then went down to eat.

Elizabeth was surprised to see Charles already seated at the table, a glass of scotch with ice in his hand. She passed by him on her way to her seat. He hardly glanced at her, and she said nothing, taking her place at the other end of the table.

Charles had been drinking most of the day. Following his encounter with Marigold, he returned to his office and finished half the bottle of scotch with his feet on his desk, looking out the window. He hadn't accomplished a thing all day—other than having an orgasm with a forced accomplice, and he didn't care. His business ran itself for the most part. Bryce would disagree, but with the many contracts in place, Charles's sole objective was to look for wrinkles, make sure deliveries and processes were in place, and things ran smoothly after the ink was dry. There was not much more that he could do other than show up at sites and businesses and micromanage, which wasn't his style.

Charles looked over his glass, watching as Faye came to bring Elizabeth a soda water. For a married couple, they had almost nothing to talk about. Charles had no desire to share his day with his wife. What, tell her about his mother showing up at his office to mouth off and demand that her cottage be available sooner, while wanting him to assure her that his wife was not stepping out of line? Should he tell Elizabeth how he entered Marigold from the back this time and describe how she lifted her ass high into the air as he expected while he pumped hard into her until he came? What more was there to share?

The ice cubes clinked against the sides of the glass as Faye delivered two more with tongs from the ice bucket before pouring more scotch. She looked down at Charles reverently, not as a father or someone she would actually worship but as a benefactor, someone whom she was beholden to serve.

"Thank you, Faye," Charles said, looking up at her unsmiling.

The tension emanating from both ends of the table was once again palpable. Elizabeth reached down and touched her belly to acknowledge the little flutter that she'd felt earlier in the day, not to draw attention, but Charles noticed.

"Everything okay?" he asked gruffly.

"Of course, Charles. I would tell you if anything was not normal." Elizabeth had no desire to tell him about the little dresses that she'd picked out from what could only have been Adria's trunk, about kissing Holden in the barn before he helped her pick out frames from the shed, and then about how that little traitor Faye helped her pin them into something she could hang as art on the walls in the nursery. Of course, if she had a boy, the girl-themed frame would come down. She didn't want to think of what might happen if she had a girl.

Dinner was then served by Faye at one end next to Charles and by Gwendolyn laying a plate in front of Elizabeth. The meal consisted of pork tenderloin and mashed potatoes with a fresh green salad from the garden. Elizabeth's mind wandered to the days of the war when there were no fresh greens, when injured soldiers were carried along bumpy roads in wagons pulled by horses—likely starving—with households along the way unable to provide them with any more than enough food to get to the next plantation.

Elizabeth suddenly wished that it was Charles going off to war and thought without a drop of guilt how she would cherish such a scenario. She imagined lying with Holden in the master bedroom, after having erased all signs of Charles ever having lived there, and being able to make love as many times as they wanted throughout the night. They would not only be free as lovers in the night, but they would stay in bed all day as well if they wanted.

She realized that she needed to find a "Liam's cousin" type of situation for outings to town, along with an excuse to spend the night. As a pregnant woman, she wouldn't be questioned if her motive was strong enough, or so she hoped. Elizabeth and Holden had time now to enjoy lovemaking before the baby took over the space, and they needed to make the most of that time. Elizabeth was brought back to the present with Charles clearing his throat.

"What in the world is the matter with you?" he asked.

"I don't know what you mean," Elizabeth said, flushing as if he had read her thoughts.

"You haven't said a word in days unless I question you, and it is beginning to annoy me," he said.

"Everything annoys you, Charles."

He stiffened, feeling his anger grow as his limbs tightened, his hand curling around the glass of scotch so tightly he feared it might break. Even his eyes felt the blood pressure from behind, pushing them out too far. He closed his eyes and took a deep breath. "What did the doctor say?" he asked.

"He said everything is okay. I just told you that," Elizabeth replied, trying to hide the amusement in her eyes for the fact he just didn't get the point of a checkup. *Nothing* was a good report, and details were few if any as long as everything checked out.

"He weighs me and talks about diet, and if I'm lucky he sticks his fingers up there and moves them around. It can be exhilarating." She said this with mock laughter in her eyes.

But Charles wasn't up for it. If he could have lifted the table and flipped it over, he would have. But instead, he forced another bite of mashed potatoes through his rigid lips and swallowed without chewing. Charles was desperate to change the subject. "My mother is coming in a month," he lied, knowing it wouldn't be that soon, noting Elizabeth's immediate disapproval.

"Great news," she said, undeniably forcing the words.

"She will be in her own quarters," he said. "She won't always need to join us here for meals."

"Yes, of course, just like grits don't come with butter in the South. There won't be a meal where Dehlia won't be right here ready to order her next course before it is offered and maybe even ask to have leftovers delivered to the cottage, all while bossing the staff to the point of tears."

That stung like a slap, but Charles was ready for the blow and to deliver one of his own. "She is more a lady of the house than you will ever be, so get used to it." With that, he took the last bit of pork in his mouth, wiped away gravy with his napkin, and threw it onto the plate. "Excuse me," he said, picking up his scotch and pushing his chair back from the table.

Elizabeth sat, smiling as Charles walked away from the table. Knowing what she knew now, there was little that he could throw at her that would disempower her. All she had to do was have this baby and—boy or girl, it didn't matter. She would somehow find Daniel, work her magic with Lillian, and find out everything more that she could about the dark nasty past of the Freeman family. Then she could decide where to take things. She knew from what she'd learned in the past few weeks that despite the efforts of this crazy, dysfunctional family, she could possibly be the one to break the cycle of abuse and confinement of the Freeman wives. She wouldn't call it blackmail, but others might.

The question remained as to how she would break through to Dehlia, who obviously hadn't been one of the Freeman wives driven mad or murdered—so she must have a secret, something she'd been able to hold over her husband before he died, something that became the ticket to her freedom, such as she hoped to obtain. The only thing remaining was for Elizabeth to find out what that secret was. That, plus the fact that she may just have a full-blown canon or two in her own arsenal, and she might find herself powerful enough to make a move.

With Charles gone from the table, the tension in Elizabeth's body released. She sat thinking about what she'd just said to Charles, about the doctor sticking his fingers up there and how it would please her if it happened. He was beside himself and had no response for once, which delighted her. He had never done that to her and never would, she was sure of it. Pleasing a woman was not part of his game. But Holden…that was another story.

Holden was a master at pleasing her. In the few short months since they'd become intimate, he'd learned his way around her body like he knew his way around the plantation—all the twists and turns in the paths like the curves and valleys of her body, front and back, the secret places where he would take his time and linger. The way he would take any part of her body in his mouth and drive her crazy by flicking his tongue back and forth. She longed for it more than she longed for anything these days. Like Adria, she couldn't stop thinking about her lover and how they might come together again. How, where, and for how long were always parts of the equation as she planned each encounter.

Elizabeth woke to sunlight streaming on her face. She'd slept late. She yawned and stretched her arms high over her head, touching the ornate headboard. Feeling the smoothness of the wood, she looked up at the carving. Thinking about the craftsman who used the fine tools required to create such a work of art made her think of Holden. She smiled, pulled back the covers, and went to the bathroom to brush her hair and dress. Today she planned to meet Holden out at their secret cabin. He was going to bring her the books from William, which until today she'd been unable to retrieve. The plan was for her to take an empty bag and head out along the path in the opposite direction. It would appear to anyone watching that she was going out for another of her walks, although she was now forbidden by Charles to do so. If anyone questioned her later, she would say she went to the bench across the lake to read.

The real plan was that she would circle the lake and take the path that led out to the old cabin, and there she would be able to stay for at least a couple of hours before she would be sorely missed. She certainly never wanted to stay long enough for them to send out a search party, whoever that might be. The first person they would call on for such a thing would be Holden, and if he was missing during the same period of time, it wouldn't look good. When she returned via the same path, taking the long way back in reverse, she would have the books in her bag, and no one would ask to see them.

Elizabeth hastily ate her breakfast, realizing that she'd slept so late that Nettie was already working on lunch—and probably dinner. Faye was minimally attending to her, as Nettie had given her tasks to start on in the kitchen, and Gwendolyn was nowhere to be seen. She quietly pushed back her chair, leaving her dishes for Faye to clear, and experienced a moment of guilt when she decided not to check in on Nettie. Instead, she padded quietly up to her room to retrieve her book bag, a hat, and a bottle of water, all of which she'd assembled the night before for today's outing.

She was nearly as excited about what was in the books that William wanted her to see as she was about meeting Holden, but once she walked through the door of the cabin that all changed. He was already lying on the freshly made bed, with the quilt and the sheets turned back, in nothing but boxers.

"Come here," he said to her, opening his arms. She dropped her bag and began taking off her shirt as she walked to him.

"Let me do that," he said, coming up off the bed. He finished undressing her in record time, and the two fell into each other's arms, the passion unleashing with a fervor unparallel to anything they'd ever experienced. It was almost as if the pregnancy made her want him more, made her orgasms stronger, and made her love him with a fervent passion she'd never known possible, knowing that the baby might be his.

When they were exhausted and couldn't maintain the lovemaking for another minute, he fell back and started laughing. He was happy and couldn't contain his emotion. He looked over at her and for the second time told her he loved her. A silence came over them both as she looked into his eyes, wondering what would become of them.

"I love you too, Holden. And no matter what happens, I will always love you as much as I love you in this moment."

Holden had thought to have a towel laying at the foot of the bed and took it then to wipe the sweat off Elizabeth's body. She took it from him to clean herself the best she could, as there was no running water in the cabin. It was a hot, humid Georgia afternoon, which would be her excuse for coming back as sweaty and disheveled as she was, or so she hoped.

Elizabeth dressed while Holden watched, then she put the books into her bag. She walked over to the bed and kissed him, still lying there naked with no plans to leave until she was gone, thinking he might even take a nap. He couldn't come back at the same time as she, so he would linger a while longer out at the cabin.

"He wants you to come back and see him as soon as possible," Holden said, looking at the books, referring to William. "I've thought of a way to get you there if you want to defy the master and take a ride on Bella this week."

Elizabeth turned, holding the knob of the door. "That sounds like a plan," she said. "I'm game. But you could get in trouble."

"I'll tell him that the lady of the house insisted, and who was I to defy her?" His smile was captivating. She let loose of the knob and walked quickly to the bed, leaning over to give him another long, deeply passionate kiss.

"Charles mentioned something about some big convention in town day after tomorrow. He told Gwendolyn, of course, not me. She mentioned perhaps going into town and visiting her sister for a night, riding in with him and back the next day, which means he also plans to stay in town for the night, likely with his *mistress*." Elizabeth emphasized the word mistress, although truthfully it no longer bothered her in the least. She was still leaning over Holden, her hair falling on his shoulders.

Holden lifted a hand to her face, tracing the outline of her jaw, then letting his finger tap her nose gently. "It's a plan. We'll saddle up just after lunch and return within two hours, again so no one misses either of us for too long. I know a path that we can take through his plantation that will bring us to the back of his house, without us ever having to ride out on a paved road. Meanwhile, I'll find out if Branson also plans to stay the night in town. Sometimes he does, rather than driving back out here. His place is just on the other side of William's. He lives there with his fiancée, so he usually likes to come home, but if Charles is going to put him up in a nice hotel, he'll sometimes drive all the way back out here to get his sweetie so they have a night out on the town, with Charles footing the bill." He paused. "That would leave only Faye to worry about. Make sure she's busy doing something. Maybe you can request that Nettie prepare a complicated recipe for Charles's return, one that requires two people and is a lot of work."

"I'll think of something. Thank you, Holden." Elizabeth turned and walked through the door, leaving it open.

A slight breeze blowing in the door from the forest gave Holden goosebumps. Whether it was from the air moving over his body or the sight of Elizabeth walking away, her long hair now somewhat tangled and her hips swaying, he couldn't be sure.

Chapter Twenty-Seven: A Plan in Motion

Charles woke up in a bad mood, as usual. He was disturbed by the way Elizabeth had acted the day before, the way she seemed to mock him, almost delighting in making him uncomfortable. The way she'd talked about the doctor putting his fingers inside her—what had that been about for God's sake? That man was her doctor!

Something in the tone of her voice had been challenging and disturbing. Did she know something that he should possibly be concerned about? What might she be up to? He had one of those feelings that gave a man pause, and for good reason, he was sure. He just did not know what that reason might be. He was good in business and knew how to trust his senses in that regard, but with women, it was entirely different.

Charles had done everything possible to keep Elizabeth in such a way that she would want for nothing, and although she had no contact with her friends and wasn't allowed company, she should find ways to console herself and find happiness in her surroundings and all that he had provided. The house, her servants, and now a baby on the way—what more could she wish for?

Indeed, Charles knew he was an asshole. His brother and his colleagues had told him so to his face. Why, even his mother had on more than one occasion. His aim was not to bring himself equal to a deity in Elizabeth's eyes, rather to be someone whom she would trust and obey "in sickness and in health" and all that other garbage he'd had to recite in order to get the final "I do" out of her. However, he realized he was failing in his endeavor to gain her respect, let alone her trust.

Charles realized he'd been harsh lately, forbidding Elizabeth from going on walks in the forest and from taking riding lessons from that stable boy Holden—a man really but Charles thought him to be more of a boy because he was young and lacking in assets—and insisting that all her trips to town be supervised by Gwendolyn or Branson. But what was he to do, if not to protect his future heir from potentially villainous predators who roamed the cities and even his own neighborhood?

Take William Stapleton, for example. Charles had been livid when Gwendolyn phoned him that day to tell him Mr. Stapleton had come to take tea with his wife while Stapleton knew full well that Charles was away in the city. Charles wasn't sure just how much Stapleton knew of the circumstances surrounding the Claytons, but he was sure that whatever he knew could not be positive or helpful in his quest to take over the plantation for good.

There was something about William that Charles did not trust, but he could not put his finger on it. Stapleton could not possibly know about Lillian and the arrangement that had been passed down through decades. Why would he? How could he? The man owned the adjacent estate-turned-museum, and although it was said that William's family and the Freemans had been at odds with each other during various eras dating back to the mid-nineteenth century, there was no reason for any bad blood to be still running in his veins, was there?

Charles pondered this as he lay in bed, staring up at the ceiling. He thought back to their first party, when Stapleton had been seated near Lillian. Charles had watched every interaction Lillian had with every person at the party that night, and he did not recall them sharing a single conversation. That was good. However, he flashed back to the moment when he walked in on Stapleton with Elizabeth in *his* room, the master bedroom. Even though he had openly invited anyone who wanted to inspect the renovation to simply ask for a tour, he never would have expected a single man to accompany his new bride on a private tour. Yet there they were, speaking in hushed tones, Stapleton extending an invitation to tour his museum, his family home, when Charles found them there together.

Something told Charles to double down on preventing Elizabeth from making her way to the plantation next door, no matter how upsetting it might be to her. He pulled back the covers and rose to greet the day, his first order of business being to check on the progress of the cottage so that he could give his mother an update, and his second being to go have a chat with the stable boy.

Charles knew he shouldn't think of him as just the stable boy, but because he owned horses—three now—and thanks to Holden the new mare was finally under control and rideable, Holden could be considered as such. Charles knew, though, that Holden also took care of everything on the grounds that needed caring for, from managing the gardener's schedule to repairing furniture and fixing siding on the barn and the shed while the spring storms tried desperately to remove any and all protection from the weather. Although Branson was great with cars, he knew nothing about any of the property maintenance, and Charles was glad to have someone like Holden on the staff to make sure all else was in good working order.

Charles also knew that Elizabeth reached out to Holden for many things, and he wondered if she might be leaning on Holden for more than horseback rides, maintenance, and the occasional ride to town. He needed to know on whose side Holden would stand in the long run, and he would demand loyalty or else.

After last night's display of defiance from his wife, Charles needed to know that everyone in his circle of employment was loyal to him and only him—not to Elizabeth, and not to anyone else. He would do whatever it took to maintain absolute control over the household. He was going to crack down even further, especially until the baby was born.

~~*~~

Elizabeth woke shortly before Charles, hoping to wait for him to leave before going downstairs for breakfast. Faye would bring her tea, and even though she woke with her belly growling, she could hold out if it meant she would not encounter Charles that morning. She had pushed her limit with him yesterday, that she knew for sure, and she did not want to interact with him until he'd had time to process and calm himself.

Tomorrow she and Holden would go see William—as soon as Gwendolyn and Charles left for the city for the night. She chose to stay in her room and read through the two books William loaned to her before she would need to return them the following day.

Elizabeth pulled out the first book, which seemed to be little more than a picture book with the history of plantations of the area. She didn't recognize the plantation on the front cover, so she flipped to the contents, which gave credit to the photographer, only to discover that she'd been looking at a picture of the original Freeman plantation, Whispering Pines, before it was decimated via years of neglect, and before the great fire brought half of the building to ruins. It was the same house that Charles had just purchased, which he had no interest in inviting her to see.

Elizabeth quickly flipped to the pages that outlined the history of the plantation, when and how it was built, showcasing her husband's great-great-grandfather and all his accomplishments prior to building the grand house that held fifteen bedrooms and later at least four bathrooms once the plumbing had been installed. After the details regarding construction, the book went on to describe the history of the family, from the first Charles Freeman as the builder to those namesakes who followed. The book did little to disguise the dark history that was said to have surrounded the plantation from its early days. It mentioned wives who had gone mad, alluding to a potential link between the plantation and their mental health, when Elizabeth knew it was certainly the husbands and the abuse. The history stopped after her husband's great uncle married into the Clayton family, making little mention of the fact that his bride, Juliet, perished in the house. The reference to her demise was brushed off as having to do with depression after the birth of their third child.

Elizabeth was livid. She knew that was not the truth. How could publications so callously refer to Juliet's demise as anything but murder, when it had been written in other books and journals—such as "Author Unknown." But here in black and white was yet another denial of the sordid history of the Freemans and the rewriting of their history of abuse.

She got up and put an ear to the door, not hearing anything stirring downstairs. She opened it slowly, walked to the hallway, and looked out the large window that faced the front, offering a view of the portico, the barn, and if she craned her neck hard, the side of Holden's cabin. She caught sight of a figure walking across the lawn, suddenly realizing it was Charles. He was walking toward Holden's cabin! What could he possibly want with Holden and why was he not taking off for the office already as planned? She tried not to panic. She knew of no reason Charles could have come to know of their affair. Yet her heart pounded in her chest, and she began to sweat.

A voice behind her made her jump. "Miss Elizabeth, are you okay?"

She turned to see Faye standing there with a tray that held a pot of hot water and her teacup, the bag already placed inside. She walked across the hall and back to her room, leaving the door open. The book sat on her bed, but it offered little more than a picture of a plantation in the area—one that Faye would not recognize—so she left it there.

"Thank you, Faye. You can leave the tray on the table. I'll have my tea, then take a bath. I'll be down after that for breakfast." She wanted Faye out of her room as quickly as possible so that Faye could not see how distraught she was. She was sure that anyone within ten feet could hear her heart pounding as she heard it in her own ears.

Faye set the tray on her table, then saw the book, which from the cover appeared to be merely a picture book about plantations. She wondered if Noble Oak might be in there. She was curious and wanted desperately to pick it up but didn't dare touch anything in the room when Elizabeth was watching.

Elizabeth looked at Faye suspiciously, then repeated, "Thank you, Faye. That will be all."

Faye turned and walked to the door, giving a last glance over her shoulder before walking into the hallway and closing the door behind her. She wondered what was outside the window that had Elizabeth so enthralled. She peeked out to see Charles walking across the lawn back to the house.

Elizabeth wanted to look at the second book, knowing she might have to return it the following day, but she was nervous and anxious to know why Charles was paying a visit to Holden. She had to calm herself, so she locked her door, went to the bathroom, and started hot water into her tub—not too hot as she'd been warned by her doctor. She opened a jar of dried lavender and added a generous amount, leaning over to allow the fragrance to fill her nostrils. It always made a bit of a mess, and usually she would leave that for Faye to clean up. As much as she didn't want Faye in her room, she would most certainly let her in to remove the flowers and clean the tub once she was finished with her bath. Elizabeth removed her nightgown and stepped out of it into the tub, but not before catching a glimpse of herself in the full-length mirror that stood in the corner of the room. She caught sight of the roundness of her belly and smiled.

Elizabeth sunk down until the water was up to her neck, reliving the previous day's lovemaking with Holden out in the cabin, delighting in the memory. As she lay there floating her body to the surface with each inhale, noting her swollen belly protruding amongst the lavender buds, she felt the stirring again. The *quickening* they called it, when a woman first begins to feel the baby moving about in her womb. Elizabeth laid there, floating in the water, feeling the tiny one inside also swimming in her own fluids, and for the first time she realized that this was a *person* inside, and her first thought was to use the word "her" to describe the baby. Intuition perhaps? Or wishful thinking.

Regardless, the baby was a person who would soon have a name and a father and a mother and who would be walking and talking before she knew it. Her thoughts turned to Holden again, and she envisioned him holding the baby—she wished it to be *their* baby—talking, cooing, cuddling, and being the father that Charles would never be. She closed her eyes and remained as immersed as she could be until the water began to grow cold.

~~*~~

Charles knocked briskly on Holden's door, but there was no answer. He knocked again. Nothing. He turned the handle and opened the door but did not enter, looking around to see that the bed was made, there were no dishes in the sink, and things were tidy. He liked that.

"Can I help you?" came a voice from behind him, and he jumped.

Charles turned to face Holden, who was holding a hammer in one hand and a piece of sandpaper in the other. "I'm so sorry," he started. "It was inappropriate to open the door when you did not answer."

"I'll say," Holden said, still wielding the hammer yet in an unthreatening manner. "What can I do for you?" He set the hammer on the table on the porch.

"It's about Elizabeth," Charles started. "I've come to talk about Elizabeth."

The hairs on Holden's neck raised in defense, but he held his gaze steady. "And? What is your concern?" Holden did not flinch at the mention of Elizabeth's name, and he was sure Charles would notice the slightest deviation in his demeanor should he falter.

"She's not to go on any more outings," Charles said. He had not really prepared for the conversation or where to take it from there.

"So, I shouldn't take her to the doctor for her appointments? I can let Branson know when that schedule is then, so that he can adjust his trips to town as needed." Holden was testing Charles now, as he had no idea what this command—seemingly blurted out as merely a random concern rather than an order—actually entailed.

"You may take her to the doctor if Branson isn't available. But nowhere else." Charles didn't want to admit that his worry specifically related to Stapleton and to Lillian at the nursing home. He didn't want to raise undue suspicion as to why, although he doubted this guy knew anything related to his concerns. He was angry, and his palms were sweaty, but he didn't want to alert Holden and specifically did not want to fight with him. "That includes horseback riding. It could hurt the baby."

Holden gave Charles an incredulous look. "Riding a horse might hurt the baby?" It was apparent he was holding back a laugh, but his eyes flashed the challenge.

Charles took three steps toward Holden, prepared to take him by the collar and shove him against the wall to make his point. Holden straightened, making fists with his hands but leaving them at his sides. When Holden stood tall, he was at least four inches taller than Charles and in much better shape. Charles was no match for him, he knew this much. But he wouldn't strike first, only defend himself if it came to that.

Charles took a step backward, still locking eyes with Holden. He regained his composure, thinking better of getting into a fight with the one person who he was aware did an excellent job of keeping his property running smoothly, and for no reason at all really other than he was frustrated with his wife. Charles did not, however, appreciate a challenge of any sort, and he read Holden's face as just that. Charles's face was flushed red, and sweat ran down from his temples as he continued to look up into the eyes of the younger man, who stood calmly holding his gaze. *Best to leave it right here,* Charles thought. He'd made his point. He turned, and without saying a word, walked off the porch, across the lawn, and through the front door of the house without looking back.

The day was uneventful for all. Charles went to work. Elizabeth laid low after breakfast, feigning exhaustion and returning to her room. Gwendolyn occupied Faye with household chores and deep cleaning. She had painters scheduled for later in the week once she returned from her sister's house, so she needed Faye's help in pulling furniture away from the walls. They could carry the lighter things, and they would stow the delicate things that might be broken by careless workers in one of the spare rooms until the painting was complete. Holden could round up the construction crew workers to get the heavy stuff out; Gwendolyn had already asked him to bring them later that afternoon. Nettie, knowing that Charles and Gwendolyn would be gone for a couple of days, worked on preparing a stock that would be frozen, as well as bread dough that could also be stored in the freezer.

Elizabeth returned to her room after breakfast, ready to dig into the journals and letters, but there were two things that were on her mind, and she wasn't sure what to do about either of them. She had to find a way to get to Lillian, and she wanted to make contact with Marigold. She realized that both would have to be accomplished using Holden as the carrier of the messages, and both could be risky if her timing was off.

Holden running into Branson at Marigold's would spell real trouble for all involved, and Lillian's state of mind was always in question. She might not recall who Elizabeth was without her showing up in person, and she certainly wouldn't know whether or not to trust Holden, if she even remembered meeting him. There was always the possibility that the staff at the facility would call Charles as he'd requested, if anyone beside himself were to inquire about Lillian or try to see her. They were not required to do so, of course, because he was not next of kin. In fact, Lillian had no next of kin. Not that she knew of, anyway, none that she'd made them aware of.

Lillian's brother had passed shortly after helping her get settled into the facility, knowing that once he was gone, she would need around-the-clock care. He'd given them the impression that she suffered more from dementia than she actually did so that she would be guaranteed a spot in the home. That was the story they'd given Charles and Bryce as well, artificially inflating their hopes that she would soon be too senile to know what was going on with the plantation. She had bad days without a doubt, but she remembered more about the past than the present, which mattered little to her.

Still, Elizabeth penned a short note to Lillian for Holden to deliver. He would pose as the son of her late brother's business partner. When he arrived to speak with the nursing staff, he would ask to deliver the note in person, a request that they would have no reason not to grant. The note simply said Elizabeth wanted to reconnect, perhaps for lunch but not at the plantation, and that Holden would bring Lillian's response back to her. She tucked a photograph inside the note, one that she'd found in the trunk underneath the stacks of baby clothes. She had no idea who it was, but it could have been Juliet. She wanted Holden to show it to Lillian to see if it might elicit a response.

Next, Elizabeth took a blank greeting card that had a simple flower on the front and wrote Marigold a brief message.

Dearest Marigold,

I'm not sure if you have any interest in meeting with me again, but I've thought long and hard about your situation with Charles, presuming it to be similar to my own, the only difference being I've not born him a son.

It pains me to no end that there is a little boy out there somewhere wishing for his mother, and I promise you that I will do whatever I can to reconnect you with him sooner rather than later, with your permission of course.

My messenger will bring back your verbal response as well as this note, leaving no trail for either of us as evidence of communication.
Warmly,
EF

Elizabeth placed the card into an envelope and sealed it shut, adding Marigold's name to the front. She would find a way to get both the card and the note to Lillian out to Holden with instructions to deliver them as soon as possible. She wrote the address of the nursing facility as well as Marigold's apartment on a separate piece of paper and folded it around Lillian's note. Depending on the responses, her idea was to plan a longer day after her next doctor's visit, unless eating lunch had also been forbidden by her husband.

Elizabeth could hear Gwendolyn and Faye walking back and forth outside in the hallway as they took things upstairs to one of the extra bedrooms for safe-keeping. Then she could hear workers downstairs moving things and furniture scraping on the wood plank flooring of the living room. She did not like the sound of that and went down to investigate.

Two men were carrying one of the sofas to the middle of the room, while another picked up an armchair by himself and moved it toward the center as well. The walls were pretty much exposed now, which would enable the painters to have the access they needed. Elizabeth heard Holden's voice as he instructed the armoire be moved carefully but covered first with furniture pads to prevent scratches. He handed the pads to one of the men, then caught Elizabeth out of the corner of his eye as she entered the room. Gwendolyn and Faye were still upstairs. He moved to her to say hello before they returned.

"I have two letters I need you to deliver tomorrow. Can you do that?" Elizabeth asked in a whisper.

"Yes of course," Holden said. "Bring them to me now if you can."

She turned and skipped up to her room, grabbing the book that William loaned to her. She'd already been most of the way through it, and she could disguise it as a loan from their library to Holden. She stuffed the letter and the card inside and ran back downstairs. Gwendolyn was standing with her hands on her hips, watching the armoire as it was scooted carefully across the floor.

Elizabeth handed Holden the book. "This is the book I was telling you about," she said casually. "I think you'll find it interesting."

Gwendolyn noticed, dismissing the interaction with curiosity as to when they'd had the opportunity to discuss books. Must have been during one of their horseback rides.

He took it, nodded, then placed it under his arm, where it stayed until the furniture move was complete, and he left the house.

Elizabeth breathed a sigh of relief, knowing that one part of her plan was in the works. Tomorrow, they would ride to see William. She knew she was moving in on obtaining enough information that could wreck the family, but why exactly did she really need to do that? At this point, she had no idea, but ideally, she would at least gain her freedom, and if she was lucky, she would part ways from Charles with at least partial custody of her child. And maybe—just maybe—she would be able to reunite Marigold and her son, Daniel.

Having delivered the messages to Holden, Elizabeth returned to her room, excited that tomorrow they would ride to William's. Before she met with William again, she realized she should look through the second book that he had loaned to her as well as dive into the war journal of John Clayton that she'd found in the trunk. She wouldn't share with William any of what she had found so far—not yet—although she knew he would be anxious to get his hands on the material if he only knew.

As always, Elizabeth wanted to start the evening off with Adria's diary. She was so deeply invested in Adria's life that she thought about it day and night, almost as if they were living the same life, only more than a hundred years apart. After locking her door and pulling out the diary and letters, she settled down to read.

Chapter Twenty-Eight: Revelations and Loss

January 5, 1861

My dear husband, John, is gone. For how long I cannot say. His absence makes me worry for him, but at the same time, it gives me a sense of freedom that I am sure I will soon come to regret, especially as I grow weary of being in charge of the plantation, which will no doubt come sooner than I can imagine. The slaves are stepping up to help in his absence, which is surprising knowing he is off fighting to ensure they are never free. But I think they realize that no matter the outcome, they have a good life at Noble Oak, and I will see to it that continues, so help me God.

John has headed off to somewhere near Virginia. Although I don't think his outpost is yet fully established, that is where he said he will be. He said he won't be able to write for a while, as things are heating up quickly, and his days will soon be filled with enlisting troops and organizing the ammunition that they will need once the war breaks out, which he said is inevitable.

The children keep me busy, and thank goodness Rae is such a motherly figure to them. They look to her for their needs almost as much as to me, seeing as I am now constantly preoccupied with one thing or another. I still put them to bed, read them stories, and sing their favorite songs. Little John is becoming concerned about his papa being gone and asks incessantly when he's coming home. I cannot lie, and I tell him I simply have no idea. I cannot explain the need for war as I do not understand it myself.

Liam has stepped in to help out in ways that he never has before, which has not gone unnoticed by the household slaves and servants. They don't see him as a replacement for the master, but they don't overlook the way he smiles at me, even when he is trying hard to be casual. I need the help, though, so I cannot deny his offers to tend to things that John would normally care for. Thank goodness, the commander of the local recruiting office agreed to allow one adult male to remain in each household, even when drafting others who do not wish to fight. John unwittingly assigned Liam to be that person, and for that I am grateful.

We've had fewer opportunities to meet in the ways we used to, and with the pending war it is becoming slightly dangerous to travel on the roads, although we still find a way to do so at least once a week. With no one to report the time of my departure and return to John, Liam and I spend more time than we used to when we venture to town. As the winter weather is a hinderance, we don't stop at the pond, but we have made use of his cousin's room during the daytime even without spending the night. His cousin is curious as to his arrangement and who the "special lady" is, as he has taken to calling me, but Liam has not divulged my name and never will. Our lovemaking during the daytime is hurried but fulfilling, and no matter how much time I have to spend with Liam, I cherish every moment.

Elizabeth closed the diary and opened the next letter in the stack. She wished she had hours to pour over everything and finish it all at once, but something always seemed to pull her away. She was determined that tonight she would make progress. Again, she took great care as she pulled another letter out of its envelope. They were always single pages. She imagined postage in that era was expensive as mail had to be carried across the country on horseback or by rail, which also explained why the paper was so thin and lightweight that it was nearly transparent, as were the envelopes.

June 5, 1864

My darling Liam,

I do hope this finds you well if it finds you at all. I've heard how disrupted the mail has been, especially with the northbound mail trains being sabotaged at times by the Union army.

I've received news from the battlefield that John has been injured. They feared his injuries to be life-threatening when he was first taken away from the fighting, after his command post was hit with cannon fire. Apparently, a small contingency of Union soldiers made their way past the front lines in the night and fired into the area where the officers had set up temporary quarters closer to where the battle had intensified.

We are now over three years into this war, and I can hardly stand another day of it. I wish you could come home, but I understand. John will be back any day. They are caring for his wounds at the hospital in Virginia and waiting for him to heal enough to travel. The last time he was home was around February just after you left, and it was awful. He complained the entire time, suffering from severe fatigue as the fighting has gone on so long. Now that he is injured, it will likely be unnerving having him around, as I hear he is not able to care for himself entirely, especially when it comes to his bodily needs. I cannot imagine having to help him in the way a nurse would, and I will consider hiring someone for that task if he is awful to me and if we can afford it. I'm exhausted, but I'm sure he would not want to hear this, instead presenting his own challenges and injuries as monumental in comparison to mine, which I'm sure they are although very different indeed.

The children are restless and hard to control as they've heard their papa is coming home, and the two of them run through the house calling for him already. I dare say they are much happier than I in this regard, but we'll see. Perhaps their presence will calm him somewhat, but there is always the chance his condition will make him nervous and unwilling to show them love, which will devastate them.

I must close this letter with the news that I am with child again. I'm sure that it happened when John was home taking leave, right after you left, although I can't be sure. I've already felt the baby flutter like a butterfly inside although my stomach has not yet begun to show signs that the little one is growing. I'm not sure how John will take it, as he will likely be so preoccupied with his wounds that it won't be a happy announcement as with the previous two. I haven't told the children yet as with John coming home, I thought he should be the first to know, officially. Hattie knows although I haven't told her. She is always the first to know, maybe even before I do.

My darling, I pray this war is drawing to a close and that you can return to me. I understand that it would be difficult, but you know there is a place for you here and as always, a place in my heart.

I love you and miss you.

Yours always,

Adria

Elizabeth carefully placed the letter back into the envelope. This pregnancy would make three children—and Adria had given birth to four. The baby that she was pregnant with that she mentioned in the letter would have been born just after John returned as was described in the book that Lillian had written. It would be John's last, as it was also written that after he returned, he was no longer functioning "down there." The baby girl who was born a year later was rumored to be Liam's, and not a single person would doubt that.

Even though Elizabeth was exhausted, she decided to delve into what seemed to be the wartime journal of John Clayton, self-described as a slave trader, husband of Adria and father of her children, and man who hoped not to die in the war. She pulled the book from the things that would remain safely hidden in her personal safe—for now anyway.

Elizabeth opened the journal past the initials branded onto the leather cover, then skimmed over the brief introduction where John described himself as a leader in the Confederate Army. He was eventually given the honorary title of general, a title only assigned to five officers by then-Confederate President Jefferson Davis, while clarifying that he was not a true general as he did not ascend through the ranks. He asserted in the journal that he was chosen because of his ranking in the county and his business influence in the state, where he had demonstrated supreme leadership skills and developed trust amongst his peers.

The daily entries consisted mostly of descriptions about their positions and how far they were from the opposing troops. He would mention the number of dead, mostly for historical records, never giving the impression that he was phased by the losses. Elizabeth skimmed the pages, looking for anything that might relate to his family, his home, and his wife. Finally, Adria's name popped out on one of the pages. Elizabeth backed up and read the entire passage.

March 21, 1864

I've returned to the battlefield after a much-needed rest at home with my wife, Adria, and our two young children. Although it was good to see them, it was nearly as exhausting being there as it is here on the front lines.

Adria bores me, and the children annoy me. Although my wife is keeping the plantation running, she could not stop talking about what needed to be done and how the fields were in disarray. Everything is in disarray! The entire country is in chaos, and this war is becoming senseless. It is evident that we are losing and that it may soon be over. At that time, I will return home and try to put the pieces of my life back together.

Without a doubt, my absence has affected my marriage. It was obvious from the way Adria looked at me when I was home that the love is lost. I never truly loved her the way she loved me. Of this, I am sure. There were whispers of something happening between her and the fellow who I left behind to tend to things on the plantation, Liam. I hope to God it is not true. If she admits this to me, and I will beat it out of her if I have to, I will track him down and kill him.

I did take her to bed several times while I was home, not because I want another child but because my manly needs were great. She would hardly look at me and would turn away each time I was finished, waiting for me to leave her room, never saying a word. She used to coo romantic words to encourage my ejaculation, but no more. It was as if she was a life-size rag doll with no emotions whatsoever.

If my visit results in another child, then so be it, but it may be our last. That will make four for me, including the child I sired with the slave, Grace. I enjoyed my visits to Grace over the years much more than I ever did when bedding Adria, but I had to send Grace away, to sell her with the son—our son—to a neighboring plantation, Whispering Pines. I couldn't have the boy growing up on our plantation as seeing him out in the fields working would be a daily reminder of my transgressions.

Elizabeth's eyes grew wide. There it was: the admission from the father himself that he had sired a child with a slave named Grace! The rumors were true, but nowhere had she heard or read that the two had been sold to Charles's family! This was certainly a new twist. Now she was more determined than ever to make the trip over to see William, no matter the cost or repercussion from her husband, should he find out.

Elizabeth understood then that the reason Liam left when he did likely had been as much to do with heading North to be with his family and avoid the war as it did with knowing Adria's husband was coming home. And she knew that John did in fact return at some point. She would have to keep reading Adria's diary and letters to find out when. She opted for one more diary entry, knowing that by then she would not be able to fight sleep any longer. She had no idea that making a baby could wear a woman out to such a degree!

April 13, 1861

Oh, dear me, it is happening. The news came late last night that the war has officially started at a fort in a bay off the coast of South Carolina. I don't know where John is, but he assured me before he left that he would be posted away from the fighting for the most part, as his duties will be more about strategy and moving men around.

In this midst of all this, I've discovered that I am again with child. I'm trying to figure out when this happened and when I will be due, but it is a mystery, as John left months ago. Unless it is Liam's baby! Oh Lord, please. Nothing would make me happier, but nothing could be more dangerous for him. And for me, for that matter. At this time, I don't plan to tell John by way of a letter. It would just upset and distract him. He would also count back the months, and he would have questions.

My life has become increasingly busy as I take on the role of managing the household. Liam is keeping the slaves busy with the garden and planting spring crops with what seed we saved. From what we understand, seed is going to become scarce, so I am buying what I can find now, before stores run out. The merchants who would normally pass through to sell us wares, seed, and the like have all but stopped coming, as the roads grow increasingly dangerous, especially the trade routes. We will have to be diligent about saving seeds from these crops in the event this war continues into next spring—but heaven forbid—please, no!

Rae told me yesterday that she is with child, so we'll soon have another mouth to feed. She's not going to marry until after the war, she says, and she'll stay in the plantation house with me until the baby is born in September. After that, we'll see. The baby can sleep with her in her room off the kitchen, but then we'll have to bring in another helper for the baby so that she can help me, or she'll have to move to the slave quarters where other ladies can watch the baby while she works.

I hate to say it, but John will be thrilled. He loves it when they "breed," as he said once, "because it gives us more stock." I hate those terms as it makes them seem like animals. They are people, some of whom I've grown quite fond of, and I refuse to treat them like animals or refer to them in such terms.

One thing that I remain curious about, though, is why we didn't keep that last slave who had a baby, if increasing the number of slaves is so important to him. I don't remember her name. I just remember that she had a boy, and shortly afterward John sold them both to the plantation down the way, Whispering Pines, owned by the Freeman family. I would have thought he would want to keep them both since the baby was a boy. And I remember she was a great seamstress. I believe she helped Rae sew the new curtains for the children's rooms.

In any case, using words to describe people that refer to animal herds disgusts me. I secretly hope we lose the war quickly and this madness comes to an end. I would welcome most of them to stay if this were the case. It would just mean we would have to increase our farming operation to make enough to pay them all. Since we would be giving up the income from the slave trade, we would have to use another parcel to grow tobacco or maybe cotton, then we could pay them and afford to feed them as well. That would make me so very happy.

Elizabeth flipped the page, determined to get through another entry before her eyes grew too heavy.

September 15, 1861

Summer is coming to a close, and finally the heat has subsided enough to throw open the curtains and even take walks around the lake. The children love it when we all go together, holding hands and walking in line like a family of ducks. Liam came with us for security, he and Little John bringing up the rear. The children love him (not as much as I do!), and sometimes he picks them up and puts them on his shoulders for a ride. One time around the lake is about as much as I can bear in the heat, now with my growing belly and all, so we went back to the house and made lemonade.

I was wishing that John could be back for the birth, but now that I've had some time to think about it, I'm glad he won't be here. I sent a letter to him, which found its way to him a month later, asking him if he could come, but I didn't expect the answer I received another month after that. It was short and to the point, and it is fair to say it was a bit cruel. I cried once I finished reading the reply. He said, "Now why in the world would I leave men fighting on the front line just to come home and watch another Freeman child be born? I have an heir. That is all that matters."

So, what are we (other than Little John)? Just a bunch of stock like the slaves? Does that make me the heifer? Now that I've given John an heir, the other children don't matter? I'm beyond caring if John ever comes back at this point. He is so cruel and callous. I'm doing everything I can to instill compassion and love in Little John and Delilah, as well as respect for the slaves as humans and love for all creatures. I'll be so terribly saddened if Little John turns out like his father, but time will tell.

Rae is going to have her baby any minute; she is walking around with her hands on her hips all day, swaying this way and that. She is trying to be helpful, but I know that it just isn't possible to assist me in her condition. I tell her to go to the slave quarters and be with her man until after the birth, then we'll figure out where she wants to live. I know she wants to live in the house, though. Those quarters out there are stuffed with people. Hattie says its crowded out there like the way she stuffs crab, "until it won't hold no mo."

I will close by saying that when I first began writing, I thought I would write every day, to create a history for my children and theirs to remember me by, even the bad parts. I had no idea that days would turn into weeks and then months would go by and I might forget to write! This may be partly because I have to keep this diary hidden. The slaves can't read, but Rae is learning, and Hattie knows a little. I used to worry about John finding it, but now that he is gone, I guess I could leave it out on my dressing table. That way, I will remember to write more often. We'll see. Evening is the only chance I have to sit down, and by then I'm usually ready for bed—especially now that the war is in full swing and all the menfolk are gone. Except Liam. Thank God for Liam and that he is here by my side. I would go mad without him.

Elizabeth closed the diary and laid it on her chest. She felt the same about Holden. What would she do without him in her life? She might not go mad, but her life would be so much more challenging, so very different. She closed her eyes for a brief moment, and soon she was fast asleep.

She woke to a knock on her door. She sat up, frightened and confused. No one ever bothered her in her room this late after dinner. She quickly pulled the covers over her chest and shoved the diary under her pillow. She noted the stack of letters still sitting on the table next to her bed and threw a scarf over them. "Who is it?" she demanded.

"It is me, Elizabeth. I need to talk to you." Charles opened the door without waiting for a response.

Elizabeth thought she had locked it before setting out to read! She must doublecheck in the future.

Charles saw her lying in bed, noting that she was still clothed. "Is everything alright? Why are you in bed with your clothes on?"

She was annoyed for the interruption and concerned for the materials that were strewn around the room. Her eyes sent a furtive glance in the direction of the table, remembering the book with his family's plantation on the cover, then she remembered she'd already given it back to William by way of Holden. "What in the world?" she asked.

"Do you need me to send someone up to help you dress for bed? Have you been sleeping in your clothes?"

"Oh please, Charles, stop it. I haven't lost my mind. I only closed my eyes for a moment, and then you knocked. What brings you to my door so late?" Her face remained calm, but inside she was shaking.

"I spoke with Holden today. He knows I'm leaving tomorrow and won't be back tomorrow night, so I wanted to make it perfectly clear that there would be no outings in my absence." Charles stood in the doorway with his arms crossed, his body not nearly filling the frame as Holden's would.

"You came up here to wake me, making it sound as though it was a dire emergency, only to tell me what I already know?"

"You mean to tell me that you were aware I'm not coming home tomorrow night? Who told you?"

Elizabeth had to think fast. "I didn't have any idea that you weren't coming home. I meant to say that I already know I'm not to have any outings. I am fully aware of my status as a prisoner." Then she sat up a bit, still keeping herself covered, giving him a defiant glare.

"You are completely wrong about that, Elizabeth. You are not a prisoner. You are the lady of a plantation house in the South, and as has been the tradition in my family for over a hundred years, a lady of stature does not go off gallivanting on her own or in an unsupervised way. If there is someplace you need to go, Branson will take you. In the rare event that he is not available, Holden may take you, but that should only be to necessary appointments, nothing more."

"Maybe you should have laid out the rules before we married, Charles. I don't believe you mentioned anything about this, not once while you were courting me to come and marry you, which we all know now was just a ploy to give you an heir." She was thinking he might say something cruel, even might want to slap her, but he softened and walked over to sit on the edge of her bed.

It wasn't that he cared. He just needed to hedge his bet and make sure she stayed until after the baby was born, praying it would be a boy. He leaned in to kiss her.

Elizabeth recoiled, pulling away from him. "Don't touch me."

Charles stood and stiffened, standing tall over her, glaring. "Good night." He walked out without turning to look at her and pulled the door shut.

Elizabeth was furious. She wished she'd had the courage to say what she wanted to say, but it wasn't time. Not yet. She had more information to gather, more ammunition to stockpile, more dirt to accumulate. Then she'd pull the trigger.

Elizabeth got up and locked the door, doublechecking this time, tugging on the knob to confirm that the lock was in place. She was trembling—partially because she could have been found sleeping with the diary and the bundle of letters, but more so because she'd just realized that in her diary Adria is carrying a baby who Elizabeth had not accounted for. Adria had two babies in the first three years of her marriage, then she is pregnant with her third in the letter Elizabeth just read to Liam, and much later Adria describes another. But Elizabeth knew that wasn't her last because Juliet was her last. So, the total pregnancies were five! What in the world happened to the baby who Adria was carrying when John was at war? She had to read on, but first she put the letters in the safe and changed into her nightgown.

November 1, 1861
    A few days ago, I started having the pains of labor and knew it was too early. Hattie quickly got the hot water ready and called the women folk to come help.

At least two of them were slaves who had delivered plenty of babies. The midwife couldn't be here as we couldn't give her enough time to travel over by buggy and the pains came at night. The pains got real bad, fast, and I thought I was going to black out. Hattie gave me something for the pain, and all I remember was that it was a thick dark drink that tasted awful. With great sadness, I must report that despite our best efforts, I lost my baby.

I was bleeding a lot. The women were working fast, and it was like I was in a dream. I couldn't feel myself pushing because of the drug they gave me, but they told me later that I pushed the baby out into their arms, but she was blue. It was a girl. I never saw her. I passed out shortly after the last push, they said, and they thought I was going to go with her.

The women worked on me to stop the bleeding, and when I woke up, I was in my bed in a fresh gown, and I wasn't pregnant anymore. My breasts were dripping with milk. Hattie showed me how to express the milk to relieve the pressure then wrapped me tight. She made an herbal tea for me that is supposed to dry up the milk.

Part of me thinks that I should share and offer myself as a wet nurse as others have done for me, but Hattie says no, it's not right. I can't nurse a slave's baby, nor anyone else's baby for that matter, not as the lady of the house.

I've never been so sad in my life. I don't know what happened. One minute, I was getting the nursery ready, and the next, I am no longer with child, and my baby girl is lying in a box somewhere ready to be buried. John is not aware, and I don't think I will tell him until he returns. It is just too much to put it all into a letter, too sad and too dark, and truthfully, I cannot in good conscious even tell him that it was his baby. He'd left four months before I realized I was going to have another baby, which only means one thing.

When John returns, I can tell him that I was much further along when I lost the baby, and no one will challenge my story. That would put the time of our being together and the time of the loss in the right months.

Creating this story is the only thing I can do besides pray and bury her. I would have named her Lily.

Elizabeth felt tears streaming down her face. She put the diary down and placed her hands on her belly. The next thing she knew, she was humming a nursery rhyme, one that her mother sang to her when she was little. *Lily. What a beautiful name.*

Chapter Twenty-Nine: History and Deception

Elizabeth woke to sunlight on her face. It was early. The light was coming in low across the lake, through her bedroom windows and onto her pillow. She pulled hair off her face that had been glued to her cheek by tears that might have kept coming even after she fell asleep. She was so sad to know that Adria had lost a baby and that it might have been Liam's.

Elizabeth thought about the stress of the war, the lack of love in Adria's marriage, and how absolutely awful it must have been for Adria to know she was going to have the baby alone while John was away fighting. And worse, how terrible it must have been that he had said in a letter that he didn't care enough to return for the birth. There was power in those words, but was it enough to cause Adria to miscarry? Or was it just the will of God?

She would never know, just as Adria hadn't, but she was feeling a lot of the same stress. Elizabeth suddenly became concerned and very protective of the child growing inside her. Not that she hadn't always been, but now she felt it in a different way. This was her baby, and nothing was going to change that. No matter how much money or power her husband seemed to have, and regardless of whatever plan he had up his sleeve for his future heir, the thought that there was a chance that her baby could grow up not knowing her was cause for great concern. It quickly grew to a five-alarm fire in her breast and in her heart.

The emotion took over Elizabeth's body as she got out of bed, followed her into the shower and next to the dining table where she sat alone for breakfast, then blazed in her head while she planned the outing with Holden that would take her to William's house in just a few hours.

Recalling the way Charles looked at her the previous night when he'd come into her room made her entire body tingle all over again. How he stood and proselytized about her not being a prisoner, but *the lady of the house*. Well, by God, if she was the lady of the house, she was going to start acting like it, and no, she would no longer be a prisoner. If anything, Adria was teaching her the consequence of not being able to live her life fully. She would go to William, talk to him about everything, and while she was there, ask him if he knew a good attorney.

Back in her room after breakfast, Elizabeth showered and changed into clothes that would not obviously give away the fact that she was going for a ride but be sturdy enough to hold up in a saddle and stirrups. She dried her hair and pulled it into a tight bun and applied just the faintest touch of makeup. It wasn't for William. She went out on the balcony to where if she leaned over far enough, she could see the stables. She noted movement out there but couldn't see Holden. It was too early to go down, as their ride was scheduled for after lunch. She was anxious, though, and so decided to try and get away earlier.

Elizabeth walked into the kitchen, and Nettie let out a low whistle. "Girl, what you got goin' on?" Nettie asked, noting the way her hair was done and that she'd even applied a touch of mascara.

"I'm going for a ride with Holden, and no one is going to stop me," Elizabeth said with a trace of indignation, as if Nettie wasn't the one person who was totally in her court.

"You not gon' get any pushback from me on dat, Miss Elizabeth. My lips are sealed." She knew Charles was gone until the next afternoon as was Gwendolyn, and Branson had driven them, so that left Faye. "What you wan' me to do wit the girl? I can keep her busy," she said as a slow smile claimed her entire face. The gap between her two front teeth suddenly became her most prominent feature, and Elizabeth smiled back as she realized that Nettie was never going to doublecross her. Nettie got it. She understood Elizabeth's situation entirely, and it appeared that she wanted to help.

"Yes, yes…good idea. Please think of something that will keep her completely busy and not wondering at all about me for at least three hours," Elizabeth said quickly, the words coming in a breathy, forced manner.

Nettie put a glass of lemonade in front of Elizabeth, pulling out the stool and pointing at it so that Elizabeth would sit. She quickly made a couple of sandwiches, wrapping them up together with carrots and an unopened bag of potato chips.

She placed everything down inside a large woven bag that sat hanging on the back of the kitchen door, added two bottles of water, then handed it to Elizabeth. "Now you go and do what you got to do. Leave the little one to me. I'll keep her plenty busy."

Elizabeth walked out the back door just as Faye walked into the kitchen. "Where is she going?" Faye asked.

"None yo business. You jus sit right down here. We gon' make a real special treat fo when Mr. Freeman returns tomorrow night. It's a recipe my grandmother used to make when she cooked in this house, and I'm gon' teach it to you." Nettie watched Faye's eyes widen, knowing she wanted so badly to follow Elizabeth out the door and that Nettie was not going to let her.

"Yes, ma'am," was all Faye could say.

Faye stood still, her eyes darting from the door to Nettie and back, wringing her hands.

~~*~~

Holden had the horses saddled when Elizabeth came into the barn somehow anticipating they might get an earlier start. They were tied up outside their stalls, and Holden was talking to them, which she could hear before she entered. His voice was so soothing, not only to the horses but also to her as she listened to him calling them both by name.

"Jack. Bella," he said. "We're going to go out for a little ride. You've not been on this trail before, so don't let anything spook you." He turned to Bella. "We need to take care of my pretty princess, Bella, so no sudden moves. Do you understand?" Holden walked around to Bella's nose and kissed her on the forehead, causing Elizabeth to pause and smile curiously.

Did he always talk to them this way? She never knew. It made her love him even more either way. Holden heard her then, and he flushed a little red as she walked up to him.

"I love you, Holden," Elizabeth said, falling into his arms. "And I love that you take care of me. I do." She stood up on her tiptoes and kissed him firmly on the lips. It was such a pleasure having the freedom to talk, to kiss, and to love him, without wondering who might be watching or listening. "Let's go for a ride." She handed him the bag that contained their lunch. She had the letters and the war journal in a satchel that she'd found in the bottom of one of the trunks. She wore it over her chest and one shoulder. She had added Adria's diary at the last minute, feeling that it was time to show William everything.

"I love you too, Elizabeth," Holden replied as he kissed her back, eyeing the bag she'd put in his hand. "I'm betting that someone packed a lunch for us. I'll put it in my saddlebag," he said, smiling. Holden untied Bella and led her to the door, holding her as Elizabeth quickly moved up into the saddle, then handed Elizabeth the reins. He stored the lunch, then swiftly rose up onto Jack's back in one smooth motion from the stirrup to the saddle.

They were off. Holden led the way, out the back of the property so as not to be seen from the kitchen window, then turning toward the same path that led to the old cabin. They rode past the cabin and beyond into the woods, causing a stir in Elizabeth's belly, wishing they could have stopped for just a few minutes. But the mission today was clear, and she knew that they didn't have a lot of time. She'd never been on this part of the path and was curious as the thick forest changed to a more exposed, winding path that followed the highway, then veered off, cutting through the forest again on the trail that would take them to the back of William's home.

How crazy, Elizabeth thought. *I could walk over here any time and never be seen.* She filed that information for another time should it be needed. Meanwhile, she followed Holden on the narrow path and was amazed when they came out of the forest in a clearing that was just steps from William's door, the same one she'd used to enter the mansion with Penny.

Per William's usual fashion, he came bursting out of the house to greet them. "Hello, hello! Just tether them anywhere for now." William was nodding toward the horses while speaking to Holden. "I'll have someone bring them water."

Holden tied the horses to a post at a shaded corner of the parking area as Elizabeth followed William up the stairs toward his side door. She turned at the top step, motioning for Holden to join her. He caught up with her and held the door after William entered. William was chattering away as he walked down the hallway, seemingly unaware that both Elizabeth and Holden were again together and behind him.

"I'm so excited, so excited that you've come," William said, opening the door to his office. He motioned to Elizabeth to enter, then paused as Holden came up behind her.

"He's going to be joining us," Elizabeth said. "He can be trusted with anything and everything we discuss here today." Elizabeth flashed Holden a smile that gave William all the information he needed to consider Holden to be safely included—not that Holden hadn't already been involved as their intermediary, but William knew that he and Elizabeth were about to go much, much deeper.

William had a spot prepared on his large desk where he had documents laid out and where Elizabeth dumped the contents of her satchel.

"It looks like we have a lot to cover," William said, eyeing the stack of letters.

"I found some things in the house that may be of interest," Elizabeth started. "And a journal that appears to be that of Adria's husband, describing his time in the war."

William rubbed his hands together as if he was about to enjoy a Thanksgiving feast. His eyes roved across the letters to the journal. "May I?"

"Of course," Elizabeth said. "This is why we are here, to set the record straight on a lot of things."

William picked up John Clayton's war journal after again putting on a pair of white gloves and caressed the leather before opening it to begin reading. It *felt* like the history that it would contain. He opened the book to the middle, letting his eyes feast on whatever day and time in the middle of the Civil War he would soon experience. He let out a deep sigh and sat back in his chair as he read.

Finally, Elizabeth cleared her throat. "I tell you what, I'll loan you this one as you've been so kind as to loan me others, and let's move on, as there is so much to cover."

That seemed to please William to no end. He closed the journal, smiling broadly, and set it on the bookshelf behind his desk. "More?" he asked.

Elizabeth began untying the bundle of letters. William lowered himself into his seat as he watched, noting the thin paper that denoted the age of the correspondence. He was nearly giddy as Elizabeth handed him the first one.

"Please sit down, both of you," he said, pointing to the two chairs across his desk.

Elizabeth and Holden watched William's eyes grow wide as he began to read, a smile overtaking his face as he nodded. It was clear there was much that he already knew, but it was also clear via his furrowed brows at times while he read, that he thoroughly understood the context but perhaps the letter contained new and perplexing information. "What a gold mine you have here," he stated.

"Yes, I know," Elizabeth said. "And everything lines up with the book that Lillian wrote and other books of yours that I've read but of course in much more detail. And then there is Adria's diary."

William's eyes widened. "You…you have Adria's diary?" he asked as if such a thing were not possible.

"Yes, I found it during a remodel of the plantation house. I cannot leave it with you as I am only halfway through reading it myself, but I can tell you that it confirms everything you probably have wondered about the time—about Adria, John, the plantation and the war, Liam, and their relationship." She paused. "They were so much in love."

William sat at his desk with his hands clasped. "Elizabeth, I have one more thing to share with you."

Elizabeth raised her eyebrows and cast a furtive glance at Holden, who had been sitting silently, now wondering what more there could be as William had given her so much already.

William pulled a manila folder from inside a drawer of his desk, set in on his desktop, opened it, and cleared his throat. Elizabeth turned to look at Holden again, who gave her a reassuring nod and took her hand where William could not see, giving it a squeeze. William pulled some papers out of the folder and turned them around to face her so that she could read them from where she sat.

Elizabeth's eyes scanned the document from top to bottom, and as she read, her eyes widened, her mouth opened, and she wanted to give a little scream. She sat back, exhaled, and looked at William, shaking her head. "You've known all along then," she said.

"Yes, but I was waiting for someone like you to take the lead on this, as I cannot," William replied.

"Does anyone want to tell me what y'all are talking about here?" Holden asked.

William looked at Elizabeth and nodded. "Go ahead. Tell him."

Elizabeth looked at the document again, took a deep breath, then began. "What this says, apparently, is that—and I admit this must be confirmed legally—any living person who is a direct descendent of the first John Clayton is the rightful heir to the Noble Oak Plantation, regardless of any transfer of title or passage of title from seller to buyer or within their family members or due to real estate transactions going back across time. It is very clear and stamped by the state of Georgia." Elizabeth turned to look at Holden directly.

"Translate?" Holden asked.

"Lillian currently owns Noble Oak Plantation, and no court in the state would dispute that, based on this document." Elizabeth paused, feeling a cascade of emotion falling around her, memories coming back to her of the first and then the second time when Charles invited Lillian out to the house— how he voiced concern about her state of mind, and how she was now sequestered in a nursing home—a *facility,* she reminded herself, not a home—and how Charles and Bryce seemed to be so concerned about whether or not her dementia was progressing. Elizabeth wondered suddenly why Lillian's brother had put her in that facility when his own health was in decline. Was he paid or coerced to do so?

Elizabeth also thought of the fact that although Lillian seemed to be forgetful about things, it was likely not much more than it would be for any other person of her age. But had she, too, been convinced that she was slipping mentally and had that been given to her as the reason for her move to a *safer space* perhaps? Elizabeth was spinning with emotion.

No wonder Charles didn't want her befriending Lillian. Things were falling into place now in such a way that she had to stuff down her anger. Anger would not serve her in this situation, and she needed to find out more, much more from William if that was possible. She didn't have much time, but she still had so many questions.

"What about the baby that John had with the slave. Her name was Grace, was it not?" Elizabeth asked.

"Yes, Grace and the baby, Henry, were sold to the Freeman plantation for about ten dollars, for the both of them, no less! After the war, Henry went on to become a free man—no pun intended—and got a job somewhere in the North. He returned to the plantation at some point, seeking to know his father, and John turned him away as an imposter, refusing to acknowledge him.

"Henry left and traveled to New York, only to return after he'd heard that John had died," William continued. "He appealed to Adria, who remembered the slave girl and the sale of the mother and baby and believed him. She opened their home to Henry. He stayed in what is now the bunkhouse, took a wife, and she bore two children there on the property." William drew in a deep breath, ready to continue, watching Elizabeth, who was sitting breathless across his desk.

"There is another twist, and I know that this will shock you." William waited a moment, but Elizabeth sat motionless, ready for anything at this point.

"Marigold."

Elizabeth sat upright quickly and became tense. "What about her?"

"Marigold is a direct descendent of Henry. Charles likely has no idea that he is having an affair with someone who is not only a descendant of a slave, but who is also the great-great-granddaughter of Henry, and who also has Freeman blood running through her veins."

William leaned back in his chair, looking from Elizabeth then to Holden and back. "How so?" she asked.

"Well, it appears that having grown up on the Freeman plantation, and knowing the freed slaves there like his own kin, it turns out his wife was sired by none other than the owner of that plantation, Charles Freeman the First."

Elizabeth sat, shocked, trying to comprehend everything that William was saying but believing it all, given the various documents that she'd read, all pointing to the same conclusion. But this was a twist that she wasn't prepared for.

"So, he's having an affair with someone he is indirectly related to from decades ago?" Elizabeth asked. "Do you think Marigold knows her family history?"

"Most likely," William replied. "But if she does, given her current situation, there is absolutely no way she is going to bring it up. Charles takes good care of her and pays for everything, and her lifestyle is nothing to complain about. She doesn't have to work, and her only job is to accommodate him."

This stung, and Elizabeth winced. Holden's hand came out to meet hers again as tears welled up in her eyes. "Does anyone but me find it ironic that the mother of Charles's son, his heir if you will as his firstborn male child, is directly descended from a slave who was conceived on our plantation, sired by his freed great-great grandfather?" Then she turned to William and in a cold, calculating tone, asked, "Could it be that Daniel is actually the heir to the Freeman trust?"

"Of course," William said. "But no one except Charles knows it, and of course, Daniel is way too young to understand, but yes." William shifted, looking at Holden, who sat with Elizabeth's hand in his lap.

"All he would need to do once he turns eighteen is get an attorney to find out," Holden added. knowing full well that a black man—a bastard heir—in the south, challenging a rich white family such as the Freemans would be a long shot. Finding an attorney who would risk his reputation presenting such a case would be even more elusive.

"Correct," William replied. "There is no clause or exception in most documents, for those blood relatives being descendants of slaves. Charles likely never anticipated that it might ever come to this possibility."

"But wait," Elizabeth continued. "Lillian may be the rightful owner of Noble Oak Plantation, for now anyway, and Daniel is possibly an heir to the Freeman family's money. Where does that leave Charles, his brother, and their mother?" She asked about them first, but she was strongly wondering about her own fate.

"In the dump, if you will, if this all comes out," William said, a smile beginning to form at the corners of his lips. "But then Charles just bought back his family plantation, so they will not be homeless! And that is *if* someone like Daniel were kind enough not to fight them for it, as it also sits currently in the Freeman family trust." William slapped his thigh with one hand, the other on his gut, stifling a belly laugh. "They'll just need to rebuild it, as half the house has no roof." He was still smiling, but then suddenly he grew serious. "Now I have one more important detail."

Elizabeth perked up, raising her eyebrows. *What now?* she wondered.

"They know. Charles and Bryce. *They know.* My copy is not the only copy of the will. I have an acquaintance at the bank where their trust monies are parked who told me about a box that he came upon one day about a year ago, before Charles bought Noble Oak Plantation. He told me he'd seen the will, the declaration page that would supersede any future sale. When Charles bought the plantation house, my friend knew the box was going to go to Charles and his brother, so he made a copy and gave it to me for safe keeping and for the historical record, of course." William sneered as he said this, then continued. "He knew our families had been at odds for over a century, and it wasn't without trepidation that he did so, making me swear to secrecy because he could lose his job for not bringing it to the attention of the title company and the bank before the money left their trust. He thinks maybe they even knew before the sale, but he's not sure. He felt that someone else needed to know, plus he was well aware that there were descendants of the Clayton family living not only in Georgia but in New York."

"New York?" Elizabeth asked, her face clearly revealing cause for concern. "Lillian's brother's children, both who live in New York, are not direct blood relatives, so have no fear, they have no claim to the Clayton's assets except those of their father. His wife died before she could conceive, and he later remarried to a woman who had two children." William swiveled in his chair, his face still contorted with contempt. "I had my friend do the digging for me so that I had all the facts before showing this to you. I'd known about the two children who showed up at the funeral when Lillian's brother died and heard the rumors that they weren't his, so I had to be sure.

Elizabeth was still sitting motionless, the look on her face betraying her emotions. She was happy in so many ways, but in others, she was terribly frightened. Charles would likely stop at nothing to make sure he did not lose control of the plantation house, which left her in a precarious position should she decide to help Lillian succeed in reclaiming her property.

And then there was the money. Technically, Daniel was Charles's firstborn, but wait, what if she had a boy growing inside her at this very moment? Might Marigold have signed an agreement with Charles once he found out she was pregnant that cut her child out of the possibility of any money? And what was the possibility that Charles had set aside a part of the trust for that child? Oh, it was all so complicated. Elizabeth shifted in her seat and asked William, "Might Charles have to go after Marigold for the Freeman money if she didn't sign any agreement and if I have a boy?"

William raised an eyebrow. "Or fight her for the plantation house as well when Lillian passes?"

"I have to give this some thought," Elizabeth said.

"Take all the time you need," William replied. "But as a side note, since Daniel is a minor, there is always the possibility that Marigold could file for the estate monies on his behalf, even before you give birth, and manage his part of the estate until Daniel turns eighteen." He cleared his throat. "The Freemans would fight hard, but in the end, they would settle, and he will win a great deal of the assets, and his mother would have the control until he turns eighteen. I must admit I've already had this all checked out by an attorney friend, who has signed a confidentiality agreement, so nothing will go past him until this all shakes out.

"Doublecheck your prenuptial agreement," William continued. "I believe Charles would have put the same option in your agreement in the event of his early demise, to make sure you can claim your son's—given that the child you are about to bear is a boy—assets, his share of the estate. If Charles goes first and your son is not yet of age, you could then sue to protect him from his family cutting anyone out of their inheritance. And that goes for you. As the mother of his child, you also need to be protected no matter what you signed." William paused, taking a deep breath after such a diatribe.

"Wills and trusts are a funny thing, are they not?" he continued. "Isn't it odd how the very rich get so much more protective of what will happen to their assets and their money long after they know they will be gone and buried even when their heirs have more than they can spend in seven lifetimes? Anyway, it is likely all in your prenup, as the same would apply to you and your child, should you have a son. And if Marigold were to keep quiet, things would be easier. But keep in mind that if she knows, and you also have a boy, the two of you may indeed end up at odds over money. Food for thought, my dear, food for thought."

Elizabeth sat looking at William while the room around her exploded into a pixelated version of itself, coming back into focus seconds later to reveal the novel tableau of what could have been an expensive attorney's office: letter opener with gold handle on a walnut desk, marble windowsill behind holding a fake fern, picture of some dead relative on the wall over William's right shoulder. Her husband's plantation home—the house where she lived and slept and was to raise a child—was actually owned by Lillian if she was to claim it as the only living descendant of the original Clayton family, and in that event they could all be kicked out should Lillian choose to ask them to leave.

And the right to manage most of the Freeman's family fortune could be challanged if Marigold had enough courage to file on Daniel's behalf as the firstborn son. Elizabeth had one shot at getting everything into the open, securing her friendship with Lillian and therefore possibly her future, and it had to be today.

Elizabeth realized in that moment just how much she hated her husband. He had tricked her, and he unapologetically continued to up the ante of control, despite the multiple times she'd tried to assert her freedom.

In a perfect world, Elizabeth would get the ball rolling and stand back to wait and see what happened, but she didn't have time. Charles and Bryce would fight hard, whether or not they realized her involvement. If things fell apart, which was likely, Charles might try to negate their prenuptial agreement and along with that, take away any support and alimony that she would rely on as a single mother—if they didn't try to take the baby from her, which was also likely.

And the baby? Elizabeth was sure that it was Holden's. She'd never been more sure of anything in her life. It was all too much. She needed to go home and lie down. But first, she needed to figure out how to get to Lillian.

She turned to Holden, who sat listening through the entire exchange watching Elizabeth and William volley, admiring Elizabeth for being so brave while appreciating William for his willingness to bring everything into the light, as he had nothing to gain other than perhaps settling a century-old rivalry. What Elizabeth did with the information was one thing, but the way forward was absolutely in plain sight, and Holden was fully on board to help her.

"We must ride back and get a car," Elizabeth said. "I need to see Lillian. Today. While Charles is away."

"Yes, of course," Holden said, rising. He turned to walk toward the door. "I'll get the horses ready and see you outside." He needed to get out of there. The tension in the air was electrifying. He was glad for the order and happy to get the fresh air.

Once Holden was out of the office and the door was closed, William leaned in toward Elizabeth. "You know what you will do to the Freeman family if all of this comes out, don't you?"

"Yes, I am aware."

"Well, good. I hope you are successful. That family has gotten away with indiscretions and abuse for far too long. My family knew it, generations before me. I grew up hearing about them and all the sordid details, and I swore if I ever had the chance, I would do anything in my power to bring them down." William shifted in his seat, realizing that it might appear to Elizabeth that he was using her as a pawn, which he was of course, but he also truly wanted to see her get out of the abusive situation she was in—and break the cycle if possible.

William had one more piece of information that he knew might help her. "Elizabeth, I'm sure you are wondering, after hearing the stories about every single woman who was ever married to a Freeman heir having gone mad or been murdered, how Dehlia escaped the torment."

Elizabeth suddenly snapped to attention. "Yes, I've been wondering what her secret was," she said.

"Money." William looked at Elizabeth, one eyebrow arched, his head tilting slightly. "Her family had more money than your late father-in-law, who needed money desperately. He'd made some investments that had gone bad during World War II, and he was deeply in debt when he married her. So, instead of carrying on the legacy of control and violence, he had to let her be whoever she wanted to be. She was the first in a long line of Mrs. Charles Freemans who could do absolutely anything she wanted. Her husband didn't dare challenge her nor lay a hand on her. And to this day, I assume she carries on—and from what I saw of her at the wedding nothing about her has changed." William cleared his throat, then continued quietly. "I dare say that although she got a pass, she knows that the cycle continues with you, and she cares little about doing anything to change this."

So that was it, Elizabeth thought. It was only money. But it had *everything* to do with money, which was how Dehlia continued to control her sons, the staff, and—if her husband had still been alive—well…he probably endured his share, but he would also still be fair game, she was sure of this.

Elizabeth thought of Dehlia coming to live at Noble Oak and how Charles insisted it was his idea "because she was getting older." She was now quite sure it was all Dehlia's doing—surely covetous as to her son's purchase of the plantation with what was ultimately her own family's money—while she lived in a seemingly modest four-bedroom bungalow on the edge of downtown with a servant quarters on the alley. She would have to find a way to have the project stalled on the Cottage at Noble Oak.

Elizabeth stood and straightened her blouse and pants, turning toward the door. "I'll get more letters to you as soon as I've read them all."

"And Adria's diary?" William asked.

"We shall see. And I would like to get the number of the attorney who is already familiar with the situation." With that, Elizabeth walked out of the office, William trailing behind her down the hall to the side door where through the glass panes he could see Holden outside holding the reins of both horses in his hands.

~~*~~

Elizabeth walked into her room and fell down on her bed. The outing had exhausted her, but she knew that Holden was out in the garage at that very moment, preparing a vehicle for their trip to town. On the ride back, they talked about how she would find a way to distract Nettie and Faye long enough to depart without either of them realizing she was gone. She'd leave a note, something about going to town for a surprise, knowing full well that Faye would try to phone Charles once it was known that she'd been able to sneak out. But Charles would either be at his function, whatever that was, or already in Marigold's arms and in any case likely unreachable.

Branson would be checking into his hotel by then with his fiancée, and Faye would have no idea where that might be. The office would close early as Charles would be out for the day, so Faye would not be able to reach anyone there either. The chances of Charles finding out about her trip to town were slim, until his return the following day, and Elizabeth was sure to be brazen enough by then to stand up to him, especially after a visit with Lillian.

Elizabeth needed to muster her strength, but she knew that without a rest she would not be able to meet with Lillian and be on her game. She needed to clear her head but couldn't sleep. She was too anxious, with all the information she'd received that afternoon and knowing how much there was to do. She had to find a way to endear herself to Lillian, hoping if Lillian took control of the plantation that she might be able to stay. Her thoughts drifted to Adria.

Of course! *Adria was the answer!* She would open up to Lillian about Adria's diary and letters, swearing her to secrecy in order that Charles not abscond with them, or worse—have them destroyed. She knew how Charles felt about the Clayton women, "not important enough to be mentioned in a portrait," and she knew that deep down Charles felt threatened—by them, by her, by all the women in his life. And now she knew the truth about his mother. Dehlia was certainly a threat to Charles, where his money was concerned, and also to his child, who would go on to manage what was actually their family's trust but that which would be under the constant scrutiny of his grandmother until she died. Elizabeth was sure now if the baby is a boy, as soon as he was born and weaned, she would be cast out—if Dehlia could even wait that long.

Elizabeth got up, removed her clothes, and stood naked in front of the full-length mirror, noting the protrusion of her belly. She stood sideways examining her profile, running her hands down from her breasts, following the curve, then stopping to cradle the little one inside. She noted the red line where her pants had been pulled a little too tight for comfort, and she realized that she had no real maternity clothes. Suddenly, she had the thought that this would be her excuse for going to town. She needed clothes. It was true, and she wouldn't have to lie if she stopped by a clothing store on the way home. It would soften the blow, the anger that would come from Charles once he was told that she'd snuck out.

She went to the bathroom and turned on the water, deciding that a cool shower would calm her enough perhaps for a nap. The day had been hot, the ride in the middle of the day had been short, but she, Holden, and the horses had all returned sweaty. After a quick rinse, she toweled off, went to her closet, and pulled the diary out of the safe, returning to bed naked. She climbed into her bed and covered up with a thin sheet.

October 11, 1862

It has been nearly a year since I've written in my diary here. I must admit that I considered throwing it away. I fell into such a deep depression after losing the baby that I also thought of taking my own life. But of course, with the children being a constant distraction and Liam being of great comfort to me—after all we are both sure that it was his baby—and with the needs of the household pulling me back from that great dark place, I have recovered.

John hasn't been home since he received the news about Lily, which also saddened me, but then again, I know that he doesn't love me, and now that he has an heir, he cares little if I have more children, or aside from Little John, if they live or die.

The fighting continues, and the news we receive here is that although it often gets close, the army is able to hold the line and that we are not in any danger currently. I don't know what I would do if the fighting got so close as to threaten the children and the house. Liam says he has family in Colorado. I can't imagine packing a buggy with the children and enough of our things and leaving this place, leaving Hattie and Rae to fend for themselves. If the soldiers came, would the slaves try to defend the place or would they hand over the keys? One can only imagine, but this is not something I can spend time worrying about.

Word came of a fierce battle down on the coast, one where the Union soldiers now occupy a fort on the Savannah River, Fort Pulaski. I don't know if this poses a danger to us, and Liam says not to fret, that we will have plenty of notice if the fighting draws near. In any case, he has sent word to his family that if it appears we are in any imminent danger, we'll head their way.

The food supply grew dangerously short last spring, but by mid-summer, we were able to harvest from the garden and replenish our supplies in the pantry and the root cellar. We never had a root cellar before, but Hattie says it is necessary in order to hide food in case the enemy soldiers make their way to our front door. They will kill for food, so by showing them we have none, or little, which they will surely take from us, we will survive with what we have hidden.

The cows and sheep all had babies this spring as well, so we were able to take a few more and preserve the meat, which should get us all through until next spring. We have to keep the livestock herds going, but we've had to mainly pasture them and give them scraps from the garden as money for extra feed is gone, so they are thin but alive. As are we!

Adria's next entry was brief.

February 14, 1863

We made it through the worst of the winter. Signs of spring are around us, thankfully. The temperatures are not so cold, which I am grateful for. The children and I spent most of the winter in bed trying to stay warm. We're all out of firewood. What we had that was seasoned enough to burn was used up sometime in December, and now that the days are warmer, the slaves will go out and cut more for next winter. I didn't know how much to stockpile, as that was always something John took care of, but now I know.

Liam is trying his best to help out. We still have two horses, which we have to keep feeding somehow in case we need to flee with the buggy. Liam has grown thin and sometimes I think he looks sickly. I don't look in the mirror anymore as I know I don't look much better.

The children cry a lot. They want their daddy, and I don't know what to tell them. We haven't heard from him in months. There was a battle up north in

Chickamauga, and I heard we did not win that one. I don't know if John was there, but I pray if he was that he is well. I ask Liam where that is and if it is close and if we should be worried, but he says no, we'll be fine. He always says that, and I pray to God that it is true.

Elizabeth closed the diary and tucked it under her pillow. She was finally tired enough for a nap, which she would be glad for later in the day. She would try to close her eyes for just a few minutes.

Chapter Thirty: A Plan Unfolds

Elizabeth woke with a start, rolling over to look at the clock. It was almost four o'clock! She'd told Holden she'd be down no later than three, but she'd fallen fast asleep. She rushed to get dressed, put the diary into her purse, then added the letters. She started to go to the door, then returned to scrawl a note to Nettie and Faye about shopping for maternity outfits. She scurried down the stairs, put her purse by the front door, then peeked into the kitchen to look for Nettie. She was nowhere to be found, but Elizabeth could smell soup simmering on the stove, so she knew she wasn't far. She had no idea where Faye was and didn't care. She had to get to the garage—fast. She laid the note on the counter and returned to the foyer for her purse, then went out the front door, closing it quietly behind her.

She nearly ran to the garage, where Holden stood polishing the chrome bumper as Branson would always do. She was out of breath but managed to get out a quick *hello* as she climbed into the front seat. Holden opened the garage door, climbed in, and started the vehicle, pulling out in time to see Faye walk out the front door with the note in her hand. Elizabeth pretended not to see her, keeping her head forward. "Don't stop," she said.

"Oh, don't worry. I don't plan to," Holden said as they neared the gate and continued out to the main road.

Once they were out of sight of the plantation, Elizabeth relaxed and took a deep breath, exhaling fully before taking another. "That was close," Elizabeth said, sending a beguiling look in Holden's direction.

"I'll say. What took you so long?"

"I fell asleep," she replied, looking down at the diary and letters spilling out of her purse. She hoped she'd not dropped any while rushing to the garage. She pulled the letters back into a bundle and gently wrapped the string back around them. "I guess I needed it. That visit to William wore me out."

"Good, I'm glad you rested. That visit wore me out too, and I don't even have as much invested in all of this." Holden paused. "Except my job." Then he chuckled. He was quite sure that this outing might put him in danger of being fired, as surely Charles would be tired of his complicit behavior by now.

"I will not allow Charles to fire you," Elizabeth said, leaning over and kissing him on the cheek. "I need you, Holden. I can't let that happen. I won't." Then she remembered their plan. "Did you call the facility?"

"Yes, I got through to the charge nurse, and she said it would be fine for us to pick Lillian up anytime this afternoon, and to let her know if we are taking her to dinner so that they won't plan on her in the dining hall."

The nurse had added that she might have to let Charles know about the outing, but Holden sweet-talked her into refraining, saying that Charles was not family and that by following *his* orders, they were not following what the wishes of the family might be. The nurse agreed and said that she would let it go "just this one time" and not call Charles. That was a relief for Elizabeth to hear, as it was one less thing she could be confronted about.

When Elizabeth and Holden arrived, Lillian was dressed in a lilac suit. She'd heard they might be going to dinner, and she rarely had a chance to dress up, so she'd picked out one of her favorite summer suits. She'd applied a little lipstick to match and had a beaded handbag on the table of her room when they knocked.

"Come in," she said from her overstuffed chair.

Holden opened the door to see Lillian sitting there, smiling, with her tiny feet resting on an ottoman and a book on her lap. He held the door for Elizabeth to pass.

Lillian's face lit up when she saw Elizabeth, her entire being engulfed with a smile. "How are you, my dear?" she asked, starting to get up.

"Please, sit," Elizabeth said as she crossed the room. She bent over and kissed Lillian on the forehead, noting the faint scent of perfume—flowery but not too strong, the way Elizabeth preferred. "You look beautiful, Lillian. Where would you like to go to dinner?" Elizabeth sat on a stool beside Lillian's chair, noting her clear blue eyes and the eyebrows that had been drawn on nearly to perfection.

"Oh, dear, I don't care, anyplace that makes a good macaroni and cheese from scratch. The stuff they serve here is horrendous. I'm sure it comes from a box—although they swear it doesn't." Lillian sat beaming at Elizabeth, glancing up to Holden every few seconds. "Aren't you going to introduce me?"

Elizabeth realized that the only time Lillian had met Holden was when she was out at the plantation. They'd also met briefly in the barn, but apparently Lillian had forgotten. "I'm terribly sorry, Lillian. I thought you'd met each other." She looked up at Holden, winked, and introduced him. "This is Holden. He works for us." The charge in the air did not go unnoticed by Lillian.

"Is that so," Lillian said and then a pause. "Is that all?" She looked from Holden to Elizabeth and back. "What a handsome fellow you are," she said.

"Why, thank you, ma'am," Holden said, blushing. He held out his hand to Lillian.

As Lillian took Holden's hand, the recollection came over her. "You're the fellow who takes care of the horses. Like Liam…" she said, letting the last words fall to a whisper.

"Yes, ma'am, that's me," he said, the redness still flushing his neck. "Let's go to dinner, shall we?" He had no idea who Liam was.

As Lillian began to stand, Holden held out his arm for her, which she gratefully took as he nearly lifted her out of the seat. She straightened her suit and picked up her purse.

Holden brought the car to the front door while Elizabeth and Lillian stood chatting in the foyer. He noticed Elizabeth's belly and how seemingly overnight she'd begun to look like a pregnant woman. He was delighted at the thought it might be his. Concerned, yes, but he planned to stick around, no matter the outcome and would support her entirely either way. He held the door open as Elizabeth helped Lillian into the backseat. Holden shut Lillian's door, then opened the front door for Elizabeth. Before Elizabeth bent to get into the front seat, Holden kissed the top of her head. She paused and looked up at him with a smile before sitting down and putting on her seatbelt. Holden closed the door. Lillian sat in the backseat smiling, having caught the entire interaction in the reflection of the glass entry doors.

~~*~~

The restaurant was crowded, but the hostess had no trouble finding them a quiet table in the back as Elizabeth requested. Once they were seated, had been served drinks, and had ordered, Elizabeth made small talk, asking Lillian about the facility and staff. "Out of curiosity, if you had a choice, would you be living there?" Elizabeth asked because Lillian seemed to be so much more alive than 90 percent of the residents. She must be bored, or maybe not.

"Oh dear, no. I'm only there because my brother knew he wasn't long for the world, and his house was going to end up going to his children." Lillian smiled at the two of them. "For the record, I do not have dementia, although I can be forgetful. My brother told the staff that to secure a spot for me more quickly, as he didn't have much time left. I have fun with the staff at times, playing it up, but no, my dear, I am not losing my faculties just yet." She let out a little giggle.

"So, you do have next of kin? Charles told me that you did not." Elizabeth wanted to hear Lillian's version of the story William had relayed earlier in the day. She was delighted to hear directly from Lillian that she had never been diagnosed with dementia and eager for more.

"Yes, I have a niece and nephew, but they've never come to see me. They inherited my brother's house, but neither of them wanted to leave New York City, so they sold it shortly after my brother, Harold, died." Lillian shifted uncomfortably. They're actually Harold's stepchildren, although I always treated them like family. When Harold died I lost contact with them for the most part," she looked from Elizabeth to Holden and back through moist eyes that somewhat blurred her vision, but fought the urge to dab at her eyes with the napkin that remained in her lap. "They just stopped calling." She paused briefly. "I do get cards from them on my birthday and at Christmas."

Elizabeth felt the hurt in Lillian's voice, noting that she would have to check on the niece and nephew and what, if any, their rights might be to the plantation. Lillian was so alone and didn't deserve to be. She had so much to share, so many stories, and had lived such a rich, colorful life. It pained Elizabeth to think of Lillian stuck in that home with drooling ninety-something-year-olds, who didn't know whether they were at dinner or in their bathrooms, incapable of being in either place unassisted. She wanted desperately to jump right in, but she didn't want to shock Lillian with too much information at once. She decided to start with the letters, then she would share the diary.

"I have something I want to share with you. Something secret. No one at the house has seen these," she said as she pulled the bundle of letters out of her purse.

Lillian's eyes widened as she noted the old-fashioned handwriting, transparent envelopes, and graying string that held the letters.

"I've read nearly all of them now," Elizabeth started. "The letters were written by Adria when John was away, most of them, until the last one that is, which she wrote after John had returned."

"Are they written to Liam?" Lillian guessed correctly, smiling, her eyes twinkling. "That would have been the only person she would have written to, I imagine." She watched as Elizabeth pulled the last one from the bottom of the bundle.

"Yes, they were written to Liam. Liam left shortly before John came home, apparently nervous about the rumors that John would surely be made aware of upon his return. I'll read the last one to you."

November 10, 1864
    My Dearest Liam,
    I have another child, another boy. I wanted so badly to name him William, after you, but I feared it would arouse suspicion amongst those who knew why you left, and so his name is Ashton. After losing the baby girl, Lily, I didn't know if I ever wanted to have another pregnancy, as it was the most painful thing a woman can endure. Knowing in my heart that Lily was yours made it even more difficult.

Elizabeth looked over at Lillian, who had her head down slightly, her eyes focused on something across the restaurant, lost in thought but listening intently. She nodded her head slightly as Elizabeth continued.

John returned home just a week after Ashton was born, and it has been more than difficult. His injuries are painful. He cannot walk without a cane and a nurse, and his abdomen is still bandaged. I haven't seen the wound and don't know if I want to. I have my own body to contend with, to heal from the birth, and I'm struggling. He doesn't want anything to do with the children, and they are devastated by this. They were so looking forward to his return. I just explain to them that their father is hurt and in pain but that he will get better and he still very much loves them. I can't say for sure, but likely only one of these is true.

Liam, I have but one request and that is that you return to me by Christmas. I cannot go through another winter without you, and truthfully, I need your help. Now with another mouth to feed—two really with the nurse who accompanied John home—and with the winter coming, I am afraid. John is no help at all. He stays in his room for the most part, and I stay upstairs in mine or in the nursery. We put up enough food from the summer harvest and slaughtered a cow, a pig, and a goat in the fall, so if we are frugal, we have enough meat to feed everyone through the winter, including you. Please, please come home.

John is not receiving visitors, and the slaves are as afraid of him as I am, so he will not be apprised of any rumors about the two of us, not until the war is over and he begins socializing again. I can find a way to deal with that should the situation arise. I've also been told that he is no longer functioning "down here," not by him but by the nurse. This doesn't bother me in the least, as you know. He never made love to me once in his life, only took me to bed for an heir or for his own pleasure.

The only person who has ever made love to me has been you. The only man who has ever loved me is you, and you, my dear Liam, are the only man I have or will ever truly love.

I realize that this letter will not reach you until mid-December, leaving you but two weeks to make it here before the end of the year, and the roads are dangerous, which makes it hard to ask you to travel. I know that what would normally be a one-week trip will likely take two, or even three if you have to hide from Union troops along the way. I have no idea where the battles are being fought, perhaps you do. I only know that without you, I don't know if I can make it through another winter.

Please be careful. I long to hold you again soon.

All my love,

Adria

Elizabeth looked up to see Lillian nodding her head still, her eyes slightly watery.

She smiled at Elizabeth. "He did. He came home, and he made it by Christmas."

"I thought he may have made it," Elizabeth replied.

"And in the fall of 1865, Juliet was born—the baby girl with the famed red hair." Lillian looked at the stack of letters. "How many are there?"

"Twelve," Elizabeth replied. "I've read them all now, but there is more." She tied the bundle and returned it to her purse, pulling out the diary. Lillian's eyes widened at the sight of the old book with the ribbon that had been sewn in to mark the page, now stained by age after having been hidden in a wall for nearly a hundred years.

"Is that a diary?" Lillian asked. "Is it Adria's?"

When Elizabeth handed Lillian the book, nodding, Lillian continued. "I heard there was a diary, that Adria kept notes during the war and that it disappeared at some point. Juliet told me actually."

"I'm sure she writes about Juliet's birth. I just haven't been to that page yet. Shall we find it?"

Lillian handed Elizabeth back the diary. "Please, let's do. My eyesight isn't so good. I'll let you look. She was born in September."

Elizabeth took the diary and scrolled through the pages, looking at the date of each entry until she came to October 1865. She had resisted jumping ahead for a number of reasons, one being that she'd taught herself not to do so, so as not to spoil a good story, and this was no exception. But here she was with Lillian, and they were both curious enough to find the entry.

October 20, 1865

I write with such joy today. I'm holding the most beautiful little girl in my arms. She is barely a month old, and I am so in love with her. She has green eyes like none I've ever seen and red hair. Her skin is like milk, and she looks nothing like John nor anyone in the Clayton family. This has led to much speculation and rumor, which we all know to be truth, as when John returned from the war, he was deemed incapable of ever functioning again in the way of making a child. It was said that he even had difficulty with his bodily functions, although I never tended to him so I cannot personally confirm this.

Liam came home when he received the letter that I wrote begging him to come by Christmas, but he stayed clear of the house and out of John's way, bringing in firewood when John was sleeping and helping me with managing food in the root cellars. He played with the children when he was around the house, outside on nice days and quietly inside on the third floor when John was napping. He could use the back stairwell to get up there from the kitchen, and John was no longer able to climb stairs, so it was a fun way for the children to see Liam and to have game time, and they knew better than to say anything to their father.

Although it was winter and extremely cold, Liam and I found a way to secretly meet at the bunkhouse, as the cabin was just too far away. He would go out ahead of time and get a fire going to warm the place and have the bed ready for me, piled with extra quilts. I will never forget the afternoon he made love to me, that day in January that our baby was conceived.

John hasn't spoken to me since I gave birth. He knew all along that the baby was Liam's. John would kill Liam if he could, but he is incapable of leaving his bed now. He lies in there ranting and raving most days, and his rage-filled screams permeate every room of the house. The nurse says that he is not likely going to live to see the baby's first birthday. This doesn't bother me as he has not laid eyes on her and likely never will.

Liam, however, is beside himself with joy and comes to see her every day. Publicly, we do not make noise about his attention and hope the slaves, who are soon to be free people, do not care enough to spread the rumors past these plantation walls.

The war is over now, and our President, Jefferson Davis, is imprisoned somewhere in Virginia as he was captured back in May when the Union soldiers effectively won this war to free the slaves. I don't care anymore, and suffice it to say I hardly ever did. Many of the slaves will stay on with us as free peoples, and they will be paid for their work. Of course, they will stay in the quarters, but as many of them planned to leave to travel to other states to rejoin their families, it won't be nearly as crowded as it has been in the past.

I have to think about Little John now, as when his father passes, he will be groomed to be the man of the house. He is so young, but I think he knows this already. The slaves and Hattie have made comments to him often enough. It will be a few years yet, but when it is time, he will be ready.

PS: I've named the baby Juliet.

Elizabeth closed the diary and laid it on the table. In between the readings, their food had come, they had eaten, and it was time to either have dessert or return to the nursing facility.

"Let's go back to my room," Lillian said. "I have something I would like to tell you."

Lillian sat back down in her overstuffed chair, having removed her shoes and hung her lilac jacket on a hook by the door. "Please, sit down," she said to Elizabeth, who took her place back on the footstool. Holden sat across from them in a second chair that matched the one Lillian was sitting in.

"Oh my, where to start," Lillian said, tipping her head back slightly. She wasn't tired, but she rested her head against the back of the chair and closed her eyes for a moment. She decided to dive right in. "A young man came to see me recently. His name was Howard MacArther. He claimed that his great-great-grandfather, Henry, was sired by John Clayton when he was married to Adria. He knew the whole story, how Henry and his mother were sent away to avoid controversy, sold to the Freeman family where he lived until he was set free after the war. Elizabeth, you remember me telling you that after the war Henry went back to Noble Oak—his mother had died of influenza during the war—and asked to live there, claiming that John Clayton was his father. John had just returned from the war with dire injuries, as we just read about in Adria's handwriting, and he was livid. He knew the child was his and that the child's mother had indeed been a slave there. Adria knew it too, and she pleaded with John to let him stay, but John went into a rage and threw the boy out, telling him he would sic the dogs on him if he tried to return." Lillian paused for a moment and asked Holden to get her a glass of water.

Elizabeth had read this same account in two other places, and Lillian had also told her parts of the story when she'd spent the night. One account was in John Clayton's war journal, where he admitted to siring the child. William had given her some of the same details, and she'd read about it again in "Author Unknown," which she now understood Lillian had written. Elizabeth had not yet admitted that she'd read the book.

Lillian continued, "Anyway, and I know I told you about this already too, but the boy Henry did leave that time. However, as soon as he heard of John Clayton's death, he returned to appeal to Adria. He'd heard that she had always been a kind, reasonable person. And sure enough, Adria let him stay. She put him in the bunkhouse, where he lived until the day he died. He worked on the plantation, was paid a decent wage by Adria, married, and had two children. One of those was a son, the great-grandfather of the young man who came to see me. How he found me, I'll never know. But he came to appeal to me that if I might ever find myself back at the Nobel Oak Plantation, he should like to live in the bunkhouse where his great-great-grandfather once lived. That was all, as he didn't come making any claims to the estate, although if he was white, he certainly might have a case as part of John Clayton's lineage."

Lillian paused, taking a long drink of water, wishing things were different. She hated the notion of slavery, and she hated the fact that a hundred years later her people still hadn't learned much about respect for each other no matter the skin color.

Then she continued, "But anyway, I told him it wasn't possible, that the plantation had been sold several times since my aunt and uncle died, and here I am in a nursing home. I can't be of any help to him. But he did leave his name and number and asked me to call in case things changed." Lillian's voice trailed off a bit as she thought about the impossible notion of returning to the great house of her youth and about those carefree days where the cousins chased each other—and geese and sometimes swans when they dare stray from the water—around the property for hours.

Elizabeth noted the moment that her attention returned to the room. It was now or never.

"Lillian," she started. "What if I told you there might be a way to return to Nobel Oak?"

"Oh, my dear, you couldn't get me to move back in with that monster living there, not for a million dollars." Lilliam realized she'd just called Elizabeth's husband a monster. She looked at Elizabeth, then bowed her head slightly. "I'm sorry. I shouldn't have said that."

"No apology needed," Elizabeth said. "He *is* a monster. And I have some news that might interest you, that might put the monster out of his misery."

Lillian raised her head. "Do tell!"

Elizabeth began by telling her about William, reminding her that he had attended the first big dinner they had. She also reminded her that William's family owned the plantation next door, the museum.

Lillian let Elizabeth know that she remembered William from both the party and the wedding, knew all about his family, and also that she had probably played with some of his great-great-aunts back in the day. She then told Elizabeth that she had in fact been at her wedding, but she had not sought to introduce herself to Elizabeth as things had been too chaotic. It would have been confusing for a new bride under the circumstances.

Elizabeth went on to tell Lillian about her visits to William, the books that he had loaned her, including the "Author Unknown" book.

That brought a smile to Lillian's face. "You know, don't you," she said.

"Yes, Lillian. He told me. I read the entire book. I learned so much, and I completely understand why you didn't put your name on it, the politics of the families involved being what they are, which leads me to the reason I came today."

Lillian sat up and leaned over toward Elizabeth. "What might that be? If not to take me to dinner, then what?"

Elizabeth took Lillian's small hand and looking into her eyes, told her the whole story about the document, how it had been sealed for nearly a hundred years, but that according to William, it was valid. She then let Lillian know that Charles and Bryce had a copy and that likely Dehlia knew of its existence.

When Elizabeth was finished, Lillian broke into another broad smile. "Do you mean to tell me that if I can afford a very good attorney and obtain a copy of that document, I might be able to take the Noble Oak Plantation back?" Her eyes teared up as Elizabeth squeezed her hand.

"Yes, Lillian. That is exactly what I am saying."

"Oh dear, then what would become of you?" Lillian asked.

"Time will tell. A lot will depend on whether I am carrying a boy. If it is a girl, I think Charles will be rather fed up with me and will likely turn me out. He may try to take the girl anyway, and I don't have the money to fight him, but either way, he would likely win." Elizabeth was the one to find herself tearing up now, and she noticed Lillian patting her hand.

"You have William come and see me, will you?" Lillian asked. "And have him bring a copy of that document."

~~*~~

After tearful goodbyes and promises of good things to come, Elizabeth directed Holden to a maternity store that she'd found in the phone book. She stood in the middle of the dressing room, clothes strewn everywhere. *My God are maternity clothes ever ugly,* she thought. She'd selected only one of every ten things she tried on, and she was exhausted. She couldn't return empty-handed as shopping was ostensibly her entire reason for getting out of the house. If she didn't come back with a substantial pile of clothing after being gone for more than three hours, her cover would be blown.

Elizabeth finally added the last pair of pants that she'd tried on to the "yes" pile. She eyed the elastic waist and how it was sewn into the fabric, cheaply made and not constructed to last more than, what, nine months? It showed. But it was one more pair of pants that would bring her haul to ten complete outfits. She added a few nursing bras and maternity stockings for dressing up—as if she ever went anywhere nice—but it would add to the take and would her her explain what had taken so long.

Elizabeth dressed and undressed rapidly between trying things on to make up the time spent with Lillian. She was sure that she would find her purchases underwhelming and possibly atrocious in the morning. She couldn't care less at this point, however, because the meeting with Lillian went exactly as she wished, even better actually, with Lillian excited and animated when they left. Holden would call William the next morning and arrange a meeting between the two; she was sure William would happily go to the facility to meet with Lillian.

Lillian had expressed that she had no idea such a document existed that might allow her to sue for possession of the plantation house, and for the new information she was grateful. After Elizabeth's departure, she found herself sitting by the window for a long time, imagining that one day she might look out again at the lake instead of a parking lot filled with cars.

Elizabeth found herself chattering excessively on the drive home, to the point that Holden pulled over to calm her down. She was nervous, excited, and exhausted.

Holden turned into the parking lot of a church and stopped, pulling Elizabeth close to him on the seat and wrapping his arms around her. He kissed her gently on the lips, then on each cheek, then her forehead, and then planted one more long, lingering kiss on her lips, whispering as he pulled away. "This will all work out. I heard what you said about Charles taking the baby. It won't happen, Elizabeth. I won't allow it. No matter what, boy or girl, the baby stays with the mother. It is just the way it has to be." He gave her a long, firm hug.

Elizabeth could feel his heart beating next to hers and knew that it was true: Everything would work out. Elizabeth also knew she could count on Holden, his love and support, and she already felt closer to him than she had with anyone in her life.

They drove home in silence. When they got back, Faye was gone. Holden carried the shopping bags from the car up the stairs and dropped them in the foyer, exiting the door with a quick goodnight toward Elizabeth, to which she replied with a quiet thank you for driving, all under Nettie's watchful gaze, Holden not looking at either of them fearing a revealing glance in Elizabeth's direction.

It was just after seven, and although Elizabeth was hungry again—she realized she'd either talked or read throughout the entire dinner with Lillian and hadn't finished her food—she didn't want to burden Nettie by asking her to fix something to eat this late at night.

"Goodnight, Nettie. I'm sorry you had to wait for me. Please get home, and I'll see you tomorrow. I overslept this afternoon and should have left for shopping much earlier."

Nettie nodded, took the bags up to Elizabeth's room as Gwendolyn or Faye would have done for her had they been there, and dropped them just outside her door.

Elizabeth followed behind her.

"There's soup in the refrigerator if you're hungry," Nettie said. "I'll see you in the morning." She had no idea what Elizabeth was up to, but she sensed it was something big. She could feel it. And boy was Charles going to be angry when he found out Elizabeth had been gone nearly half the day.

Chapter Thirty-One: The War Begins

At seven the next morning, Faye walked through the front door. She had tried to call Charles the previous afternoon once she realized the horses were gone. Then she tried to call his office when she saw Holden speeding off with Elizabeth in the front seat of the car. There had been no answer either time, and his assistant apparently had the day off due to the conference. Faye knew she should have tried to call Gwendolyn, but truthfully, she didn't want to disturb her on her day off in the city. Elizabeth had brazenly left not once but twice, even after Charles had told her that her outings had to stop.

Part of Faye didn't like that Charles put her in such a position, and she understood why Elizabeth didn't want Faye in her room any longer. The snooping was no longer a secret. In addition to recording Elizabeth's every move outside the house, Charles had put Faye up to that, as well, and she was sure Elizabeth knew this.

"Find out anything you can, if you suspect something, that is, and let me know right away," he'd told Faye during one of their meetings in the library. "I personally have too much at stake, then there's the family's reputation and our standing in the community, and everything is centering around this marriage and birth going as planned. I will reward you handsomely." Charles referred to it as "the plan," and of course Faye knew exactly what that meant. She'd overheard him talking to his mother one day when he and Dehlia were taking tea in the library. Dehlia had dropped in for a visit while Elizabeth was on one of her longer walks, the kind that aroused suspicion.

"Well, just where is she?" Dehlia had asked.

"Out for a walk." Charles never knew exactly where Elizabeth went, but that particular day, she'd left with a book bag, so he presumed she had walked to the bench on the other side of the lake and found a place of solace where she could read uninterrupted.

"She should have been back by now. Who in the world can walk for so long in this heat?"

"Mother, just leave it alone. Things are going according to plan. Once she conceives, and once she has a boy, I'll find her a nice house in the city. She can visit the boy supervised, on occasion, and otherwise she can go on her merry way as the ex-Mrs. Freeman."

Faye had been careful that day to make sure her retreating footsteps had not given away her position outside the cracked door.

Faye had seen infrequent deposits into the account Charles had started for her at his bank, and there was more now than the previous month—she'd just checked again the day before—so it was trickling in. It seemed the deposits were larger when she came up with the goods. The bigger the tip (as in when Elizabeth was fertile) or the find, (as in the plantation book that William had loaned to Elizabeth), the bigger the deposit.

Although Faye hadn't recognized the plantation on the cover, she'd flipped through the pages the day after spying it on Elizabeth's table as she brought her tea. Faye was sure it had not come from the home library as she'd dusted every shelf a hundred times. Her suspicion was confirmed when she found the sticky note William had placed on the page that began the history of the Freeman family with "I think you'll find this interesting" printed in bold handwriting—and not that of Charles.

Faye knew that after finding the book and telling Charles about the note, Charles had gone out to talk to Holden. She didn't know what transpired, but she was sure that Holden had been able to lie his way out of that one. However, a nice fat deposit had shown up the next day.

Faye knew there was something going on between Elizabeth and Holden. She just had not been able to find a way to prove it. When they left on their long horseback rides, she couldn't hardly follow them like she had the day she followed Holden to the bench across the lake. Faye had been spooked by an animal in the trail just as Elizabeth, spooked by Holden, let out a little scream. That scream covered up Faye's own, simultaneous squeak, both of which caused her to turn and run all the way back around the lake without stopping. She'd burst into the kitchen, red-faced and sweating.

Nettie had taken one look at Faye and suspected what had happened, given Elizabeth had just left a few minutes prior with a book and a bottle of water and she hadn't been able to find Faye. Nettie knew Faye had been trying to follow Elizabeth—Faye had asked too many curious questions about Elizabeth's excursions—and Nettie also knew that Faye was terrified of the woods. Nettie had silently handed her a glass of lemonade, but not without first giving her a wide staring side-eye that spoke volumes as she turned slowly back to the stove.

There was also something in Elizabeth's safe. Faye just *knew it*. She had caught Elizabeth hurriedly coming out of the closet on several occasions after she'd knocked to announce herself holding a breakfast tray or with tea, as she pushed opened the bedroom door. Faye thought she should perhaps tell Charles and wondered what Elizabeth might be hiding. The safe was installed when the workers had been remodeling the master suite, presumably to protect what few valuables Elizabeth owned in the event an errant day-worker went sniffing around on his break, most of them given to her by Charles either while he was courting her or as engagement or wedding presents. Charles had many valuables as well and had mentioned this when he came home with the safe, but he'd let the staff know at that time that all his were in a safety deposit box in the bank— perhaps as a way of discouraging any notion of pilfering— because he trusted no one.

Charles returned later that afternoon, immediately hailed by Faye near the library door as he was headed down the hall toward his room for a nap. Marigold had been particularly rowdy during their encounter the night before, replacing the normal low moans and groans with wilder primal vocals that gave rise to a full-on melodic meltdown during her last orgasm. At one point, she took the lead, climbing on top of him and riding him like a rodeo pony during a barrel race. He'd never quite seen her like that, and he had no idea what it had been about, but suffice it to say it had worn him out.

"What is it?" Charles asked as he turned to close the library door.

"She's hiding something in the safe," Faye said. "I just know it. Several times, she's been in the closet, spinning the dial to lock it after I've knocked to come in with her breakfast. There is something in there she doesn't want me to see."

Charles stood with his back against the door, studying Faye, the girl who agreed to spy on his wife essentially for the opportunity to buy a car. It was extreme, but it was necessary. He couldn't have Elizabeth put him in any compromising position, not like the last girl he'd almost married. That had been a close one. The girl had found out about Marigold before he'd even proposed—he guessed that she had stalked him or had him followed—and had threatened to reveal his affair with the woman of slave ancestry, trying to blackmail him even before a prenuptial agreement was discussed, to make sure he knew she had something on him. That something could destroy his standing in the community, and he'd had to let loose his lawyers on her with a proactive threat that *he* could destroy *her* and make sure she never got another job in the entire state if she didn't go away and never speak a word of anything she knew about him.

"Thank you, Faye," Charles said, closing the door dismissively. "I'll look into it." He was tired and didn't have the energy for that right now. But if Faye was right, he would have to confront Elizabeth. He recalled giving her the combination but wasn't sure he'd actually written it down anywhere. Apparently, he had a few things to confront her about, none of which was more disquieting than the fact she'd been gone the entire previous day, according to both Faye and Nettie, who he'd had to question relentlessly to get a firm response. Why Nettie might want to stick up for Elizabeth was also troubling. But in the moment, a nap was Charles's highest priority.

~~*~~

Lillian opened her door to find William and another, taller man standing on the other side. She was expecting William, but she held the door, waiting for an introduction. "And you are?" she asked the stranger.

The stranger extended one hand for a shake, and in the other, he presented his business card. "Attorney Benjamin Crowell, ma'am."

Lillian took his outstretched hand, declining to take the card. "Come in, sit down," she commanded. She presumed the attorney was there at the behest of William, as she'd mentioned to Holden when he rang the day before that she wanted to see William that afternoon and also if William knew of any good attorneys who dealt with wills and trusts, he could feel free to pass along her information. William had brought an attorney to her instead, which was fine. She would only have to explain once.

Lillian sat in her usual spot, motioning to the two available seats. "William and I have some things to talk about. Some of it I'm sure William has already made you aware of, the rest maybe not, but if he trusts you, I'm fine with you being here."

The two men each took a seat. Benjamin began. "William here, Mr. Stapleton, is a friend and long-time colleague of mine. We went to school together. I also grew up in the county. You might remember the plantation on the far eastern side of the county, Chestnut Arms. It was in my family for eighty years, sold in 1940. I moved to Boston to go to law school in 1952, and after graduation, I decided to come back and serve my community and my neighbors." He took in Lillian's air of grace and her hair—perfectly coiffed although she probably went next to nowhere—and the way she watched him intently as he described himself.

Lillian was satisfied. She turned to William. "I'm sure you are well aware that Elizabeth and I have become friends and that she has visited me here. She has shared information with me, and I've shared a little with her, some of which you probably already know, some perhaps not."

William nodded his head.

Lillian continued, "One of the most shocking things that came out of our last visit was the existence of a document that you have in your possession. Did you bring it?"

William was still nodding as he withdrew a single sheet of paper, a copy of the original note attached to the trust of John Clayton the first. His signature appeared at the bottom of the document, although faded, the enhanced copy clearly showing his original signature.

Lillian recognized it because she'd seen it on other documents, some that she'd found after Juliet died and that she still had in her possession. Next to John's signature was a line naming the attorney who had executed his will, as well as the trust, with another signature.

Lillian put on her glasses, feigning a read-through of the document, although her eyes were so bad that she could hardly make out a complete sentence. "Since it is more or less a legal document, can you read it to me and translate?" Lillian directed her request to Benjamin.

Benjamin took his time reading through the document out loud, stopping to explain after every couple of sentences, whether he felt it was needed or not. He kept his explanations to a minimum and easy to understand.

Now Lillian was nodding along. What she heard from the attorney was just as Elizabeth had stated: The documents that had been handed down from generation to generation originally included the financial trust, and they also added in the legal description and that the property was part of a larger trust, managed by the estate and whichever John Clayton was living on the plantation at the time. It went on to state that under no circumstances would the plantation be sold nor subdivided as long as any descendant of the original Clayton family was still living. Also, it said that any sale made of the property or any of its assets would be deemed null and void should any said descendant petition in writing before any court in the state of Georgia.

Lillian looked at Benjamin. "Mr. Crowell, if I am hearing this correctly, I can hire you to represent me to petition the state and that there is a chance I could reclaim my family property without buying it from the Freemans."

Benjamin nodded. "That is exactly correct, Mrs. Clayton. And I have taken the documents to the state archivist to confirm authenticity of both the document and signature. Because Mr. Clayton was of high standing in the state—as you are well aware, our fine county was named after him—his signature is on many documents filed within the state, and this document was deemed to be authentic." He handed the document back to Lillian. "This copy is for you. I made others."

He continued, "Furthermore, I've discovered with William's help that the Freemans are well aware of the document's existence, and they may even have a copy themselves. They did their research before purchasing the plantation and deemed you to be the only viable descendant who would possibly step forward to claim the property. But given your being relegated to a nursing facility with dementia, or so they thought, they proceeded with the purchase. I also understand their banker might have given them a box that was being held at the bank and who may have also been aware of the document. If that is true, he could be on the hook for allowing the sale to go through, since he manages the family's money."

"The bottom line," William added, "is that although the Freemans might put up a fight, several people knew through the entire process—the Realtor excluded no doubt—that you could stake your claim at any time. They were probably hedging their bets that you would pass before you were ever made aware, or that without a copy of this document should you make a claim to its existence, they could use your dementia as their defense."

Lillian sat calmly with her hands folded in her lap. "Let's start the process."

The knock on her door startled Elizabeth. She had clothes strewn across the bed, one pile she'd tried on again and taken off the tags, another pile she'd tried on and changed her mind about (she'd have to go to town again to return them), and a third pile she'd just dumped out of the bags.

Charles again came through the door without announcing himself, as he had the last time. The habit was becoming annoying. He looked on the bed and at Elizabeth, who stood in front of the mirror wearing leggings and a matching maternity top. She looked absolutely beautiful. But he had come on a mission and was not going to be dissuaded from his purpose for the visit.

"Elizabeth, I need to see your safe," he demanded.

Elizabeth's face went white.

"Why in the world would you need to see inside my safe?" she asked.

"I just do. Please do not ask questions. If you refuse, I will simply take the entire thing down to a locksmith and have it opened." He stood in the door with his arms folded.

Elizabeth walked to the closet, pulled back the dresses that obscured the face of the safe, knelt, spun the dial back and forth until the last number elicited a faint "click," then pulled the door open. She stood back. "Go for it. Have a look," she said, walking back to the middle of the room. It was her turn to stand strong, arms crossed, furious and frowning.

Charles turned on the light in the closet, knelt, and peered inside the safe. The pearls that he'd given Elizabeth as a wedding present, his grandmother's ring, and a diamond necklace and matching earrings all sat neatly next to each other in their respective boxes. There was nothing more. He stood, looked at Elizabeth then around the room, seeing nothing that would be cause for concern or suspicion, gave a glance at the piles of clothes, then said simply, "Excuse me," before walking out the door.

He went down the stairs and past the library, embarrassed and exasperated. Whatever Faye had imagined Elizabeth to be hiding in the safe simply did not exist, and he had gone to her room unnecessarily. Charles gave Faye a furtive glance when he saw her standing at the dining table next to Gwendolyn, readying the place settings for dinner. He would have a word with her later about this. He was restless and hungry. He pushed through the swinging kitchen doors, immediately noticing the ribs, barbequed and resting on the counter. Greens sat simmering in a pot, and Nettie was mashing potatoes with her back turned.

"You make sho dat the good silverware is set out there and dat Mr. Freeman's scotch is already on the table when he come down," Nettie said without turning. She thought that it had been either Faye or Gwendolyn who had entered.

"You take such good care of me," Charles said, causing Nettie to turn sharply, embarrassed that she'd been caught off guard.

"I'm flattered, really, Nettie. Thank you," Charles said. He knew he needed to keep Nettie buttered up after the round of questioning he'd unleashed on her earlier in the day. "I was just wondering if anyone has mentioned to Elizabeth that dinner is about to be served." He noted that she was upstairs trying on clothes—the massive piles that had been added to his credit card bill—but he'd left in such haste he hadn't thought to ask if she was coming down for dinner.

"She knows," Nettie replied. "Faye don' knocked on her do' a few minutes ago while you was restin'."

Charles turned and headed out to take his place at the table and get started with a drink. "Thank you, Nettie. I'll wait for her in the dining room," he said before disappearing through the doors.

~~*~~

Elizabeth watched as Charles closed the door behind him, exhaling what was certainly a breath that she'd held for far too long. She went to the bed and fished around underneath the clothes that she'd not yet tried on and found her purse. Since her visit to Lillian the day before, she'd hardly left her room, so she'd not bothered to take the letters and the diary out and return them to the safe, but she did so now.

Thank God, she thought. It would have been awful to lose the diary before she finished it and to have to turn over the letters that she planned to give to Lillian eventually. Elizabeth was now furious—not just angry and untrusting of Faye—and ready for battle.

She came into the dining room wearing a new, totally different outfit from the one Charles had just seen her in, and again she looked stunning. Whatever it was that they said about the beauty of a pregnant woman was certainly true. He didn't notice it so much, never actually, in any other women he'd seen out an about, but he'd seen the change in Elizabeth, and it was quite becoming.

Elizabeth did not so much as look at Charles, nor at Faye nor Gwendolyn. As far as she was concerned, Nettie was her only ally in the house now, and of course Holden out in his cabin. No one else could be trusted.

Charles had finished his first drink in three long swallows and signaled for Faye to pour another. Faye looked down at the glass, not at Charles and certainly not at Elizabeth, as she loaded ice cubes into his glass with tongs, then filled it to the brim from the bottle of scotch. She sensed Charles to be in one of his moods, and she couldn't tell if it was bad because he'd found what she'd been concerned he might find or if he was mad that he'd found nothing. She looked down at Elizabeth's glass of lemonade, noting that it was still full, and hastily left for the kitchen.

"So, I heard you went for a ride against my wishes," Charles started. "Then you went to town." He was holding his glass firmly, too firmly as he did when he was angry. He did not want to reveal that his hand would have been shaking if not.

"I needed clothes. If you haven't noticed, my belly is growing, and none of my clothes fit anymore." Elizabeth ignored the comment about the ride.

"Damnit, Elizabeth. I told you." Charles glared at her.

"Told me what, exactly, Charles?" she asked. "You've told me a lot of things. Anyway, the ride was short, just around the fence line," which he knew to be a lie.

Faye had already described to Charles seeing Elizabeth and Holden exit the property from the third floor and head west down the side of the narrow lane toward William's house.

Charles slammed his glass down on the table, causing it to shatter. Elizabeth calmly stood, pushed back her chair, and went to the kitchen. Nettie had just put a serving tray into Faye's hands to take to the table. At the sight of the ribs, Elizabeth's hunger was heightened.

"Can you please make a plate for me that I can take to my room?" she asked.

Faye returned the tray to the counter while Nettie took a plate from the shelf and dished up a little bit of everything, then added a second helping of greens. She handed the plate to Elizabeth with silverware and a napkin. "Faye will come up with a pitcher of lemonade, Miss Elizabeth." Nettie had heard the glass shatter. "Faye, first go in there with a towel and a fresh glass for Mr. Freeman."

Elizabeth turned and went through the kitchen doors, detouring through the foyer so as not to pass near Charles, went to her room, and locked the door. The war had officially begun.

~~*~~

Elizabeth ate at her table, recalling the look on Charles's face when she defied him, knowing if she wasn't pregnant that she might have been in for a physical altercation. She pulled the diary out of the safe, where it would remain locked until she gave it over to Lillian. She couldn't believe her luck in the timing of having temporarily removed it. Lillian could keep it safe, but she wanted to finish it first. She decided to skip a few entries and move on to the one following what she'd just read to Lillian the day before.

February 27, 1866

I write today with sadness, regret, and resolve. John has passed from the injuries he sustained in the war. His last days were filled with anger and rage, as they had been since his return, but he was louder, more forceful, as if he was screaming at God to take him.

The funeral is in three days, and the men are busy preparing his burial site, Liam included. The women on the staff washed and prepared his body, then dressed him in his uniform.

I couldn't bear to look at him. I've held so much hatred for him over the past few years that it is now a burden off my heart to know that I will never again have to listen to him scream nor have to cringe when he raises his fist high above my head.

I have black clothing for myself and the children to wear to the funeral, although part of me wishes to wear lilac for the coming spring and the lightness in my heart. The children are happier, suddenly singing and running through the halls, which they were forbidden to do all winter lest it disturb the master, Hattie would tell them.

I dare say they do not miss their father, not one bit. They constantly ask about Liam now, asking if he can move in from his quarters and live in the big house with us. They ask if he can be their daddy now.

I can't explain to the children how complicated it would be to have him living here, but yes, I yearn for that to be the case. Of course, the scandal of such a thing would bar me from seeing people in our former social circles, many of whom have begun hosting parties again now that the war is over and the men have returned home. But nothing would delight me more.

I've never been a Confederate at heart. I'm happy the slaves are free people and delighted that so many chose to stay on and help us with the place. None of us will miss John, especially those who suffered beatings at one time or another, not by his hand but his orders.

Many of them, free people and paid servants now, come to me often and tell me how much they appreciate the way they were treated, telling me stories of others they know of who suffered and even some who had died during beatings. Some were hanged and burned after the war by plantation owners who would rather kill them than set them free. It has been awful, but it is amazing that we have lived through such a dark time and we are all still doing well. It is also comforting to know that my departed husband is finally at peace. God rest his soul.

Elizabeth finished her dinner and set her tray and the empty lemonade pitcher outside her door, much as she would have at a hotel. Faye would undoubtedly come to check on her and would find it there, a sure sign that she did not wish to be bothered. She'd never done that and felt awkward about it, but she no longer cared—not about Faye, her husband, or the house. Nothing mattered now, except finding a way to free herself of Charles and make sure he didn't take her child. She was growing sleepy but was anxious to finish the diary and give it to Holden to get to Lillian for safe-keeping.

August 20, 1866

I am writing today with such exciting news! Henry has come back. I felt terrible the day that John threw him out of here, threatening to unleash the hunting dogs on him. I knew the girl Grace, Henry's mother, and remember when John sold them. I never could figure that out at the time. Anyway, Henry is an orphan, and John was indeed his father, I firmly believe, and so I've taken him in. He will stay in the slave quarters for now. There is room there because with the slaves gaining their freedom, many have gone to find family in other states. He'll be a good helper too; he promises. He just wants to be back where he was born.

Funny thing is that he and Little John were born just months apart. My husband was a busy man! It's not funny, actually, as it breaks my heart to know that this went on for some time, and I never figured it out. And it's worse that John felt he had to sell them to avoid possible scandal, instead of accounting for his misdeeds. However, I must also remind myself that while John was busy out in the forest siring a child with Grace, there is a good chance that I was in another part of the forest, or in a room in the city, making a baby with Liam. May God forgive us both for our transgressions.

Elizabeth closed the diary, unable to keep her eyes open. During her reading of the last entry, she heard dishes rattling in the hall, so she knew that Faye had taken away her tray.

Chapter Thirty-Two: The Reveal

Lillian sat at the long table in Mr. Crowell's office, reading the gold-leaf stenciled letters backward on the closed door—Crowell and Banks, Attorneys at Law. William sat across from her, and Benjamin sat at the head of the table, organizing papers into piles. Everything required an original signature, and he had all the documents in triplicate: one for his files, one for Lillian, and one that he would submit to the court.

Once the documents had been passed to Lillian for her signature, she signed then handed them to William, who was keeping everything in order. It seemingly took hours, and once completed, she sat back in the leather chair that swiveled, stretched her neck back and forth and took a long drink from the glass of water on the table. "What is next?" she asked.

Benjamin carefully explained, "I take the documents to the court tomorrow and file the petition. Depending on the load, meaning what the judge has on his plate, he'll either take a first look tomorrow or the next day. Then he'll set a hearing date. The first will be just us with the judge to present our case. If he agrees that we have a case, Mr. Freeman will be notified, and the judge will set an initial date with the other side to present the petition. The other side may bring counsel, and they may want to depose you, but I'll be present every step of the way."

"Depose?" Lillian had never heard the term.

"Ask you questions under oath," Benjamin responded.

"What kind of questions?"

"They will be served with a copy of the document with the petition, which we suspect they've already seen and may have a copy of. They will have a few days to prepare a defense, decide how to proceed in arguing that you have no right to the property. They will ask you about your lineage, how exactly you are related to the first John Clayton, and why you waited until now to file for ownership." Benjamin cleared his throat. "They might ask you how you came upon the knowledge that the document existed. You must be truthful and tell them Elizabeth was the one who informed you of its existence."

"Oh, dear," Lillian said. "I would fear for her safety at that point, then."

"We have a plan," William said. "I have a carriage house behind my plantation that is set up for guests." He looked at Benjamin. "Benjamin here has already put together papers for a restraining order to keep Charles away from Elizabeth until the court settles the matter, and further into the future as is needed. We may have to depose the household staff who can confirm how Charles often goes into a rage and that Elizabeth would not be safe in her own home given the situation. When the baby is born, we will suggest a blood test to confirm paternity, as Elizabeth has informed us that the baby might not be Charles's."

A smile formed at the corners of Lillian's lips. She'd seen the way Elizabeth looked at Holden. She'd never seen her look at Charles like that—not at the wedding nor the dinner party, not once. Lillian noticed that Charles never touched Elizabeth, not in her presence. But that young man Holden, he took great care around Elizabeth, helping her with bags and getting her door, then that kiss that he stole—thinking no one could see—outside the facility as he helped her into the front seat. How charming. She certainly hoped it was *his* baby.

Lillian thought of Adria, Liam, and Juliet, and she found it uncanny how history was repeating itself at the Nobel Oak Plantation. She found that for the first time in a long time, she was happy.

"She will live with me," Lillian declared, looking from Benjamin to William, who formed a slight smile with that remark. Lillian's face was suddenly glowing, like a moonlit visage of a whitewashed building.

"She'd probably like that," William said.

"And Holden, he will stay. And Nettie and Branson and maybe Gwendolyn, we'll see. But that Faye, you can draw up her termination papers right now, and I'll sign them."

"Let's get you the property first, Mrs. Clayton, and then we'll arrange for whoever you wish to remain and see to the termination of anyone you don't wish to employ." Benjamin assiduously divided the signed papers into separate, marked folders, handing Lillian the one marked with her name. "Let's get you home before dinner is served."

"Ha! If you can call it that," Lillian said as she gathered her purse from the long table. "Eating Nettie's cooking until the day I die will bring me great joy."

~~*~~

The next morning, Elizabeth woke to the sounds of Charles barking orders downstairs. She heard Gwendolyn's voice as well, then Branson's. What in the world was going on? She dressed quickly, then went out into the hall and waited at the top of the stairway. She could still hear Charles talking, but the voices had moved to the front porch. She took the steps quietly, stopping in the hallway where she could see out the front door.

There, under the portico was a large, white box truck with a logo emblazoned on the side that she could not read from where she stood. Two men had unloaded a piece of furniture off the back and were carrying it toward the house. Another followed with boxes stacked high, nearly obscuring his view. Elizabeth noted that the man had to look around them to see the steps, nearly toppling the boxes at one point, then deftly recovering just before they teetered over.

Gwendolyn had returned to the foyer. Elizabeth could see her stealing furtive glances in the direction of the stairs, then she raised her arm and pointed in Elizabeth's direction. The two men came toward her with a large wooden crib. Suddenly, Charles moved around them, and Elizabeth put her back against the wall as Charles and the three men moved quickly past her and began climbing the stairs. Charles gave her a brief, unsmiling glance as they passed.

Elizabeth walked up to Gwendolyn. "What in the world is going on?"

"The nursery has arrived."

Elizabeth shook her head and walked past Gwendolyn wordlessly, entering the kitchen. Nettie sat at the counter making a list. "Good morning, Nettie. May I have some tea?"

"Sho 'nuff, Miss Elizabeth," Nettie said, jumping up as Elizabeth sat down at an adjacent stool.

"Charles ordered the nursery furniture without asking me a single question about what I might like," Elizabeth said quietly.

Nettie placed a teacup in front of Elizabeth and poured scalding water over the bag. This was followed by a small plate that she'd pulled from the refrigerator. She pulled off the plastic to reveal a fruit salad and handed Elizabeth a fork.

"Not a single question," Elizabeth said as she took a bite of a cold apple slice.

Elizabeth could hear the truck's back door being rolled down outside, landing with a thud, then more metallic noises as the latches were put into place. Then tires on gravel. She could hear Gwendolyn telling Faye to take the bedding out of the boxes and wash it, then take it to the nursery. Elizabeth wondered what pattern he'd picked out without asking her for input. Surely, it would be masculine. Blue with little trumpets, she imagined. Nothing frilly. She knew without looking that the entire nursery would be set up to welcome a boy.

Gwendolyn entered the kitchen where Elizabeth sat watching Nettie, slowly sipping her tea but saying nothing. Elizabeth suddenly felt like throwing up. She hadn't done that since the first days of her pregnancy, but she stood and rushed past Gwendolyn, up the stairs to her bedroom, and vomited into the wastebasket by the door, unable to make it as far as the bathroom. She put the trash bin outside the door and locked it, then went to her bathroom to take a shower.

"Mr. Freeman said to tell her he has gone to town," Gwendolyn said to Nettie. "He has an early meeting and won't be taking breakfast with her," Gwendolyn had missed the crushed glass incident the previous evening, and Faye hadn't told her yet how glass was scattered across and under the table and how she refilled the fresh glass three more times before Charles, still red-faced and angry, stood up and walked to his room without a word.

"I don't think that gon' bother her none," Nettie said. Then she looked at the kitchen doors, still swinging from Elizabeth's rushed departure. "What in the world is that man thinkin'?" Nettie shook her head. Gwendolyn had no answer.

Once Elizabeth had showered and dressed for the second time, she decided she needed to see Holden. She went up to the third floor and down the back exit that skirted the kitchen door but just barely. If someone happened to be standing by the window, they would have seen her go out the back door and rush across the lawn to Holden's door, then knock quietly. Nettie watched the entirety of it all, also seeing the door open and Elizabeth rush into Holden's arms. The door closed, and

Nettie turned her back to see Faye standing in the kitchen with an empty wastebasket.

"She threw up. She left the bin outside the door."

"Take it outside and wash it with a garden hose," Nettie replied sarcastically. "You can figure that out." She shook her head. "Then put it back where she left it." Nettie went back to pushing dough around on the floured board, curling the long pieces into spirals that she then dusted with cinnamon and sugar and dotted with butter.

Nettie knew things weren't good. She just didn't know how bad it was going to get. She needed the job, and she was willing to keep her mouth shut and keep working. She thought of the image of the three little monkeys, "See no evil, hear no evil, speak no evil." She, Gwendolyn, and Faye were in that position, although Faye, she was a troublemaker. Faye needed to learn a few things if she was ever going to get a good job or be in the position of running a household. You just pretend you don't notice some things to maintain harmony.

~~*~~

Holden stood with Elizabeth sobbing into his shirt sleeve, his arms wrapped around her. He'd seen Branson pull up to the front door and take Charles away minutes after the delivery truck left. He wondered what the men had taken inside the house, but he would wait to ask. It was likely the reason that Elizabeth was crying. When her sobs finally subsided, he pulled her back far enough to see her face. Her eyes were red and a tiny bit swollen, as were her lips. He took a clean handkerchief from his back pocket, dabbed the tears from her cheeks, and leaned over to kiss her gently. His telephone rang. He let it ring two, three times.

"You should get that," Elizabeth said.

Holden let her go and picked up the call on the fifth ring. It was William. Holden listened while William went on, grunting "Uh-huh," and "Oh boy," then "Alright, I'll tell her." He hung up and turned to Elizabeth.

"I think you need to sit down."

~~*~~

Two hours later, a driver pulled up under the portico. Elizabeth came downstairs with a box and put it into the backseat of the car along with her purse. She returned to her room and pulled two packed suitcases out of her bedroom door, one at a time. She walked back into the room and looked around, satisfied. She noted the closet door sat open, revealing the open, empty safe. She walked back in and closed the closet door. She didn't want that to be the first thing Charles saw when he stormed into her room looking for her.

The driver helped Elizabeth load the suitcases into the trunk. She turned to see Gwendolyn, Faye, and Nettie, with tears in her eyes and wringing her hands in her apron—standing in the doorway.

"I'll send word through Holden. Everything will be alright." Elizabeth said as the driver stood holding her door opened, closing it once she was in and settled in the backseat.

~~*~~

Penny's phone rang. She was shocked to hear her sister's voice on the line, suddenly needing to steady the full cup of coffee that she held in her other hand.

"You were allowed your one phone call for the month? How much time do we have?" Penny asked somewhat sarcastically, but the truth was she was about to buy a plane ticket and show up unannounced because she'd been so concerned about Elizabeth's well-being.

"We have all the time in the world," Elizabeth said. "I've left him."

Penny nearly dropped the phone. She sat down in an overstuffed chair in the living room, placing her coffee cup on the end table. "Please tell me what is going on. Where are you? Are you safe?"

Elizabeth told Penny everything that had happened since they'd last spoken—about the visit to Lillian, the document, William, the lawyer, and the outburst from Charles the night before, ending with the nursery that had arrived that morning by truck. "So, they have me in an undisclosed location," she said almost jokingly. "I'm only a half-mile away but tucked in a luxurious guest house. He'll never find me here." Elizabeth looked around the room. The floor-to-ceiling windows letting the northwest light in at such an angle that she could tell the sun would be setting soon. She described the tall curtains that would be easy to pull closed after which she would make herself something to eat.

The kitchen had been fully stocked, the refrigerator was full of everything she needed (Holden had helped with the grocery list), and the pantry was also laden with soups, a variety of boxed teas, and a large wicker basket filled with fruit. Elizabeth told Penny about the canopied bed that had been made with a ruffled comforter that matched the settee in the corner. It was feminine but not over the top.

Elizabeth walked Penny through on the phone to the bathroom, describing the white fluffy towels that were stacked in the corner cabinet with more hanging on the bars next to the clawfoot tub. The tub had a cloth shower curtain surround for privacy with a tall post holding the shower fixture. Black-and-white tiles checkered the expansive bathroom, which was bigger than the one she had back in her room. Everything was bright and cheery.

"I feel safe for the first time since I married that monster," Elizabeth said, then she plopped down on the bed, wishing her sister was with her.

Charles would be served the papers for the petition tomorrow at his office, to spare him the embarrassment of being served in front of his driver and staff at the plantation house. Following that, a sheriff would come to serve the restraining order.

Nettie had given a statement to a man who had come to the house. He'd pulled up in a long black car just after Elizabeth left. He was wearing a three-piece suit and shoes that cost more than her monthly salary, she guessed. He asked to speak with her privately, so she sent Gwendolyn and Faye, still in shock and unsure if they should stay or go home, to the third floor where they were sure to be far enough away not to eavesdrop.

The man asked Nettie lots of questions, including if she'd ever seen Charles hit Elizabeth, to which she nodded *yes*. He went on to describe other incidents as relayed to him by Elizabeth, and she affirmed each one of them. Once he was finished, he asked for her signature, then added his to the bottom as the witness: Benjamin B. Crowell.

"Can you come?" Elizabeth asked Penny.

"Of course! Give me some time to figure it out. Can I call you?"

Elizabeth hadn't realized that now she actually had a phone and would be able to make outgoing calls. And she could accept a call from her sister at any time! She looked down at the pad next to the phone where someone had written *Your Number* at the top, with the area code and number below it. She recited the number to her sister, her voice wavering with excitement and happiness. She laid back on the bed, noting for the first time that she could no longer see her feet over the bump that was her baby.

Chapter Thirty-Three: Resolution

Lillian stood in the foyer, directing the movers as they maneuvered the large heavy bed out to the truck, followed by the massive dresser that matched and the leather chair, all of which had been part of the furniture at the plantation house for decades.

She walked into the master bedroom, noting the difference and the lightness that now permeated the room—not just because of the blonde oak furniture and the new curtains that had been installed the day before. The bassinet stood tucked in on one side—Elizabeth's side—the other where Holden would sleep. She looked approvingly at the stained-glass lamp and the ornate bedside table she'd found on the third floor. She'd found the furniture tucked away up there in an unused room, stacked and covered with sheets. Lillian remembered the furniture from when she was a girl; she had slept in that bed.

Lillian just had to get rid of the furniture that had been slept in by John Claytons going back generations, and most recently by Charles Freeman. The memories and the madness that lived inside the wood grain shouted at her as the men took the furniture out the door. She wanted to give Elizabeth and Holden the master suite, and she would take the room that had the pulley to the kitchen bell. She'd always loved that room. She could summon Gwendolyn from there, after which she would be brought tea if she felt like taking breakfast in her room, or she would go down to join Elizabeth and Holden in the dining room.

Nettie would keep the kitchen humming as she had for years, and Gwendolyn would stay on to manage the household. Faye had been replaced by a new girl, Catherine. She was the girlfriend of Harold, the young man who had shown up at her nursing home asking to stay at the plantation house. She couldn't turn them away when he came again after hearing about her move back to the place, this time with a lovely woman whom he introduced as his fiancée.

Catherine would work in the main house, and Harold would tend to the cars and the horses. They would stay in the bunkhouse and start a family, just as his great-great-grandfather had done.

The divorce had gone much more smoothly than anyone had expected. Once Charles found out the baby wasn't his, he relinquished all rights—and any desire to see the child. He'd already moved out of the plantation house and into his family's original plantation. He was livid, of course, what with finding out the baby was Holden's, but with the embarrassment of having been served a restraining order, he remained mostly calm through the process.

The lawyer, Mr. Crowell, had done an excellent job navigating the prenuptial agreement, again finding favor with the judge as Charles could not control himself at all during that day's hearing. Charles did not understand or agree with how Elizabeth could end up getting more than was even stated in the original agreement, but the judge told him exactly why after admonishing him for his behavior a third time, taking pity on the poor girl, who he realized had been conned into marrying for the sake of an heir.

Elizabeth and Holden planned to move into the master bedroom, temporarily staying at William's guest house until after the baby was born and waiting for the judge to issue the order for Charles to vacate. The birth was beautiful and uneventful, with Holden at Elizabeth's side, where he would have been regardless of the positive paternity test that was confirmed days later.

The trial for possession of the plantation house had not gone quite as well, with Charles's outbursts disrupting the proceedings multiple times a day, none of which weighed in his favor with the judge. But the documents told the story, given what they were and deemed to be authentic, and the judge determined that Charles in fact was apprised of the situation by someone at the bank prior to the purchase, one who managed to remained nameless due to the old South's politics and for purposes of saving the face of the institution, but who was fired the day after the trial ended.

Lillian sat silently through those proceedings. She had already been deposed and therefore did not have to answer any more questions during the trial. Once it was over, she rose and walked out of the courtroom unaided and unescorted to a waiting car.

Lillian walked through the dining room to the large patio doors, opening them wide. She noticed the shimmering waves on the lake and welcomed the breeze that wafted from the water through the doors and into the house, rippling the curtains throughout the living room. She stood still, imagining that she heard laughter of the children who would come to inhabit the house. Elizabeth and Holden planned to marry out on the lawn in the coming months, and surely more children would follow.

Lillian loved Elizabeth for her courage, tenacity, and boldness in standing up to Charles. She loved that Elizabeth was cunning enough to find her way to Lillian and trusting enough to allow William to intervene and manage the attorney and the proceedings to get the plantation house back. For this, Lillian would be eternally grateful, and with legally removing her niece and nephew's names from all documents relating to her and her brother's assets, who had both become fabulously wealthy when their father passed, she was able to legally change the decades-old document to read that the heirs to the plantation house would soon be equally Mr. and Mrs. Holden Grady Harding.

Epilogue

June 15, 1979

I'm sitting at an old desk in the master bedroom at Nobel Oak Plantation. As I write, I am looking out at the lake, watching sunlight dance on the top of tiny waves, just as it did on my wedding day. I can hardly believe that this is my life. After enduring months of crushing control from the man who married me hoping for an heir and then finally escaping, I found myself once again reciting my vows—but to a man who truly loves me.

Lillian was there, and my sister, Penny. She and her husband and children all flew in for the wedding. Everyone who wasn't invited to my ceremony with Charles came and danced, and there was much laughter. I only wish my parents were alive to see me so happy. Holden and I danced until the wee hours, in between my leaving to nurse the baby when called by the nanny.

Friends from my old job showed up, those deemed to be so beneath Charles that I was disallowed contact from the moment I accepted the engagement ring. It was good to see them all, especially Beth! We used to be inseparable, and we may be once again. She is married now and expecting a baby in a few months.

When everyone was gone or shown to their rooms, Holden and I settled into our new house as husband and wife, and for the first time, I feel like the lady of the house. Holden treats me with such dignity, respect, and love, love like I've never imagined. He actually carried me across the threshold of our bedroom and after closing the door, undressed me and suggested we start immediately on baby number two.

Marigold's son, Daniel, did in fact turn out to be in line for a good part of the Freeman family's money.

After I went to her with Benjamin Crowell and William in tow, we were able to convince her to file for what was her son's rightful portion of the trust. Before the papers were even filed, I invited her to come and live in the newly remodeled quarters, and she was able to bring Daniel out to live on the property with her! I hold no animosity toward her; she was only doing what she needed to do to survive. She was truthfully happy to be free from the clutches and control of Charles, thrilled to have her son with her again, and what a surprise we all had when her brother Harold showed up with his girlfriend, Catherine!

They had been separated after his birth, both being raised in foster care, and neither had been aware of the other although they bear the same last name. They are actively looking for their mother, who is probably in her sixties by now, and if they find her, who knows, maybe we'll have her join us here as well.

I've heard that Charles isn't doing well and might be on his deathbed. I can't say that this saddens me. Hearing this reminds me of Adria and how she described the torment of her husband, John, after he returned from the war. I wonder if Charles is bedridden and angry, barking orders to the staff, and making everyone miserable. If so, surely Dehlia is at his side, relieving him of any last sense of decency and reminding him that it was her money that bailed his father out.

I was told that Bryce and Aimee had their third child, another boy, so they will likely take over the Freeman plantation.

I look over at my baby sleeping next to me in the bassinet, and I am filled with love. Her eyes flutter behind closed lids as she dreams. Her blonde curls, just like Holden's when he was a boy he says, frame her little round face. I now know the love that Adria spoke of when she described her daughter, after giving birth to Liam's baby. The experience of having a child with someone you love is vastly different than with a man who is only seeking a path for his money and assets to land so that his lineage is carried down.

I feel that we have broken the cycle of murder and madness, of cruelty and control, and replaced it with love, laughter, dignity, and respect.

Lillian decreed herself to be the adopted grandmother, and our baby has begun to think of her as such, reaching out to stroke Lillian's gray hair as she is rocked, looking up into her eyes, bonding.

We named our baby girl Lily.